PRAISE FOR

What a Woman Wants

"Fans of Fennell's quirky style will enjoy the entertaining misadventures." —*Publishers Weekly*

"The dialogue was fun and witty." —*Night Owl Reviews* (Top Pick)

"Fennell's latest will have readers laughing as they turn the pages." —*RT Book Reviews*

PRAISE FOR JUDI FENNELL AND HER NOVELS

"The opening . . . is one of the best hooks I've read. I don't know who could set it down after the first few pages . . . An excellent choice." —Joey W. Hill, national bestselling author

"One of the most exciting and fun reads I have ever encountered." —*Fresh Fiction*

"Phenomenally written novel . . . One of the best stories I have read this year, and I highly recommend it to anyone who loves a happy ending!" —*Sizzling Hot Books*

"Will keep the reader enraptured." —*Publishers Weekly* (starred review)

"I had a smile on my face and a sigh of contentment . . . Lighthearted but full of emotion. The story stirred in me feelings of falling in love all over again. It was just downright enjoyable to read!" —*That's What I'm Talking About*

continued . . .

What a *Woman* Gets

JUDI FENNELL

BERKLEY SENSATION, NEW YORK

THE BERKLEY PUBLISHING GROUP
Published by the Penguin Group
Penguin Group (USA) LLC
375 Hudson Street, New York, New York 10014

USA • Canada • UK • Ireland • Australia • New Zealand • India • South Africa • China

penguin.com

A Penguin Random House Company

WHAT A WOMAN GETS

A Berkley Sensation Book / published by arrangement with the author

Berkley Sensation Books are published by The Berkley Publishing Group.
BERKLEY SENSATION® is a registered trademark of Penguin Group (USA) LLC.
The "B" design is a trademark of Penguin Group (USA) LLC.

For information, address: The Berkley Publishing Group,
a division of Penguin Group (USA) LLC,
375 Hudson Street, New York, New York 10014.

ISBN: 978-0-425-26831-5

PUBLISHING HISTORY
Berkley Sensation mass-market edition / November 2014

PRINTED IN THE UNITED STATES OF AMERICA

10 9 8 7 6 5 4 3 2 1

Cover art by Daniel O'Leary.
Cover design by Judith Lagerman.
Interior text design by Kristin del Rosario.

This one is for my mom and dad.
A parent's love is a wonderful thing.
Thank you for being here.

Guys' Night . . . Plus One

⋘⋗

believe, dear brothers, you all need to be fitted for Manley Maids uniforms."

Liam Manley bit his tongue at his sister Mac's announcement as she laid her winning hand on the green felt poker table. She'd played him—him *and* his brothers, and she'd played them good.

She'd played *poker* good. Who knew she even *played* poker?

And that bet . . . Four weeks' worth of free cleaning service for her company against their vacation homes and expensive sports cars. Why did Liam feel like a sucker?

"I am *not* wearing an apron." Bryan, the youngest Manley brother, sounded so offended it made Liam bite his tongue even harder—so he wouldn't laugh at him. You might think Mac had asked him to wear . . . well . . . an apron.

Sean, his middle brother and fellow loser, kept stacking the poker chips, avoiding Mac's jack-high straight flush like the plague while keeping his mouth shut.

Bryan's mouth was hanging open. Any second their movie-star brother was going to start gaping like a fish.

Where was a camera when he needed one? Bry would pay anything to keep *that* unflattering picture out of the press, and Liam could use a new hot tub for the house he was renovating—make that, had just *finished* renovating, which meant he had some time on his hands.

No time like the present to get started paying off the ridiculous bet. "When do you want us to start, Mac?"

"I have extra uniforms, so whenever you have the time."

Extra uniforms? Since when did she have extra anything when it came to the business?

Something was going on.

He never would have thought Mary-Alice Catherine would resort to dirty tricks to get her older brothers to do what she wanted. Hell, when they'd gone to live with Gran after their parents had been killed in a car accident, they'd practically tripped over each other to take care of their baby sister. Now he was going to be tripping over brooms and mops and vacuum cleaners. Ugh.

"Hey, can I do my own house?" That was Bryan, working whatever angle he could to come out on top.

"You'd put Monica out of a job to weasel out of the bet? Really?" It was Mac's turn for mouth-gaping.

"I'm not weaseling out of anything." But Bry didn't look happy. "You can count on me for Monday, too. I've got a month between projects and was looking for something to do anyhow."

Liam highly doubted Bryan's choice would be to play maid, however. It wasn't Liam's, either. Still, he'd made the bet . . .

And so had she.

He finished off his beer then gathered the cards, dragging Mac's winning hand across the felt last. Bryan's gaze was on those cards the entire way. Sean kept his on the chips. They were probably the most anal-retentively stacked chips in the history of the game.

"I didn't know you had guys working for you, Mac." Liam kept his voice even. Controlled. And if there was the slightest hint of something else in it, well, he'd be fine with

Mac assuming it was anger at losing. But why would Mac (a) want to play poker so badly with them when she couldn't afford the cash if she lost and (b) make that bet *and* win? Something was rotten in the state of Manley.

"Wha . . . what?"

Yeah, that startled look in her eyes confirmed exactly what he'd thought. There *were* no guys employed by Manley Maids, so those uniforms weren't "extra." She'd had them made in advance. For them.

Mac had planned this. Her winning was no fluke. He'd call her on it if he had any proof other than his gut, but he didn't. And God knew, he couldn't always trust his gut. It'd let him down before.

"Never mind." He shuffled the offending cards in with the other forty-seven, then tapped the long edge of the deck on the table. "I'll be there Monday."

And he'd use the mindless monotony of cleaning to come up with some way to pay his sister back.

In spades.

Chapter One

❧

IF there was one thing Cassidy Davenport hated, it was to be kept waiting. And if there was one thing her father did best, it was keep her waiting.

"But, Deborah, I just spoke to him." She had to go through her father's executive secretary for every little scrap, but that's the way Dad's empire worked. No one got to him without going through Deborah. The woman seriously ought to demand the title of CEO because Cassidy doubted her father ever made a business decision he didn't run through Deborah Capshaw first. She had been with him for nearly thirty years and kept the business running while Dad *went* running.

Running around, that is.

"I'm sorry, Cassidy, but he's in a meeting he can't be pulled out of. I'm sure you understand."

Oh, Cassidy understood all right. She wondered how old this one was. Probably blonde—most of her father's "meetings" were—and probably had an impressive degree. That was the weird thing. Somehow Dad always managed to snag the Harvards and Yales of the world. You'd think those women would know better, but there was something about Mitchell Davenport that made women lose their minds.

Cassidy was about to join their ranks.

She ran a hand over her Maltese, Titania's, soft fur. "All right, Deborah. I understand." They both knew she *didn't* understand. "Have him call me when he's free." *And showered*, she wanted to add, but Deborah didn't deserve crass. Poor thing had to deal with it on a daily basis.

Or hourly.

Cassidy ended the call, then stroked her cheek over the little dog's soft head. When was she going to accept the fact that her father only came through for her when it garnered him something? And the "meeting" in his office was garnering him a lot more than she ever would.

Lunch and, more importantly, the conversation she wanted to have with him were now going to be curtailed time-wise.

She set Titania down on the floor and picked her iPad off the glass table in front of the glass wall that looked out over the glass-like lake twelve stories below her condo, the riot of wildflowers reflecting off all surfaces.

She'd love to spend the day painting, trying to capture this scene. The oils she'd bought yesterday would bring out just the right shimmer of the flowers' reflection on the gray blue water. Her fingers itched to get to her brushes.

Cassidy tapped the calendar app to make sure she had enough time today. There was nothing worse than getting all psyched up to lose herself in her art only to find out she had other commitments.

Which she did. *MANLEY MAIDS* was written in for ten A.M.

Ah, yes. Today was the day Sharon, her housekeeper, had been going to train the new girl the service was sending over, but Sharon had gone on maternity leave early over the weekend.

Cassidy checked the time. Nine fifty-five.

She tapped the calendar and set the iPad back on the table. Nothing like having to introduce someone to the

Davenport world she inhabited. At first they were awestruck—Dad did like to do *showy* in grand style, with a side helping of *decadent* just to make himself look good, and he'd had the designer outdo herself with this placc.

It usually took less than a week for a newcomer to see beneath the veneer and start with the pitying looks—the ones she had to pretend she didn't see because it made no sense for anyone to pity someone who lived a life as fabulous as hers.

Wasn't that what Dad always said?

Actually, Cassidy didn't know what Dad said anymore. If it weren't for email, she'd rarely hear from him.

Right at ten, the doorbell rang. Cassidy shooed Titania into her enclosure, brushed her chestnut waves over her shoulder, straightened the lapels on her beige silk blouse, then smoothed the braided belt at the waistline of her matching linen pants. She'd test the one-week theory with this one.

She opened the door to the condo's vestibule. It took the hunk in the Manley Maids uniform less than one *second* to start with the looks.

Only his weren't the pitying kind. They also weren't leering, which was another reaction she'd come to expect.

No, if she had to guess, she'd call his look angry.

C ASSIDY Davenport stood before him in the flesh. Flesh-colored pants, flesh-colored top, and enough buttons unbuttoned to reveal a lot more flesh.

Liam worked hard to keep from groaning. Mac had assured him she wouldn't be here. Not on Mondays. Yet here she was.

Cassidy Davenport. Pampered socialite whose daily clothing bill was probably more than a blue collar worker earned in a week—and he doubted she'd know a blue collar worker if he came up and bit off her ridiculously priced manicure. The woman was frivolous with a capital F.

He was done with frivolous. Been there, done that, spent a fortune on designer clothes and rhinestone-studded T-shirts for his ex, Rachel, that had matched the diamond studs she'd insisted on having.

The scene in Flannigan's Pub came back in blinding clarity. Rachel giving a lap dance to that damn pretty boy frat guy with a tab longer than his dick, one hand down the back of his pants while she rubbed her chest all over the kid's face.

Liam had stood there in stupefied disbelief, watching her talented fingers—that he'd thought had been reserved for his pleasure alone—slip the wallet from the kid's pocket and into her own, and no one at the table, least of all the kid, had been any wiser. A socialite-wannabe stealing money because *he* wouldn't pander to her shoe-and-pocketbook habit.

He'd backed out of the place, sick to his stomach over the loss of what he'd thought had been his future, questioning everything he'd thought he'd known, then he'd driven home in a fog, hurt and disillusionment overshadowing everything else.

Eventually, anger had risen like a phoenix from the ashes of his love, so when she'd shown up later with that new Louis Vuitton bag she'd said was a knock-off, he'd called her on it. On everything.

Rachel hadn't denied it. Hadn't even tried to manipulate him with tears into taking her back—for once—when he'd demanded his key. He'd been almost as surprised at that as the bar scene. She'd merely shrugged, handed it over, thanked him for a good time, and sauntered down his front walk, shredding his heart beneath the damn Manolo What's-their-names he'd bought her.

No, women like Rachel—and Cassidy Davenport— women who lived off the hard work of the men in their lives . . . he was done with them. He'd been played once, but luckily, not to the point of no return. He'd learned his lesson: stay away from the high-maintenance types who only had looks to commend them.

He was really going to have to work for this job. And *not* to keep it.

"*You're* the maid?"

Liam winced. Surely there had to be a better term, but *domestic goddess* didn't exactly fit, while *housekeeper* brought up an image of the Brady Bunch.

He gripped the vacuum cleaner and straightened his shoulders. His pecs flexed—purely involuntarily of course. "Um, yeah. I am."

He didn't have to be a college graduate—though he was—to read what she was thinking when her gaze ran over him from head to toe. Mac didn't run *that* kind of a business.

"They didn't tell me they were sending a guy."

"Is that a problem?" God, let her say "yes" so he could get the hell out of here, because he felt a sudden need to clean something—himself. Women like her got under his skin and not in a good way.

They used to, but what was the saying about repeating history's mistakes? Liam had zero intention of doing that.

"Well, no. I guess it's not a problem." She tapped one of those ridiculously priced nails on her surprisingly non-collagen-enhanced lips. "Won't you come in?"

"Uh, yeah. Sure." Mac would kill him if he said no. This had been his baby sister's first account. That's why she'd selected it for him, she'd said; she knew he wouldn't lose it for her.

So he sucked up his innate prejudice against the Cassidys and Rachels of the world, and took the step up into the foyer beside her.

She was smaller than she'd first appeared now that they were on the same level.

Then he got a look around the place. No way would they ever be on the same level.

Rich dripped from the chandelier with the pear-sized crystals. It wove through the gold-threaded rug, vined through the marble floor, and scented the air with the hint of millions.

Liam had money, but this . . . Even the froufrou little dog had a gilded cage. This was on the level of the Donald Trumps and Conrad Hiltons of the world.

And Mitchell Davenports. The Trump-in-training had turned a small construction business into a residential and commercial design and management firm in an enviable amount of time. But none of this was actually Cassidy's of course. She lived off *Daddy's* money.

Cassidy Davenport was more Bryan's or their pro-ball player friend Jared's type than his these days. He was done with women who looked down their noses at men who couldn't give them what they wanted.

He glanced at Cassidy's nose. Perfectly pert in that rhinoplastic way of the rich, but she'd never get the chance to look down it at him. He'd learned his lesson, and women like her, while not a dime a dozen—because they upped the ante to about a hundred thou a dozen—were so far below women who knew how to make their own way in the world that all he felt for her kind was anger at such uselessness.

But he wasn't here to judge; he was here to clean. For four frickin' weeks.

He should have folded that last hand. Taken his losses and lived with them. But Manleys didn't go down without a fight. It was how he'd made his own fortune, inconsequential though it was when compared to this place. The one he was supposed to be cleaning.

He gripped the vacuum wand and planted it in front of him. "Where would you like me to start?"

"I guess the bedroom's as good a place as any."

Seriously? Did she really think he'd fall for that? Was she slumming today? Pissed off at the boyfriend or something? Wanting a little spice?

"Sharon always started in the bedroom, then worked her way out. She said it kept what she'd already cleaned from getting messed up again before she finished. Makes sense to me, but if you've got another routine, I'm okay with that. Whatever you want to do is fine."

Sharon. The maid. The one he was here to replace.

Liam glanced at the bucket of cleaning supplies and vacuum cleaner as if he'd never seen them before.

That's right. He was here to clean house; not *play* house.

Liam bit back a chuckle. As if she'd be interested in him that way. He'd forgotten he was in the green golf shirt and cotton pants that constituted a Manley Maid uniform. He didn't feel very manly in it, and with the vibe he *wasn't* getting from Cassidy Davenport, he probably didn't look it, either.

He should be glad. He could get through this nightmare without having to fight off a society babe who thought she'd have some fun with *the help*. Been there, done that, ripped off the diamond-studded T-shirts. And wished he could have shredded them, but he'd been the one shredded.

He adjusted his grip on the bucket, took a deep breath, and headed into Cassidy Davenport's bedroom. If he wasn't involved with a woman, going into her bedroom should be no big deal. And if he couldn't even stand to be in the same room with that woman, her bedroom was just another room.

Then he saw the silky baby blue robe tossed over a padded chair. A piece of black lace peeking out from the top drawer of the dresser. Something peach and frothy lying in a puddle beneath the flowered bench at the end of her rumpled bed. It'd landed near a pair of shoes.

Black shoes.

With really high heels.

And ankle straps.

Black lace. Peach nightie. High heels. The spiked kind.

Cassidy bumped into him from behind.

He'd called this *just another room*? He seriously needed to have his head examined and his sense of smell shut off because the scent of her—still of millions but this time with a good dose of *woman* threaded through—wrapped around him the way that silk robe had embraced her curves.

And those curves, the ones her unbuttoned shirt hinted at, were every bit as lush and soft as he'd expect—except that he *hadn't* expected them to be lush and soft. Most women in her income bracket underwent the knife as if it were a day out with the girls, but the few nanoseconds she was plastered against him were enough for Liam to learn that she hadn't subscribed to that particular social custom.

She jumped back. "Why'd you stop?"

Because the image of her in those heels and that nightie, all wrapped up in silk, had nailed him to the floor.

"You don't make your bed?" Anger was always good for dispelling tension, sexual or otherwise, and right now Liam knew which one he needed to focus on. Not focus on. Whatever.

"I forgot you were coming."

Did she have to use that particular word?

What was *wrong* with him? He didn't even *like* the woman.

"Are you going to hover over me while I do this?"

These were going to be four really long, hard weeks.

He so wished he hadn't used *those* words.

And when he saw the look on her face—fleeting though it was—he wished he hadn't used that tone. It wasn't her fault that he'd reacted this way to her.

"Um . . . well, no." She backed up, her green eyes wide and—shit—teary.

"Hey, I'm sor—" Damn it. He wasn't going to apologize. He'd learned his lesson when it came to women's tears. Rachel had been a master of the waterworks and he, fool that he'd been, had bought them. Every single time she'd used them.

"I guess I'll leave you to it." She spun around on her sexy-as-hell stilettos and strode out of the room, her ass-hugging pants leaving nothing to his imagination. Which sent it into overdrive.

Liam cursed beneath his breath and turned around—

To stare at the rumpled, unmade bed with sheets that had been wrapped around that curvy ass, those long-as-sin legs, and her perfectly natural breasts, and Liam didn't know if he was going to make it four *hours* in this place let alone four weeks.

Chapter Two

❧

CASSIDY gulped the San Pellegrino and blamed the fizz for the tears in her eyes. They certainly weren't caused by Mr. Manley Maid in there. Mr. Rude-Obnoxious-He-Man Manley Maid who probably expected every woman to fall at his feet for one small glimmer of his interest.

Well she'd seen the interest—fleeting though it'd been—but she was still standing. Bastard.

She would have thought he'd have been a little nicer. After all, all she had to do was make one phone call and his ass would be canned.

Cassidy fumbled for her cell phone and hit her contacts list. Yeah, she didn't have to put up with his attitude. Who did he think he was? Did he *know* who her father was?

Her finger hovered over the Manley Maids' phone number for a second.

Two.

Was she *really* going to throw her father's name around to demand respect? Seriously? Where was her backbone? Her sense of pride? Self-esteem?

Cassidy set the phone on the counter.

She couldn't make that call; she'd be just as bad as her father. Wasn't that what today's lunch was all about? To prove to herself that she didn't need him? That she had her own talent, her own skills, and she didn't need him and the made-up position at his company to support herself?

She took a deep breath, not really looking forward to the conversation. It would be a battle. Dad always expected everyone to jump to do his bidding, her included.

Look where that'd gotten her.

Cassidy walked into the living room. Okay, so this wasn't a bad place to be, but while it might be a giant, gorgeous room with the best furniture and view money could buy, a Steinway in the corner, a sound system fit for a Philharmonic, and enough artwork to feed a third world country, it was still just as empty and devoid of warmth and hominess as any of the other top-of-the-world penthouses or hotel rooms or boarding school dorms Dad had put her up in over the years.

If he'd let her, she could've made this place a home. With splashes of color and personal knick-knacks, and that granny-square afghan she'd found at a flea market in college and had kept hidden in the steamer trunk in her closet ever since for the day she'd have a house of her own.

If she didn't get this lunch with him, that day was going to be later rather than sooner.

Something crashed in her bedroom and Mr. Rude cursed. Cassidy bit her lip to keep from smiling. It wasn't funny, really, but served him right for being so testy. Normally her room was in pristine shape when Sharon showed up, but she'd been more focused on the lunch with her father than the fact that someone new was coming by.

Titania growled and that *did* elicit a smile from Cassidy. She picked up the teacup-sized dog and nuzzled her top-knot. "Hush, Titania. I can't hear him cursing if you start barking."

Titania licked Cassidy's neck, little tail brushing the side of Cassidy's breast, reminding her all too well what her breasts had felt like pressed against the guy's hard, muscular back. She'd had to jump away to keep him from noticing her body's reaction. He was one giant pheromone in a way Burton, her father's right-hand man and her semi-regular date these past eight or so months, wasn't.

Mr. Maid cursed again and Cassidy winced, waiting for the crash. Luckily, it didn't come, though, honestly, there wasn't anything in that room that she'd mourn the loss of. She'd learned long ago not to put out anything personal that wasn't designer-selected or Dad would have a fit. Everything had to be picture-perfect for her father. Everything. Including her.

She twisted one of the diamond studs her father had given her on her birthday. The ones he'd picked up in Dubai. She'd seen them when Deborah had unpacked his briefcase, both of them figuring they were for the flavor *du jour*, neither one of them certain what that flavor's name was since it'd only been one *jour*. But that's all that one had lasted and Dad had given them to her. What was there to be said for getting a bimbo's cast-offs?

Cassidy sighed and set Titania, the show-dog-caliber pet, back in her pen. She needed to talk to Dad; this living in a gilded cage thing was over. She was almost thirty years old and after her mother had walked out, she'd practically been in limbo waiting for her real life to start.

Well now it was time and Dad was just going to have to face it. He couldn't go jet-setting all over the world and expect her to sit here, twiddling her thumbs or arranging flowers or meeting with women old enough to be her grandmother on some charitable board to discuss which tea sandwiches to serve, waiting for the moment he needed a hostess. "Event Director" was her official job title within the company, but it was as shallow as she used to be. This was no kind of life, and after twenty-nine years of being a Barbie doll he put on display when the mood suited, she was sick of it.

Not that Dad would ever understand. He'd think she was nuts. But then, his life hadn't been changed by witnessing one young boy's battle against a disease that didn't care how

much money someone had. It'd put life in a whole new perspective for Cassidy and she'd changed hers the day they'd
buried poor Franklin.

She slid the deposit slip from the bank for the gallery's
check from her pants pocket. Her first sale, and now that
she'd actually sold a piece of handmade furniture—*without*
Dad's help or his name attached to it—Cassidy finally had
the proof and the resolve to show him she was more than
just a pretty face.

Dad owed her this lunch, whoever the hell he was "meeting" with. She grabbed her purse and the keys to the Mercedes and left a card with her phone number on the kitchen
counter, then decided to let Mr. Rude know he could now
clean without having to suffer her presence. She poked her
head back into her bedroom to tell him so.

That was her first mistake.

Mr. Manley Maid was bent over, those green pants
stretched tight across the finest backside she'd seen since
that last World Cup match she'd attended. So she stared at
it. After all, it was there, just begging to be stared at.

Staring was her second mistake.

"Need something?" He stood up and looked over his
shoulder at her, and her third mistake was taking a few
nanoseconds too many to take her focus off his backside.

When she finally did, it was to find his blue eyes boring
into hers. Gorgeous blue eyes. Cerulean, like the sky she'd
painted on the bombe chest she'd sold.

"Is there something I can do for you, Ms. Davenport?"

She ignored the slight sarcasm on the *Ms.* and instead
thanked God she didn't make a fourth mistake and tell him
exactly what he *could* do for her.

"I'm going out," she answered calmly, willing herself not
to clear her throat to cover her embarrassment. Those Swiss
finishing classes came in handy. "There are extra cleaning
supplies in the hall linen closet, and if you have any other
questions, my cell number is on the kitchen island. Please
lock up when you leave."

She willed herself to smile warmly and turn slowly, the

perfect tilt to her head that said *I am in complete control*, and walked calmly out her front door.

With his gaze boring through her shirt the entire way.

JESUS, the woman could light a fire in him. Standing there, looking so unbelievably cool, yet so utterly hot in that nude outfit, with her head held high and that lingering glance on his ass . . .

He'd wanted to turn around and call her on it, but he hadn't been *able* to turn around. Let her think he was arrogant—he could be—but in this instance, it'd been all about self-preservation. She'd had him harder than the stupid vacuum cleaner wand he'd been holding and just as thick.

Liam threw the wand away in disgust. God, comparing his anatomy to a vacuum cleaner only brought images of suction and that went down a road he had no business—nor interest—in going.

Liar.

Hell. Yeah, he was lying. He was definitely interested—at least physically. Any other way? Out of the question.

But she packed one hell of a punch to his libido, so he'd better keep his guard up. Forget kissing her or he'd be kissing this stupid job goodbye. And in under twenty-four hours, no less. Mac would kill him.

Liam sank onto the bed and swiped a hand over his face. He couldn't let Cassidy Davenport get to him. She was everything he hated in a woman: spoiled, pampered, self-entitled, condescending . . .

Sexy, gorgeous . . .

He exhaled. The physical part had been his downfall with Rachel. He'd been so infatuated with that part of her, that he'd missed the rest—who she really was beneath the gorgeous veneer. It was time to go on a date. Find someone else. Someone new. Someone *real*. All these months—all eighteen of them—since Rachel, he'd steered clear of women, even for the most basic of his needs. Rachel had done one hell of a number on his heart, his goals, and his judgment. To find out she'd been using him solely for the things he could give her . . .

The yippy little dust rag Cassidy Davenport called a dog started imitating a mouse on steroids, dragging Liam back to the present. Christ. Mac hadn't mentioned anything about dog-sitting for this job. He'd ignore the thing, but unlike its owner, the dog wasn't to be blamed for being a spoiled little monster used to having its demands met with the first shrill bark. Liam headed out to see what was wrong.

The thing was running circles inside its pen, hopping onto its back legs when he walked up to the enclosure, a rippling bundle of white silk, complete with a stupid little bun on the top of its head, its little pink tongue hanging out as if Liam were carrying a steak.

It'd probably expect Chateaubriand.

"What do you want?" Liam practically growled when it yipped at him again. He couldn't even call it a dog. Dogs were animals of substance. Man's best friend. Saver of kids who'd fallen into wells. This thing was a feather duster on paws. An animated accessory and he couldn't believe Cassidy Davenport had forgotten to take hers with her. That purse she'd been carrying had been big enough for this little thing.

The dog yipped again.

"I don't know what you want, dog."

The thing ran clockwise around the pen a few times, then stopped, yipped again, and ran the other way a few more times.

Liam walked into the kitchen to get it some water.

The room looked like a mausoleum. White marble floor and countertops, pristine white cabinets with glass doors, everything lined up inside like a showroom. And of *course* the dishes were white china rimmed in gold. He wouldn't be surprised if Evian came out of the faucet.

He took a bowl of water out to the dog. The thing sniffed once, then ran circles around it.

Oh hell. It probably needed to go out. Mac definitely hadn't mentioned dog-walking in his duties.

But the other choice was to let it do its business on the floor and that he *would* have to clean up.

No thank you. Besides, he didn't have any issues with the dog.

"All right, hold on. Where would she have put your leash?"

After some deductive reasoning because he did *not* want to go searching through her closets and drawers—that peach nightie he'd picked up probably had a matching thong to go with it that he did *not* need to see—Liam found the leash in the closet in the foyer.

It was pink. Not that he'd expect anything else. This dog and its owner screamed pink.

He wanted to scream when he saw the leash was covered in rhinestones. Christ, he couldn't get away from the stupid things. What was it with women and sparkly things?

He clipped the leash onto the dog's matching pink and rhinestone collar—which matched the pink bow around the silly bun—and headed out of the condo.

Just before the front door closed behind him, however, he tossed that stupid pink bow back inside. Bad enough people were going to see him walking this stuffed animal; that ribbon was too much.

The building's elevator operator smiled politely as he got in with the dog, but laughter hovered at the corner of the guy's mouth.

Liam couldn't blame him. It was funny—*if* it was happening to someone else.

"I'm assuming you know this dog's name?" he asked the guy. Marco, his name tag read.

Marco nodded. "Titania."

Figured Cassidy Davenport would name her dog after the queen of the fairies. Nobility and fairy tales. Could be a metaphor for her life. She even lived in a gilded tower.

"She likes the patch of grass beneath the dogwood tree," Marco said. "It's to your right out the front door."

He probably also knew what Titania ate for breakfast, the last time she'd taken a constitutional, and what designer costume her owner had put her in for Halloween. That was the kind of service buildings like this offered and what people paid millions for.

But the guy was making an honest living, so Liam couldn't fault him. Instead, he tucked a few bills into the breast pocket of Marco's uniform as the doors opened into the lobby.

"Thanks." Liam patted the pocket. "For the info and for not mentioning this to anyone." He might not have many friends in this part of town, but if word somehow got back that he'd walked a froufrou piece of fluff for some spoiled socialite—on a pink sparkly leash no less—he'd never hear the end of it. Bad enough he was going to take ribbing for being a cleaning lady.

Thankfully, Titania took care of business quickly and bobbled back to the building as quickly as her stubby little legs could take her, while Liam could only imagine the laughs the guys monitoring the security cameras must be having over this scenario. Hopefully, the management had a restriction about posting security videos online.

He put Titania back in her pen, hung the leash back in the closet, then resumed his job of cleaning Cassidy Davenport's bedroom.

The woman was a piece of work. He always straightened up before Sharon came to clean his place. Funny that he was taking over for her here, since she also cleaned his house. Clean*ed*. Mac was going to have to send someone new over now that Sharon's leave had come earlier than expected because there was no way Liam was going to play maid here then go home and do the same.

He swept the dust rag over what he'd guess was a high-priced piece of artwork on the table beside her bed and— shit! A pewter sphere rolled off and under the bed.

Liam got on his hands and knees and looked for it. He could just hear the woman now, complaining that he'd broken it, and it'd probably cost more than he'd made all year.

There it was, smack under the middle of the bed. He flattened himself on the floor and inched toward it. With his head, shoulders, and practically his entire back under the bed, he finally reached it. Jesus. What size bed was this? It certainly was bigger than his king. What came after king? Monarch? Sovereign? Dictator?

Whatever. Liam grabbed the ball and backed out.

Except his shoulder snagged on the bed frame. He stopped, not wanting to rip Mac's uniform, then tried to reach back and free the shirt, but there wasn't enough space to maneuver and he wasn't a contortionist who could get his fingers back there.

He wiggled a little, shimmying like a snake. Tried rotating his shoulder to see if that would free it.

Nope.

Christ. Liam lay on the floor, those black, ankle-strapped stilettos directly across from him. Perfect line of sight. He did *not* need the visual.

He headed back toward the middle of the bed and felt his shirt come loose.

Shimmying down and over, Liam managed to extricate himself from Cassidy Davenport's bed. He wondered how many men would think him stupid for wanting to.

He stood up and something dropped at his feet.

A photo and something else.

Liam picked them up. The photo was of a woman with a dark-haired little girl on her lap sitting on a beach somewhere, palm trees and a grass hut behind them, buckets and shovels and sandcastles all around.

Cassidy Davenport, no doubt. The child had the same smile, and the same brilliant green eyes. He flipped it over.

Mother. Martinique. The last vacation.

That *last* bothered him.

Obviously Cassidy Davenport had had a mother, but as far as Liam knew, Mitchell Davenport wasn't married. Divorced? Widowed? Was his daughter the result of a love affair?

Liam picked up the other thing that had fallen out. A bracelet made of seashells. Cracked, the cord fraying, it was a match to the ones the two in the photo were wearing.

Why hide these under the bed? Or had she lost them? Would she be glad that he'd found them? Or upset?

He had no idea and he didn't want to give Cassidy any reason to complain to Mac about the service, so he knelt down and felt around for where they'd come from. Out of sight, out of mind.

But that word wasn't out of his mind. *Last*. And the four other words with it: concise, stark. Practically devoid of emotion.

Liam tucked them away and stood up. Those words—that picture—were too real. Too raw. Too honest. He didn't want to see Cassidy Davenport like that.

It would make her too human.

Chapter Three

❧

CASSIDY'S father's pitiful grab for youth had only gotten worse since he'd turned the dreaded six-oh. It was as if he knew the date of his impending death and was determined to do everything on his Bucket List. Three times. Including any bimbo he could entice into the back of his Rolls. It was utterly sad how many of those women there were.

Case in point: the one leaving his office now, trying desperately to cover up the fact that her blouse was mis-buttoned.

Cassidy just rolled her eyes at the chick who couldn't be older than she was. Why these supposedly smart women with great degrees and good jobs opted for sleeping their way up the corporate ladder was beyond her. Didn't they have any self-respect?

"Thank you, Mr. Davenport, for your time." The poor thing was actually trying to make it look as if the sales call had gone as planned.

Or maybe a quickie on his desk had been her objective all along.

Cassidy could tell her it was futile. That the blondes came

and went—she coughed to cover the inappropriateness of *that* thought—at regular intervals. Her father was a dog, which made the media's moniker of Hound From Hell for him so very apt. He was tenacious, and once he'd set his sights on a project, watch out anyone who got in his way.

Mother had been his first victim. Or, at least, the first one Cassidy was aware of. And that'd been over for twenty-five years.

"He'll see you now, Cassidy," Deborah said after touching her earpiece.

Poor Deborah. Mitchell had her on an electronic leash, able to reach her at any time or anywhere by buzzing in her ear. Did she ever take it out? Like in the bathroom or when she went home to her husband?

Cassidy just hoped her father paid the woman what she was worth, but doubted it. He hadn't gotten where he was today by being generous. Everything had a price, according to him. Including his daughter's obedience.

She stood up and smoothed the linen pants. Funny that her father hated if she showed up wrinkled yet the woman who'd just left his office had looked like something someone had left in the washer a few days too long. Ah well. Not her problem. For much longer anyway.

She took a deep breath before pushing open the door to Dad's office. Thankfully the girl hadn't latched it; Cassidy was loathe to touch anything in the office for fear of what DNA might be lingering and from whom.

"Hello, Cassidy." Dad did his usual throw-his-arms-open-wide, politician-style hug as he walked out of the full-sized bathroom he'd had custom-designed for his office. "To what do I owe the pleasure?"

The word *pleasure* coming from him made her shudder. "Lunch? Remember, we have a date?"

"Ah . . ." He looked at his desktop calendar and tapped it. "Yes. I see it right there. Lunch with my daughter."

His smile was indulgent, but it set Cassidy's teeth on edge. He still thought of her as a malleable sixteen-year-old, kept in line by the promise of a cool car and credit card privileges. God, she'd been so shallow. So easy.

"So where would you like to go? Chinese? Thai? Indian? Italian?"

"It doesn't matter to me, Dad." She wouldn't be able to eat anyway. She'd been psyching herself up for this conversation for almost a year. Now it was finally time to have it.

"All right, then. How about Padraic's? It's been a while since I was there."

That's because, to her father, Padraic's was "slumming it." Which showed her the importance he put on this luncheon.

One more reason for her to go through with it.

"Actually, you know what? I would like to go to La Maison. It's my favorite." Until the words came out, she'd had no idea she was going to contradict him.

Dad was just as surprised that she was finally getting a backbone. At twenty-nine, it was about time.

No, she wasn't going to dwell on that. She wasn't exactly proud of herself for playing into his world order. Most people were sucked in; it was hard not to be when the charismatic Mitchell Davenport put his plans in action. It'd made him a good businessman but a shitty father. And she, who'd been starved for some sort of parental affection after Mom had walked out, had chosen to ignore the fact that she was living a sycophantic lifestyle. But no more.

He wasn't going to like what she had to say.

He also didn't like her lunch suggestion—his left eyebrow was arched almost into his hairline. As a kid, she'd dreaded that eyebrow. Disappointment, anger, disinterest . . . it was all there. And had been for way too long.

She had a feeling there was going to be a lot of eyebrow arching in the next hour.

He punched a button on his phone. "Deborah, have Paxton bring the Rolls around." He smiled his business smile when he disconnected the call. "I'm guessing this is a special lunch today?" Hence the Rolls.

Cassidy would have preferred anything but the Rolls. He took his "meetings" in that car. But she'd give him this one; he was going to have a lot more to deal with than her unwillingness to ride in his love-mobile.

But he had to see, once she explained it, that this was what she was meant to do. She could only be an ornament for so long; she needed a purpose in her life. She needed to *do* something. Her artwork was good. Someone had paid real money for it—someone who hadn't known who she was.

The feeling of getting by on her talent, her efforts . . . It was heady. It opened the door to all sorts of possibilities, not the least of which was her own career and her own place. One she would be able to afford on her earnings instead of the monthly allowance Dad liked to call her salary. But she wasn't sixteen anymore; she knew exactly what that money was. It was a way to keep her in line and make his life easy. It was also the physical embodiment of her marking time.

Franklin's death had shown her how little time anyone could have. He'd left behind a legacy; what did she have to speak for her? The byline on the programs and agendas she put together for her father and the photos in the society pages weren't enough for her. Not anymore.

Dad had to understand it. He'd made a name for himself; was it so wrong that she'd want to do the same?

He was solicitous on the ride to the restaurant, holding the door for her, offering her a glass of wine in the car. Noon was a little too early for her to start drinking, though with what she was going to tell him, maybe she ought to get *him* liquored up.

The doorman opened the car door when Paxton pulled up to the restaurant's *porte cochere*. "Good afternoon, Miss Davenport."

"Hello, Dennings." She'd grown up calling those in the service industry by their last name, but it'd never felt right or comfortable to her. But if she didn't, Dad would start in on an embarrassing cringe-worthy "lesson" of how to comport herself.

He was *really* not going to like what she had to tell him.

Fifteen minutes later, after the pleasantries had been discussed and their orders delivered, Cassidy took a fortifying sip of the wine she'd caved in and ordered, set it down, folded her hands in her lap—so he wouldn't see her wringing them—and took a deep breath. "Dad."

"Yes, Princess."

She tried to keep the cringe off her face. She'd hated that nickname when she'd heard every one of her friends called the same thing by their wealthy never-home-and-typically-divorced fathers. Just once, she'd wanted him to come up with a new one. One that meant something. But after twenty-nine years, she was finally reaching for her own happiness and her own self-esteem and not relying on him to come through for her. It'd been a lesson she'd learned the hard way.

"I did something that I'm very proud of."

"Oh?" He signaled to the waiter to refill her wine.

She ground her teeth. He might as well just pat her on the head and give her a lollipop. Her nails bit into her palm. "I sold my first piece of art."

Dad set his fork down and for the first time since she'd seen him today, he actually *looked* at her. "You did what?"

"I've been collecting old pieces of furniture, painting them, and selling them."

"You sell furniture?"

"No, Dad. It's art. I refinish old furniture and turn them into collectibles."

"Where?"

"Where do I paint them?"

"No. Where are you selling them?"

"At Marseault's Gallery. On commission."

"What name are you using?"

Of course. He was worried about his reputation. "Don't worry. Not Davenport. I'm using C. Marie."

There went that damn eyebrow again. "Your full name has been published often enough in the papers, Cassidy."

"Which is why I didn't use it. No one's going to know that C. Marie is Cassidy Marie Davenport."

"Does the gallery owner?"

"Well, yes, of course, but—"

"No buts, Cassidy. The owner knows. Do you think he's going to miss out on the opportunity to cash in on my name? That little immigrant came to this country to make his fortune and you handed him the perfect opportunity. My God, how short-sighted can you be? After all the years I've put into building my name, now you've gone and ruined it with some paint-by-numbers hobby."

"It's not a hobby!"

The diners around them stopped talking and stared because of her raised voice—a bigger sin than her "hobby" if Dad's reaction was anything to go by, but Cassidy didn't care. A *hobby*? How *dare* he! She'd worked her heart out on the pieces she'd finished and had almost a dozen more in the works, squeezing in time between his "engagements" where she was supposed to show up looking elegant and glamorous, the perfect Davenport, all so he could say his properties were as beautiful as his daughter. She'd always found the pitch tacky, but now . . .

"Who bought the piece?" Mitchell dabbed at his mouth with the linen napkin, then tossed it onto the table and grabbed his phone. One punch and poor Deborah was again summoned. "I want you to find a piece of furniture. No Deborah, listen. It belongs to a—" The damn eyebrow went north as he glared at her.

"I don't know." And she didn't. Jean-Pierre, the gallery owner, hadn't told her who'd bought the piece, just that it'd been sold.

"That's not helpful. Nor professional." He shook his head. "No, Deborah, not you. I want you to track down the owner of the Marseault's Gallery and buy back a piece sold by C. Marie. Yes, that's right, you heard me. C. Marie, *not* Cassidy Davenport. And I don't care what the price is; you buy it back." He turned off the phone, picked up his napkin and placed it back in his lap, picking up his fork and spearing one of his snails as if he hadn't just completely dismissed Cassidy's life dream.

"Now that that unpleasantness is out of the way, what did you want to talk to me about?"

She ought to throw her fork across the table and storm out, but Cassidy was so sick at heart at her father's callous disregard for her feelings and dreams she couldn't summon the energy. Plus, he and the headmistress of her boarding school had ingrained proper behavior into her so much that she wouldn't dare create a scene—

"Is it about this evening? I know Burton had to attend the ground-breaking ceremony in Charleston, but he has the helicopter. He'll make it in time to escort you. I guarantee it."

The gala. Another one. Number forty-two for the year. She knew because she'd just donated forty-one dresses to a local auction to raise funds for underprivileged children. It's what she did with all her dresses. Dad had pitched a fit over her giving away designer clothing until the publicity had started rolling in, extolling her generosity and giving the Davenport name kudos left and right. Now it was a matter of pride for him that her wardrobe constituted the majority of the donations.

"I'm not worried about Burton not making it." Because, God knew—and so did Mitchell—that *nothing* would keep Burton Carstairs from making it to one of her father's command performances with the boss's daughter on his arm. "But, Dad, about my art. You can't just buy it back. What'll that say about me? Jean-Pierre will never sell any of my pieces again if he thinks you're going to hunt down the buyer. It won't look good for his gallery—"

"You're assuming I care about this man's gallery. I don't, Cassidy." He examined the snail he'd pulled from the shell as if it were more important than a conversation about her life. "He's a businessman and he should have thought things through. At the very least, a phone call to me as a professional courtesy would have been in order. But he didn't make that call, so this is the price of doing business his way. I protect my name at all costs."

"But it's not your name; it's mine."

"Last I looked, my name is on your birth certificate. Therefore, it *is* my concern." He popped the snail into his mouth as if that was the end of the conversation.

Cassidy almost gave in. She'd had too many dealings with him in the past to think he'd ever go along with it now.

But if she didn't fight now, for herself and what she wanted out of life, when would she? She had proof that this wasn't some fly-by-night career choice. She had talent and there was a market for it. If she dropped the ball now, she'd have an even harder time getting the chance to pick it up again because her name would be sullied by Dad's little clean-up act.

She leaned forward, gripping her fork as if it were a lifeline. "Dad, look. I didn't use Davenport on purpose. I didn't want it to affect you if things didn't go well." She crossed the fingers on her other hand resting in her lap. That *wasn't* why she hadn't used her last name, but she'd let him think so to show him she was still on his "team." Dad had a thing about loyalty and her going out on her own would challenge it. "But things have gone well. And I don't *have* to use my last name. That's the beauty of this. I did it on my own. Jean-Pierre thought enough of my talent to take on my pieces, and someone else thought enough of it to buy it. I can have a career at this, I know I can."

"You already have a career, Cassidy. You don't have time for both."

She bit back her retort that wearing designer gowns and schmoozing his business associates only constituted a career if she worked for a call girl service. Because honestly, that's pretty much what she'd felt like ever since she'd met Franklin. Her life had been so shallow compared to what she'd learned in the short time she'd known him. It was the connections, the honesty, the relationships between people, that gave life meaning. Mitchell Davenport used people for his own gain. And that was fine for him; his dream had been to make it big in his industry and he'd accomplished that. But it wasn't her dream and now that she finally had one, he *couldn't* pooh-pooh her for it.

"But I do have time for both, Dad. I managed to finish the piece and more, *and* find a gallery all while working for your company."

"Then why are we having this discussion? Why bother telling me at all?"

"Because . . ." She took a deep breath, going for broke—and she hoped she didn't mean that literally.

Nah, that wouldn't happen. Dad wouldn't cut her off simply because she wanted this. At the very least, she was his daughter and he'd never do anything scandalous to sully his reputation.

She tapped her fork on the linen tablecloth. "Because I *do* want to focus on my art full-time. I can train someone to take over for me in the office for the daily stuff—" not that she had much to do since she'd been "promoted" *off* the design team; her new job and new title were shams and everyone knew it—"and I can still be there for the evening functions."

She had it all planned out. Once her father accepted her chosen path and she'd trained her replacement—probably one of those Harvards or Yales—then she could wean herself from the events. Dad wouldn't even notice as long as the woman who replaced her looked just as good in the gowns and smiled at all the right places, which was pretty much the job description anyway.

He speared another snail and contemplated it again. "That's a nice plan, but you forgot the most important part, Cassidy."

"What?" She'd wracked her brain to cover all her bases because she'd known he would fight her; she hadn't missed anything.

"I don't agree to this plan of yours." He pulled the snail from the shell and popped it into his mouth. "Now, about this evening. Did I mention that I have Corcoran by the balls and when he shows up tonight he's going to see . . ."

Cassidy nodded at all the right places, making the appropriate "mmhmmm" when required, but her mind was far away. He'd dismissed her dream. She hadn't *really* thought he would. Sure, he wasn't going to be happy with it; she'd expected that. But she was his daughter for Pete's sake. His child. Surely he wanted her to have the same chance to make her dreams come true as he'd had? It wasn't as if she was irreplaceable at the firm.

This was supposed to have been her *out*. Her declaration of independence. Granted, the commission on the bombe chest wasn't enough to live on, but it was a start. And once C. Marie's name started getting around, she wouldn't have to rely on the Davenport Properties paycheck and dress up like a toy poodle to prance about on gala nights.

God, she was sick of this life.

And now, once the gallery owner had been tracked down and convinced to buy back the bombe chest—a feat Cassidy had no doubt her father's secretary would be able to accomplish given the almost bottomless coffers of her father's company—there was no way she'd sell any more. Matter of fact, she should probably pick up the rest of the pieces first thing in the morning because no one was going to want to touch a piece they were going to have to return sooner rather than later. Though if Mitchell kept buying them back at a premium, the buyers might not be upset about it.

But she would be. And so would Jean-Pierre. It was bad business all the way around. And given that Jean-Pierre knew who she was—knew who her father was—he wasn't going to come near her with a ten-foot pole once Dad's displeasure was known. No one wanted to get on Mitchell's bad side. She was screwed. Stuck in this life she hated.

"Dessert?" her father asked, the first direct question since he'd shot down her dream.

"No. I'm not hungry."

He looked her over. More along the lines of sizing up a prize thoroughbred instead of a caring father wondering if something was wrong. "Yes, you are getting a little round in the face. That won't photograph well. Try one of those diuretics my trainer gave me. It'll thin you out before tonight."

She'd thought nothing could make her more dejected than her father dissing her career choice. She'd been wrong.

"Really? You want me to have an eating disorder?"

"Stop being dramatic, Cassidy. I've seen your room service charges. You'll never have an eating disorder. Which is why we're having this discussion." He laid his napkin on the table again and tapped her hand. "Use the diuretic. And be sure to have your makeup gal hollow out your cheeks." He stood up and held out his hand. "Can I drop you anywhere?"

Off a cliff. At an orphanage. How she wanted to tell him to shove it, but the reality was, without her custom furniture, she was still dependent on him for her income.

She shouldn't have taken that trip to the Riviera. And the one to Carnival. And the month in Fiji with her favorite designer's summer line she'd bought out had also been completely irresponsible. If only she'd saved the money, she'd be that much closer to financial independence. But it'd all been Mitchell's money and she hadn't yet had her wake-up call.

Then there was the huge chunk of change she'd dropped at the hospital—No. She wasn't going to wish she'd never done that. That was the best money she'd ever spent.

"Cassidy? Time's wasting and you know time is money."

So was taste and breeding and early rising and a whole host of other things her father held dear. Which would be why she wasn't on that list. Her existence served one purpose and one purpose only for Mitchell: to serve as his hostess so he'd never have to marry again and give away half his fortune in alimony.

"No, I'll grab a cab."

His eyebrow arched yet again as he stood. "Suit yourself." He shuddered then straightened his tie and shook his head as he turned to leave the table. "A cab. I have a fleet of corporate cars and she wants a cab."

That was *exactly* the reason she wanted a cab. It was something her father couldn't control and didn't have a hand in. One of the few things in this town that didn't bear the stink of Davenport money.

She laughed at herself. *She'd* borne that stink and had done so willingly. Proudly worn it, actually. All until that fateful dinner when she'd met Franklin.

She shook her head and stood as the waitress brought the bill. Typical. Mitchell had left her holding it. Luckily, she had an account at La Maison, so she charged it to that. Which Mitchell would end up paying anyway, so it was sort of poetic justice.

She exited the restaurant and checked her phone. Fifty-one minutes since they'd entered. Fifty-one minutes in which her carefully laid plans had gone up in flames. Mitchell could suck the air out of any sail. She shouldn't be surprised. She'd known he wouldn't be pleased. But she'd obviously placed too much importance on the father-daughter relationship and the mistaken assumption that he wanted her to be happy. She should have learned from her mother; the only person Mitchell wanted to be happy was Mitchell.

She just wanted to go home and curl up in a ball and forget this day had ever happened, and she was just about to hail a cab when she remembered: the hunky guy was at her place. She did *not* want to go home and lick her wounds with his derisive sneer following her around.

Sighing, she looked around. She didn't feel like grabbing a latte, and spending Mitchell's money was the last thing on her list of things she wanted to do. Okay, second to last. Hunky maid guy was last. Actually, he *could* be on her list of things to *do*, but her father would go into orbit if she canoodled with *the help*.

Hmmm . . . Actually, that'd be the perfect reason *to* do it.

Except she wasn't a user like Mitchell. Well, not anymore.

Sighing, Cassidy turned left and started to walk. Maybe some air would clear her head. The park was this way. At worst, she could spend a few hours tossing coins into the fountain. Mitchell's money would do more people good that way.

Chapter Four

LIAM swiped his forearm across his forehead, but that was futile. His arm was just as sweaty as his forehead. Hell, as the entire rest of him. The AC was cranking in this place yet he was still sweating bullets. That was because of all the damn nooks and crannies that made the millwork something to be envied by everyone except the person charged with cleaning it. He was going to have to talk to Mac about Sharon's lack of cleaning. Though, to be fair, climbing twelve-foot ladders *did* pose certain health risks to pregnant women. Still, maybe Mac could add a specialty line to her services for items beyond the norm. And this place was definitely beyond the norm.

He'd tried not to be impressed, but it was hard not to, from the seamless piece of granite that'd been carved for the kitchen counter, to the see-through fireplace between the living room and dining room, to the architectural wonder that was the balcony. He'd almost taken a header over the railing trying to see the suspension. Mitchell Davenport was a leader in the industry for a reason, and as much as Liam hated that Cassidy was living off her father's spoils, he was thoroughly enjoying the opportunity to see one of the flagship properties up close and personal. The fact that he had to clean the other condo on this floor when he was finished in here so Davenport could put it up for sale just meant he'd have more inspiration for his own growing business.

Walking back into the living room, Liam closed the French doors. They, too, were an engineering marvel, swinging easily with the touch of a finger and latching without a sound. The glass was tempered yet crystal clear in a way he'd never seen. The doors probably cost about as much as he'd made last year, and there were three sets of them in this place.

The froufrou dog pranced on her hind legs when he walked back in. Put a tutu on it and Cassidy would have a circus act. "Sorry, nugget, but she put you in there for a reason and since I just cleaned this place, I'm not letting you out to mess it up. Still, I guess you could use a treat or something for not barking my ears off."

He went into the kitchen to search for some treats and got a shock. The insides of the cabinets were a mess, a jumble of empty plastic containers, canned food, paper products, and dog food, a direct contrast to the rest of the place. Even the frothy negligee on the floor in her bedroom was neat compared to this. The woman had a lot of repressed messiness.

I wouldn't mind getting messy with her . . .

Okay, it was time to leave.

He dug a dog treat out of the mess, managed to close the cabinet door without any of the contents spilling out, and tossed the eraser-like treat to the dog.

Now she started yipping. Of course.

Liam sighed and went around the place to make sure he hadn't left anything. That'd be a rookie mistake and Mac didn't hire rookies.

The muffin with four legs wouldn't stop yipping. It was so high-pitched Liam couldn't call it a bark, but it got on his nerves worse than any bark he'd ever heard. Their next-door neighbor growing up had had a beagle, and while that dog had had a spine-tingling howl, that dog had nothing on this thing. Liam couldn't get out of here fast enough.

Which meant, of course, that he was stuck there when he couldn't find the extension attachment for the vacuum. Shit. He retraced his steps, starting in her bathroom—yeah, yeah, that made no sense, since there was nothing to vacuum in there, but best to start at the beginning and work his way out.

He was on his hands and knees half under her bed again when she returned home.

This wasn't going to look good. Especially since the attachment was all the way by the wall, which meant he had to do that stupid snake-move to grab it and get back out without ripping his shirt or dislodging that bracelet and picture.

"What are you doing?" she asked.

"Fishing." Ask a stupid question, get a smart-ass answer. He humped his way back out—and snagged his shirt again. "Dammit."

"Catch something?"

He could hear the smile in her voice. She knew exactly what'd happened. "Everything's fine."

"Uh huh."

The bed creaked.

"What are *you* doing?"

"Taking my shoes off."

Damn if she wasn't. He had a bird's eye—and ankle—view. And it was a hell of a nice ankle. So was the arch in her foot. And the bright blue nail polish on her toes . . .

Hmmm. She didn't look like the bright blue sort of woman. Not with that flesh-colored outfit. Muted, understated, but reeking of money—*that* was Cassidy Davenport. The blue nail polish was some hippie chick he wouldn't mind tumbling into bed with for an afternoon of hot, sweaty, amazing sex.

Oh hell. Now he had the image of tipping Cassidy Davenport back onto the bed and peeling the muted, understated things off her one inch at a time and kissing his way right behind them.

Good thing his groin was pressed against the carpet.

Then she knelt down beside him. "Here. Let me help."

He didn't need her kind of help. And he was just about to tell her so when she put one hand on his lower back and the other one under the bed between his shoulder blades.

Holy hell, the woman's touch shot fire through him. Fire Liam didn't want or need. It *figured* she'd affect him like this. He'd thought he was immune. That he'd learned his lesson, but apparently his hormones hadn't gotten that memo.

"You're caught."

In more ways than one. "You go to college to learn that?"

"Smart ass." She flicked her fingers and his shirt was free.

Which meant he could come out, but only if his dick decided to cooperate.

Of course it didn't. Especially when she stumbled as she was getting up, and her hand landed square on his ass.

"You did that on purpose." He got himself out of that position pronto, turning the verbal tables on her to cover up the fact that he was still hard under these stupid pants. Pants that left nothing to the imagination—both his hard dick and the feel of her fingers on his ass. Mac needed to get another uniform.

"Don't flatter yourself." She managed to get herself back onto the bed—why???—and smoothed her blouse into place.

Her nipples were hard.

Liam smirked. Couldn't help himself. He affected her like she did him.

Which probably wasn't a good idea for him to know. Now it'd be harder to stay away from her.

"So are you finished?"

Sweetheart, I haven't even started yet . . .

"Why? Got a hot date?" Damn. Why'd he ask that? It was none of his business. And she probably did.

"As a matter of fact . . ." She stood up and unbuttoned the top button. Which was between her breasts to start with so that meant her breasts were on their way to being exposed.

He walked past her. "Then I'll be out of your way."

"Um, you forgot your rod thingie."

He slammed to a stop. His *rod thingie*? Last he checked, his *rod thingie* was still in his pants.

He looked over his shoulder to see her bend over to pick something up off the floor, which gave him unimpeded access down her shirt. God, her breasts were gorgeous. And real.

He licked his lips. "My . . . what?"

"This." She held out the vacuum cleaner attachment. "Don't want to forget this or you'll have to come back tomorrow."

And she thought that was a hardship? "Actually, I do have to come back tomorrow. I still have the windows to do."

"Really?" She tossed her hair back as she held out the *rod thingie* that he was forced to take while trying to shove the image of her holding his real *rod thingie* out of his head. "Sharon can clean this place in a day."

"No offense to Sharon, but this place needs a little more touch-up than she's capable of. A pregnant woman isn't able to do as much physical work as me."

If he weren't mistaken—and he usually wasn't when it came to a woman's interest—she ran her eyes over him.

Shit. He didn't need that. Didn't want it. And if she'd only put a bag over her head, it'd be a non-issue.

Jesus, he had to remember the pain Rachel put him through. Remember what it was like to get figuratively kicked in the teeth to see her for what she was. And she was small potatoes compared to Cassidy. Rachel's father had done well for himself, but he wasn't in Mitchell Davenport's league, so Rachel's expectations had to be lower than Cassidy's. No, the man who ended up with Cassidy was going to have to make major bank or his life was going to be a living hell. Liam had no inclination to sign on for that sentence whatsoever.

No matter how sexy she was.

"I guess you're right about Sharon."

"Yeah. So I'll be back tomorrow, then. Nine o'clock late enough for you?"

"Let's make it eight. I'm an early riser." She crossed her arms and damn if that didn't bunch her breasts together, giving her way more cleavage than the average man could handle.

"Think you can handle that?"

"Princess, I've completed half a day's work by eight. No problem whatsoever."

"Then I'll see you then."

"Fine."

"Good."

They stared at each other for a heartbeat or two longer than they should have and awkwardness set in. Cassidy raked her hair off her forehead and turned around while Liam shoved the *rod thingie* into his back pocket hard enough to tug the front of his pants tight enough against his dick to get *that* rod thingie to calm the fuck down.

"Well, uh, I have to get ready for—"

"Uh, yeah. I'll get out of your hair." Shit. He wanted to get *in* her hair. Spread it out all over that monstrous bed and have her moaning in under a minute. He could, too.

So much for his resolve . . .

Run, Manley. This is not a safe place for you to be right now. Get the fuck away from temptation.

He took his own advice and got the hell out of there, only to come shin-to-snout with the nugget who decided to growl at him.

"You have got to be kidding me." One well-placed kick and—

No. He didn't kick dogs. Or cats. Or small children.

Sexy brunettes who didn't have the sense God gave them (or then again, maybe not) to stay at least a hundred yards behind him, however, were another story.

"Titania! Stop that! He's been here all day. You know him!"

The fluff-ball uttered one last growl and made a beeline for her "Mommy." Fine. Whatever. God save him from temptation-in-heels . . . and her little dog, too.

He couldn't get out of there fast enough.

Chapter Five

❧❧

"YOU look lovely, Cassidy. As usual." Burton held out a glass of Clicquot to her.

Cassidy resisted the urge to down it in one swallow. She and Burton hadn't gone much beyond attending these sorts of events and the occasional dinner together, so he'd probably be stunned if she did guzzle it. Her father would have a cow at her appalling lack of breeding, but, man, wouldn't it feel good to shock them?

She did drink a third of her glass. Champagne flutes were too small anyhow, and after the day she'd had, she needed the pleasant fuzziness the bubbles could provide. Not enough to get her drunk, though. God knows what she'd unleash on her father if she had a buzz going and he decided to mention her painting.

"So your father told me you have a new hobby." Poor Burton. He'd walked into the trap with no warning. But it was interesting that her father had thought to share the info with Burton. Dad was pushing this relationship a little too much.

"Actually, I don't. I have a career."

"A career?" Burton smiled the smile that had always left her feeling a bit icky but she'd never figured out why.

At this moment, she knew. It was Mitchell's smile. That patronizing, isn't-that-nice-dear smile he gave most of the women in his life. Actually, now that she thought about it, Deborah was the only one Cassidy had never seen be the recipient of it.

"So what is this new *career*?" Burton sipped the champagne with his pinkie finger slightly extended.

God, what an affectation. Why hadn't she ever noticed before now? What else was an affectation?

She looked at him. The gold cufflinks, the Rolex, the diamond pinkie ring . . . Oh my God. He was becoming her father. Burton hadn't had all the trappings of *über*-wealth when they'd first met. Mitchell had recruited him out of Wharton, and while she knew he'd been groomed to fit in with the company, she'd never realized until right this minute that Mitchell had groomed him to *be* him.

Oh God. Her father was grooming Burton to take over his role in the company when he retired. Not that Cassidy could see that happening any time soon, but this was suddenly as plain as the diamonds on that Rolex's face. And if he was planning *that*, she got why he was pushing Burton on her. He wanted Burton as a son-in-law to keep the company in the family.

It'd be a cold day in hell before Cassidy would *ever* marry a man handpicked and tutored by her father.

"So what is it?" Burton, to his credit, tried to look interested, but Cassidy could see the little darts out of the corners of his eyes as he looked for some advantageous conversation to become a part of. He'd obviously already been given Mitchell's blessing to pursue her—none of her other boyfriends lasted long if Mitchell didn't approve. Since none of them had been her Prince Charming, she hadn't really minded, but this . . .

Burton was a nice guy, could hold a conversation, and had actually seemed to find talking to her interesting instead of merely staring at her cleavage, but marriage material he was not.

Maybe Mitchell ought to marry him.

"Cassidy?"

Oh. Right. He'd asked a question. "I paint."

"What, like watercolors and stuff?"

"No. Furniture. I turn old pieces into custom-painted pieces of art."

"You mean with flowers and butterflies and rainbows?"

And unicorns and fairy princesses, too, she wanted to add. Did he really think she was that shallow?

Maybe he did. In which case, that just proved how much he *hadn't* been paying attention to her for the last eight months. "No, Burton. I paint landscapes or faux finishes or textures on them."

"Like Thomas Kinkade?"

Kinkade had had talent and he'd certainly had marketing savvy, but she did not want to be classified with him. "No, not like Kinkade. More along the lines of Davenport. Cassidy Davenport."

Burton didn't seem to get the point, but he raised his champagne flute to her—extended pinkie finger and all. "Well, congratulations, sweetheart. That's quite a handy talent to have. You could paint murals on nursery walls. You know, I was thinking . . ."

Oh God. She didn't want to know what he was thinking. Not with that lead in. And the champagne and the cuff links and her father's knowing smile as he chose that moment to look over . . .

"Excuse me, Burton." She didn't even look as she handed him her champagne glass and turned away. The ladies' room was always a handy excuse and the truth was, she could use some cool water over her wrists—to cool down her heated temper. Mitchell was behind this. No wonder he'd dismissed her at lunch. If he was hoping she'd marry Burton and raise little Davenports, of *course* she wouldn't have time for a career . . .

Best to head this cataclysm off at that pass before it ever got a chance to gather strength.

And then she ran into Mitchell.

"Cassidy. Enjoying yourself? Why isn't Burton with you? He's looking rather well tonight, don't you think?"

"He's talking to someone over there." She did a vague wave of her hand, hoping Mitchell would go off in search.

Of course he didn't. Instead he lowered his voice and actually moved closer.

Never a good sign.

"Deborah tells me that that hobby of yours is costing me five figures. You'll want to contribute your profit from it, I'm sure, to defray the cost. I'm willing to take the loss on paper, but not quite that much in actual cash."

"You're kidding me. You buy my artwork that I've already sold and expect me to pay for it?"

That damn eyebrow went north. "It should never have been sold in the first place."

"Why not? It's a good piece. Enough that someone thought enough of it to pay a decent amount of money for it and display it in their home. You should have left it where it was and kept your precious money."

"My *precious money* is what's keeping you in your designer clothes and that penthouse, young lady. I suggest you remember it."

"As if I could forget," she muttered.

"What?" Now the other eyebrow arched and he lowered his head as if he were looking over the rim of glasses.

"I said that my earnings from my art would help with my budget so you wouldn't have to."

At that Mitchell laughed. "Oh please, Cassidy. You couldn't keep to a budget if it was a million dollars. You have no idea what it costs to keep you in your lifestyle. It's nice that you want to contribute, but don't get yourself all concerned with it. I have more than enough to take care of you."

Walk. Away. Do not say something that you're going to regret. Save it for later when you're alone.

Cassidy wanted to listen to her subconscious, knew she *should* listen to it. But that condescending tone just did her in.

She couldn't just let it go. Couldn't let him think that he

could manipulate her into doing what he wanted. She was going to find *some* way to live on her terms.

"You know, Dad, I am actually capable of providing for myself. I just proved it. I haven't before because you needed me to be available for the company. *You* put me in that penthouse. I was happy in the loft."

"The penthouse is more your style—"

"No, the penthouse is more *your* style and you like letting it be known that I live there. I've always been a figurehead for you. The single dad who took his daughter under his wing and set her up in the company. Only you and I know that my role is completely superficial and my job description is to be a size two and look good. Any one of your bimbettes could pull that off."

Oh shit. That comment had gone too far. She knew it by the narrowing of his eyes and the V of his eyebrows. More than the arching, that shape meant a hell of a lot of trouble.

"Look, I should go. This isn't the time or the place."

"You're right about that. I'll be at the penthouse tomorrow morning and we'll finish this."

"Oh, but, the maid is going to be there." There was just something so completely *wrong* about calling that guy a maid.

"So get rid of her. After all, I pay her salary. She'll do what I want."

Doesn't everyone? Cassidy almost said it out loud before she left, but figured she'd done enough damage for one night.

Tomorrow was time enough to say it.

Chapter Six

❦

don't care how it got in the paper, I want the story killed,"
Cassidy said into her phone as she opened the door and
waved Liam in the next morning, looking way too artfully
messy with a pair of shorts hanging low on her hips and an
off-the-shoulder professionally torn-and-frayed T-shirt
like the chick from that eighties' welder-dancer movie, showing way too much skin for his liking and definitely too
much leg.

On second thought, none of it was too much in the normal
male-female interaction. But with *their* interaction . . . Yeah,
definitely too much. He didn't need to be any more attracted
to her than he was.

"Deborah, you always work miracles for my father. Can't
you do something for me? I mean, how hard is it to kill a
story?" Cassidy flicked the newspaper she was carrying and
Liam got a glimpse of a large photo of her in one hell of an
evening gown.

Okay, *that* was too much skin to be flashing around at
*any*one, let alone having it plastered on the front of the
society page.

"But it makes me sound like a spoiled brat."

Liam's ears perked up. He'd never met a society chick who *complained* about being spoiled.

"But I didn't say any of those things. Can I get a retraction?" She groaned. "Well how about a rebuttal?"

"Never heckle the hecklers," Liam muttered. Bryan, his movie star brother, had imparted those words of wisdom. You couldn't win when someone started heckling. Usually, the story grew.

She glanced at him, her eyes narrowing.

"I'm just sayin,' if you make a big deal out of something, its importance will grow. Whatever's in that article, let it go."

"Look, Deborah, I'll have to call you back. But please see what you can do in the interim."

She punched the face of her phone with her thumb. An unnecessary act, since the thing shut down with a swipe, but still, Liam could feel the anger rolling off her in waves from across the living room.

"Did you have something you wanted to share?" Cassidy asked, sounding *just* like her condescending father.

Liam had been to a few events and tradeshows where Mitchell Davenport had been the speaker. The man had an opinion on everything and his was the only one that counted. Granted, the guy *had* built an empire out of practically nothing, but he should never forget the people who'd helped him climb that ladder to success because those same people could pull that ladder out from under him.

Ah, but what did it matter to Liam? He wasn't—and never would be—in the same league as Davenport. And perhaps that supercilious, I'm-better-than-you attitude was the reason.

Well that was okay with Liam. He was perfectly content to maintain his business and style of living at a level he could live with. Being an ego-inflated know-it-all wasn't for him.

"All I said was, if you make something a big deal, so will other people. Let it go."

"Let it go? Do you know what this says?" She rattled the paper at him, the skin above the neckline of that top turning a nice shade of pink in anger.

It was a good look on her. Her green eyes were flashing like gemstones, and her breathing quickened enough so that those gorgeous breasts shifted beneath the clingy fabric in a way only a dead man wouldn't notice. And even that was questionable.

God, it was only 8:16 in the morning and already he was lusting after the client.

"I hear you, but this is slander. Libel. One of the two." She raked her hair back off her forehead and that perfectly coiffed *do* she'd had yesterday had become a jumble of untamed waves that bounced over her shoulders in a way designed to make a man want to run his fingers through them. Tug on them. Hold them tight as he drove into her—

Shit. 8:17 and he was sweating again.

"I mean that it's lies. All of it is lies."

"What's it say?" Damn, he didn't want to ask that. Didn't want to know. Didn't want a damn thing to do with Cassidy Davenport other than to get in and out of her home in the quickest time possible and still allow Mac to call her a client.

The things he did for his sister.

"It says, first, that I got engaged." She held up her ringless left hand. "Do you see a ring here?"

"No." Thank God.

And he'd examine why he was thanking the Lord for that later.

"Damn right you don't. Burton's a nice guy, but definitely *not* the man I'm going to marry."

It was on the tip of Liam's tongue to ask *Burton who*? but he didn't really want to know. He wasn't interested in Cassidy Davenport or who she dated.

"And I didn't storm out of the gala. I walked out nicely. Serenely. Said my good-byes. No one could take issue with my manners. I have no freaking clue if Burton's ex-fiancée was there, nor do I care. She can have him."

He really shouldn't feel any satisfaction whatsoever at hearing those words, but for some reason, he did.

Dammit. Cassidy Davenport was nothing to him. Nothing. And never would be.

Yeah, keep telling yourself that, buddy. That'll explain all this hypersensitivity to her and the way she smells like peaches, and the way her nipples have hardened, and the flutter across her abdomen as she sucks in air to calm down. And how you've noticed all of this about her. Yeah, you're not into her at all.

". . . as if I'm this stuck-up snob who can't lower herself to talk to the common people." She waved the newspaper at him. "Can you believe it? It actually uses the term *common people* in the article! What are we? Living in some feudal village? Who *does* that?"

She turned around and stormed across the room, those stomps doing some mighty nice things to her ass.

"I'm not going to stand for this. I'm just not. My father had to have planted at least part of the story."

"He wants people to think you're stuck up?" Since Mitchell Davenport was all about image and this would not be the best public relations, Liam didn't buy it.

She spun around, her hair fanning out behind her, swinging around to curl over one shoulder, leaving the other bare, enticing him to kiss his way from her shoulder up the curve of her neck and lose himself in that scent of peaches.

"No. That I'm engaged to Burton. I'd hoped last night that he wasn't intending to propose, and I left before it could get awkward. Now my father is forcing my hand, so to speak, so that I can't turn him down. What would it look like if Mitchell Davenport's daughter said yes, then no, to his hand-picked son-in-law? I'll be the most ungrateful, spoiled, willful child there ever was."

"So you're not getting married?" Why on God's earth was *that* the question he asked? Jesus, her perfume must have infected his brain.

"Not to Burton Carstairs I'm not. It'd be like marrying my dad, and that's the last thing I'm ever going to do."

"Yeah, but who are you going to find except Daddy's hand-picked henchman to be able to afford this place?"

She stormed back across the room toward him, one finger

pointed right at his chest. "Seriously? You actually have the *nerve* to say that?"

Liam stepped up onto the foyer level from the sunken living room so she wouldn't be eye-level with him.

That finger hit him in the chest. Ouch. Damn manicure was sharp.

"How *dare* you say that. You don't know anything about me. Don't believe what you read in the papers. Today's story is the perfect example of the lies they'll make up to sell advertising. I am not some spoiled, useless doll that my father puts on the shelf when not parading me out in public. I actually have a job at his company."

Liam decided discretion was the better part of valor when it came to that statement. From what he'd seen of her over the years, her so-called job *was* to come out and look pretty. Just like a doll.

Luckily, her cell phone rang then, saving him from making the matter worse. Sure, she could boast all she wanted that she wasn't going to marry this Burton guy, but she ought to know that Mitchell Davenport had rarely lost a battle he'd wanted to win. It would take a certain kind of man to marry Davenport's daughter, and Carstairs sounded like the perfect toady. Hand-picked and modeled after the man himself. That way, he'd never have to worry what Carstairs was going to do with his company or his daughter.

"No, Stacey," Cassidy said into the phone, "it's not true. Burton didn't propose, so I couldn't have turned him down." She raked a hand through her hair again, which hiked her shirt up a little bit.

Shit. That curve of her waist was enough to get his mouth watering.

Utterly inappropriate.

"Yeah, I know. It's going to be a major pain in the ass to set the record straight. I should just go away and let the whole thing blow over." She tapped her finger against the corner of her mouth.

Yes, Liam was watching her a lot longer than he should— but he wasn't about to look away. Her toes were bare—except for that blue nail polish of course—and the way they curled into the thick carpet had him imagining how he'd get them to curl when he kissed his way down her body—

Back the fuck off, Manley. You are not going anywhere near this woman. Have you forgotten about Rachel?

Right. Rachel. His disillusionment and almost-downfall.

"Oh, that's right. I'd forgotten you are. Well, what about Donna? Isn't she going to Monte Carlo? I haven't been in a whi—Oh. I hadn't realized. Well, what about Janet? Wasn't her father buying her that house in Marbella? I love that town. The water's gorgeous and the atmosphere is just—" She tucked a shank of hair behind her ear. "She said that? Well I don't know what I did to her that she'd—" She sighed. "I guess. But Jean's in Long Island with her relatives, so that's out, and Mary's at the Cape with her new boyfriend, and Joy's in Europe for the rest of the summer, and with you going to LA, it looks like I'm stuck here, and alone to boot."

Liam didn't say anything about the poor little rich girl having no place to go. Poor her; she had to stay holed up in this swanky penthouse with a doorman, concierge, and room service—not to mention a *maid*—while she rode out the "bad" storm of publicity surrounding her supposed engagement to a man who could afford to keep her in this lifestyle.

Even socialites got jaded, he supposed.

God, it was really hard for him to swallow. The woman had it all and was too damn spoiled to realize it and thank her lucky stars that there were still men in this world who wanted to treat the women they were with like the china dolls they wanted to be.

But Liam wasn't one of them. No way in hell. He wanted a woman of substance. A real human being. A partner. Someone he could count on to be by his side, not off spending his hard-earned money and complaining that he never took her anywhere or did things with her.

Now if only he could squash the physical attraction he felt for her, he might just be able to complete this job without losing his sanity.

* * *

CASSIDY swallowed the question she really didn't want to ask, but hell, all of her friends were tied up or on vacation and she was going to be stuck here. But she'd love to go to LA with Stacey, except Stacey was off on her father's corporate jet to visit the movie star she was currently dating. Some women had all the luck while she got to sit home in her father's showplace and fend off rumors of her being spoiled. Hell, being stuck in this place was the epitome of being spoiled, but she didn't want to ask her father for the beach house or the place in the mountains because then he'd have one more thing to throw in her face. And no public hotel was as security-conscious as Dad's buildings, so she wouldn't have to face the paparazzi unless she went out.

She said goodbye to Stacey and turned off the phone. She was stuck.

Everything had been so clear when Jean-Pierre had called about the sale. Cassidy had been nervous to even approach him about displaying her work, but Franklin's memory had given her the courage. Then, when Jean-Pierre had been enthusiastic, Cassidy had felt the hope she'd tamped down for so long come out of hiding and blossom. Then there'd been the sale, and she'd finally felt as if she was someone. As if she had something to contribute. Granted, it wasn't what the doctors and nurses had done for Franklin, but it was a hell of a lot more than sitting on her butt while clothing designers flaunted their latest fashions in front of her.

"So you'll be here today while I finish up?"

She looked up, startled. That's right. Maid guy was here.

Damn. What was his name again? She didn't want to ask. She didn't want to come off as shallow as everyone thought she was.

"Um, yes, I will." How was she going to find out his name? "Do you have a business card, by any chance?"

He cocked an eyebrow at her. Funny how her father's

eyebrow-cocking only instilled dread but this guy's . . . That wasn't dread flooding her insides.

Or her thighs.

What was *wrong* with her? She had some big-time PR snafus to fix and she was lusting over the guy who cleaned her toilets because he was hot?

Oh, God. She *was* that shallow.

Still, she took the business card he handed her. "It doesn't have your name on it." Just the logo and the contact info. Plain, functional. Which was nothing like the guy standing in front of her.

The guy shrugged. "I'll have to get Mac on that. I guess it should, though, so people can request people specifically."

She'd request him specifically.

"Right. I mean, how else will people know who you are?" Damn, she still needed to find out his name.

He cocked his head. "You don't know my name."

"What? Of course I do. You introduced yourself yesterday." She kept replaying the scene in her mind, but all she could remember were the tingles that had run through her as he'd stood in her living room while she'd prayed he was a stripper her friends had sent—the ones who'd all but abandoned her this week—and not the actual maid.

How wrong she'd been. And now she was paying for it.

"You *don't* know my name."

"You're crazy."

He crossed his arms, and, oh my, what that did to his shoulders. She wouldn't mind being wrapped in those.

"Okay prove me wrong. What is it?"

"What's what?"

"My name?"

Crap. She'd forgotten the question; why couldn't he? "You don't know? That could be a problem. You might want to get that checked out."

"Funny." He uncrossed his arms and put his fists on his hips.

Oh my, what that did to his washboard eight-pack—

"So what's my name?"

Dammit. She licked her lips. "Seriously, buddy, if you're not remembering your name, you might want to see a doctor."

Liam took a step toward her. "You can't back out of this, Princess. You either know my name or you don't. I'm either important enough for you to remember or I'm not."

"That's not really fair." Because she'd *never* forget him. Maybe she wouldn't remember his name, but him? No, he was definitely memorable.

"And looking down your sculpted nose at us poor working slobs is?"

"My nose isn't sculpted. This is the nose I was born with."

The arched eyebrow said he thought differently.

"It is." She crossed her arms. "Just because most people in my social circle have nose jobs or boob jobs, don't assume I have as well."

"Oh, sweetheart, I already know you didn't have a boob job."

He had no business thinking about her breasts.

But, damn, her breasts liked that he did, her nipples hardening beneath the sports bra and flimsy painting shirt she was wearing.

Turn around, Cassidy. Walk away from the hot guy. Whose name you still don't know.

Oh God. She didn't know his name. How freaking shallow was she?

Cassidy took a deep breath and closed her eyes. She could admit she didn't remember. Lots of people had trouble with names. It didn't mean she was shallow. Plus, she'd had a lot going on these past twenty-four hours. She'd been nervous about lunch with Dad; that's why she couldn't remember his name. He'd probably only said it once and it'd probably been so fast that she really hadn't heard it.

Still, good manners dictated that she should own up to her memory loss. It could happen to anyone.

A key turned in the front door lock.

Maid guy's head swung around at the sound.

Cassidy's didn't. There was only one person who'd use the key without knocking.

Funny, she hadn't thought she'd be happy to see her father after last night, but if his arrival was going to save her from the embarrassment of having to admit she couldn't remember the maid's name, well then, there was a first time for everything.

"Who the hell are you?"

Dad's question, though well-timed, was as arrogant as Cassidy not knowing his name was shallow.

Maid guy, however, didn't seem intimidated. He stuck out his hand and met Dad on equal footing. "Liam Manley. Of Manley Maids."

"Your company?"

Liam (!) shook his gorgeous head of hair. "My sister's. I'm just helping out."

"You work for your sister?" There went Dad's damn eyebrow arching again. "Shouldn't that be the other way around?"

Cassidy wanted to shrivel up and die. How condescending could Dad be? She didn't want to see Liam squirm, but a morbid sense of something had her looking at him.

He looked like a Liam. Big and strong and strapping, like someone from the old country you could depend on to take care of you when the going got tough.

Now why the hell had she thought that?

"I don't really see my sister climbing hip roofs or installing insulation, but I'll mention it to her if she feels the need for a career change." Liam ended the handshake and turned ninety degrees so her father got the side view.

She, lucky woman, got the front view.

"So, Cass, I guess I'll head into the bedroom to finish up in there. Give you two some privacy to discuss your, ah, issue."

Cass? Since when did he call her *Cass*? Since when did he call her *anything*? Well, except for Princess of course, but that'd been said with a healthy dose of sarcasm that she could do without.

Dad watched Liam head into her bedroom. Then he arched an eyebrow at her. "*Cass*? Don't tell me you've made the maid your boy-toy and that's his nickname for you."

Dear God, her father could be crude. Which was really laughable considering he made every blonde twenty-something his bimbo. And even if she *had* made Liam her boy-toy—not that it'd be any of her father's business—*Cass* would be the last thing she'd let him call her. She hadn't let anyone call her that since, well . . . since Mom had left.

"I'm not dating Liam."

Dad just arched his eyebrow again.

But this time, Cassidy wasn't going to squirm. His innuendo was ridiculous and, besides, she had another bone to pick with him.

"Why'd you tell a reporter I'm engaged?"

Her father sighed as if he couldn't be bothered to have this conversation. "That's what your frantic call to Deborah was about? Seriously, Cassidy, I do have a company to run. People are counting on me for their livelihood. To feed their families. I can't be at your beck and call over everything someone says about you. Haven't I told you that we *want* to be mentioned in the society pages?"

"But you don't want any word getting out about my painting."

"That's different. We control the flow of information. Your hobby won't do a bit of good for my company."

"But my faux-engagement to Burton will?"

"Of course." Her father picked up one of the throw pillows and turned it about three inches to the left. Damn perfectionist. Just had to show her that what she'd done wasn't good enough for him. "Burton is a valued member of my executive team. A trusted member. He's worked hard to earn his place and he cares for you a great deal. He's the perfect man for you to marry."

"You make it sound like a business deal."

Dad looked out the large glass windows. "Love matches certainly don't work out well. Look at this country's divorce rate."

He wasn't talking about the country. He was talking about him and Mom. He hadn't spoken about her since two years after she'd left. Which was about the time he'd starting looking at boarding schools . . .

"I am not going to marry Burton, Dad."

He took a deep breath, stuck his hands in his pockets, and turned around. "Yes, you will."

To say she was shocked would be an understatement. Cassidy had never, in a million years, thought he'd be so controlling as to tell her who she was going to marry and actually expect her to. Or go along with it.

"You can't be serious."

"Oh, I'm serious. And with the announcement on the front of the society pages, it *will* happen."

"No it will not." She was not going to budge on this. He might have picked out her wardrobe, her house, even her name, but he was *not* going to pick out the man she was going to spend her life with.

"It will, Cassidy, and when you calm down you'll see it makes sense. Burton's the perfect man for you. You'll continue to live as you're accustomed and he'll work at Davenport Properties. It's all planned."

"Really? By whom? Because I certainly wasn't consulted in this plan."

"You'll do as I see fit, just as you've always done if you want to continue with the benefits of being my daughter."

"Well maybe I don't want to." She shocked even herself when she said that, but the look on Dad's face was priceless.

Too bad she couldn't sell it. Especially when he uttered his next statement.

"That's up to you. And it's a decision that needs to be made in the next thirty seconds."

He tugged back his jacket sleeve and stared at the Rolex that was the model for Burton's. "Twenty-eight, twenty-seven."

"Your intimidation tactics aren't going to work this time, Dad."

He arched an eyebrow. "This isn't a tactic, Cassidy. You either play by my rules or you don't play at all. And that includes all the trappings that go with being my daughter."

"Dad, this is ridiculous. We aren't living in the Dark Ages. I can choose who I want to marry."

He looked back at his watch. "Fifteen, fourteen."

He wasn't serious. He wasn't going to disown her just because she didn't want to marry Burton. He was just used to getting his own way. Plus, he needed her too much. It was a power play. Well, she'd been his daughter for twenty-nine years; she wasn't intimidated.

"Nine, eight." He didn't even look up at her. "Seven, six."

She crossed her arms. "I'm not giving in, Dad."

"Four, three, two, one." He tugged his sleeve down over his Rolex. "I expect you out of here in the next fifteen minutes. You will, of course, leave everything my money has purchased. Except the dog and what you're wearing. I can't turn my daughter out naked on the streets."

"But you'll turn her out onto the streets just the same?" He was trying to scare her into doing what he wanted.

"Exactly. That's what you get when you think you know better. Prove it." He tucked his hands into his pockets. "Aren't you going to get moving, Cassidy? I'm sure it will take you at least five minutes to pack the dog's things. Your things, however, won't take as long since I have paid for everything in this penthouse. Since I'm not without a heart, however, I will permit you to take your toiletries. But be quick about it. I now have to go to my real estate broker to put this place up for sale."

"Sale?" Geez, he was really pulling out all the stops.

"Of course. I can't have an empty property sitting around costing me money. It'll help the other units sell." He pulled out his cell phone. "Hurry up, Cassidy. I don't have all day. Let's make this quick and devoid of unnecessary emotion, shall we?"

"Dad, I'm not going anywhere."

"Perhaps I haven't made myself clear." He punched a button on his phone. "Deborah, I want a locksmith at the Davenport Towers penthouse. Yes, Cassidy's apartment. No, there's nothing wrong, it's just that Cassidy has decided she isn't going to be living here any longer. And call Shel once you've arranged for the locksmith. I want him out here with his photographer right away to get pictures of the place. The maid's here and should be finished within the hour. This place will be in perfect shape for the listing photos."

Cassidy glanced at the phone. Holy shit. He really was talking to Deborah.

Oh my God. He *meant* it.

He was kicking her out.

No, that wasn't right. He wouldn't just toss his own flesh and blood out on her ass.

Though he *had* tossed Mom out if Deborah's recounting could be believed and Cassidy had no reason to think it couldn't. A few years ago, after Deborah's sister had died and Dad had been on safari in Africa where cell service had been spotty at best, Deborah had had some free time to accompany Cassidy on a site inspection for an upcoming event. One glass of wine at the bar had led to four, and a few stories about her father had come out. Mom had been part of that disclosure.

Mom had had an affair with Dad's head of security. Cassidy would like to say the affair was what had made her father a cold-hearted bastard, but the way he was barking orders at Deborah to arrange the locksmith, the broker, editors of various real estate and architectural magazines, even a spot on the local morning show wasn't something that'd happened because his wife had cheated on him.

"Cassidy, you're down to seven minutes. I suggest you get packed or you and your dog will be left with nothing."

Yeah, her father had been born a bastard.

Chapter Seven

❧

"J ESUS, are you all right?" Liam stared at the zombie-like creature that had woodenly walked into the bedroom. Cassidy looked as if she'd seen a ghost.

She stared up at him on the ladder but didn't say a word. Her green eyes that had sparkled in anger were dull and lifeless, and she was looking around as if she didn't recognize a thing.

"Cassidy?"

She didn't seem to hear him as she walked disjointedly toward her bathroom, grabbing a bag from her closet almost as an afterthought.

He practically jumped off the ladder and ran after her. She did not look good.

He found her tossing toiletries into the bag. Silly things like loofas and toilet paper and razors.

He slid the bag from her grasp. "Cassidy, honey, talk to me. What happened?" Her father had just arrived. Had something happened? Her mother maybe?

She picked up the scale and put it into the bag, then headed over to the basket of bath gels and stuff, aimlessly picking through them, but not with any real idea of what she was doing.

Liam took the scale out of her bag. He was pretty sure wherever she was packing to go would have a scale. And what did she need one for anyway? The woman was as thin as a socialite should be.

"Cassidy, what's going on? What are you doing?"

She looked over her shoulder at him. "I'm packing."

"I get that, but for what?"

"The rest of my life, apparently." A little laugh escaped. A maniacal little laugh.

He took the basket of bath products she'd picked up out of her hands. "Explain."

She looked at the basket as if she didn't know what it was, which was odd, since she'd been pawing through it as if every item was a crown jewel, then looked around the rest of the bathroom and made her way, shakily, over to the toilet lid to sit down.

"My father's evicting me."

Liam set the basket down and wiggled a finger in his ear. "Come again?"

"My father. He's kicking me out."

"Of here?"

She raised her eyebrows. "Isn't that what evicting means?"

"But why?"

Another laugh came out but this one wasn't really amused. More along the lines of a snort. "Because I'm not getting married."

Oh. Liam got it. Daddy was putting his two-thousand-dollar-shod foot down. "If you don't marry that guy, he's making you leave?"

"You got it."

"He can't do that."

Cassidy's eyebrows went even higher. "Do you *know* who my father is? There isn't much he can't do."

That was true. "So what's with the rush job?"

"Oh shit." She jumped up. "I don't have time to talk. I've

got to get my stuff and get out of here." She grabbed the bag, plopped it into the sink in front of her medicine cabinet, shoveled those contents into it, then tossed in an assortment of hair appliances and brushes.

Jeez, she had a brush for every strand of hair.

Figured.

The front door slammed shut.

"What was that?"

Cassidy hefted the bag onto her shoulder. "Damn. That was my father. I have to make sure he didn't take Titania with him." She almost fell when the bag slammed into the door frame as she tried to run out of the bathroom.

"Here, let me get that." Liam winced as he slid the handles off her shoulder. Damn it. He didn't even like the woman; why the hell was he helping her?

"I've got it." She tried to yank it from him.

"Go. Get your dog. I'm not carrying *it* out for you."

She looked at her bag, then out to the living room, then at him. "Thank you."

He almost said, "Sure thing, Princess," but right now wasn't the time for sarcasm she wouldn't get. He was carrying her bag for her while she was being evicted from her penthouse apartment by the man who paid the bills. He ought to be gloating over this. One of *them* had just gotten a dose of reality.

Too bad none of those vacations she'd tried to glom on to earlier had paid off. She could've waited out Daddy's change of heart after teaching his little princess a lesson in style if her so-called friends hadn't bailed on her.

"Titania, no!"

Liam winced when he heard the crash. He had a feeling it was one of the crystal knick-knacks on the end table right where the carpet ended and the marble foyer began. Which meant at least five grand now in shards—that he was going to have to clean up.

"Titania, come here. I don't have time for this."

Liam heard the cabinets in the kitchen slam and the plastic containers and assorted cans scatter all over the floor.

"Bad girl, Titania!"

"Oh please." Liam walked in and hunkered down beside the little terror and scooped it up. "Look, mutt, chill. Your mom doesn't need you freaking out right now. She's got an agenda and you need to help out."

The little yipper-snapper calmed down, thank God.

"Here, give her one of these." Cassidy tossed him a cardboard canister covered in pink felt and rhinestones.

"Uh, I'm not sure, but I'm thinking rhinestones aren't good for her digestive tract." God knew, they weren't good for his. He loathed rhinestones, and juggled the canister and the dog as if they were a game of *hot potato.*

"There are treats inside. She likes those."

"I thought you weren't supposed to reward bad behavior?" He set the dog down. She was looking at him a little too interestedly as he peeled back the lid. For all its designer outside, the inside still smelled like liverwurst dog treats.

"She quieted down. I'm rewarding that."

"No, you're encouraging her to bark so she'll get a treat when she quiets down. You don't just give these to her randomly throughout the day for being quiet, do you?"

"Really? Is that what you think is most important right now?" Cassidy stretched her arm to the back of the cabinet, her cheek smashed against the drawer above it. "I have a few more important things on my mind at the moment." She grimaced and leaned into the cabinet some more. "Ah, there it is."

"What's that?" It was some sort of pink plastic concoction with curled edges and, oh for Christ's sake, a tiara carved into the back of it like a throne. A dog throne.

"This is her bed."

"And it was in the cabinet why?"

"My father wouldn't like it in the living room or my bedroom. It doesn't go with the décor."

That was for damn sure. The thing looked as if it'd come right out of a Disney movie.

"Since he's making me leave, I figure it won't matter that Titania sleeps in it now."

"If you say so." Personally, he'd have nightmares if he

had to sleep in something like that, but then, he wasn't a spoiled socialite's pampered accessory.

But it could be fun to be hers.

He shut that thought down real quick—until she stood and brushed off her thighs.

Her bare thighs.

How had he missed that amid all the clutter falling from the cabinets?

Damn, Manley. Losing your edge.

Actually, that was a good thing. The last thing he needed to be noticing was Cassidy Davenport's legs.

Except when she leveraged herself on the counter to stand up, and her shirt managed to get caught under her hand and she gave him a quick flash of pink bra and cleavage and *that* was the last thing he needed to be noticing.

Especially with these damn pants that were way too tight to begin with for his liking. And then he had to stand up in them.

Luckily he still had her bag, so he covered his hard-on with it and scooped up the mutt.

"So do you have everything you need for now or are you going to pack up all the closets?"

An odd look crossed her face and he could have sworn her bottom lip trembled. But she regained her self-control quickly, and straightened her shoulders as she purposely closed the cabinet door.

"No, I'm done. This is all I need." She looked around the kitchen, grabbed a bag from the pantry and dumped the cans of food and boxes of biscuits into it. "Oh, and her leash. I need that."

"I got it." Liam headed out to the closet in the living room.

She followed him, slinging the bag—a brown paper bag with twine handles—on her forearm and rearranging the drapey shirt so it covered some parts of her.

"Where's my iPad?" She walked to the sofa back table and rifled through the magazines there. "Did you move it to clean?"

"Last I saw it, it was there."

"He took it. The bastard."

Probably better not to point out that the bastard was the one who'd *bought* said iPad. He didn't feel like dealing with tears. The day had started out so promisingly; he didn't want to ruin the rest of it.

"So should I call you a cab or is your car here?" Anything to help the cause along of getting her out the door.

"My car's downstairs." She held out her hand after she shoved her feet into a pair of sparkly flip-flops. "If you'll hand over the leash and my bag—and my dog—I'll get all of us down to it."

He was tempted. Man, was he tempted. Get her out the door in one fell swoop. Problem was, she looked as if she was going to collapse before he could.

"I've got your stuff. You have your keys?" He didn't wait for her to nod, but headed to the door and held it open for her. "After you, Prin—Ms. Davenport."

She stuck her nose in the air, perfect socialite behavior. "Don't call me that. I'm changing my name."

He rolled his eyes after her. Worthless threat since it was that name that opened doors for her and would continue to, he was sure. Like the ones at the Ritz, or the Hyatt, or hell, especially her father's hotels.

Marco greeted them by name—including the dog. "Your father said you'd be down. Should I call you a cab?"

Cassidy looked at him absentmindedly. "A cab?"

"Yeah, you know, a yellow car?" Liam interjected. "Takes you where you want to go?" He hefted the pooch and stage-whispered in its ear, trying to diffuse the situation because Cassidy still didn't look so hot and there was no need to feed the gossip mill. Marco appeared to be a stand-up guy, but who knew what he'd do if the tabloids came calling for dirt with the right amount of payola. "Your mommy seems to have forgotten how us common people live."

"That's a really nasty thing to say."

Good, he'd gotten her Irish up. It worked. Anger was a much easier reaction to deal with than tears.

"Hey, babe, if the Jimmy Choo fits."

"You think you're so funny, don't you? Acting all holier-than-thou because you were there when my father—" She glanced at Marco. "Uh, just now."

Liam shrugged and handed the fluff-ball to her. "Just sayin.'"

"You can keep your comments to yourself." She hiked the pooch and kissed the silly knot on its head. The thing licked her on the lips.

Yeah, the *lips*. Not a big deal, Liam was guessing. The pooch probably made regular trips to the doggy dentist.

The extremely fast and extremely quiet elevator made quick work of the twelve stories to street level, and Marco was the epitome of the not-seen-and-not-heard help as he held the door open for them. Liam would have tipped him, but since Cassidy made no move to, he figured good ol' Mitch's daughter either didn't have to or had an account that paid out handsomely at holiday time. He wasn't sure what the protocol was for this level of high life.

Liam was heading for the front door when Cassidy took a left toward another bank of elevators, fully expecting him to tag along, her flip-flops flopping furiously on the marble floor. It'd serve her right if he dropped her bag right there in the lobby for assuming he was her lackey, but—dammit—he felt sorry for her and didn't want to make a scene after the one she'd just had.

THE second bank of elevators opened into a parking garage unlike any he'd ever seen before. It wasn't just *any* old parking garage. The floors looked like brick, the support columns were Ionic, and he wouldn't be surprised if there were cushioned benches in the shape of that stupid dog bed all over the place. The lap of luxury for luxury cars.

"Son of a bitch."

Liam did a double take. One did not expect to hear such language from a socialite who'd gone to all the best finishing schools. Not that he knew which schools those were, but that'd been her claim to fame every time she was mentioned in the newspaper. He was fairly certain Cussing 101 wasn't on the curriculum.

"That supercilious, sanctimonious bastard."

If it was a course, she'd get an A for delivery because the words sounded so incongruous coming from that angelic face.

And then he saw what she was looking at.

There was a boot on the Mercedes.

A boot.

Man, that was fast. But then, Mitchell Davenport probably had people lying in wait to do his bidding.

"He booted your car?"

Cassidy inhaled so deeply her breasts rose a good four inches—which made her shirt rise a good four inches, showing a delicious four inches of silky, tanned skin.

Why couldn't the woman be fat and dumpy? Why'd she have to be straight out of every erotic fantasy he'd ever had *and* be a pampered princess? Was the universe *trying* to torture him?

"How the *hell* does he expect me to go anywhere without my car?"

"That explains the taxicab comment from Marco."

She twisted her lips. "Great. Marco knows. I wonder who else does. It's not bad enough my father evicts me, now he makes me a laughing stock." She set the puffball down, dragged her pocketbook off her shoulder, and started rummaging through it. "Dammit."

He was almost afraid to ask. "What?"

"I don't have any cash."

Of course she didn't. The super rich didn't have to carry cash.

"I'm sure you can charge cab fare."

She looked at him as if he were an idiot. "The man put a boot on my car. It takes about a tenth of that time to cancel my credit cards and, oh hell, my debit card. You can bet *my* money that my father didn't overlook those."

Liam wasn't betting anything. Betting had gotten him into this predicament—and smack dab in the middle of hers.

"What about stopping at a bank? You can make a withdrawal."

She shook her head. "He'll have closed the accounts if he's cancelled everything else."

"So I'm guessing that means a hotel's out."

"What?" Cassidy's eyes got wide. "Oh my God. Where am I going to go?"

"The boyfriend?"

"Burton? I don't think so. Not after last night."

"He doesn't know you don't want to marry him, right? You didn't actually turn him down. I bet he'll come to your rescue." And she could go live happily ever after in a castle her father paid for. Rachel would be so jealous.

"Oh sure. I call him and see if I can move in? That's *exactly* what my father wants me to do. And then there will be the guilt and the pressure to give in to Burton." She tugged the shirt back onto her shoulders, but Liam could have told her not to bother. That shirt had been designed to hang provocatively off a set of very sexy shoulders and Cassidy possessed just such a set. "Now what am I going to do?"

"Give your friends a call." There had to be one she hadn't been turned down by.

"I did. Everyone's away and those who aren't have probably already heard about last night. There won't be any grand gestures of letting me stay with them now. My father's name and influence is bigger than mine in this town, and when word gets out . . . No one is going to want to be on his bad side. In the face of social ostracism, friendship with me falls by the wayside." She leaned against the hood of the booted car. "Besides . . ." She pulled out her cell phone and swiped her finger across it, then held the screen toward him.

The black screen.

"He turned it off."

Liam didn't like where her logic was leading him. He really didn't. He also didn't like his stupid, fucking bleeding heart. "So where are you going to go? Don't you have any family that'll take you in? Your mom?"

Now it was her turn to roll her eyes. "I guess you haven't

read *all* of the society pages. My mother took off with her lover when I was just a kid. Wanted to get as far from Daddy dear as possible. Mexico's pretty far."

"She could wire you money."

This time she looked away. "That's not an option." Her tone said that was the end of the story.

It must be one hell of a story if she was willing to live on the streets instead of calling the woman who'd given birth to her.

So what was with the picture and bracelet under Cassidy's bed? He ought to find it interesting that she hadn't gone for those in her almost catatonic state when she'd been throwing anything and everything into her bag, but maybe not. Maybe she hadn't wanted any reminders of her parents. She hadn't taken any of her personal items like clothing—

Oh hell. All she had to her name was what was on her back and in her bag. Without a freaking dime.

He was going to regret this. As sure as he'd lost the bet to his sister, he was going to regret this. But he couldn't stop the words.

"Come on. You can come home with me."

Chapter Eight

CASSIDY shook her head. She couldn't have heard what she'd thought she heard. "Did you just invite me to come home with you?"

"Yeah, I did. And I'm just as surprised about it as you are."

"But you don't even know me."

"I know you just got tossed out, don't have two nickels to rub together, have nowhere to go, and no one to help you. That leaves me."

"How very Prince Charming of you." He seriously thought she would be grateful to go home with him? Here she was at her darkest hour and he was probably trying to get in her pants.

"Okay, Princess, if that's the way you want it. Seems to me I'm the only option you have. But, hey, if you'd rather not . . ." He dropped her bag on the stamped concrete floor. "Don't let me stop you from finding your prince. I'm sure Burton will come looking for you at some point."

"That's not happening." She wouldn't let it. She was *not* going to sit here and wait for Burton to show up. That he would, she had no doubt. It was, after all, Dad's master plan.

Well, she was not going to go along with it. Not this time. This was too important.

"Fine. So stay at my place until something else comes through. A day or two. A week even. I'm sure that when your friends come back from vacation, this will have blown over and you can stay with one of them."

"That's not going to happen either."

"Huh?"

"Once they find out about this eviction, I'm going to be a topic of discussion. A *scandal*. These women can be vipers, Liam. They *live* for scandals. For talking about other people. For making themselves feel better by crushing others. No one's going to risk Mitchell Davenport's wrath to take in his daughter. No, I'm pretty much a pariah now."

Which meant she damn well better take *him* up on his offer and be grateful about it.

And quick. Before he changed his mind. Or saw the light in not pissing off her father. "Okay, I'll do it. Stay with you."

She didn't know who was more surprised: her or Liam.

"You will?"

"Unless you changed your mind?"

"What changed yours?"

"Brutal reality. I have nowhere to go." Dammit, she could feel the tears well up behind her eyes. But she was *not* going to let them fall. *Not* for Da—Mitchell Davenport. The man wasn't worth it.

Silence filled the space around them, thick and uncomfortable. But then, that went part-and-parcel with brutal reality.

Oh. My. God. Her father had kicked her out. He'd cut her off. No phone, no credit cards, not a single luxury. Not her car, and no one who'd come near her with the scarlet specter of his ire hanging over her head.

She was on her own. Totally. Completely.

And broke.

A chill washed over her and her knees wobbled. She shouldn't be surprised. Not really. This feeling, this itchy floating-above-it-all-knees-wobbling feeling was the same one she'd felt when her mother had walked out. Dad had been just as unemotional then, a bland, "Your mother is gone, Cassidy. She doesn't want to live with us. It's just you and me now," as if he was discussing a field trip or what was for dinner. Then he'd closed her bedroom door without one whit of emotion and left her there. Alone.

She'd cried herself to sleep and even then she'd understood it was because she had no one.

She wasn't going to cry now. Not this time. Being evicted was merely the physical manifestation of the emotional desert she'd been in since she was four years old.

And hey, at least she'd have time to paint. She'd show her father. He didn't have a hold on her any longer. She'd crank out those pieces so fast, it'd make his head spin.

Except . . . Crud. She'd left her paints in the penthouse.

"All right, then." Liam picked the bag back up. "Let's get going."

"Um, Liam?" She really hated to ask him this, but she had no way of getting any other supplies, what with being cut off and all. "Could you . . . I mean . . . That is . . ."

"Spit it out, Princess. I don't have all day. I have to get you situated at my place, then come back here to finish the job I was hired to do."

"About that. I was wondering if you wouldn't mind getting something of mine I left back there."

"I am not taking anything out of that place and having your father accuse me of theft."

"Oh, trust me. He'll probably give you a reward if you do."

Liam's gorgeous blue eyes narrowed. "What is it?"

"My new paints. I left them in the bottom drawer of the credenza in the dining room."

"You paint in the dining room?"

She shook her head. "I stuck them there after I bought them the other day. It's the least-used room in the place, so it's the last place Dad would think to look for them. *If* he'd even think to look for them. After last night, I'm sure he'll be more than happy not to have them around as a reminder. So if you could get them for me, I'd really appreciate it. It will allow me to start earning some money to pay you for my stay."

Liam rubbed his chin. "We'll worry about you paying me back later, but, yeah, I'll get the paints. Anything else? Jewelry, gowns, shoes?"

She shook her head. "No. Nothing. If I know my father, and unfortunately I do all too well, he'll have Deborah inventorying everything against the charge slips. I don't want anything of his."

"Then you might want to leave those rocks on your ears here."

She fingered the diamond studs. "I'm keeping these. I earned them."

"Doing what? Entertaining visiting dignitaries? Hosting heads of state?"

She glanced away and blinked back more tears that sprang up at his sarcasm. Silly really, since he was right, but oh how she wanted to be valued for what she could do instead of what she looked like. And the ironic thing was, she *had* earned these. Chit-chatting with people she had no desire to speak with, attending events that left her bored to tears, and being thought of as nothing more than a pretty face with the occasional pass-by ass-patting deserved recompense.

"Look, I get what you think of me. I know what people think of my life. That it's all wine and roses and I should be happy as a clam living in the gilded tower with my clothes and jewelry and nice things. I get that. The thing is, that's who he wanted me to be. I bought into it for a while, but I'm not that person anymore. There's more to me than that."

She wanted to wipe that skeptical look off Liam's face, but words alone would never do it. She had to show him. She had to show them all. And she would, dammit. This was her chance. Her shot at making over her life as she'd planned to do during the lunch yesterday—had it only been yesterday?—with Dad.

"If you say so." Liam picked up her bag. "Okay, then. Let's get going. My truck's over here."

She watched him swagger ahead of her. Oh, it wasn't an intentional swagger; those, she could spot a mile away. His was all natural grace and athleticism, with one hell of a nice butt—

Okay, not thoughts she ought to be having at the moment. She was going to stay with the guy just until she got on her feet, not move in with him forever. No sense starting something like that and risk having him think *that* was how she was going to pay him back—

Uh oh. That wasn't what he thought, was it? He'd talked about paybacks . . . He didn't think she was going to . . . That she would . . .

Titania wriggled in the crook of her arm and started to whine. "Um, Liam? Could you hold up, please? Titania needs a potty break."

Liam looked back over his shoulder with his eyebrow arched. "Don't tell me you got her a throne-shaped one of those as well."

"Not funny." She juggled her bag, her purse, the dog, and the leash to get the last two attached to each other. Normally, Titania wouldn't run away, but with the way Cassidy's luck had gone the past twenty-four hours, she wasn't risking it.

The dog kept wiggling. "Hold still, Titania. The bushes are over there." She hurried to the edge of the garage where the landscaping was above the chest-high wall, and plunked the cutie-pie among the petunias. "Go ahead. Do good girl."

She caught Liam rolling his eyes in her peripheral vision.

Titania, being Titania, took her time sniffing the flowers before finding the perfect spot.

Liam's foot started tapping.

All finished, Titania yipped her sweet little happy bark, then licked Cassidy on the nose before practically leaping into her arms. There was nothing like the unconditional love of a dog. That would be why Titania barely left her side. The Maltese was six years old and Cassidy could remember each day as if it were yesterday—especially the day she'd brought her home.

Dad had had a conniption. Cassidy had heard the term but never known exactly what a conniption entailed.

Bringing a dog home to his new pristine, "highpoint of my career" penthouse induced the conniption. And what a thing it had been to behold. Exactly what she'd been trying to avoid yesterday at lunch by breaking the news to him gently.

Yet he'd gone and had one just the same. Granted, it'd been in her—*his*—home, but still, it was the second time she'd ever seen that reaction from the normally calm and unflappable Mitchell Davenport.

She still couldn't believe he'd cut her off. She hadn't seen that coming. How could she have been so wrong about her own father?

"Are we all set, then? You don't have softly scented, individually wrapped doggy wipes, do you?"

The sarcasm was rolling off Liam's tongue, yet still the man held open the door of the truck *and* helped her into it. Thank goodness because it was really high off the ground, even with running boards.

"This is a big truck," she said after he walked around the front and climbed in the driver's side.

"Yes, it is."

And that was it. There wasn't another word spoken by Mr. Liam Manley the entire way, for which she was grateful because she was still trying to wrap her brain around the past hour. Dad had cut her off. He'd tried to force her to his will with money.

God, how pitiful. How utterly shallow did her own father think she was? How shallow was *he*? And Burton? How shallow was *he* to marry her just to become Mitchell's heir?

Okay, well that might be incentive, but did he really want to marry someone who wasn't in love with him?

Scratch that. People did it all the time, and being CEO of her father's conglomerate was reward enough for a loveless marriage.

He'd. Cut. Her. Off.

Cassidy shook her head. Her own father, manipulating her—an almost thirty-year-old woman—into an arranged marriage. What was this, feudal England?

Cassidy looked out the window as Liam turned onto a quiet, tree-lined street with the houses spaced close enough to be called neighbors, but far enough apart that they wouldn't know their neighbors' intimate business.

Intimacy. Burton would have expected it. And with money as the basis for their marriage, her father would be consigning her to being a very well-paid prostitute.

She was going to be sick. She'd never even *thought* of him doing something like this. Oh, sure, the passing "being broke" comment had risen its head every once in a while when she'd thought about going out on her own, but she'd expected the "broke" part to be temporary while she waited to sell more furniture, *not* because every cent she possessed would be frozen due to her father's long reach.

What was she going to do? When she'd first envisioned this, she'd expected to stay in the penthouse or maybe one of his other properties until she had enough income for a small mortgage. She'd planned to live simply. Make do with a thousand square feet instead of the four thousand she'd just been booted from.

Now, if it weren't for Liam's generosity, she wouldn't even have *one.*

Liam pulled down a long driveway. Cassidy had to keep her mouth shut. And not shut, as in, she wasn't going to say anything nasty, but shut as in preventing her bottom jaw from dropping. She was worried about *one* square foot? Liam probably had four thousand of them himself—and that was just the front yard.

"This is yours?" she finally had to ask him, not taking her eyes off the beautiful landscaping. She hadn't known what to expect on a maid's salary, but it certainly hadn't been this. Tree-covered except for a small clearing that was lit as if from a beacon, with a lily pad pond in the center and stone-carved benches around it, with an old-fashioned water pump used as a fountain, and a beautiful array of annuals at the pond's edge, the place actually looked like a fairyland. Titania would have a blast curling up by the rocks. "Are there fish in there?"

Liam nodded. "Koi. I have a few that are over a foot long."

"Wow. I'm impressed. Koi need just the right touch to live so long."

Seemed to be a metaphor for her life.

Liam drove over a narrow arched stone bridge, then circled around to the left, going behind the A-frame cabin-like structure with a front wall of windows that reminded her of the penthouse. The difference was (a) it wasn't owned by her father and (b) it was in the middle of nature, not above it. She'd always wondered about people who liked to live above nature. Who thought looking down on it was so much better than living within it. After all, a patio-sized waterfall couldn't even begin to compare to the beauty of Liam's oasis and its gurgling water pump, or the butterflies flitting among the flowers, and the dragonflies hovering just above the surface of the pond with their wings humming in the silence.

It was so peaceful. So beautiful. A place where someone could go to escape the stresses of the day and just relax.

"Something wrong?" Liam's voice had a sharp edge to it. "I know it's not the Ritz or the Hilton or anything like that, and the water's dirty, and the bugs are buzzing around, but this place suits me. I like sitting on the bench and watching the air bubbles on the surface from the fish, or the frogs jumping to catch the insects flying by. Or the occasional plop as one jumps in."

"Sounds peaceful."

"It is. Sometimes there's nothing better than a little solitude in nature."

It was a hell of a lot better than solitude in her gilded cage. She was going to like it here.

Titania squirmed around in her lap, put her paws on the door by the window, and started yipping.

"Aw, look. She wants to play."

"She's not going to keep up all that yapping, is she? She does go to sleep at some point, right?"

"Of course she does. She's just excited right now."

"What about accidents? I spent too much money on the flooring to be her potty-training service."

"Titania's been housebroken since the day after I got her. You don't have to worry about a mess."

"Oh, I wasn't worried, since you'll be cleaning it up."

"Well, of course I will. She's my dog. I clean up after her."

Liam pulled into the garage and was around to help her out of the passenger side before she'd gathered Titania and the rest of her things.

"Put her down. She might as well learn the place from the get-go." Liam set Titania on the floor. It was so strange to see her little dainty dog in Liam's large, strong hands. It reminded her of an Ann Geddes photo with a baby cradled in its father's hands.

Whoa. She was being way too fanciful here. Liam was just trying to help and she was the one weirding the situation out with her stupid imagination.

Save it for the artwork, Cassidy.

Exactly—Uh oh. Her art. The furniture. It was in the warehouse that she—fortunately—had leased in her own name. The rent was paid up to the end of the month, but if Dad found out about it before then . . .

She needed to get all the pieces out of there.

Thank God Liam had a two-car garage. Now hopefully he'll be amenable to letting her furniture move in for a few days as well.

She followed him through the garage to the laundry room where the heater, laundry tub, and a contraption of pipes that might be a tank-less water heater greeted her.

"Leave your shoes here in the mudroom," he said, taking his own off.

Really? The man took off his shoes in his own home?

"I try to keep the mess to a minimum so I don't have to clean a lot."

"I guess you don't want to after doing it all day for your job, huh?" Made sense. She slipped off her flip-flops and put them on the shelves in the closet along the back wall.

"Here's where I keep all the cleaning supplies." Liam pointed to the shelves on the left. "Broom, dust mop, a wand for the blinds." He pointed to the things lined up on the pegboard along the far side of the closet. "The attachments for the central vac system are in here." He opened a cabinet. "I also have a hand-held vac, and the bags and attachments are here." He flicked a hanging black vinyl pouch thing. "Extension rod and gripper for the light bulbs, which are up here." He opened a cabinet within the closet to show her various types of light bulbs and a couple of big batteries and flashlights. "Trash bags, batteries, duct tape, some tools . . . This is where you'll find everything."

Because she was going to need duct tape and hammers why?

Titania scratched at the door leading to what Cassidy presumed was the rest of the house.

"She scratches? Dammit, I just finished painting the doors."

Cassidy scooped the dog up. "She doesn't usually. I guess you have something that smells really great behind that door."

"Dinner." He opened the door. "I put salsa chicken in the Crock-Pot before I left."

The scent of salsa filled the air. "That smells really good."

"It is. Easy and good, too. Crock-Pot cooking is a godsend."

Cassidy didn't mention that though she'd heard of a Crock-Pot she wasn't quite sure what one was or how to use it. Probably better to leave out that bit of info, since he was all "yes, Princess" this and "yes, Ms. Davenport" that. She didn't need to know how to use a Crock-Pot to survive on her own.

Or maybe she did. Cooking on a budget hadn't been included in any of her curriculum. *Cooking* hadn't, either. Menu-planning, on the other hand, and how to deal with staff, had.

Well, maybe cooking was something she could learn while she was here. Guys liked when women cooked for them, right? Surely Liam wouldn't mind. Most guys probably never set foot in their kitchen except to get beer and pizza from the fridge.

Apparently Liam did more in the kitchen than that. His was a mess.

"What happened here?" Cassidy set Titania down and surveyed the cardboard-box-covered quartz countertops.

Liam sighed and raked his hands through his hair. "My grandmother. She stops by every so often to restock my fridge, as she calls it. I guess today was that day." He grabbed a box and started breaking it down. "We moved her to an assisted living facility and she misses cooking, so she borrows the facility's kitchen and cooks up a storm." He opened the stainless steel fridge door. "See?" He stepped back. Plastic container after plastic container lined the shelves. "She thinks I'm going to eat all of this before it goes bad."

He grabbed two of the containers and shifted them to the freezer—except he couldn't. It was stuffed to the gills, too.

"Looks like you're set for the apocalypse."

"Well, I guess I can take cooking off your payback methods." He looked her up and down. "You do know how to cook, right?"

She almost let him believe it, then decided she better not. Easiest way to get caught in a lie was to have to prove it. "Not really. Dad had chefs. They didn't like kids in their way."

"And I'm sure coming up with menus is more important than learning to cook what's on them at those finishing schools."

"I didn't have any say in my schooling, you know."

He grabbed another box and broke it down, starting a stack on the island. "And you're how old?"

She sucked in a breath and was about to unleash a tirade but . . . didn't. What was the point? They could argue all they wanted, but the truth was, she didn't know how to cook and hadn't considered it a necessity for moving out on her own. That's what take-out was for.

"What does it matter anyway? Your grandmother has made my culinary skills"—or lack thereof—"a non-issue."

"Okay, fine. So then you can move straight to straightening this place up."

Say what? "Your kitchen?"

"For a start. Then the living room, the bedrooms, and the bathrooms. There are two downstairs and one up."

"There's an upstairs? Where?"

He pointed another box toward a spiral wrought-iron staircase. "Leads to the loft. Two bedrooms and a bath. Shouldn't take long."

"Long to do what?"

"To clean, of course."

She heard the words, but they weren't making sense. "Wait. What? You want me to clean your house?"

"Got it on the first try. Good. We shouldn't have any communication issues, then."

She shook her head. "You want me to clean your house."

"Didn't we just address that?"

"But why?"

He looked at her with an arched eyebrow. "Because the place is dirty?"

"But why me? Don't you have a Manley Maid to do it for you?"

"I do, but why pay someone when you said you were going to pay me to stay here?" He stacked another flattened box on the countertop.

She wasn't liking his logic. Or his payback method. "Why can't I pay you in cash?"

"Do you have any?"

"Well, no. But I will."

"Then we'll discuss it when you do. In the meantime, you can save *me* some cash by doing it yourself." He held out a box to her.

"But I don't know how to clean."

"Oh come on, Princess." He shook the box when she didn't take it. "It's not that hard. I showed you where all the supplies are kept. You wipe up dust and vacuum up debris. A couple of chemicals in the bathroom. It's not rocket science. If you can figure out how to play pinochle, I'm sure you can clean a toilet."

"How do you know I play pinochle?"

"Isn't that what all the finishing schools teach these days?"

"Well, yeah, but I never liked it."

"But you know how to play it, don't you?"

Of course she did. She'd actually taken courses in bridge and pinochle and mahjong and a whole other assortment of pastimes considered suitable for the country club set.

God, how pretentious they all seemed now. Where was the practical experience like . . . well, cooking and cleaning and managing money?

And she was going to have to manage her money. When she got some, that was.

Liam set the box—intact—on top of the stack. "Look, I have to get back. Your dad wants me to get to work on the condo across from yours, er, your old one, because he wants to sell it. The photographer is coming this evening to take pictures."

"Yeah, Dad's big on taking moonlight photos. He spends a fortune on tiny white lights for all his patio gardens and loves how they're reflected in the glass surfaces. Says it makes the place seem warm and inviting."

"It does."

"The outside maybe. Inside, it's cold, austere, and utterly devoid of any personality."

Liam stared at her a heartbeat too long for her liking so she turned away. She probably shouldn't divulge her inner angst to the man who wasn't all that fond of her to begin with, but who, for whatever reason, had taken pity on her and taken her in.

God, she hated pity.

But it was all she had going for her right now because there was, literally, no one she could call. She hadn't been exaggerating earlier. No one was going to want to help her and risk getting on Mitchell's bad side. She knew it as surely as she was standing here.

But then she almost wasn't standing. The enormity of what Dad had done—*and* how she hadn't seen it coming— washed over her again and, this time, her knees did buckle. She grabbed hold of the breakfast bar to stop herself from collapsing and managed to wiggle her way onto a bar stool there. She just needed a few moments to regain her composure. She'd be fine. Really.

"You okay?" Liam walked around the bar, the concern on his face making her feel guilty because he'd already helped her more than he should have; she didn't want to add concern to the rest of what he was doing for her.

"Yes. Why?"

"Because you were as white as a ghost there for a second."

"Probably because I didn't have breakfast."

"Well help yourself to what you want. Gran, I'm sure, brought quite the assortment. She usually does. Doesn't want me to go hungry." He patted his eight-pack. "As if that'd happen."

Cassidy wished he hadn't slapped those rock-hard muscles. She didn't want to notice them. She didn't want to notice anything about him. Not when she'd be staying under his roof and feeling more grateful than was prudent.

"Okay, so I'm going back to finish the job and should be home by six at the latest. The chicken should be done by then. If you want to throw on some rice and a vegetable, I'd appreciate it."

"Uh, sure." Once she figured out *how* to cook rice, that was. She could probably manage some steamed broccoli.

If she knew how to steam something . . .

"Do you, uh, have a computer here that I could use since I don't have my smart phone anymore?"

"In the den. You can sign on under a guest account." He walked over to the whiteboard above the desk area in the kitchen. "I don't have a house phone, but you can IM me through the computer." He wrote on board. "Here's my cell. Holler if you get into trouble."

"I should have been hollering all the way here then, shouldn't I?"

A sexy little smile crossed Liam's face and Cassidy so wished it hadn't. She was indebted to this guy. Being attracted to him was not a smart idea.

Tell that to her hormones and the stupid butterflies in her tummy that'd been dormant for months.

"You'll be fine for the next few days until something else comes along. Just get the place cleaned up and we'll go from there." He brushed past her and darn if she didn't catch a really awesome scent of sandalwood and Liam. The man was a walking pheromone.

Yepper . . . Staying here ought to be *real* interesting.

HAVING Cassidy Davenport at his place was going to be *real* interesting. Liam just prayed he didn't strangle her.

She didn't know how to cook or clean. Seriously? How hard was it to figure out? He and his brothers had been young but they'd gotten it real quick that a rag and some furniture polish equaled hours of drudgery. But that same rag and polish also equaled a happy grandmother who made amazing chocolate chip cookies and smothered them with hugs for all their efforts. They'd hated cleaning, but had understood the mess they made was their responsibility. That they were all in it together and Gran couldn't do everything. So they let her do what they couldn't—cook amazing things—and they picked up the slack in other areas.

Cassidy Davenport had probably never had to pick up slack in anything.

Liam backed out of his driveway, praying he wasn't making a mistake by having her here, but what else could he do? She had nowhere to go.

God, wasn't that ironic? The woman who'd had more money than he'd ever hope to see in his lifetime was homeless. And dropped by all her rich, so-called friends. Hell, with friends like that, who needed enemies? And the whole situation with her father . . . Didn't people realize how special the relationship was between parents and children? How, once that other person was gone, there was no going back? He missed his parents every day of his life and he wouldn't care whatever the fight was between them, he'd fix it in a heartbeat. But Cassidy and her father couldn't. Or didn't want to.

Sad. Just sad.

He turned right toward the penthouse. No. He was not going to feel sorry for her. It wasn't his problem that she was a spoiled brat who'd taken everything for granted. Why wouldn't she have any money of her own? Why not sock some of Daddy Dear's allowance away into an account he'd know nothing about for just such a day?

Because she'd probably been off partying in LA or Cannes or any one of those zillion jet-set places her friends were now staying at without her, not thinking that the money train would ever end.

Just like Rachel. Spoiled, selfish users.

Yet he'd just put her up in his home.

To *clean*.

Liam couldn't stop the chuckle as he pulled into the underground garage at her father's building—the one used for the "common folk." The one without the painted concrete and pretty landscaping.

Cassidy Davenport was at his home, right this minute, *cleaning*. He probably should have mentioned the box of rubber gloves on the top shelf. Wouldn't want her to ruin her manicure.

He nodded to Marco in the lobby as the guy was going on break from his elevator-operating job. Wonder how much he got paid to do that? Must be a nice sum if that was his main source of income.

Liam shook his head. He'd never understand the super rich. But then, since he'd never *be* super rich, he didn't have to. He was perfectly happy with the home he'd renovated, the ones he flipped, and his one indulgence—the vacation home on Kiawah Island in South Carolina. Not that he got there a lot, but it was there for him if he ever wanted to.

Maybe he ought to let Cassidy stay *there* instead. That way, he wouldn't have to worry about walking in and finding her in his bed.

There was a thought. What *would* it be like to have her waiting for him at the end of a long day?

He let himself indulge for a second. Okay, maybe thirty of them.

It was a nice dream. A good fantasy. But this was Cassidy Davenport he was lusting over, the exact sort of woman he'd vowed to stay away from. The exact *wrong* sort of woman for him. Because she might say she's not going to do what her father wants, but once reality set in, she'd go back. Her kind always did.

The penthouse was eerily quiet when he entered. No yipping dog—Christ. He hoped that thing didn't scratch his leather furniture.

Liam walked through the living room, everything picture-perfect. No one would ever know it'd been the scene of someone's life-changing moment. Of a fight so big between father and daughter that she'd been cut off. No phone, no credit cards, and no Mercedes.

Okay, he wasn't feeling all that sorry about the last part for her, but still . . . It sucked having everything yanked out from under you at once, as he and his siblings knew firsthand.

He headed toward the dining room, a massive spread of glass and pastel upholstery with a birchwood credenza along the one solid wall in the room.

He opened the bottom drawer and saw the paints, along with an assortment of power tools that was surprising, to say the least. As was the fact that nothing was stored with any sort of organization or care. Just like her kitchen cabinets, everything had been tossed into the drawer as if she'd been in a hurry.

He looked down the hallway toward her bedroom. Were her dresser drawers just as messy?

No, he was not going to snoop. The peach nightie and spiked heels had been enough; he didn't need to imagine her in anything more. Or less. Or nothing—

Hell.

He turned back to the living room and took a few steps when he thought of something. The picture and bracelet.

They had to have meant something to her for her to keep them all these years, though he didn't know why she hadn't taken them with her. Maybe she'd been too upset to remember. Maybe she'd even blocked them out—another parent abandoning her had to be tough. At least he and his siblings had known the reason they didn't have their parents was because of the accident, not because they hadn't wanted them.

Liam knelt down beside Cassidy's former bed and felt around under it until he found the items. Cassidy and her mother looked happy there on the beach. She had her mother's smile. The same shaped face and the same nose. The eyes were different though, her mother's much smaller and closer together than Cassidy's wide green ones with lashes so thick people would probably think they were fake.

He shoved the picture into his back pocket and tucked the bracelet in the front one. Enough about Cassidy's looks and her thongs and anything else he had no business noticing. He was here to do a job and get out. One month and then he'd never have to see Cassidy Davenport agai—

Except she was living with him. Hell. What had he gotten himself into?

Chapter Nine

S HE was in his bed.
Liam looked heavenward. *Really?*

He stood in the doorway to his bedroom after a long, fairly shitty day of cleaning, and ran his hand over his mouth. She was willing to pay with her body to get out of cleaning? Did she really think he'd fall for that? Memories of Rachel sashayed through his brain.

The princess must have decided that this would be easier than an honest day's work cleaning his place. Too bad she didn't know him.

She's offering to know you very *well.*

Not going to happen. He wasn't the same idiot he'd been with Rachel.

He walked toward the bed. "Who's been sleeping in my bed?" he asked loudly.

Cassidy sat up as if he'd electrified the sheets, her hair flying around her head in a mess of waves.

A sexy mess of waves.

Dammit.

"Huh?" She blinked those green eyes at him.

Double dammit. That act wasn't put-on; she was too groggy to be trying to entice him.

"I said, who's been sleeping in my bed?"

"Me?" Her eyes widened. "Oh my gosh. I'm sorry." She scrambled off the bed. "I don't know what I was thinking. Well, yes, obviously I thought I could just take a quick nap, but since you're here—"

She flipped her hair over her head with her forearm and it settled behind her like a fluffy cloud he wanted to tangle his fingers in—

Dammit. *Triple* dammit.

He took a step back from the bed. And another just to be safe. He was trying to do a good deed and help the woman out, and her sex appeal was following him around like a rain cloud. "So did anything get cleaned today?"

"I did the kitchen, the living room, your bathroom, and I was cleaning in here when—"

"When you decided to play Goldilocks?"

"I did not. I'd just thought I'd"—she yawned—"take a five-minute or so catnap."

He looked at the mess her hair had become and the sleepy puffiness to her eyes. "I'll go with the 'or so' option."

She winced then scratched her head. "I'm sorry. I really didn't intend for you to find me on your bed."

Everyone knew the road to Hell was paved with good intentions, and she was practically dragging him down this one.

"Oh, Liam, I was hoping I could ask you a favor."

Of course she was. Just like Rachel. If he ever stopped thinking with his dick, he'd remember that he couldn't trust women like Rachel and Cassidy. Didn't seem to stop his stupid libido from wanting them, though. Damn libido.

"I'll pay you back. I promise."

"Look, sugarbritches, not everything in *my* world is about money."

She winced and he, idiot that he was, felt bad about causing it. It'd make things easier if she made him angry, but no. With her, he got the guilts.

"I . . . I'm sorry. I didn't mean to offend you. I just wanted you to know that I'm not expecting you to do things for me simply because you're nice enough to do them. I will pay you back. I promise. It's just that, today was . . . um, well, I'm not exactly on top of my game. It's been kinda rough, you know?"

"Yeah." He didn't want her to get to him, but he apparently didn't have any more control over his empathy than he did his stupid libido. "So what's your favor?"

"I was wondering if I could borrow your truck."

"You want me to lend you my truck?"

"Just for an hour or two."

"For?" What would a woman like her want with a *truck*? And did she even know how to drive or was she used to chauffeurs? He wasn't giving her his truck for her to crash it into a tree.

She turned her head to the left fast enough so that her hair swung in front of her face. "It's, um . . ." She tucked the hair behind her ear with a big sigh and looked at him head on. "It's for my furniture."

"I thought you said you left with just the clothes on your back. And your paints, of course. They're out in my truck along with your power tools. Oh, and I grabbed a few things for you to wear." The underwear had been an issue, but he'd sucked it up and grabbed a handful without going through the rest of her drawers—it was better than knowing she was walking around his home without any. "There was a pile of clothes at the bottom of your closet without any tags, so I figured your father wouldn't be able to account for them."

"Oh wow. That's so sweet of you. Thank you so much!" She hugged him.

Hugged him. As if they were best friends.

Or more.

The moment got awkward in a hurry. Especially when his hands—no more under his control than his libido or his empathy apparently—stole up to her waist and hung on.

Her smile disappeared.

His stomach clenched. He needed to let go. Step back. Get away.

He didn't.

She slicked her tongue over her lips then tilted her head, exposing a long line of tempting skin from beneath her ear, down her neck, and along her shoulder to where the shirt barely clung to the curve to her arm. If he took just a bit of it in his teeth and tugged . . .

"I, uh . . ." She let go of his shoulders. One finger at a time, perhaps, but still, she let go.

He'd better, too.

He took one last lingering look at the curve of her neck and removed his hands from her waist. Took a step back, too. "I'll get your stuff."

Then he got the hell out of his bedroom before he did something they both might be happy with for a few moments, but would ultimately regret in the long run.

SHE'D almost kissed him—and she was pretty sure he'd wanted to kiss her, too. If that didn't just make this all that more complicated . . .

She was attracted to him. Talk about the wrong place and time. Her goal was to move out on her own. *Be* on her own. *Make it* on her own. Staying here was temporary. Just until she sold a piece of furniture or two and had enough money for an apartment. She just needed a little time to get on her feet, and him sweeping her off of them was not part of the plan.

"Come on, Titania." The dog had been curled up on the pillow and hadn't even barked when Liam had come in, the traitor. "Let's get out of here before he gets back." *And* before she lost whatever strength it was that had made her let go of his shoulders. His big, broad shoulders—

Yep, she got the hell out of there.

He wasn't any less appealing when she met him in the living room.

"The room looks good. You did a nice job."

"Glad you approve." If only he knew the effort she'd put into getting it that way. She'd almost had to pick up cracked glass from the sofa back table when Titania had tried to help out by pushing the mop around. Then there were the three times she'd had to polish that table.

Yes, three. First, there'd been streaks on the glass, so she'd cleaned it again. More streaks. She finally read the fine print on the back of the cans only to find out she'd been using wood polish that wasn't designed to be used on glass.

So then she'd had to *find* the glass polish in that scary thing he called a mud room that was filled with gadgets and hoses and way too many chemicals for her sensitive skin, until she'd gotten lucky and found a box of rubber gloves and glass cleaner.

Then there'd been the whole what-to-use-in-the-bathroom-and-does-it-work-in-the-kitchen-as-well investigation, followed by wet mop/dry mop analytics. The whole mold/mildew thing had turned her stomach. When she had her own place, it was going to require only three bottles of cleaning solutions, one mop, and one vacuum. Anything else was overkill. Who had the time or the money for six different bottles, a mop for tile, a vacuum for a hardwood, a vacuum for carpet, and some weird attachment for steps? Thank God his steps were wrought iron and the dust mop worked for them because she wasn't quite sure how all those attachments hooked together.

"So where do you want this?" He held up the bag that'd been in her closet. Good call on his part, because Dad wouldn't know those clothes were missing.

She just wasn't sure she'd be able to wear them around Liam and not feel self-conscious, though. They were her painting clothes. Ones Dad would never sanction her being seen in, which was half the reason she'd bought them. The other half had been because they were completely opposite of what she usually wore and she'd been feeling rebellious. That whole trip to the flea market with Stacey one weekend had been rebellious and a hell of a lot of fun. Wearing the clothes had made her happy.

She could use that feeling right now.

"I guess my bedroom." Whichever one that was. There was one more downstairs next to his and two upstairs.

Common sense would dictate that she use the one down-stairs, since it was on the main level, but self-preservation said to head upstairs.

He didn't help matters by just staring at her.

"Or . . ." She'd already asked for the truck; she ought to get everything out in the open. "What about the empty side of your garage? I was hoping I could use it for storage and a temporary studio. I have a few more pieces in a warehouse, and once my father finds out about its existence—if he hasn't already—he'll have it sealed and I'll be out of luck. Hence, the need for your truck. I'll put a tarp down so you won't have to worry about the floor, plus the smell and mess would be outside. The sooner I can start working on the furniture, the sooner I can sell something and begin paying you for taking me in. You won't even know I'm here and I'll be out of your hair, so it really won't be that much of an imposition—"

"Stop." Liam held up his hand. "Take a breath before you pass out on me. I don't need a trip to the hospital on top of everything else."

Instead of taking that breath, she swallowed her panic. She'd sounded desperate, spewing everything to him all at once, but she needed his cooperation with the plan or she'd be stuck here for a long time.

"Fine. You can borrow the truck. But I'm going to put pads in the back. I don't need the bed scratched. Are you going to be able to get the furniture in without my help?"

Oh crud. She hadn't thought about that. "Well . . ."

He exhaled and wiped his forehead with his arm. "Yeah, that's what I figured." He set the bag on the floor by the wall and stuck his hands on his hips. "And how many pieces are we talking? Am I going to be able to park the truck in the garage if it's your art studio?"

"You will. It's not that many. Maybe half a dozen."

"Okay. Fine. Let's go after dinner."

"Dinner?"

"Yeah, you know. The meal that comes at the end of the day? The thing in the Crock-Pot?"

The Crock-Pot. Oh. Crud. She'd forgotten about that.
"Um, Liam, about that—"

He held up a hand and exhaled. "I'll make the rice. The sooner we get out of here, the sooner we keep your father from finding your secret stash."

Was this the same guy who'd mocked her by calling her *Princess*? The same one who believed all the hype about her life? Yet here he was, being nice to her, taking her in, and wanting to one-up her dad. That could be career suicide for the guy should Mitchell ever find out.

If he wasn't careful—hell, if *she* wasn't careful—she could find herself falling for Mr. Liam Manley.

*T*HIS is what you wanted to salvage?" Liam stood in the doorway of her storage facility with his mouth hanging open after their hurried meal. "Princess, I hate to tell you this, but no one's going to buy this stuff. It's . . . well . . . it's junk." He pinched the bridge of his nose. "I don't mean to be harsh, but this stuff looks like shi—uh, crap. Old. Run down. You're not going to make money with any of this."

"I'll have you know, the piece I just sold was in worse shape than most of these, and it sold for five figures."

"You're kidding."

"Nope."

"So where's that money? Why can't you use that to get your new lease on life going?"

Now she did take that breath. And a second. "I deposited the check. In an account with my father's company's credit union. You know, the one my debit card is attached to. And since Dad didn't think painting and—heaven forbid—*selling* what I painted were dignified pursuits, he bought the piece back when he found out about it. *And* demanded that I forfeit my commission. So, yeah, that account's closed."

"You're kidding."

"Do I look like I'm kidding? Would I move in with you, a virtual stranger, if I were kidding?"

He dragged his palm down his face. "I guess not, but shit."

She exhaled. "I know, right? I can't believe he did that." Or that she hadn't seen it coming. Why oh why hadn't she opened her own secret bank account? Hindsight truly was twenty-twenty. All her frivolous pursuits keeping up with her friends and their families . . . If only she'd thought ahead.

If only she'd seen her father for who he truly was.

"I can't believe he thought the furniture wasn't a good idea. People love that sort of thing."

"I know. There's a market for my work. A few hinges, a hammer or two, and a good coat of paint can transform an old piece of furniture into something useful and decorative. Just because it's old doesn't mean it's out of the game."

"I hear you. I buy old houses, fix them up, and flip them. Make a decent living doing so, too."

That was how her father started out. "What about cleaning? I thought that's what you did."

"Uh, well, yeah. I do that, too. To help my sister out."

What a nice guy. Hardworking, too. And then there was the good-looking thing.

Yeah, she better watch out or she could get attached very easily, and then where would her grand plans for her future be? Liam had come along at both the right and the wrong time.

"So did you do your own house?"

Liam's back got a little straighter, his chest puffed out a little more. "I did."

He had a right to his pride. "You do great work, Liam. I mean, I don't know what your place looked like before you bought it, but you have great taste."

A flash of something crossed his face, but he covered it with a shrug before she could figure out what it meant. "I just pick out what I like." He cleared his throat. "So shall we do this before your father shows up?"

Big fat yes on that one. "Let's grab the credenza first, but be careful of the front leg. It's hanging on by one thread of the screw."

He arched his eyebrow at her. "And you thought you were going to get this in the truck by yourself?"

"I wasn't thinking, okay?" About a lot of things, obviously. "Besides, I'm imposing on you enough as it is and didn't want to ask. I would have figured something out."

"And broken it while doing so. Then where would you be?"

She flicked open the cabinet door and it *thunked* lopsidedly open. "It couldn't be any worse than it already is."

He stared at it for a second or two, then looked at her. There was something in that look . . . Dare she think it *might* be admiration?

"I can't wait to see this when you're finished. If you can turn this piece of junk into something worth five figures, I owe you dinner."

"You're on."

"That means that if it doesn't, you owe *me* dinner."

"I'm not worried." She wasn't because either way, she'd have dinner with Liam Manley.

Though maybe *that* ought to worry her.

LIAM kept his eyes glued to the rearview mirror as he drove away from his home for the third time today. The princess was ensconced in his garage, tarp on the floor, her furniture strewn around her, and the look on her face was one he would've expected to see on a sale day at the mall, not for a bunch of broken hunks of wood and marble that were going to require some decent carpentry skills, not to mention a hell of a lot of talent in the artistry department. He didn't have the heart to tell her that the reason she'd gotten five figures for that other piece had to have had more to do with her father's name than some finishing-school art class.

He hoped she wasn't living with him when the realization

sank in. He didn't want to test his resolve against a woman's tears; he doubted he was as immune as he'd like.

He definitely wasn't immune to her smiles. Or her frowny looks as she studied the chest of drawers from every angle. Or the sexy tilt of her chin as she tapped a paintbrush handle against it.

Luckily, he looked out the front window then—just in time to avoid a tree that was about six inches from his bumper.

He swerved, cursing himself for getting distracted. He needed to have his head examined.

Normally, he'd go visit one of his brothers to talk about what was bothering him, but he didn't want the looks. The lectures. They'd heard enough of his bitching when Rachel had pulled her stunt; he didn't want to go running back with his tail between his legs again because of a gorgeous smile and that damn spunky determination he'd never have thought Cassidy Davenport would have in her.

Figured. The latest socialite he was stuck with was starting to defy the stereotype.

Chapter Ten

～⟨✿⟩～

PINK rhinestone T-shirt, white embroidered capris, black yoga pants, long flowing tie-dyed caftan her father would probably order her to burn, short-shorts he *definitely* would, and a leather jacket that looked as if it'd come right off some motorcycle gang chick . . . Cassidy was smiling as she pulled the outfits Liam had brought her from the bag, trying to not get all tingly at his thoughtfulness.

But when she hit the peach nightie, blue silk robe, and black stilettos with the ankle straps, she lost that battle. Only it was a different sort of tingle. There was something about the idea of him handling those silky things that did deliciously naughty things to her insides.

Not a good idea. You wanted to be on your own, remember? No guys. Not your father, not a sugar daddy, and no boyfriend. This time is for you. About *you. Remember that.*

She was trying to, but he had to go and be so darn nice on top of being so sexy.

Titania yipped by her ankle, then jumped to her knee. The Maltese was normally a perfectly behaved little lady, except when she was hungry.

"Is it dinnertime, Titania?" Cassidy felt naked without her cell phone. She couldn't believe her father had turned it off. And booted the car. And let her walk out with nothing but the clothes on her back.

She looked at the pile she'd folded into the dresser drawers in the room Liam had given her and smiled. One dilemma solved. She'd love to hug him for that.

Among other reasons.

Titania yipped again.

"Okay, okay." Cassidy tucked that thought out of the way and closed the last dresser drawer before heading to the kitchen to find the dog food packets she'd brought from home. She took inventory. There were enough left to last about a week. Which didn't leave her a lot of time to finish the credenza if she wanted to sell it for dog-food money. A tough schedule on a normal day, and that was *if* Jean-Pierre would even *consider* taking on another piece. Which would necessitate her rounding up some courage, putting her mortification at her father's antics behind her, and plead with him to risk her father's wrath.

And if he even *did* agree, she'd have to pray the credenza would sell as quickly as the chest had.

Those were a lot of *if*s. And her entire future—as well as Titania's—was resting on them.

So she stuck her rhinestone-studded protective glasses on and got to work.

A few hours later, she was covered in sawdust and dried wood glue, and had repaired the droopy hinges on the credenza's doors. The wobbly leg was no longer in danger of breaking off, and after a few more passes with the chamois, the piece would be ready for the first coat of paint.

Cassidy removed her glasses and dust mask, swiped some sweaty, sawdust-laden hair off her forehead, then glanced outside. It was dark. She was always amazed how time passed when she was engrossed in her work.

Poor Titania had been locked up in Liam's laundry room

since she'd come out here. Good thing the dog had answered the call of nature before Cassidy had locked her in, but now it was Cassidy's turn. And she ought to take a shower to clear this crud off.

She looked out through the garage door. Not a sign of Liam. Good.

She turned off the lights, then stripped off her T-shirt and shorts, not wanting to clean up a trail of sawdust all the way to the bathroom, and ran back into the house in her underwear.

Liam sure knew how to treat his guests—or his indentured servants, but she wasn't going to let that stop her from enjoying the luxury of a full marble shower with an overhead sprinkler showerhead and the full body accompaniment. After the cruddy day she'd had, she could use a little pampering.

And as she stepped into the perfectly timed pulsing spray with the toiletries she'd appropriated from her own bathroom, it felt as if she was stepping into heaven.

LIAM, however, was in hell.

He'd stepped out of his truck—right onto a pile of clothes.

Cassidy's clothes.

The ones she'd been wearing earlier.

There was only one reason a woman would drop her clothes in the middle of a garage, especially when they were covered in sawdust.

She was running around his house naked. Or in her underwear, which—seriously—was not any better.

What had he done to deserve this torture? He'd tried to do a *good* thing and now he was paying the price of the dammed. God help him.

He pinched the bridge of his nose and walked around the front of his truck and into the laundry room, making as much noise as possible, praying she'd hear him and duck into her room or the bathroom, and at least wrap a towel around herself.

"Cassidy?" He said from behind the room door.

Nothing.

"Cassidy?" he said a little louder, this time peering around the door frame.

Still nothing.

He walked into the house and then he heard it.

She was singing in the shower.

Off-key.

Well, hey, there was something Daddy's money couldn't buy—the ability to carry a tune. He liked that flaw in her.

But he didn't *want* to like *any*thing about her.

She hit a high note . . . sort of. A little pitchy, but that wasn't making her give up.

He liked that about her, too.

Hell.

He skirted the door to the hall bath as much as possible, since he had to pass it to get to his room, where he, also, would take a shower.

There was a certain irony to the fact that the two of them would be naked at the same time, but Liam knew the best way to avoid temptation: take the coldest shower known to mankind.

Unfortunately, he could still hear her singing even with the water pounding on his head.

He tried to drown out her voice with soap in his ears, but that key of hers . . . It'd make the hair on his neck stand up if it weren't wet.

So he washed off as quickly as possible, taking a little longer to get all the suds out of his ears, wrapped a towel around his waist, and tossed another one over his shoulder. He'd dry off in the bedroom with the buffer of the bathroom between them.

It was the perfect buffer actually, since he didn't hear one note as he grabbed his boxer briefs from his dresser.

That should have been his clue.

He'd just dried off and tossed the towels onto the bed when he heard a "Titania!" followed by a gasp.

He turned around.

Big mistake.

There stood Cassidy, wrapped in a towel that left her covered her from chest to thigh, but still too naked for his liking, while he . . . he *was* naked.

"Oh shit."

"I'm sorry."

"What do you—"

"I should go—"

"Yeah. Good idea." He reached for the towels and had to half crawl onto the bed to get the damn things. Which gave her more of a show than he wanted.

He looked at her. "You can go, you know."

"Uh, yes. Right. I will. It's just—"

He sat on the bed and plopped the towel on his groin. "Princess, in case it's escaped your notice, I'm naked." He fluttered the towel.

"Technically, you're not now, and I think Titania came in here."

"Is that the best line you can come up with?"

She rolled her eyes. "It's not a line. She ran out of the bathroom and I checked the front of the house. She hasn't mastered your spiral staircase, and since she took that nap in here with me, I thought she might have come in. It would help if you'd closed your door."

She was right. He should have locked it, too. But it wasn't as if he was used to living with someone, and he'd *thought* he'd closed it.

"Titania," he called.

There was a scuffling under his bed.

Of course she was here. Which meant more torture for him as Cassidy got down on her hands and knees—kill him now—to peek under the bed. If he were standing in his doorway, he'd be getting one hell of a show.

"Come on, Titania. Get out here."

The scuffling moved toward the head of his bed.

Of course.

"Titania!" Cassidy slapped the floor. "Come here!"

The dog didn't move.

Liam rolled his eyes. And stood up. And wrapped the towel around his waist.

Keeping his eyes off the rounded curve of what he was sure was a delectable backside with the towel almost hiked over it, he got down beside Cassidy. "Titania. Come."

The little fur-ball belly-crawled right up to him and licked him on the nose.

He snaked his arm around her and slid her out from under the bed, cradling her like a football.

"Here you go," he said once they were both back on their feet.

Cassidy took the dog, almost dropping her when her towel started to fall.

Liam went to catch the dog, got a handful of breast, and yanked his hand back as if he'd burned it.

"Uh, I'm sorry. I didn't mean—"

"I know." Cassidy grabbed her towel with the dog teetering on her arm and there was no way in hell Liam was going to help out this time.

He turned around. "Let me know when you're out of the room."

"Thanks. I will."

He heard her run from the room and he took a huge breath. That'd been too close. *She'd* been too close. His *hand* had been too close. As the hard-on beneath the towel attested to. And the feeling of her breast in his palm . . . That was going to be a hard thing to forget.

He strode to his closet—towel *securely* wrapped around his waist—and grabbed a T-shirt, the boxer briefs he'd dropped in favor of the towel, and a pair of basketball shorts.

Too bad he didn't choose a suit of armor because, just as he walked by her door on his way to the kitchen, the dog bolted from her room, leaving the door open just enough to see—

Now Cassidy *was* naked.

She held the towel to her chest so he only got a side glimpse of a long, shapely leg, and a butt that, yeah, was delectable. Then there was the tiny waist that he'd had his hands on earlier, plus the added bonus of the curve of her breast, a visual he really didn't need, since his memory was working just fine.

Unfortunately, so was his dick. It went to full mast in two seconds.

"Titania, come back here!" She spun around, clasping the towel to her chest, and headed toward the door—stopping the moment she saw him. "Oh."

"Yes. Oh." He looked. He shouldn't, but he couldn't help himself.

"I, uh, need to get dressed."

"Yes. You do."

"So, could you, you know . . ." She fluttered her fingers.

Yes. He knew. But the dog was resting on his feet.

So he scooped Houdini up, spun around, and carried the little yipper—though now she was a little licker, lapping up the remnants of his shower off his wrist—out to the kitchen.

He grabbed a container of Gran's beef stew. The little troublemaker was going to eat in style tonight. Just because.

"Oh you don't have to feed her. She already ate."

A soaked-hair Cassidy came running into the kitchen in a tie-dyed dress that clung to those damn curves of hers way too much for his liking—well, that wasn't exactly true, but the sight was too much for him to take right now.

Then she bent down to pick the dog up and the torture just continued as he got a straight-shot view down her dress.

Seriously, what was he? Eighteen? He should really stop ogling her.

But why the hell couldn't she wear a bra?

Because you didn't happen to pick one of those up while you were grabbing her lingerie.

The pooch's growl was an effective *snap out of it* call to arms.

"I guess the dog has other ideas."

"She has a name, you know. Titania."

"I know. I used it, remember? In my room. When I was naked, remember?"

"Look, I said I was sorry. If you'd locked the door, this wouldn't have happened. I didn't know you were home."

"Hey, don't put this on me. It's my home. I'm entitled to walk around naked if I want."

"Then why were you all out of sorts when I walked in?"

"Did *you* like it when I walked in on you?" He was sort of hoping she'd say yes to that.

And he'd deal with the *why* to that thought later.

"Look, Liam. I'm sorry. I'm sorry my dog got into your room and I'm sorry I walked in on you. It's not as if I did it on purpose."

"Then what's with the clothes all over my garage?"

"They're not all over the place. They're in a pile, covered in sawdust. I didn't think you'd appreciate me tracking sawdust through your house."

She was considerate. That was something he hadn't foreseen. If she ended up having any other nice qualities, he was going to have a hard time ignoring her effect on him. "As long as you clean it up, I can't say anything about it."

"Well you weren't home and I didn't feel up to more cleaning on top of working on the credenza. I fixed the door, by the way. It works just fine now. No one will ever know it didn't. If you're interested, that is."

She put her hands on her hips and tilted her chin and—

Yeah. He *was* interested.

Chapter Eleven

❧❧❧

CASSIDY stopped at the supermarket entrance and stared. Seriously? How was she supposed to find anything in here? The last time she'd been to a grocery store was when the nanny had been sick and the chef had needed a few last-minute items. Now, she had a list and some cash and she was supposed to make the list fit the cash.

That finishing school education of hers had been sorely lacking in day-to-day skills, but she tucked some hair that escaped her ponytail behind her ear and looked at the list Liam had written. She could do this. It wasn't rocket science. Millions of people did this every day. She had to do it sometime; might as well be now.

She had sixty bucks for things his grandmother hadn't brought. Things like milk, eggs, cheese, and . . . and she'd almost lost it when she'd read this—dog food.

She blinked back a few tears even now. She was not going to cry. Liam, the sarcastic pain in the ass, had a heart. Unlike her father, the man whose DNA she carried.

It was *because* of that DNA that she was going to do this. And she was going to do it in style. Dad was not going to see her fail. She was not going to cower and go crawling back to him. Or Burton. She was on her own. Well, once she left Liam, that was.

Rolling back her shoulders, Cassidy headed for Customer Service. "Hello. I was wondering if you could help me."

"Whaddya need?" The girl behind the counter didn't even bother to look up. Good. Cassidy didn't want to be recognized. Not only would Dad have yet another conniption, he'd know where she was.

She cared more about the latter than the former.

"I was wondering if you could tell me where to find dog food and eggs and milk and—"

"Dairy's on twelve. Pets six."

"I'm sorry, but what does that mean?"

The girl finally looked up and arched a pierced eyebrow. "Aisles twelve and six?"

"Oh. Okay."

"Hey, aren't you somebody?"

Cassidy's stomach *thunked*. "Well, sure. Aren't we all?"

The girl straightened up and tapped her pen against the counter. "No. I mean, *some*body. Like famous or something."

Crap. She'd worn the most anti-Davenport clothes from the pile of anti-Davenport clothes, pulled her hair back, and sworn off makeup. She didn't look anything like her former gossip-pages self. "Nope, sorry. I'm just me."

The girl's lips twisted. "Well you sure look like someone. I just can't figure out who it is."

"Aisles six and twelve, right?" Cassidy tapped the countertop. "Thanks."

She headed for the dog food first, then managed to find everything on the list within a half hour. Not too shabby for a first-timer. She could do this. She could learn the normal, everyday things that most of the population took for granted, but for which those of her father's crowd had "people."

She was in the checkout lane when that afterglow of success dimmed.

"Did you hear about Mitchell Davenport's daughter?"

Actually, the afterglow *tanked*. Way beyond *dimmed*.

"You mean the pretty one who's always all over the news? Born with a silver spoon and leads a charmed life?"

The other woman shook her head. "Not anymore she doesn't."

Cassidy couldn't see the woman's face, but she heard the glee in her voice.

Ah. A Hater. She'd run across more than a few of them in her time.

"What do you mean?"

"Here. Look at this."

Supermarket tabloids. Dammit. Cassidy's glow went up in a *poof* of mortification.

"Her dad kicked her out. Made her fend for herself."

"About time. How long did she think that self-made man was going to keep paying for her party lifestyle? What I wouldn't give if my old man had funded even half my teenage party-hopping. Still, gotta admire a girl who's managed to get her father to pay for it for ten years after graduation."

"She shoulda found a sugar daddy to continue the tradition. In those circles, shouldn't have been too tough."

"Next."

Cassidy heard a buzzing in her head. She looked at the conveyor belt, expecting something to be caught to make that god-awful racket, but all she saw was the checkout girl looking at her.

"Next."

Oh. Right. Her. That buzzing was probably the beginnings of a whopper of a migraine.

"Poor baby didn't get to take the 'Benz. And the reporter even managed to get a shot of the car."

Cassidy jerked to the register, somehow managing to get her hands to coordinate with her brain to get the contents of her shopping cart onto the conveyor belt, and her fingers to negotiate her pocketbook for the sixty bucks.

The total came to sixty-two fifty.

She didn't have it.

God. This had *never* happened to her before. Where was

that damn silver spoon that woman had been talking about? She'd sell it for cash to make this transaction happen.

"Sure, I could sleep with some old guy for his money," said the Hater. "Not as if it'll be for too long, know what I mean? A few good Os and the guy'll blow a gasket and die on me. Then it'd be all mine."

"Too bad we don't run in that Davenport girl's circles. I wouldn't even be picky as long as his bank balance was in the seven figure range."

That would make the woman a prostitute, but Cassidy kept her mouth shut. Oh, not because she was some sage human being, but if she opened it, she was fairly certain something she shouldn't say would come out.

That wasn't who she was. It wasn't who her friends were. Did it happen in her social circle? Of course, but that didn't mean everyone had the morals of an alley cat and the conscience of a flea.

"Sixty-two fifty, please." The checkout teenager cracked her gum.

Cassidy shook her head to clear the fog of screaming reprimands from it and focused on the total. What was she supposed to do? She'd never had to return food. Could she even do that? And was it a return if she never took it out of the bag?

"Um, could you take off three of the dog food packets?" Titania would just have to do with more beef stew and less commercial food. The dog wouldn't mind.

The kid, however, obviously did, rolling her heavily made-up eyes, and huffing loud enough that those women overheard.

They turned around. And one of them got a look on her face Cassidy dreaded.

"Hey, you look a lot like that Davenport girl."

"Who? Me?" Cassidy couldn't pay the checkout girl and get the bags off the turnstile fast enough. "I get that a lot. Wouldn't mind having her bank account, though."

"Not these days you wouldn't."

"Bet she can't even afford to buy your groceries."

That's right; she couldn't.

And it'd made the tabloids. Everyone she knew would know.

Cassidy practically ripped the last bag off the turnstile and headed toward the door before the women got a look at her earrings. Those would be a dead giveaway and she didn't want to have to stand here apologizing for being born with a silver spoon nor hear their ridicule anymore.

God, if only she'd met Franklin sooner in life. The lessons his thirteen short years had taught Cassidy were worth more than any private school education her father had paid for.

She blinked the tears from her eyes. She'd met Franklin when she'd attended a charity dinner for the hospital's pediatric unit in her father's place. Yet another chance for Dad to parade her out on his behalf.

Not that she'd minded. She'd known almost everyone and had had the opportunity to wear her new Stella McCartney dress and drink champagne—her life's staples up to that point.

Then Franklin had been seated next to her.

The kid had won her over in about thirty seconds and changed her life in the next thirty days. He'd been at the end stage of his treatment with no hope for remission, but he'd been determined to leave his mark on the world. He, who'd had every reason to be bitter and to give up on life—from his cancer to the family who turned him over to child services because they hadn't been able to deal with it—had refused to do so. He'd wanted to enjoy himself as long as he was able, and dwelling on the negative and petty things in his life had been a waste of the time left to him.

Cassidy had made sure to stop by at least three times a week, more as the end neared. Being with him so much had put those frivolous time-sucking things like shopping and gossiping and "being seen" into perspective.

And then he'd been gone.

Cassidy still remembered the pain as if it were yesterday. As if her heart had been ripped out and trampled. As if she'd never catch her breath again. The only reason she'd known she would was because she'd gone through the same emotions when Mom had left.

But hearing those women talk about her—*laugh* at her hard times . . . Times like these were when she wanted to give in to the self-pity and just cry. But then she'd remember Franklin and suck it up and go on. Because what she had to deal with wasn't as bad as what Franklin had faced and he hadn't succumbed to self-pity.

Neither would she.

Those women's attitudes, the whim of fate, the insidiousness of disease, and life . . . none of it was fair. It was how she chose to deal with it that would make or break her. And Cassidy, like Franklin, was *not* going to be broken. She would rise above.

She blew a kiss heavenward—as she did whenever she thought about Franklin. She wasn't going to let his death be in vain.

She took a deep breath, pushed the women from her mind, and headed back to Liam's truck. He'd loaned it to her for the day, since he was going to be tied up at her father's building. It'd been bittersweet to see the place she'd called home for six years when she'd dropped him off there this morning, but, interestingly, there hadn't been any of the sadness or anger she would've thought she'd feel to be there again. It was as if the building belonged to a different place and time. One she didn't want to go back to.

She stowed her shopping bags in the back seat of the four-door cab, then climbed inside, remembering when Liam had helped her.

Damn if that didn't elicit tingles. It was strange, really, how just the thought of being near him, standing beside him, having him touch her put Cassidy in touch with her feminine side in a way she'd never been with Burton or Carlton or Helmsford, or any of the other men her father had arranged for her to date.

She winced as she put the truck in gear. There'd always been some eligible guy at her father's gatherings. A representative of another "well-bred" family to create the perfect offspring. She'd often joked with her friends that the guy who examined her teeth would be the one her father would pick for her to marry.

Burton hadn't gone that far, but then, he hadn't gone far at all. She hadn't let him. Hadn't felt the need to delve into a physical relationship with him—a big glaring neon flashing light that said he wasn't the man for her.

What about Liam?

She scooted around a wayward shopping cart that was rolling across the parking lot. There was nothing about Liam. He was a nice guy to help her—and sexy as hell—but he was a temporary measure. A stopgap.

He can stop my gap anytime—

Oh for heaven's sake. Cassidy exhaled and deliberately yanked the truck to the right. Seriously? Did her subconscious *have* to be so crude? So banal?

Hey, get crude and banal with Liam and see if you don't enjoy it.

She had to smile at that. Yeah, that would be pretty fun.

But she had a job to do and it wasn't to do the maid, no matter how hot he was. There was more to life than sex.

But it does make life sweet . . .

She pulled out of the parking lot and turned right onto Davenport Drive. She couldn't even escape her father *when* she'd escaped him. There was the Davenport wing on the library and the Davenport Properties roadside clean-up signs, and the playground she'd tried to get her father to rename Franklin's Field but he'd refused. Of course. Nothing was more important to her father than the Davenport name.

Not even his daughter.

She made a quick left into another strip mall and was just about to circle back to the alley behind it—anything to get off Davenport Drive—when a storefront caught her eye.

Pawn Shoppe.

A cutesy name for a nice solution to that two-fifty deficit.

She parked in front and headed inside, unscrewing the backs of her earrings as she went.

* * *

LIAM reread the blurb in the newspaper beneath a picture
of Cassidy in a knockout evening dress on the marble
steps of a ritzy restaurant.

PRINCESS BECOMES A PAUPER

Local socialite, Cassidy Davenport, is learning that the
grass on the other side of the fence is far less green than
the professionally landscaped lawns of her high-rise and
country club these days.

An insider reports that Ms. Davenport's father, renowned
entrepreneur Mitchell Davenport, has evicted her from her
penthouse condominium, forcing her to seek employment
among the masses.

Friends say they last spoke to Ms. Davenport yesterday
morning before the eviction. No one has heard from her
since, prompting questions of what else her father has cut
from her lifestyle. No statement has been forthcoming from
the Davenport Properties' stronghold in the downtown
business district.

Is this true or just another PR ploy by the man many
refer to as the Hound From Hell for his marketing savvy
and entrepreneurial style?

And if not, how will Ms. Davenport fare in this
challenge? Where will she live? What will she do? And will
she look as fashionable as she does in this photo from the
Todd Best Art Show last fall?

Freaking vultures. One more insult for Cassidy to endure.
A public one, at that. Poor woman.

Yeah, he was feeling sorry for her. He probably shouldn't,
given that life in a fishbowl also came with millions and fancy
cars and luxury vacations, but he'd seen how her father's
actions had hurt her. Now she'd have to endure them all over
again, this time knowing it was out there for everyone to see.

He hoped she'd gone home and not food shopping after dropping him off this morning, and missed finding out about this at all. Maybe he could get her so focused on painting that she wouldn't find out until the hype blew over.

Then he looked out the windshield and that theory was blown to hell.

Cassidy was out and about all right—and heading into a pawn shop.

With her fingers working the ice on her ears, he had a good idea why, but the woman was going to get raked over the coals and taken for every dime she didn't have. Going to the pawn shop wasn't like going to a jeweler. Not that a jeweler gave the best prices—as he'd found out when he'd tried to return the bracelet he'd bought Rachel. Didn't get close to what he'd paid for it, but at least it'd kept him out of Vito's shop.

"Hang a right, Jake," he said to his buddy who was driving. Jake had been on a job site nearby, and they'd decided to grab some lunch.

"Thanks. I'll get my own ride back." Liam stashed the newspaper under his arm and was out of Jake's truck before it'd stopped, running to the pawn shop door about thirty seconds after Cassidy.

He was almost too late.

"How much will you give me for these?" Cassidy was at the counter.

"Hey." He put his hand over her open palm where the two hunks of diamond sat glinting in the fluorescent lighting, while Vito salivated all over them. Probably the first time in Cassidy's life that a guy was salivating over something other than her when she was in the room, but Vito had an eye for business. *His* business. And he wasn't in business to make other people a profit, which was why this was the last place Liam wanted to see her.

"Liam? What are you doing here?" She curled her fingers closed beneath his palm. The diamonds, for the moment, were safe.

"I saw you head in here and wanted to make sure you didn't make a mistake."

Uh oh. Wrong choice of words. The princess turned even icier than the rocks in her fist.

"I am *not* making a mistake. I know what I'm doing."

"No, you don't. You don't want to sell those to Vito."

"Well of course I don't. I'm going to pawn them."

"You don't want to do that either."

"Yo, Manley. Butt the fuck out, man. I don't tell you how to do your business." Vito's testosterone went into an uproar.

"Chill, Vito. You're not taking her diamonds."

"Like hell I ain't. If she's sellin', and they're what she says they are, I'm buyin.'"

"She just said she isn't selling."

Vito's sausage-sized finger almost slapped Liam's nose. "I like you, Manley. Your brothers, too. And that sister of yours . . ." Vito didn't have to say anything for Liam to get what Vito thought of his sister. "But this is business. So you back the fuck away or I'm gonna have ta call out my boys. You don't want me to call out my boys."

No, Liam didn't. He looked at Cassidy. "Can we please talk about this before you do it?"

"Why? You're not my boss."

"Actually, technically, I am. And you're on the clock, so you shouldn't be here. I could fire you."

Her eyes narrowed and he prepared himself for the fight. He arched an eyebrow.

She looked at him, then at Vito. She tugged her hand out from beneath his and looked at the earrings for a few seconds.

Then she folded her fingers around them again and stuffed them into her shorts pocket. "Okay, what do you want to say?"

He looked at Vito. "Not here." He gripped her upper arm. "Let's go outside."

"Motherfucker," Vito muttered beneath his breath, shaking his head as he headed toward his back room. The inner sanctum back room that probably had a couple mil stashed there on any given day, along with Vito's weapons of choice. His shop might be in the nice part of town, with its name all prettied up with the extra *PE* on the end, but the fact remained that this was Vito's place of business and sometimes that business wasn't always so nice. Or friendly. Or legal. Or all three.

Liam led her outside toward his truck. This was the last time he was giving her the keys. Here, he'd been worried about an accident, never thinking she was a walking accident just waiting to enter the right *shoppe*.

"So what do you have to say, Liam?" She rounded on him right in the middle of the parking lot.

"Could we go someplace less public?"

She looked around and flung her hands wide. "You want private in a parking lot? Good luck with that."

"You're the one who needs the luck." Liam was working very hard to keep his temper. He didn't have a bad one; typically he never had *any* temper. He was the easy-going brother.

But not this time.

"Fine, Cassidy. Let's air your dirty laundry in public. This morning's headlines of you being booted from your home aren't enough, is that it?"

"Don't tell me you read those trashrags. Everyone knows that stuff isn't true."

"Trashrags? The *Herald* isn't a trashrag."

"The . . . the *Herald*? It made the *Herald*?" Her face went white.

"You didn't know." Shit. This was not how he'd want her to find out her picture was on the front page of the daily newspaper with a lot more than a one-line caption beneath it. Hell, he'd love to avoid her finding out at all, but Mitchell Davenport was a big name in this town and what he did or said made the papers.

He'd love to find out how the reporter got his info. Had it been Marco? The guy had seemed so innocent, but maybe he needed the money a juicy story like this would command.

"You're sure it's in the *Herald*? Not just the tabloids?"

Liam grabbed her arm. "Look, it doesn't matter where it is. The point is, you were about to sell your soul and those diamonds to the devil."

"I wasn't selling them. I told you, I was pawning them."

"Same difference. If you don't have the five grand he'd give you for those—*if* you're lucky to get that—now, what makes you think you'll have it when the payment's due? Not to mention the interest he'll charge if you're late. Are you prepared to lose those earrings just to prove to me that you know what you're doing?"

A myriad of emotions crossed Cassidy's face and Liam wasn't sure what to expect when they finally coalesced into a definitive reaction.

"Please tell me it's not on the front page."

Shit shit shit.

"Cass, don't go there. Just forget I said anything."

"Liam, *tell* me."

Where was this backbone when her father was tossing her out? If she'd grown it then, she wouldn't be in this position and he could leave the freaking day job behind when he came home at night. But no; he was plunged right back into the chaos that damn poker game had wreaked upon his life the minute he walked through his front door.

He opened the door to his truck cab. "Get in and I'll show you."

He waited for her to climb in. She might be in a state over the headlines, but when that haze of anger faded, she was going to be grateful to him for not letting her be out in the open where anyone would see her. A woman should have her privacy for what was to come.

He pulled the paper from under his arm. "Here."

"Son of a bitch."

He didn't think it was possible for her face to get any whiter.

She proved him wrong as she read the article. "Oh my God. That son of a bitch." She dropped the paper onto her lap. "And I was just about to . . ." She looked back at Vito's shop.

"Yeah. You were about to let Vito know exactly who you were. The second he knew, he'd figure out why you need the money and adjust his price accordingly. It's like any negotiation; you want to be in a position of strength. Knowledge is power, and the minute Vito knows you're desperate is the minute he's going to undercut you. And now that I pulled you out of there . . ." He wanted to go back in and threaten Vito to keep his big mouth shut, but that'd only send Vito to the tabloids faster. "Vito's out to make a buck any way he can."

She blinked faster and stared at something out the windshield, but she didn't say anything.

He was waiting for the tears. They'd come; they always did. Rachel had been a master at pooling her tears and looking up at him with those watery big eyes and he'd melt . . .

"So." Cassidy exhaled and to Liam's surprise, cleared her throat, *didn't* cry, and faced him. "What do you suggest I do? It's not like I can expect to sell thirty-thousand-dollar earrings online and get a decent amount for them."

It took him a second to make the shift with her. She was moving forward. Not wallowing in the morass of hurt and anger she had to be feeling.

Damn, the woman could surprise him.

"Why not try? People sell cars; why not jewels? I'm sure you're not the first." Thirty *grand*? She had thirty grand hanging off her ears and she was mooching off him? "You know, thirty grand is nothing to sneeze at." Unless it was in gold-leaf handkerchiefs. "You don't need to work for me."

"That's *if* I can get it, Liam. Do people just have thirty K lying around for online shopping?"

"Good point." Those who could afford the earrings probably didn't go online to do so. They'd go to their own personal jeweler. Probably being driven by their own personal chauffeur. After having lunch at their club. On a yacht.

Okay, bitterness was starting to gnaw at him and he didn't like it. Rachel's defection could have done a number on his self-esteem if he was that guy, but he wasn't. He did well for himself and if that hadn't been good enough for Rachel, well, hell, she wasn't good enough for him. He didn't need a yacht. He didn't need a club. He just needed his friends and family and his business to do well. Money, so important to the Rachels and Mitchell Davenports of the world, wasn't the be-all end-all to him.

"Will you take them as payment?"

"Earrings? What am I going to do with diamond earrings? I'm not a jewelry kind of guy."

"No, I mean, would you take them and sell them and we'll be even?"

"You're willing to give me thirty-thousand-dollar earrings in return for room and board? And I can keep whatever I make on the sale?" He raised his eyebrow. "Seriously, Cassidy, you're never going to make it on your own if this is how you operate."

"I—" She sat back against the seat and crossed her arms.

Liam could see the words foaming at her lips, but he was right and she knew it. Yeah, sure, he'd take the jewelry and make a nice profit, but he didn't need the hassle. All he'd need was for Davenport to list them as stolen and Liam would find himself answering a whole lot of questions from behind bars. That thirty K would be gone in a minute if he had to get attorneys to fight off Davenport's stable of lawyers.

"You're right. I should sell them because I'm never going back now." She sat up a little taller in the seat. "But I have no clue how. Will you help me?"

He wanted to say no. Wanted her to do it on her own, but there was so much worry and hope in her eyes that he'd feel like the world's biggest jerk if he didn't help her. Navigating the online bidding system could be a struggle if someone wasn't familiar with it, and he'd bet all thirty thousand of those dollars that Cassidy Davenport had never bought anything online. Why would she when all she'd have to do is call the jeweler and fling Daddy's name around? The stuff probably showed up, hand delivered, that afternoon, in pink cushioned boxes with sparkly bows tied around them.

"Yeah. Sure. At least I'll get my money out of you."

"Don't worry, Liam. I intend to pay you for everything."

He hadn't meant to be so brusque. He wasn't heartless and she was going through a bunch of shit. Maybe not his idea of shit—thirty-thousand-dollar fallback options were kinda hard to ignore—but this was Cassidy he was talking about. She wasn't used to this sort of stuff.

And there you go, wanting to take care of her.

"And I'm going to clean your house so well, you'll be able to eat off the floors."

"That's okay, I'll stick to the table, but by all means, show me what you got."

"I intend to." She crumpled up the newspaper and looked out the window, muttering something that sounded an awful lot like, "You *and* my father."

Chapter Twelve

❧

ASSIDY had never worked so hard in her life.

She'd *had* to open her big mouth. *Had* to tell him she'd show him what she was made of.

Right now that felt like the love child of a limp noodle and a wet dishrag.

She flung said wet dishrag over her shoulder, wincing as a stream of yucky, chemical-laden water dripped down her shirt. The bleach was going to leave a mark.

Oh, well, it wasn't as if she'd be wearing this shirt anytime again soon. She'd torn it on the curtain rod when she'd batted the dust from the curtains, then caught it in the oven door, leaving a grease line right across the middle.

And now, Titania was jumping at her knees again and leaving dirty paw prints on the beige tile and her skin.

"Titania, what are you doing?" She tossed the dishrag into the sink and scooped up the dog—there went paw prints on the shirt she was never going to wear again. The little dog licked Cassidy's nose. "What? Where'd you get that dirt on your paws?"

Titania licked her again.

"I've been ignoring you, haven't I?" Cassidy grabbed a

damp paper towel, then sat on the edge of the leather sofa in Liam's living room and cleaned Titania's feet. He probably called this room a great room since this was the only room like it in the place. No formal living room versus family room, but then, he didn't have a family.

Neither did she, apparently.

Whose father sold them out? Seriously. The son of a bitch.

But it'd gotten his name in the papers, hadn't it? And put pressure on her.

But her father didn't know her as well as he thought he did if he thought public humiliation would bring her back to the fold. If anything, it made her more determined to succeed.

She checked the pay-as-you-go-phone she'd borrowed money from Liam to buy. More debt she owed him. But, seriously, she couldn't live without a phone. If, at the very least, to tell what time it was.

"Hey, Cass, I'm home. What's for dinner?" Liam's voice echoed in the big room, startling shivers up her spine.

"Dinner?" She was too tired to even bother to tell him that she hated that nickname.

"You know, the meal that comes at the end of a long day when someone's been out earning a living for eight plus hours and someone else has been home keeping the hearth fires warm." The cute smile he had going took the sting out of his words.

She tried to return the smile as she ran her arm across her forehead. "No fires here. I'm sweaty enough as it is."

For a heartbeat, there was no sound in the room. Even Titania seemed to stop breathing.

Then Liam cleared his throat. "Well, good thing, since it's hot enough outside. So I guess that means that I'll grab us something my grandmother made. Sound good?"

"I'm not hungry."

"Bull. You've had a shitty day and have been going nonstop. I'm sure you've worked up an appetite." He waved her over. "Come on. You need to eat. You sit; I'll get it."

She really wished he wasn't so darn nice to her. Why him? He didn't even know her and he wasn't related to her.

Oh no. She wasn't going there. She was *not* going to feel sorry for herself or question her self-worth. Her father was the one with the issue—a lot of them, apparently—not her.

Cassidy took a seat at the breakfast bar, exhaustion and guilt warring with each other as Liam warmed up two—no, make that three—bowls of beef stew.

Titania sat at his feet, worshiping him as if he were a god, the little glutton.

Of course, she, too, couldn't stop the grateful smile she gave him when he set the bowl in front of her with a nice hunk of crusty French bread that had shown up out of nowhere.

"I stopped at the store on my way home. Thought this would go great with the stew."

He had that right, but Cassidy couldn't tell him because she'd torn off a piece, dunked it in the stew, and was savoring the flavor before he was finished speaking. His grandmother was an angel. Anyone who could cook like this—outside of a high-end restaurant—was divine.

Her father would have a fit if he could see her now. Sweaty, in torn clothing, slurping stew off her fingers.

Cassidy smiled. Good.

"What are you grinning at? You look like you're about to take over the world."

Cassidy sucked the sauce off her fingers, then wiped them on the napkin Liam handed her. "I'm thinking about it."

"So you sold the earrings, then?"

"Uh, no. Haven't even thought about it, actually. I've been too busy since I got back here."

"How much did you get done?"

"There's still the loft and bathroom upstairs to do. I'll finish up tomorrow."

"Just in time for the next project: the garage."

"The garage? Nobody cleans a garage."

"They clean *out* garages, but I meant the room above it. I was planning to make it a work-out room, but it's ended up as storage. If you clean it out and organize it for me, I'll move my equipment up from the basement so we can have a gym."

He wanted her to organize it? Had he *seen* her cabinets? "There's a basement?"

Liam pointed to the door by his bedroom. "Where did you think that door went to?"

She'd been afraid to look. After the whole nudity thing, she was staying far away from his bedroom. It was going to be pure hell to have to clean it again.

If her luck, her sales, or the earrings sale panned out, she'd be gone before she'd have to.

"I was hoping to be able to work on the credenza tomorrow."

"And I was hoping to sleep in, but we both have jobs to do."

"Liam, your house isn't that dirty. It's just you; how much of a slob are you?"

He arched his eyebrow again and, man, that distracted her. The man really was gorgeous, what with his black hair that refused to lay flat on his head but curled around it in *run-your-fingers-through-me* abandon that made her want to do just that.

"We had a deal, Cassidy. You don't renege on your deals, do you?"

He had to put it like that. "Of course not. But it's not as big of a deal as you made it out to be."

"Then it works to your favor, right?"

Shoot. He was right. He didn't owe her anything; all he wanted was his house to be cleaned. She needed to work her personal stuff in around it.

If only she'd planned better before talking to her father.

She sucked up her frustration and nodded. "You're right. I'll get to the garage tomorrow."

"Thanks. I've wanted to get the gym operational. And feel free to use the equipment once it's up."

Was it wrong that her mind went right to the rock hard abs she'd glimpsed? To the biceps straining against the sleeves of his T-shirt? The pants that stretched tight across some well-defined thighs? What did this man need a gym for? And with what she'd glimpsed during the après-shower debacle, she could speak with authority.

What would it be like to make love with Liam, a man so masculine he could be the advertisement for testosterone?

Cassidy almost choked on her stew. She shouldn't be having thoughts like that. She wasn't here to play house, just clean it.

Titania slurped up her meal, then pranced on her hind legs, twirling like a ballerina beside Liam's chair. All she needed was a tutu—and she had one, but unfortunately, it was back in the condo.

"Looks like you have an admirer." Cassidy nodded at her dog, who was practically apoplectic with happiness, her little tongue darting in and out in excitement.

"As long as she doesn't try to hop into my bed tonight, I'm fine with that."

Cassidy wisely kept her mouth shut.

Instead, she picked up her bowl and slurped the rest of the stew, effectively blocking him from sight. She needed distance.

Luckily, Liam headed to his room after putting his and Titania's bowls in the sink. "I'm going to shower, then go over some paperwork. I'll hang in my room if you want to watch TV in the great room."

Watch TV? She didn't think she could keep her eyes open long enough. And she'd thought shopping was exhausting. Nothing compared to manual labor. She was feeling bad that she hadn't insisted Sharon take her entire pregnancy off. To have to clean while carrying a child . . .

For a second, something shifted in Cassidy's stomach. A baby. She'd thought she'd have one someday—the requisite heir for whatever dynastic merger her father finally sanctioned—but for some reason, the reality of having one never clicked with her until just this moment. She thought of the way Sharon had always rubbed her belly. She'd been caressing her child. Thinking about it, worrying about it, loving it. Cassidy had even heard her talking to it on a few occasions.

None of it had seemed real. It'd been as foreign a concept to her as, well, as selling diamond earrings online or cleaning someone's house. Mom hadn't had any problems high-tailing it out of town away from her, and Dad just kept her around for his image, so it wasn't as if children were something she had any experience in looking forward to.

But for whatever reason, being here, in Liam's home, cleaning his things—a job so personal that she couldn't help but think about personal things—the idea of a child, *her* child, suddenly became real.

As did the matter of the kid's father.

"You want to keep an eye on this little dust mop?" Liam walked back into the kitchen within about six inches of the bar stool Cassidy was still perched on, Titania yipping at his heels and once more prancing like a ballerina. "She followed me back there."

Smart dog.

Cassidy bent down to pick up said genius, hiding the fact that she was thinking about *back there*. About what she'd seen the last time she'd been *back there*. What *he'd* seen . . .

No. She was not going to think about getting involved with Liam. It would make this situation awkward. It might even get her kicked out if things didn't go well. And there was no guarantee *he* was thinking along those same lines anyway, so it was pointless to go there. In a few (short, she hoped) weeks, Liam and this place would be a distant memory.

You don't really believe that, do you?

She had to. She had to believe that she'd move on from here into her new life. She had to believe in herself.

Because there was no one else who would.

She tucked Titania against her hip. She was *not* going to feel sorry for herself. So many people had it tougher than she did. Today was the second day of the rest of her life, and while she may have spent it cleaning, she had a whole world of possibilities open to her now. All she needed was the courage to seize it.

Well, that and money.

"You know? I think I will get started on the garage. That way I'll be able to start painting sooner."

She *was* going to do this. She'd show her father what she was made of.

And herself, too.

Chapter Thirteen

LIAM couldn't sleep. That shouldn't surprise him, given that he was sharing his home with his worst nightmare: a sexy-as-hell daddy's girl.

Who wasn't the spoiled selfish brat he'd thought.

The last part of that was worse for his equilibrium than the first. The first, he could deal with. The second . . .

He had very little defense against the second. Cassidy Davenport wasn't turning out to be like anything he'd thought. And it was that that had him up tonight.

Definitely up.

He tossed off the covers and sat on the edge of his bed, his toes digging into the carpet. He didn't want to take another shower. Especially a cold one. Not at—he winced as he glanced at his phone—three A.M.

He scratched the back of his head, creating more of a bedhead than he currently had. Not that he cared. The best thing for him would be to be such a turnoff that Cassidy wouldn't look at him twice.

Unfortunately, he'd caught her looking at him a lot more than twice. Which only added to this nightmare.

He stood up. No sense trying to go back to sleep. Not without taking matters into his own hand, so to speak, and how pathetic was that? A beautiful woman in the next room and he's jacking off alone. Not gonna happen.

He could use a beer.

He stepped into his shorts, pulled on a T-shirt, things he'd never done when he lived alone, but he wasn't risking any sort of temptation with her around, then headed toward his kitchen.

Only to hear two sets of little snores emanating from the sofa in the great room.

The princess and her mutt had fallen asleep there.

Turn around and go back to your room. Now.

It was sage advice. Good advice. The best for the moment. So why did he ignore it?

Because curiosity got the best of him.

Oh, yeah, sure. Curiosity. That's the latest term for sex drive these days?

He wouldn't know. It'd been a while since he'd had sex.

That's part of your problem. Go find some chick and take the edge off. Then you won't be noticing how Cassidy's finger is resting on her bottom lip in sleep. How tousled her hair is, so soft and silky it'd trail over a man's skin, evoking shivers in its wake. Or how supple and soft her skin is. Her legs, so perfectly shaped as they curled up against her in sleep—and would curl around him when awake. Her dainty ankles would lock behind his ass and she'd urge him into her, deeper and—

Fuck.

Yeah, that's the general idea here, Einstein.

Liam practically stumbled out of the great room before he did something they'd both regret.

"*Yip!*"

Of *course* the dog would wake up. Great.

"Shhh." He held up his hand.

And of course the dog didn't listen. And it *definitely* wasn't going to stay put.

It squirmed out of Cassidy's arms and bounded over to him with a pink tongue flapping as fast as its tail, and another excited *yip* doing exactly what Liam hadn't wanted it to do.

Cassidy woke up. "What . . . ?" She flipped her wavy froth off her face as she sat up, and it jumbled over her shoulders as if he'd spent the better part of the night running his fingers through it.

Which he really wanted to do.

"Uh." He cleared his throat. "Sorry. I, uh, couldn't sleep. Came out for a drink. Didn't realize you and the dust mop had fallen asleep out here. The dog's uh, a good watch dog."

"Titania?" Cassidy scrubbed her fingers through her hair, which only made him want to do it more. There was something about a woman's hair in wild disarray that called to him to make her as wild and abandoned as he could.

God, did he want to. Right now. Right here. With her just like that.

He was in serious trouble.

The pooch was jumping on his leg, those pink frosted nails of hers a little too sharp for his liking.

Now if they were Cassidy's, raking down his back—

"I, um, am just gonna grab a beer and, uh, head back to my room."

Don't ask her to come with you.

"Want one?"

Oh even better. Keep the contact going, genius. You have one hell of a way of avoiding temptation.

"Not a beer, no." She scrubbed a hand over her face and even without makeup, she was beautiful. Hell, she was flat-out gorgeous. The quintessential girl next door with a Victoria's Secret model's sexiness added in just to make his life miserable.

She followed him into the kitchen. "But if you have some OJ, I'll take that. Or cranberry?"

"I've got both." He set the bottles and a glass on the counter. "Take your pick."

She tapped the OJ bottle as she slid onto the barstool with

the slinkiest move he'd ever seen someone make to sit at a bar. He'd swear it was intentional except the yawn that came with it should've undone the sexiness.

He sloshed some OJ over the edge of her glass when he poured it. Cassidy *couldn't* undo sexiness. The woman was a walking pinup poster.

Who burped like one of the boys.

"Oops. Excuse me." She covered her mouth and blushed all the way up to her hairline as she set the glass of juice she'd gunned onto the island.

Liam laughed. "I hear that's a compliment to the cook in some countries."

He got the smile he'd been hoping for.

"I didn't realize *you'd* squeezed the oranges."

"Hey, it's tough work lifting those bottles." He flexed his bicep. "Takes a lot of muscle."

"Well then, my regards to the bottle-lifter." She picked up the glass and waggled it. "Any chance I could have round two?"

"And risk another moment of indignity?"

She shrugged and it sent her hair cascading over her shoulders. "It's a risk I'm willing to take."

But would she if she knew how close he was to hauling her up onto the island and making them both forget how thirsty they were for beverages, and find out how thirsty they were for each other?

What was *wrong* with him? Had he learned *nothing* from Rachel?

Except she's not Rachel and you know it. Keep waving the Rachel flag, but that's not why you're staying away from Cassidy. Matter of fact, why are *you staying away from her? She's nothing like Rachel—not where it counts. Could you see Rachel cleaning your house with no complaints? Rachel trying to start a business? Rachel giving up on the easy money of marrying her father's heir apparent? Rachel wearing the clothes Cassidy has or sleeping on a sofa? Selling diamond earrings?*

Not a chance in hell.

You're in trouble, here, Manley, because the one argu-

ment you have against Cassidy is fading away. So now whatcha gonna do?

He was going to pour her another glass of OJ, which he did, then head back to the fridge to put the bottles away. And, yeah, maybe just bask in the cold for a bit to cool himself down.

He grabbed the beer he'd forgotten about and twisted the cap off, taking a bigger swig than normal.

Coming into the kitchen hadn't been a good idea. Inviting her to come with him, even worse. He would've been so much better off staying in his room and acting like a teenager instead of being out here thinking like one with her in touching distance.

"Titania didn't wake you up, did she? She's usually a sound sleeper. Barely moves when I try to get her off my pillow. She might look small, but she spreads out all over a bed and it's hard to sleep."

He was hearing the words but the images were completely different. He was seeing *Cassidy* spread out on a bed and he definitely wasn't sleeping.

"No. I was up anyway." In every way. "Figured a beer would take the edge off."

"Edge? Are you worried about something?"

Yeah, like how he was going to get back to his room without yanking her off that stool and taking her with him. "Not really. Well, my brother Sean has a deal going on that I'm part of and there could be complications, but not enough to keep me up at night. Not yet anyway." No, that honor would belong to her.

"So what do you think it is?" She ran her finger over the rim, and damn if Liam didn't imagine her doing that to him.

So much for the mellowing effects of beer.

"Probably just not used to another person in the house." He guzzled some more. "I'll get used to it."

"I'll try to be out of here quickly. I really do appreciate your generosity, Liam."

Yeah, he was so generous he was working her so hard that she fell asleep on the sofa. What a prince he was.

"You know, the garage doesn't need to be done tomorrow. Take your time. Get some of your painting done." That way he'd get her out of his vicinity and him out of temptation's way. And wasn't that the goal all along? She now knew how the "other half" lived; he'd made his point.

"No, no. We have a deal and I'm going to uphold my end of it. I'll finish upstairs and then start on the garage. I'll fit painting in there somewhere."

He finished the beer so he could finish this conversation because with each sentence Cassidy uttered, she was knocking down his wall of misconceptions about her. Instead of whining and taking him up on his offer to get out of working, she was going to work harder. He really hadn't wanted to like this woman, but he was starting to.

The dog yipped by his feet.

"She wants you to pick her up."

"I'm not picking her up."

"But why? She just wants to give you a kiss."

"And you know this how? Don't tell me you talk to animals."

She rolled her gorgeous green eyes. "Her tail's wagging and she can't take her eyes off you."

"And that means she wants to kiss me?"

Cassidy arched perfectly arched eyebrows at him. "Come on, Liam. Looking like you do, you can't tell me you aren't aware when a woman's interested."

"Considering the not-so-nice correlation between female dogs and women, I don't think I can answer your question without getting myself into a heap of trouble." He set the beer bottle in the sink. "And on that note, I'm calling it a night."

"It's morning."

"Morning. Whatever. I'm going back to bed and I'd invite you to do the same."

For a heartbeat he heard her thoughts. Or maybe they were his. Whoever they belonged to, yeah, he wanted her in his bed.

Chapter Fourteen

❦

ALL in all, the room above Liam's garage wasn't the nightmare Cassidy had envisioned. She even had enough time to finish most of the credenza afterward. Another couple of hours to finish the swirls around the flowers that would link the design throughout the piece, a few more shadows and highlights, plus the final finish, and she could give Jean-Pierre a call. If he refused to take her on, maybe he could recommend someone else.

She winced. It wasn't the best plan, but it was the only one she could come up with at the moment. Dad's reach was a long one and finding someone willing to risk his wrath was going to be a lot tougher than cleaning a house if Jean-Pierre did shoot her down.

Well, she'd deal with that later. Right now, though, she'd settle for a shower and a massage.

Too bad someone knocked on the front door as she was headed toward her room.

Titania went ballistic, hopping and twirling as if she were auditioning for a talent show. It took a last-minute sprint by Cassidy to grab the dog before she scratched Liam's door.

Cassidy scooped up her pet before she opened it. Who knew if a dog lover stood on the other side?

Turns out, it was a little old lady with blue eyes and a smile identical to Liam's. Cassidy was guessing the woman wasn't selling encyclopedias.

"Hello?" The woman offered her a polite smile with a quick sweep over her disheveled hair and clothing with a look that said—

Oh God. The lady didn't think that she and Liam had been— That she and Liam were—

"Hi." Cassidy stuck out her hand, then saw all the paint on it and shoved it behind her back. "Um, sorry. I'm covered in paint."

"You're a painter?"

"Um . . . yes." Yes. She was. Dammit. "An artist." That felt even better to say.

"May I come in?"

"Oh I'm sorry." Cassidy stepped back. "Please. Yes."

"Thank you. I'm Liam's grandmother, Cate Manley."

"Hi. I'm—" She didn't want to tell the woman who she was. Who she *really* was. Things changed when people knew who she was. "Cass. Cass Marie."

The nickname her mother used to call her fell from her lips. She hated it, hated the memories, but Cass Marie was not Cassidy Davenport, so it worked for now.

"It's very nice to meet you, Cass." Mrs. Manley walked toward the kitchen. "Is Liam here?"

"He's working."

"Oh. So what room is he having painted? I thought he finished decorating this place."

"I'm not painting a room. I'm working on custom furniture. In the garage."

Mrs. Manley turned around. "Liam's having furniture painted?"

"It's not for him. I'm going to sell the pieces."

"So you're renting space from him?"

"Well, not exactly. I'm, um . . ." Damn. She didn't know

how enlightened Liam's grandmother was or how she'd feel about Cassidy living here.

Still, one lie was one too many.

"I'm cleaning for him in return for a room. Until I sell another piece of furniture and can afford a place on my own, that is."

"Oh. Well that's . . . new." Mrs. Manley looked a little confused. But not horrified, thankfully. "So do you sell a lot of this furniture?"

"Not yet. That's why I'm here." Cassidy walked past Liam's grandmother to the cabinet to the right of the sink. "Are you thirsty? Can I get you something?"

"Thank you. I'd love some iced tea. It's on the second shelf on the back right."

"Ah, yes. You stocked his fridge. Your food is amazing, by the way."

"Thank you." Mrs. Manley slid onto the bar stool, apparently planning to stay for a bit. "So how did you come to be exchanging cleaning services for room and board?"

"I, uh, was evicted from my condo. The owner wanted to sell it." That wasn't a lie. Technically.

"Sounds like a quick turnaround."

That was putting it mildly. "Yes. It was."

"And you know Liam from . . . school? Another job he did? One of his friends? Or do you work for Manley Maids as well?"

"No, I don't. He was cleaning the place where I lived. He heard the whole eviction thing and was kind enough to offer me a place to stay."

Mrs. Manley sat back with a smile. "Good to know my lessons weren't wasted."

"I'm sorry?"

"Liam. I raised him and his brothers and sister after they lost their parents—my son and his wife—in a car accident. Because of the rabble-rousing three young boys are capable of, they learned to help out around the house, cleaning and doing yard work, and even some of the cooking. It's why I like to do for them every so often. Of course, my granddaughter, Mary-Alice Catherine, she says I go overboard." Mrs. Manley shrugged her shoulders with a slight blush on her cheeks. "I guess I do, but for so long we had to worry about every bit on the table that it's nice now to be able to be generous, you know?"

Cassidy, unfortunately, now had first-hand knowledge of what Mrs. Manley was talking about. Before Dad's marriage ultimatum, she'd never had to worry about where her next meal was coming from or where she'd live or if there would be clothes in her closet.

"It did bring us closer. Made us appreciate each other more. I'd always loved my grandchildren of course, but there's a difference between visiting and having them go home, and taking on four small children at my age. And I was a widow who'd raised only one child. Four was quite the handful." •

"I can imagine." She could imagine Liam as a child, running around with his brothers and sister . . . Kids. Children. Family. What would it be like to have that? Being an only child with absentee parents gave her zero frame of reference.

"You did an amazing job raising him, Mrs. Manley."

"Why, thank you, dear. That's nice of you to say. Have you known him long?"

"Not very long, no." It would probably shock the older woman to know just how few days it'd actually been. Seriously, who moved in with a complete stranger after knowing him for such a short period of time?

Which also begged the question of who invited someone to live with them after knowing them such a short time?

Someone special, that's who.

"May I see this piece you're working on or are you one of those artists who won't let anyone see it until it's finished?"

"If I had the luxury of people batting my door down to see my work, maybe, but at this point in my career, I'm willing to show it to anyone who's interested."

Mrs. Manley set her glass onto the countertop and slid

from the stool. "Then let's see it. I've always wanted to be a patron of the arts."

Cassidy felt kind of funny walking Liam's grandmother through his home. She must have been here countless times. More so than Cassidy. It ought to be the other way around. But somehow, this felt right.

Knock it off, Davenport. You're not going to play house with Liam, so don't go getting your hopes up that Liam's grandmother can be yours, too. Just because your grandparents were as worthless as your parents doesn't mean you get to claim Liam's. You ought to be thankful for the room and board and forget anything else.

She *was* trying to forget anything else. Truly. The problem was, she *liked* Mrs. Manley. Anyone willing to take on four kids and raise them all those years was someone special in Cassidy's book.

"Watch your step. I haven't cleaned up yet. I was going to"—nope, not going to make the woman feel guilty that she'd interrupted her shower—"do that right before you arrived."

"Well then, I won't keep you." Mrs. Manley turned around and looked at the credenza. "This is lovely." She reached out to touch it then pulled her hand back. "I'm sorry. I shouldn't touch, but it's so pretty I just felt compelled to run my hand over it."

There was no better compliment.

"I must have this piece. How much are you selling it for?"

Okay, maybe that was a better one.

But as thrilled as she was with the validation, this was a high-ticket item. She could get a lot for it and she didn't want to take that much from Liam's grandmother. And she couldn't really afford to give it away, not when she needed every penny.

"I'm sorry, but it's already been sold on commission. It matches another piece and the owner wants the set." Cassidy crossed her fingers so tightly she lost circulation. "I do have that end table if you'd like it."

Mrs. Manley looked at the table. Cassidy was surprised to see her smile. Most people wouldn't see the possibility in the worn old piece of furniture.

"That would be perfect. I recently moved into a new home and I'm still trying to set it all up, you know?"

Cassidy nodded, though she hadn't even begun "setting anything up" because she didn't *have* anything *to* set up.

"It'll be nice to have beside the chair my granddaughter bought me. It's in front of a bay window. With a nice table, it'll be the perfect spot for the lamp Bryan bought me on his first trip to London. Waterford crystal."

"I had Wa—er, I've always wanted a Waterford lamp. They're lovely." Phew. She'd almost blown her cover. And *technically*, what she'd said was true. She *had* always wanted one of her own because the ones she'd had were her father's.

"I told Bryan he shouldn't have spent so much on me. Really, I would have been happy with a little memento from his trip, but he insisted. And it *is* beautiful. One of the nicest things I own. They've all done well, my grandchildren, and they like to bring me gifts. But it's enough to me that they're doing well in life. Now if I could just get them settled, I'd be happy."

The image hit Cassidy like a lightning bolt: Liam married. His grandmother wanted some woman to move into this house and into his bed and have his babies. Give her great grandchildren.

Some other woman living here . . .

Cassidy pasted a smile onto her face. Being jealous was just plain ridiculous. She had nothing to be jealous about because she had no claim on Liam.

And at this point in her life, nice as it sounded, she didn't want one.

Uh huh . . .

CATE Manley let her smile loose the minute Liam's houseguest shut the door behind her. Cass Marie, indeed. Even covered in paint and sweat, with questionable taste in clothing and her hair in complete disarray, there was no hiding the fact that Liam had Cassidy Davenport working for him.

Funny, according to Mary-Alice Catherine, *he* was supposed to be working for *her*. That's why Cate had stopped by: to get his impression of the socialite *she* had personally picked for him.

Turned out she'd gotten quite the surprise of her own. Cassidy was as interested in Liam as Liam had to be in her to invite her to stay.

Cate allowed herself a little chuckle. Obviously God was on board with her plan, since things appeared to be working out just the way she'd wanted.

Chapter Fifteen

❧❦❧

LIAM loaded the last of the cleaning supplies into the back of the work van the next morning. He'd left his truck for Cassidy to use because he'd co-signed the loan for Mac's first company van yesterday—with the condition that he'd be using it the rest of the month. If Cassidy hadn't left by then, well, he'd figure something out.

About a lot of things.

In the meantime, he'd finished the second condo for Davenport, glad to get that out of the way before having to go back on Monday to clean Cassidy's place again.

Not that it'd be a big deal, since no one was living there, but the place wasn't the same without her.

Don't go there. She will *be leaving your place.*

True, but not right away, so he ought to grab a few other things for her when he went on Monday. Things like sweat pants and baggy shirts. Her skimpy little T-shirts and long flowing dresses that probably looked like muumuus on other women but just slid over her curves to tease him weren't helping maintain the comparison to Rachel he was trying to cling to like a lifeline. And if that broke, he'd have no reason not to want her.

He slammed the tailgate a little harder than necessary, but it relieved some of the tension. Thank God his latest property's settlement had closed earlier than expected so he had something to keep himself occupied with instead of having to head home where *she*'d be.

Except she showed up at his property. He shouldn't have mentioned where he'd be.

"Liam?" Cassidy knocked on the front door of the Cape Cod where he was in the middle of stripping the hideous seventies' green paint the previous owner had chosen for some unknown reason off the teak built-in bookcases.

He didn't understand the choices some people made.

Like his opening the door for her. "What are you doing here, Cassidy? Don't you have something to clean?"

"Still grumpy from your interrupted sleep the other night, are you?"

"It was yesterday morning and I'm fine. I'm just busy and wasn't expecting to see you." Otherwise he would have prepared himself for her. She was making him think things he thought he shouldn't—and made him not care that he did. "Where's the mutt?"

"*Titania* is at home in her pen."

For a second, Liam imagined the white marble hearth and fireplace that the pampered pooch's gilded cage had sat in front of in her condo, then he realized that she'd meant *his* home. It ought to sound strange for Cassidy to call his place home, but . . . didn't.

She cracked her knuckles, a habit so incongruous to her runway model image that it took him a moment to realize she was still talking. ". . . more wood glue, so I thought I'd run to the store. A few dovetail joints on the drawer of the piece I'm working on are broken."

"You could always make another side rail to maintain the integrity of the piece." He was a jack-of-all-trades when it came to construction, but woodworking was his specialty.

"Painting is my area of expertise, not construction. Plus I don't have the right equipment."

"I do."

"Are you offering to help?"

Apparently. "If you need it."

He had to grit his teeth when she put her hand on his bicep. Between the home thing, that outfit, and her touch, the woman was going to kill him.

"Liam, really, you've done more than enough for me. You're busy with this place. I'll get the glue, but um . . ."

She looked too sexy in another tie-dyed T-shirt with an angled hem that someone thought was a good idea, but wasn't for him when the image of sliding his tongue over the skin of her peek-a-boo waist flashed into his head and wouldn't go away. Then she went and tucked her hair behind her ear and he wanted to suck on her earlobe, too.

"I need a few dollars. I promise I'll pay you back."

He had his wallet in his hand before he thought about it.

So much for learning his lesson with Rachel. In many ways.

"Here you go. And I left my laptop on my bedside table. Feel free to use it to list the earrings. I set up the account for you and linked it to my bank account. We'll work out the logistics after they sell."

"Oh. Right. The earrings. I'll do it as soon as I set the drawer." She took the twenty. "Is there anything you need while I'm at the hardware store? More paint stripper or sand-paper or anything?"

A lock for his bedroom door . . . "How is it you know so much about construction and furniture refinishing?" He'd bet those weren't courses in her fancy finishing school.

"My dad's in the construction business, remember? He made sure I knew every aspect of it, since it was apparent he was never going to get that son he'd wanted."

Surprisingly, Liam didn't hear any sarcasm. She wasn't the kid her father wanted, the man had kicked her out of her home, she had to work for her bed and board for the first time in her privileged life, yet she was considerate enough to ask *him* if he needed anything. Without bitterness. It was getting really hard not to like Cassidy Davenport.

And if she played with her bottom lip one more time, something else was going to get hard.

"No. I'm good. Keep the change. Add it to what you owe me. I'll collect when you sell the earrings. Or your furniture. Whichever comes first."

And then she could get out of his life so it could get back to normal.

She tapped him on the forearm. Even that turned him on. Dammit.

"Oh, by the way, since you came home so late last night I didn't get a chance to tell you that your grandmother stopped by yesterday."

He'd been late to make sure he wouldn't see her, after helping his buddy Jared and wearing himself out with a lot of manual labor on the estate where Sean was working off his bet. Lucky bastard didn't have a hot chick staying there with him to drive him nuts. Liam was seriously thinking of camping out there for the rest of the month. "Gran did? Why?"

There she went with playing with her bottom lip again. He'd think it was an affectation, but she'd done it in her sleep on the sofa.

"Actually, I don't know. She didn't say. I introduced myself and we started talking about my furniture, then she wanted to see it, and then she ordered a piece. The end table I'm working on."

Liam bit back a groan. Gran had been feeling Cassidy out. She made no secret of the fact that she wanted great-grandchildren. But once she'd met Cassidy—learned who she was—she had to have known he wouldn't be interested.

But he *was*. And that was a problem on so many levels.

But Gran didn't need to know about it. It was one thing to be attracted to the woman, but kids were out of the picture. The last thing he'd want would be to have Mitchell Davenport as a father-in-law.

Father-in-la—was he out of his fucking mind? How did he go from Gran stopping by to marrying Cassidy?

"So the glue is for my grandmother's table?"

"Yes, but don't worry, Liam. I do know what I'm doing. The drawer will be fine and it'll be the original piece of wood."

"With modern glue. You're going to devalue it."

"I'm fixing a broken piece of furniture and custom painting it. Any intrinsic value from its original state is going to be shot to hell anyway. But the fact that it's a C. Marie original will up its value. And I'm not gouging her, by the way. She wanted the credenza, but I told her it was already sold."

"But it's not."

"It'll command a higher price than the end table. I didn't want to have to bargain with your grandmother. I couldn't in good conscience take as much from her as I want for it."

Liam knew for a fact that Mitchell Davenport's ethics could be rewired to fit whatever circumstances he found himself in, so it was nice to see that Cassidy's ethics were a step up. He'd bet she wouldn't be caught giving a lap dance while she stole the guy's wallet.

Okay, he did *not* need to think about Cassidy giving anyone a lap dance. Including him.

"Thank you for that. I'm sure she would have paid whatever you'd told her you wanted."

"That's because she's a nice lady."

"Too nice."

"I should be offended, but you're right. She *was* being too nice, though I think she might have gotten the wrong idea about us. Or she might be hoping. She wants you married, you know."

"Yeah. I know." He scraped a hand across his face. If Gran knew how he was thinking about Cassidy, she'd be dancing for joy.

"But that's because she loves you and wants to see you happy."

He knew. And it wasn't a discussion he wanted to have with Cassidy of all people. Not in light of recent events. Mitchell Davenport for a father-in-law . . . He must have sniffed too much of the paint stripper. "I hope you didn't feed into her delusion."

"Feed into—?" Cassidy slammed her hands onto her curvy hips. "What do you take me for? I didn't even tell her who I was so she wouldn't get her hopes up that you'd hit the mother lode."

"Hit the—?" It was his turn to be offended. "Look, Princess, I'm doing fine on my own. Just because my lifestyle hasn't reached the Baccarat-and-Dom-Perignon echelon yours has doesn't mean I'm not doing well on my own. I don't need a rich woman to take care of me." And he sure as hell wasn't taking care of anyone else, either. "I make my own way in this world." And had the vacation home to show for it. No *time* for the vacation, but that was beside the point.

She held her hands up and Liam noticed that the nail on her ring finger on her left hand was broken.

There was a whole bunch of symbolism in that, but Liam wasn't examining it any closer. Cassidy Davenport's love life—or lack thereof—was of no concern to him.

"Whoa, there, mister. You can get off your high horse. I didn't lead her on in any way, and for your information, I didn't even tell her who I was. I said I was Cass Marie, which, technically, isn't a lie, but I didn't think you wanted her to hear you had me staying at your place. Trust me, I know how people get once they learn my last name. I'm tired of dealing with their reactions and misconceptions. You might think living in that high-rise was a treat, but these last few days of not having to worry what I look like or if there's going to be some paparazzo staked out in front of your place waiting to catch a glimpse of me without makeup in ratty clothing"—she held out the frayed hem of this T-shirt—"has been eye-opening. In a good way."

He really should have checked the clothes before he'd brought them home for her. Cassidy's casual clothing left a lot to be desired—namely, her—and didn't leave much to the imagination. Two things designed to drive him nuts.

"For the first time in my life, I'm able to be me. Who that is, I'm not quite sure yet, but I'm definitely *not* the Cassidy Davenport you see in the papers. It was nice being just some woman in your house to your grandmother."

Except there'd never been just "some woman" in his house—Gran hadn't even seen Rachel in his home because Liam had made sure to keep those parts of his life separate. He knew Gran wanted the four of them to find matches like she'd had with their grandfather, so he'd been hyper-conscious of *not* having women over until he'd found The One.

It *figured* that Cassidy Davenport was the woman Gran had seen in his place. He knew for a fact that Gran would recognize her no matter what name she'd used because Mitchell had been in grade school with their father, and Gran liked to follow the local-boy-turned-tycoon stories in the press. She used to tell them that they—like Davenport—could do anything they put their mind to. She knew a lot about the guy. And his daughter.

Cassidy had seemed like a spoiled princess living in the gilded tower from Gran's stories. Funny, how he hadn't seen the same thing in Rachel. Or rather, the same wannabe thing. Rachel had downplayed her ambition. He'd thought she'd been real.

Showed what he knew. She'd been all over Mr. Ivy League Frat Boy, trying to pass for a college co-ed, looking for someone with a fatter checkbook and entrée into the world Cassidy inhabited. He'd missed it until it'd been staring him in the face. Or rather, the face of the frat boy motorboating her.

Liam kneaded the back of his neck. Why couldn't Cassidy be what he'd thought she was? "So, great. You've made a sale. Is it enough for you to move out?"

For a second, a hurt look crashed over her face, but she masked it so quickly that he realized she'd had a lot of practice hiding her hurt.

But why would she be hurt that he wanted her out? It wasn't as if this was supposed to be a permanent thing. And sure, she might be enjoying the anonymity at the moment, but no way was she going to trade the high-rises of her world for his Handyman Specials for the long term. *Not* that he was going to ask her to.

"What kind of person would I be if I charged your grandmother that kind of money?"

She crossed her arms now, and that wasn't much better than when they'd been on her hips because it only emphasized an area he was trying hard not to notice.

"I charged her a nominal amount. I can pay you back for the glue, but I'll need the rest for the phone."

"Okay. Fine. Whatever." He dipped the brush into the stripper again. He didn't want to talk money with Cassidy. Money was at the root of all evils. Case in point: Rachel. And money was, after all, the reason she was in his home. The irony of one woman thinking he didn't have enough of it and another needing what he *did* have was laughable.

Too bad he wasn't laughing.

CASSIDY chewed the inside of her bottom lip. Something had crawled up Liam's butt, but it couldn't be her. She was going to pay him back and she'd been nice to his grandmother. He couldn't be mad at her.

Well, he probably could, since she'd pretty much barged into his life, but she was trying to be as unobtrusive as possible. Her side of the garage was as neat as she could keep it and still be creative. She'd cleaned his house, cleared space for his gym, kept Titania out of his hair, been nice to his grandmother, and was custom painting a piece for her only slightly above cost. And that markup had only been because she hadn't wanted Mrs. Manley to figure out that she was cutting her a deal. Cassidy wasn't going to make anywhere near what she should for her time and talent, but there were some things more important than money. Her integrity being one of them.

Hmmm, which parent had she gotten that from? Or maybe it was a latent gene in the family tree.

"So what are you planning to do with this place? Are you going to live here?" She couldn't imagine him wanting to leave where he was now, since it was such a beautiful house, but she'd seen the peaceful look on his face when he hadn't been aware she was outside the six-paned front door. He'd been scraping the paint from the shelf, his attention focused yet relaxed. His mouth had been curving up a bit at the corners and there hadn't been all the tension in his shoulders that was there now.

She'd put that tension there. She had to have. The minute he'd answered the door with his gruff greeting, his hackles had risen.

Her first instinct had been to call him on it. After all, no one treated a Davenport with disrespect. But then she'd remembered she wasn't throwing her father's name around anymore and being a Davenport hadn't really done much for her these past few days.

"I can't live here. Zoning's changed in this part of town and it's no longer residential. My real estate guy has a couple of professionals interested in this place for their office."

"What about a daycare?"

Liam pointed to the fireplace. "Not a good idea with the fireplace that's still operational. I don't want to seal it up. It's a good feature for the sale, especially once I stain these floors walnut."

"What about cherry? Give it a high-gloss finish?" It was a Cape Cod; he ought to embrace the characteristics and go full force on the New England feel. "Paint the walls hunter green with white trim and maybe re-point the brick surrounding the fireplace with black mortar? That'd punch up the impact when you come through the front door. Make it a focal point of the room."

Liam looked at her as if he were seeing her for the first time.

She got that look a lot when people actually took the time to get to know her—as if they didn't expect her to have a brain in her head. Thank God she wasn't blonde; she'd never even get the opportunity to show them she had brains if she were. "I studied interior design. My father wanted me to be part of his design team." But then one of his Flavors of the Month (who'd lasted longer than a day) had had an issue with "Mitchell's daughter" giving her advice, and dear old Dad had switched Cassidy's status to Showpiece. When the Flavor had been dismissed, Cassidy had been too mortified to head back to the team. Everyone knew she'd gotten the job because she was Mitchell's daughter and had been replaced because of his lover. Bad enough her parents had ping-ponged her between them while Mom had been around; Cassidy wasn't reliving it in her career. So she'd pasted her perfected smile on and been the best damn Showpiece anyone could want.

And look where it'd gotten her. On the marriage block and, now, out on the street.

Still, she did have her talent and her eye for design. Dad couldn't take those from her. "You'll want to have a couple of plant stands with ferns when you stage the room."

Liam arched one of his eyebrows in a sexy, rakish way that made her stomach flutter. "I don't stage a room. The agent brings buyers to an empty space."

"Seriously?" She ordered the butterflies to quiet down. "You ought to try staging it. Not everyone can visualize the opportunities of an empty room, plus the place looks cold and impersonal without anything in it. Even if someone's going to turn it into an office, seeing the hearth with a rug and seating group in front of it, a few pictures on the wall . . . It'll do wonders for people's impressions. And I bet it'll up the offers you get."

The arched eyebrow settled back on his brow and if she weren't mistaken, moved downward with the other one. "Look, Princess, that might be how you do it in your world, but I've been flipping properties for years and know what I'm doing."

"I didn't say you didn't. Just trying to help, but you're right; this is your business. But if you change your mind, I could pull a few pieces together to help out when you're ready. If you're interested, that is."

Yes, she might be shooting herself in the foot by not trying to sell the pieces immediately, but she could see the sideboard beneath those leaded windows. She might go with a hunt scene on it, or maybe just a cascade of fall leaves. She could finish the top in the same high-gloss cherry stain as the floor, tying the room together—

Except that it wouldn't be staying in the room. Still, the round plant stand had the same claw-foot design as the sideboard and there was a hutch that she could tie in with them that'd look perfect in that nook.

She crossed the room and paced off the space. She'd have to check it against the width of the hutch, but it would look perfect there if it fit. She'd suggest ivy in a tarnished brass pot on the upper shelf, trailing down the side with a matching planter on the stand between a set of Queen Anne wingback chairs and a matching upholstered settee squaring off the hearth—

"What are you doing?" Liam's voice cut through her vision.

"Measuring."

"For?"

"There's a hutch that I think would fit here—"

"Cassidy, I appreciate the suggestion, but I'm not staging the room. The professionals my agent will be bringing through already know what they want. It'll be a matter of the right price per square foot. If I have to rent furniture, it'll cut into my profit, which I'll have to pass on in the square-foot cost. I'll be priced out of the market. Besides, that's unethical. Or at the very least, coercive. Artificial. As if you're trying to pull something over on them. If I walked into a space like this that'd been tricked out, I'd be lifting the rugs to check for termite damage or something."

She refrained from pointing out that there would *never* be termite damage in a Davenport property. Dad was all about branding and the last thing he'd do was let an insect damage his image.

His daughter, too, apparently.

"Okay, then. I'll just be out of your hair and head back home after the store. I have a lot of work to do." And she didn't need to stay around here and have him patronize her "little ideas" like her father had done for years. That was what she was trying to get away from.

So she'd head back, get to work, and get those pieces ready for sale. She could do this, and she would.

Then they'd all see who the real Cassidy Davenport was.

Chapter Sixteen

"TELL me you brought beer." Liam reached for the cooler Sean carried, praying his hand didn't shake.

What the hell had come over him? Cassidy had made a couple of innocuous comments and he'd immediately gone off on her, defending his business as if she were an authority he had to answer to.

"Yeah, it's five o'clock somewhere." Sean flicked the lid open when Liam set it on the sawhorse table he'd set up in the middle of what would be the entrance foyer of someone's new office. *Without* a hutch or a sofa or anything. "Domestic or imported?"

Liam grabbed the first bottle he found. "Doesn't matter. I just need something to quench my thirst." And calm his spinning mind. He couldn't decide if it was anger at Cassidy for insinuating he didn't know his business, or the fact that she'd looked so damn appealing and he didn't *want* her to look appealing. Whatever it was, the last thing he needed was for Sean to find out. Thank God she'd left fifteen minutes before his brother had shown up unannounced and unexpected. If Liam had known he was coming while Cassidy had been here . . . He didn't want to think about it.

"So how's working for Cassidy Davenport?"

So much for that.

Liam twisted off the top without answering. Not sure *how* to answer it.

"What?" Sean tilted his beer away from his mouth. "Is it some big secret?"

"Me working at her condo? No." Liam took a tentative swallow, still waiting for Sean to warn him off getting involved with another high-priced user.

"Well at least we don't have to worry about you with her."

Liam choked on the swallow. "Me *with* her?"

"Yeah, you know. Having a thing for her. I mean, you have to admit, the woman is hot."

Liam started to get hot. Sean shouldn't be noticing how hot Cassidy was—

Oh. Damn. Not cool. Not cool at all. Bros before hos. And she wasn't even his ho—

Liam shut down that train of thought because that's *exactly* what he'd thought of Rachel when he'd found out she wanted to live off the fruits of his—or any guy's apparently—labor, simply by putting out to reap all the benefits. Classic definition.

But the same didn't apply to Cassidy. Why that was worried the crap out of him. He had to keep some perspective here.

"Yo, Lee?" Sean waved a beer in his face. "You in there? Or did I just wake you up to the fact that your client is one hot babe?"

"Could you stop saying that, please? You don't know her or you wouldn't say that shit."

"*Shit*? Are you blind? Or, wait. Did she turn out to have a soul after all? One that hasn't been sucked dry by her father's millions?"

"Drop it, Sean. I'm not in the mood."

"Protesting too much perhaps?" Sean couldn't keep the shit-eating grin off his face.

Liam wasn't finding it funny at all. "I'm not protesting anything. You're a moron if you think I'd go down that road again. End of story. I just want to get this place in shape to put it up for sale. The realtors are bugging me. Seems there's a pending zoning change that's going to make this area a hot market."

Sean looked around. "Uh, Lee? Do you realize how much work there is? Those steps outside are hazardous."

Liam nodded and took another chug of his beer, thankful to be off the subject of Cassidy. "The rot on the outside wall. Water wicked through the subpar stucco repair job the last owner made to them."

"Good thing you didn't get Mac's live-in job that I did or you'd never have time for this. Hell, it takes me a whole day just to clean a suite."

"Yeah, but you're at the estate, so that's like getting two birds with one stone."

Sean had convinced Liam and Bryan to invest with him on a gorgeous estate in the Pocono Mountains to create a luxury resort closer to Philly than the Catskills and more affordable than hightailing it to New York City, DC, or Atlantic City. A great place for high-salaried executives to relax and get away from it all, with a championship golf course, once Sean bought the place from the deceased owner's estate. Sean had been working on this deal for years, even buying some of the surrounding properties for privacy and possible future expansion. It was Sean's chance to make his dreams come true, and they had had the extra funds to back him, with the idea that Sean would buy them out some day. Liam didn't care when; he still had his cash flow, and he liked being involved with his brothers on a project. It was a stroke of luck that Mac had the estate on her client list. It'd been Sean's the minute they'd lost the bet.

"Yeah, but I'm working my ass off. That place is huge. Mac's gonna need to hire some more guys once we're done because I'm definitely going to need the help if—I mean, when—I take over."

Liam set down the beer. "If?"

"I meant when."

"But you said if."

"I meant when."

Liam looked at him. Sean had a good poker face, but he hadn't been prepared for Liam to question him. "Spill."

Sean sighed. "There might be a glitch."

"How much of a glitch?"

"I'm not sure yet. But I'm going to fix it. I *will* get that property."

Liam didn't push. If there was a "glitch," it was bigger than Sean wanted to let on, otherwise he wouldn't have made that slip. Sean had a load on his mind. No use adding to it by pushing him. When he was ready, he'd tell them.

The good thing about being so close with his brothers was that they knew when to back off. Just like Sean had about Cassidy.

"So why are you here if you're so busy at your place?" Liam picked up the scraper and headed back to the shelves. There *was* a lot of work to do on this place, and for once, he was grateful there was. It'd keep him out of his house and away from Cassidy.

"I needed a break. I'm starting to talk to myself in those long empty hallways, you know? Wouldn't mind something else to do. You up for another poker game? We could call Bry."

"What, the last poker game turned out so well you want a repeat?"

"We won't invite Mac."

"Ever again."

He laughed with Sean, half tempted to share his theory, but . . . why? There was nothing to do about it now except suck it up and finish out the next three weeks.

Or longer if Cassidy couldn't sell enough of her furniture to move out.

The bet's ramifications just went on and on.

God help him.

CASSIDY flipped her safety goggles back into her hair as another set of lights drove past Liam's house. One more car that wasn't his.

She shook her head, wincing as the goggles slid onto the

bridge of her nose with a *clunk*. Cockeyed. Seemed to be her natural state of being around Liam these days. One minute he was being all nice and thanking her about his grandmother, the next he was telling her to butt out when she was offering her expertise for free.

Cassidy adjusted the glasses—the rhinestone-studded ones that she'd thought were so cute when she'd been painting on her own but in Liam's home just felt out of place—and finished sanding the credenza's wood top. A few passes of the top coat, a couple rounds of buffing, and this thing would look like it had a marble top. Faux finishing had been her specialty, especially *trompe l'oeil*.

She'd found an antique mirror surround at an estate sale to use that technique on. A magic mirror, she was thinking. Perfect for a little girl's room. A nice fit for her creative side, and her businesswoman side liked the fact that people typically spared no expense for their kids. Marketing a piece for someone's daughter upped its odds of being sold and selling well. Marketing was also a talent of hers, one that Dad hadn't given her credit for unless it came to looking good for the rack brochures and sales pieces.

Cassidy cracked her knuckles, her hand cramping from holding the brush and palette so long, not wanting to think about all the things she couldn't do right in her father's eyes. Was it because she was a reminder every single day of the woman who'd cheated on him and left?

She didn't think it had bothered her father all that much emotionally—aside from the obvious embarrassment at the whole sordid affair being public, that is. And if it had, he'd pretended it hadn't. He'd shown her how to be strong when Mom had left, but that hadn't stopped her from curling into a ball in her bed at night, wrapped around her favorite stuffed animal—a plush Maltese puppy she'd named Tinkerbell—and wondering why Mom had left *her*.

Well there was nothing she could do about being a reminder of her mother—

Speaking of, she'd left the photo and bracelet at the condo. Ah, the irony. She'd kept those things for years, tucked out of sight, hoping against hope that Mom would come back for her—and then she hadn't.

She didn't need the photo anymore, and the bracelet was falling apart. Reminders of the last good time she and Mom had had. The last good time in her life.

Well that was going to change. *This* was going to be the best time of her life.

A crash came from the mudroom.

Or maybe *tomorrow* would be the best time of her life.

"Titania!" Cassidy set the sander on the floor and flew into the house, not caring that she was covered in sawdust.

Her dog was covered in just plain dust. She'd somehow managed to knock an electric broom off the wall and it broke apart, *poofing* a cloud of dust throughout the room. Great. There went all her hard work keeping the place clean.

TWO hours later, the dust was off every surface in the room, though she was pretty sure it was covering every inch of her. Titania had been banished to the quickly dog-penned bathroom, yapping her cute little dust-covered head off. She really *was* a dust mop right now and Cassidy had to smile at Liam's description, though she doubted he'd be smiling if he could see the two of them.

Then again, maybe he would be. Lord knew, the man had surprised her already. He'd let a complete stranger into his home, gave her the keys to his truck, some money, and a job. He hadn't needed to give her a place to stay. He didn't owe her anything. He'd known her for all of what? Half an hour? Who *did* that?

Liam Manley. Some woman was going to get very lucky someday.

For a second, she imagined it was her. That she could live here, with Liam, be a part of his family. Call Mrs. Manley Gran, have a few brothers-in-law, a sister-in-law— hell, make that *sister*. She'd always wanted a sister.

She'd always wanted a family. And Liam had a ready-made one just waiting for someone to be a part of it.

Was it so wrong to imagine that someone being her?

Chapter Seventeen

OKAY, I'm ready to work."

Liam dropped the hammer. On his foot.

He hopped around to see the menace of his nightmares standing in the doorway of his new project, looking way too perky and . . . and . . . *sunshine-y* in her hot orange shorts and bright sunshine yellow top. "You're what?"

"I'm here to work. I'm wearing my painting clothes so put me to good use."

Don't think it, don't think it, don't think it.

Too late. Seeing the non-Rachel actions had opened the doors to an image he'd never thought he'd seen in Cassidy. And after the dreams he'd had of her and him for the past two nights while he'd slept on a pile of drop cloths in front of the fireplace here so he wouldn't have to go home and be tempted by her, *not thinking it* wasn't possible. He was imagining it in all its vivid colors—which were orange and yellow apparently. "What are you talking about?"

Cassidy held up a paint brush and a bunch of what he guessed were rags, though they looked more like someone's non-ironed handkerchiefs to him. "Paint. Here. With you. This place."

No no no. Not happening. "Don't you have some furniture to refinish or something? Dog to walk? Earrings to auction off?" Apartment to find, furniture to sell . . . Something that would get her out of his house sooner rather than later so he could get off this *was she/wasn't she* merry-go-round. Painting *this* place wasn't going to do that.

"Earrings are listed, house is clean, and I spent the morning repairing and sanding the next pieces I'm going to work on so I have some time on my hands while the dust settles in the garage. And because of it, I can't paint anything new. Not that I have room for anything new. It's an obstacle course in there as it is."

No surprise, given the state of her cabinets in her condo. "So you thought you'd come here and work?"

"Got it in one." She dazzled him with her smile and Liam had to literally blink the sun spots out of his eyes.

"*That's* what you thought?" Painting certainly wasn't his first thought when it came to her.

"Well, yeah." For the first time since she arrived, her smile dipped a little. "Don't you want the help? We'll get the place ready for sale sooner. My father's always after people to come in under budget and under deadline. I do know what I'm doing and with two of us working, we can finish that much faster."

That wasn't going to happen. Not with her in some ridiculous pair of hot orange shorts that might not be skimpy enough for Daisy Duke but worked just fine—*too* fine—for him, and a T-shirt covered in—good God—rhinestones.

"*Those* are painting clothes?" He looked down at his own drab khaki painter's shorts and the sweat-stained T-shirt that used to be blue. Or maybe green. Hard to tell because it'd faded from all the times he'd washed it. He had a few painting outfits; no sense ruining new clothes, just wash the old ones until they wore out.

"These are all I had, remember?" She tapped the end of the paintbrush to her lips, and Liam tried hard not to stare. Or wonder what they'd taste like. "So what color are you going to do the trim?"

"White."

"That'll be a nice offset with hunter green walls."

"The walls aren't going to be hunter green."

"They should be."

"They're going to be beige."

"Beige walls and white trim? Why don't you just cover everything in plastic while you're at it and remove any personality from the place?"

"It doesn't need personality; it needs to be neutral so someone can come in and make it theirs. With *their* personality."

"But if you spruce it up, you'll get more interest."

"Just how many houses have you sold?"

Her sexy lips thinned into a straight line that she twisted sideways. And even that was a good look on her.

"I'll have you know that I studied with some of the finest European designers who are on the cutting edge of interior design. People who work at *Architectural Digest*, who design hotels and luxury penthouses. My father has a whole team to design all the rooms in his buildings, down to each and every knickknack."

"Those are hotels. They're supposed to be all done up. People don't want an empty hotel room."

"He has condos, too, remember? I used to live in one."

"And wasn't that just the homiest place?"

"It wasn't supposed to be warm. It was supposed to be striking. All that white and glass . . . The place shows well. It'll sell and it'll go for big bucks. Because it's a Mitchell Davenport property and all the standards he's set for his properties are there, meeting the customer expectations he's built. You should do that. Make Liam Manley projects have a statement, a certain panache, so people know what they're getting when they buy something you've created. Build a brand for your name and it won't matter what color you put on the walls as long as it *is* a color. *Not* beige." She actually shuddered.

"Weren't you wearing beige the other day?"

She cocked her head. "I was?"

Jesus, she didn't remember? He couldn't get the image out of his head. "Yeah, your whole outfit was beige. Top, pants, shoes." The bra he'd seen when she'd bent over in front of him, and probably her damn thong. And God knew, her skin was the same color—every mouth-watering bit he'd glimpsed.

She shrugged. "So what if I was? I'm not a house and we're not talking about me anyway. I'm designing the furniture with my brand in mind. You should think about yours. What have you done across all of the houses you've flipped that's identifiable to you? That makes the place say it was done by Liam Manley?"

"My name on their check."

Cassidy rolled her eyes that were still gorgeous even when devoid of makeup. "Do you want to keep doing manual labor until you die, Liam? You have to think of the big picture. Make a name for yourself, for your brand. Then you can teach it to someone else and either sell your business or pass it on to family when you want to retire and still earn income from it. You have to create the need for your products. Give people a reason to seek you out as opposed to finding another place. Make everyone want a Liam Manley property because they are so economical or functional or innovative or something that it's a real coup for them to own it. Create your niche so people will come to you instead of you having to go out and find clients every time you have something to sell. It's always better to have a line waiting than echoes of silence when you open the door for business each day."

"Sounds like you paid attention when Dad spoke."

She cocked her head and put a hand on her hip. "The guy might be a jerk, but he does know what he's talking about and you don't live and work with him without picking up a few things, so don't patronize me."

Liam flinched. He had, actually. Hadn't meant to, but that conversation with Sean still hung in his head, and in all honesty, he'd never thought Cassidy Davenport would have even one iota of a clue about business.

But he did, and he'd been doing this for a while. "I

appreciate your offer, Cassidy, but this is my place. I'll do it in my time, my way."

Damn if the corners of her mouth didn't turn down and he'd swear her bottom lip quivered.

"All right, then." She inhaled and looked him in the eye. "If you don't want my help . . ."

"I didn't say that."

What are you doing? You want to invite her to hang around?

He pinched the bridge of his nose. This was probably the stupidest—okay, second-stupidest—thing he'd ever done. But she *wanted* to help. How many times had he wanted Rachel to even take an interest in what he did for a living? "Okay, fine. You can help. But the walls are *not* going to be green."

She opened her mouth and Liam geared up for a fight.

Instead, she surprised him. "Okay, Liam. Whatever you say."

He blinked. Really? She was going along with him? Not fighting? Not giving in to tears to get her way?

Liam's eyes narrowed. She was up to something.

And then she kissed him.

Chapter Eighteen

❧

SHE didn't mean to do it. Really, she didn't.
It was just . . . just . . . well . . .

He was giving her a chance. For whatever reasons, Liam was giving her the chance to work with him on something important to him. She was so used to her ideas being pooh-poohed that she'd been expecting him to turn her down flat. When he'd said she could help, well, she was so surprised, so happy, that she didn't really think how she should react.

Jumping into his arms and planting one on his lips probably wasn't the best choice.

Then he started kissing her back and, yeah, well, maybe it *was* a good choice. The man was *primo*.

And, man, could he kiss. If Burton had been able to send her senses into the stratosphere like Liam could, she might not have run from Dad's ultimatum.

But then she would have missed this.

She would have missed the play of Liam's lips over hers—almost biting but much softer. Tantalizing enough to send little shocks through her and take out her knees. Then there was the way his large, calloused hands gripped her back and spanned her waist, even dipped down to her butt.

It was as if someone had plugged her into a wall socket. She lit up in flames and all of a sudden, she didn't care that she was supposed to be thanking him instead of kissing him. There was no way she was stopping.

His lips traveled from hers to just below her jaw near her ear. "Cassidy."

Yes, that was her name and oh, God, it sounded so good coming from him.

"Cassidy," he said a little more forcefully, his hot breath fanning the flames a little more as it caressed her skin.

Yes, yes, she wanted to answer, but her breath had disappeared so she couldn't. She just couldn't. Besides, why bother talking when they could be kissing instead—

"Cassidy."

Wait. He was talking. He wasn't kissing. And he didn't sound out of breath or have wonder in his voice.

The electricity turned to ice and Cassidy couldn't move. She'd thrown herself at the guy—literally—and he wanted no parts of her.

Well, okay, his hands hadn't strayed from her ass, so maybe there were a few parts he wanted, but he didn't want *her*. His tone said it all.

Mortification crept through her veins and her knees weakened for a whole other reason. God, the humiliation.

She cleared her throat and pried her fingers from the knot they'd made in his hair as she unwound her leg from his calf—oh God, she'd wound herself around him like a vine— and she stepped back with one painful, legs-about-to-give-out step at a time. "I . . ." She brushed her hair off her face—hair that had escaped her ponytail and gotten all tangled and sweaty from being caught in the heat of their kiss. "I'm sorry. I don't know why I did that. I—"

"Bullshit."

"I—what?"

"Bullshit. You know exactly why you did that."

Well, yeah, she did. She found the guy incredibly

attractive and she hadn't been thinking; she'd been reacting. "I . . . do?"

"Look, I'm not some puppy dog hanger-on your father lined up for you to marry. I'm not some guy you can drag around by my dick. I don't do women like you."

"Women like . . . like me?"

"Yeah." He took the final step that put him out of arm's reach and raked both hands through his hair. "Jesus. I give an inch and you take a highway. When am I going to learn my fucking lesson?"

Something wasn't computing here, but Cassidy was still trying to slow her heart rate and figure out what the hell he'd meant by *women like you*. What did that mean?

"This isn't going to work, Cassidy. You need to go home."

Home. That was the problem; she didn't have one.

"Why? Afraid you can't resist my charms?" She let sarcasm cover her humiliation. She'd never thought he'd be repelled by her—whatever type of woman she was. It'd never happened before. She'd always been the one to pull back because she'd never been sure what a guy had wanted from her.

"It's no secret I'm attracted to you."

That answered that question.

"A man would have to be dead not to be."

She didn't think that was a compliment.

"But I'm not looking for complications in my life. I'm not looking for a woman."

"Whoa. Hold on there, Casanova. If you think I did that to try to rope you in or something, you have another thing coming. That was gratitude. Thanking you for letting me work with you on this. Don't go blowing it out of proportion." That was her story and she was sticking to it.

She did, however, cross her fingers behind her back.

He raised an eyebrow at her. "Really."

She raised her chin. If he hadn't been out of control during their kiss, she sure as hell wasn't about to admit she had. The less he knew of the attraction he held for her, the better.

"Okay, fine," he said. "I misinterpreted your leg wrapped

around me and the death grip you had on my hair, not to mention your tongue sweeping every part of my mouth."

Damn him. Her cheeks flamed, but Cassidy hadn't stared down haughty ambassadors' daughters at her boarding school for nothing. "I *can* control myself, you know. It's not as if you're God's gift to women, Liam. So I kissed you. Okay, so I got carried away. It's no big deal."

She was lying to his face but she wasn't lying to herself. The man was prime. And perfect. And if the visual wasn't proof enough, the way he sent her hormones into orbit was. But she wasn't going to pander to his ego, nor was she going to let him think he was her be-all.

Is he?

Oh, for God's sake. It was just a kiss.

Uh huh.

"But you weren't exactly pushing me away, either. I distinctly felt your hands on my ass."

He clenched his hands and his lips tightened. Yeah, he remembered.

"So are we going to do this or are you going to get your boxers in a twist and kick me out because you can't resist me?" She went for the challenge, and stuck her hands on her hips for good measure—and to remind her legs not to buckle.

Was it her imagination or did she see a flicker of something—dare she think it was admiration—as he stared at her?

"Fine. You can stay. But there are ground rules. You stay on your side and I stay on mine and if there's any meeting in the middle, there's no contact. Agreed?"

"Wow, after that romantic statement, how do you expect me to stay away?"

He sighed. "Yes or no?"

"Yes. Of course. It's not like I can't live without kissing you again." Though the thought did *thud* in her stomach a bit.

"And that holds true for back at the house, too."

"Don't flatter yourself, Liam. I'll stick to my side of everything, especially the side that has my bedroom." She tossed her head to get the damp hair off her cheek. She needed no reminders that they'd been lip-locked not a minute ago—and that it'd be the only time she'd ever have that with Liam. Which was a damn shame.

"So." She picked up her paint brush from where she'd dropped it for that lip-lock-that-wasn't-happening-again and tucked it behind her ear. "Shall I start on the trim?"

He studied her for a minute and looked like he wanted to say something, but instead, gnawed on the inside of his cheek for a second. "I was planning to do the trim after the shelves."

"Okay. I can help with those."

He arched an eyebrow. "Didn't we just discuss opposite sides?"

"So? Opposite sides of the shelves."

If she wasn't mistaken, he swallowed a groan. But she wasn't mistaken about the heavy sigh he made no attempt to hide.

"Cassidy."

She held up her hands. "I get it. Distance. Because I'm so irresistible you can't help yourself."

"Oh I'm resisting a lot right now. And I don't mean about kissing you."

Damn. That actually hurt.

He raked a hand through his hair and kneaded the back of his neck. So maybe this hadn't been the best idea. She ought to go.

But that would be admitting to more than a gratitude kiss. For all her big words, if she walked out, he'd know that it'd been about more than just gratitude.

She picked up a can of paint. "Okay, Liam. Looks like the trim's going to get done sooner rather than later. I'll start over here. On the *opposite* side of the room."

How ironic was it that the one man she *did* want was the one man who didn't want her?

Her father would call it poetic justice.

Well, she deserved more than he wanted for her, be it Liam, her art, or her independence, and she was going to get what she deserved.

Chapter Nineteen

✥

TWO torturous hours later, he and Cassidy had made little progress.

Well, *he'd* made little progress. Cassidy had gotten much more done because she was obviously taking his *opposite sides* edict literally. Her gaze hadn't strayed even once in his direction.

It was stupid that that bothered him, but every time he turned around, she was in some pose that punched him in the gut. The last one had been a doozy: she'd been bent over the top of the ladder putting painter's tape around the edge of the trim, giving him the perfect view of her butt. The one he'd had his hands on. His palms still felt the curve and softness. If he had to spend even another second staring at her butt, he'd go nuts.

Which, of course, was the universe's code for Make-Cassidy-Bend-Over-In-Front-Of-Him-On-The-Ladder-Again, thereby putting her butt at eye level once more when he went for another gallon of paint.

He looked heavenward. *Seriously?*

"Liam? Can you come over here for a second?"

Not a chance in hell. "Why?"

She tossed her ponytail over her shoulder and looked back at him. An escaped curl got caught on her nose and she blew it out of the way.

The move also went straight to his gut because he could completely imagine her doing the same thing after being bent over him like that—

"Hello? Because I need help?" She pointedly looked at the blue painter's tape that had come unstuck and the dribble of white paint on the wall below it. "I could use a wet rag before the paint dries. Unless you're just going to stand there and stare?"

Standing here staring definitely had a lot to recommend it. Which was the reason he got moving.

Twelve seconds, six deep breaths, and one wet rag later, Liam was trying to figure out the safest way to get it to her without having to go anywhere near her.

"Liam?" She nailed him with her gorgeous green eyes. "Any day now. Unless you want the wall to be white, too?"

"I'm sure you'd take issue with that color as well."

"As you could see from my condo, white isn't a color any more than beige is. It's a backdrop. Now, yes or no to the white wall?"

"Hang on." She was a bossy thing. And, surprisingly, on her, he liked it. Better than being a covert manipulator like his last girlfriend.

Cassidy is not your girlfriend.

"Here." He practically threw the rag at her.

"Seriously?" She looked where the rag landed on the bottom rung and rattled the paint tray and brush she was holding. "Which hand was I supposed to catch that with? I mean, I know we'll be violating the opposite side of the room thing, but I'm thinking dripping paint supersedes that."

Dammit. She was right and he hated that she was almost as much as he hated that he was going to have to stand behind her on the ladder to wipe the paint off.

He climbed up, trying to keep as much air space between them as possible. The problem was, her scent filled that space. Something floral and female; it'd been tough to resist from the other side of the room, but up close and personal? She was killing him. He should have driven her to a hotel, paid for a month, and left her there. He hadn't had a moment's peace since moving her in to his house.

"Yoo hoo, Liam."

Right. He mentally shook his head to clear it. Christ, he wasn't some teenager with his first crush. So he was attracted to her. That didn't mean it had to go anywhere. He was a grown man; he could control his urges.

But the one he had as he leaned over her to clean up the drip . . .

It took two passes with the rag to wipe off the paint, then Liam was down that ladder and out of temptation's way before he took another breath.

"Thank you," she said, her breathing sounding perfectly normal.

Liam strove for the same thing when he said, "No problem."

Total lie. *Huge* problem. That kiss was sitting right there between them and he'd wanted to take up right where they'd left off.

"If you say so," she mumbled. "So you're still set on this beige non-color?"

Yeah, focus on the paint. On what they were doing here. Not what he *wanted* to be doing here. "Better than hunter green, given your little accident, sweetheart." He walked back to his side of the room, which wasn't far enough away from her, but was as far as he could get, that *sweetheart* comment sticking in his head. It'd slipped from his lips way too easily.

"So what color are the shelves going to be? Also beige?"

He chuckled. Couldn't help himself. Especially when he saw the mischievous twinkle in her eye that said she was teasing him.

If only she knew in how many ways.

He needed to get a grip. "No. They'll be stained mahogany to match the floor." Liam took a deep breath. Shop talk was the perfect way to get his head back into the project where it needed to be and off her.

"I still think you should use cherry. It goes with the house so much better."

"Mahogany is a perfectly fine color, Cassidy."

"Okay, but if you're still stuck on the whole beige thing, cherry would offset the black mortar around the fireplace really nicely. Much better than mahogany."

"I'm not going with black mortar."

"You should." She tapped her lips with the end of her paintbrush. "It'd look great."

He looked at the fireplace, focusing on it instead of her lips. The ones he'd kissed.

Black mortar. The woman was right. That would look nice.

And with a property this small, dark mahogany floors and shelving would make the place seem smaller. Plus, he had enough cherry stain left over from another job, so the cost would actually be less.

Hmmm. She'd said she'd studied design; maybe she did know what she was talking about after all.

"So, Cassidy." He put the kiss behind him and thought carefully about what he was about to say. She might drive him nuts physically, but business-wise, she made sense. That discussion about branding and bringing clients *to* him rather than having to reinvent the wheel made sense. "If I do elect to go with a cherry floor, what would you suggest for these shelves?"

"Well . . ." Cassidy descended the ladder with all her eighty-gazillion inches of leg, and Liam had to remember to breathe the entire time she climbed down. "If I were you, I'd go with a custom paint job on the shelves. Maybe autumn leaves or a padded-leather look that'll go with the house. Play into its character."

And again, it was a good idea. It was only paint after all, not the commitment of wallpaper or architectural elements that a prospective buyer could take issue with.

"So . . . if we do this, we'll barter room and board for your design expertise? I don't have the money in my budget for extras like knickknacks or things, and we're not talking furniture. We're talking design. The color on the walls, the stain, the trim, the shelves. Does that work for you?"

"Work for me? Absolutely."

Her smile was worth the offer alone.

Get a grip, Manley. She's just a woman. A pretty one, but still . . . Let's not forget Rachel.

God, he sounded jaded. He'd never realized it until right now. He'd judged Cassidy on his preconceptions, and if her father hadn't kicked her out, he'd still be thinking them.

It wasn't a moment Liam was proud of.

It was also the moment he realized that he was painting her with the same brush Rachel had waved around like a banner.

"Bartering will help me pay you off quicker."

That idea no longer held the appeal it used to. "Okay, so we do the walls and trim, then you can think about what you want to do for the shelves, and we'll go from there. Sound good?"

CASSIDY made sure not to jump off the ladder and fling herself into Liam's arms this time. They'd worked past the kiss and gotten to the point where he was hearing what she was saying. She didn't want to jeopardize that.

"That works." She tried to keep the emotion out of her voice. He was giving her a shot and putting his trust in her vision. It might not seem like a big deal to anyone else, but being taken on her own merit, her own idea, was huge. All her life, things had come to her because of who she was. Liam didn't *have* to do this. He'd actually fought her on it until he'd taken the time to listen.

No one had really listened to *her* before.

The fact that Liam had, that he valued what she had to say . . . That opened a can of worms.

Because while her father's eviction made her angry and determined to prove him wrong, Liam's respect made her worried that she wouldn't prove him right.

Chapter Twenty

꒰꒦꒱

"HELLO, dear." Mrs. Manley stood on the front porch the next morning with a genuine smile on her face and a plate of cookies in her hand. Liam was off to work on some issue with the steps, so Cassidy let her in.

"Good morning, Mrs. Manley. It's nice to see you again." Except for the fact that Cassidy was wearing a pair of cut-off shorts made out of an old pair of Liam's sweatpants and one of the drabbest T-shirts she'd ever seen that she'd found in the old chest of drawers in his garage where he stored dust rags and drop cloths. It was better than her remaining wardrobe choices, the best of which was a ridiculous pair of studded jean shorts and a cotton shirt that tied beneath her breasts. Daisy Duke or male grunge? That the latter was the better pick said a lot about her wardrobe. She should have taken a few of her real outfits, Dad's edict be dammed.

"I haven't come at a bad time, have I?" Mrs. Manley looked almost hopeful at the question.

"Liam's on a job, but of course you're welcome to come in." Cassidy toed Titania out of the way. The Maltese was sitting smack dab in the center of the foyer as if she owned the place. Cassidy had told her more than once not to get too comfortable.

"I can only stay for a minute." The woman came in and headed to the kitchen, placing the cookies on the breakfast table, not looking as if she was only staying a minute. "I was in the area and thought I'd see how my little table was coming. I'm not pushing, mind you. It's just that I'm so thrilled I can hardly wait. I've had the maintenance workers at my facility move my chair into place and polish the lamp Bryan bought me. The sun hits the spot just right in the morning. It'll be perfect to read the paper while I have my coffee."

"Oh, would you like a cup?" Cassidy wasn't a coffee drinker, which was why the pot wasn't going, but Liam had one of those single-cup makers and an assortment of coffees in his pantry.

"I'd love some. Liam keeps a coffee maker here for me. Such a thoughtful man. He even bought different flavors for me to have an assortment to choose from."

"Well then, let me make you a cup." Cassidy brought out a selection from the pantry and prayed she could figure out the coffeepot, since she'd never actually *made* coffee.

"Your dog is awfully cute." Mrs. Manley sat at Liam's kitchen table and patted her lap for Titania to jump onto it.

"Thanks. Titania's a great dog."

"I never had a dog when the kids were growing up. One more mouth to feed. One more thing to clean up after. Four young children at my age, and having lost my son . . . It was a bit much."

"I can't imagine how you did it. The thought of one child terrifies me." But not for the reasons Mrs. Manley would think. Half the reason she'd bought Titania was to see if she *could* care for another living being. (The other half might have been to give her father agita.) But dogs were different than children, and while Titania was a success story, Cassidy didn't harbor any thoughts that a child would be as easy. Titania required two meals a day, a patch of grass, and some loving—none of the psychological, esteem-building sort of caring that kids did. The sort of caring Cassidy had been sorely lacking.

"Oh, it's amazing what you'll do for love." Mrs. Manley tapped the Hawaiian Kona packet. "We didn't have a lot, but those kids knew they were loved. And they loved me right back. I was very fortunate to have been able to know my grandchildren as I've come to know them, and to have them be such a part of my life. There was nothing like having them with me all those years."

Cassidy had to clear her throat on her walk to the coffee maker. It was either that or start blubbering all over the woman. Here, she'd been the only child to *two* parents and hadn't gotten even a tenth of the love the lone Mrs. Manley had shared with *four* children. Liam and his siblings were so lucky, and it just showed what Franklin's life and death had taught her was true: that all the *things* she'd had weren't what was important in life. Look at her now: she didn't even have *one* person she could go to for help, just some stranger with a big heart—that he'd obviously gotten from this woman.

"So what about you, Cass? What's your family like? Do you have siblings? What do your parents do? Oh, and press that button on the top there."

It might be a better idea to just get a kitchen knife and slice a vein than have this conversation. For all that she'd had everything, she'd had nothing when compared to Liam and his family.

She pressed the button and the coffee maker opened. "Um. My parents. They're divorced." Yes, stick as close to the truth as possible when lying. Not that she was going to lie, just omit a few things. Like her father's name. "Mom lives out of the country, so I don't see her a lot, and my father's a workaholic. I'm an only child. Needless to say, my upbringing was a bit tame compared to Liam and his siblings'."

"I can imagine." Mrs. Manley set Titania on the floor and took a seat at the counter. "Put the water in that clear plastic part, dear. The lid lifts, I believe. The mug goes underneath and then press BREW." She rested her hands on the counter, fingers intertwined. "My husband and I only had Neil. Liam's father. I'd wanted more, but it wasn't to be. Having four took

some getting used to, but I must say, having them certainly
made the grieving process easier. I didn't have time. Plus,
they were hurting so badly. My poor little Mary-Alice Catherine . . . She clung to me as if *I* was going to leave her next.
As it is, I only moved out of the house she and I shared a few
months ago. That girl wouldn't let me go even when she grew
up, though I think it was out of a misguided sense of guilt. I
finally had to sign the papers on my new place behind her
back to push her out of the nest, as it were, though I was the
one who left. It's time for her to be on her own and live her
life. She's too young—and so am I—for her to start taking
care of me. I have some living left to do, you know, and I
don't think my grandchildren see me as a real person. As
someone other than their grandmother."

She winked at Cassidy and it was all Cassidy could do
to keep her mouth from dropping open. Did Mrs. Manley
mean what Cassidy thought she meant? Was there a *gentleman friend* in the picture, by chance?

She looked at the woman with new eyes. As a woman,
not as a grandmother. She looked to be in her late sixties,
early seventies, and in great shape. Obviously her mind was
still sharp, and she was very beautiful. Why shouldn't she
date? Find someone to spend her twilight years with . . .

That image hit Cassidy with the force of an arrow right
to the heart. Why? Why was she thinking about this now?
It wasn't as if she'd never contemplated the rest of her life,
but it'd never hit her with such force.

And the sad thing was, she was seeing herself alone in a
penthouse like the one she'd just left. Oh, sure, she'd probably
have her father's millions, but what about having children and
grandchildren around her? Would marriage with one of Dad's
flunkies give her the family she so desperately wanted?

No. She knew it as surely as she was standing in Liam
Manley's kitchen conversing with his grandmother, and it
only enforced her decision not to marry who Dad chose. It
was merely another business deal to him, but to her . . . It was
her chance to get what she wanted. Needed.

A family.

"Cass? Are you okay, dear?"

Cassidy took in a shuddering breath and pasted that big ol' Showpiece smile on her face. She was no stranger to pretending everything was fine, to sucking it up and pouring on the charm when need be, and Mrs. Manley didn't deserve to have all of Cassidy's baggage unloaded on her.

"I'm fine. Just imagining what it must have been like growing up with three siblings. It must have been loud." She took the mug from the pot, grabbed a spoon and the sugar bowl, then set them in front of Mrs. Manley. "Cream and sugar?"

"Just sugar." She scooped out two teaspoons. "It was loud. I was used to just the one boy, you see. Three almost put me over the edge. And then Mary-Alice Catherine was doing everything her tiny little legs could do to keep up with them. There was never a dull—or clean—moment."

"Liam told me that you taught them to clean."

"It was that or drown in a mess. There were too many of them with too many needs and only one of me. They had to help out or my home would have been condemned." She chuckled and took a sip of her coffee. "I just never thought they'd end up using what I'd taught them like this. I'd love to see Bryan cleaning a bathroom. This is wonderful, by the way. Thank you."

"You're welcome." Bryan. Manley. Bryan *Manley*. Oh wow. Cassidy hadn't made the connection. Bryan Manley was a movie star. This town's hometown hero. He was actually a bigger celebrity than her father—which rankled her father to no end. The only saving grace in Dad's eyes was that Bryan spent most of his time in Hollywood, and when he was here, he kept a low profile. She'd seen him at a few charity events, but hadn't had the chance to meet him because of the throngs surrounding him. Dad felt it was undignified to be a member of a throng, so they'd waited for Bryan to come to them.

He hadn't.

And she, in her pre-Franklin all-about-her days, had been miffed. Had decided he wasn't worth her time or attention.

What a stupid idea. He was probably just as nice a guy as Liam.

Though Liam was actually better-looking in her opinion. But then, she might be a tad biased.

"So may I see my table?" Mrs. Manley asked after she'd shared more of Liam and his siblings' childhood stories and finished her coffee. "I'm so excited. I've never had anything custom-made before."

"Well, I've only sanded it and fixed the drawer. I haven't started painting it."

"I'd still love to see it, if you wouldn't mind. The before part of my masterpiece."

"Well I don't know about masterpiece—"

"Nonsense." Mrs. Manley tapped Cassidy on the arm. "If you don't think your furniture is an artistic masterpiece, no one else will either. You have to have faith in your work. Confidence. People can tell. Act as if they're doing you a favor and you'll devalue all your hard work and time." Mrs. Manley hopped off the stool. "Let's go see my diamond in the rough."

Mrs. Manley was the gem here. The only gem that was really important in life. Cassidy wanted what Liam and his siblings had.

If she and he started something, maybe she could.

Of course, that would have to mean he *wanted* to start something with her, and she wasn't sure he did. Oh, he was attracted to her, but a kiss did not a relationship make. She couldn't let herself hope. Couldn't let herself dream. She couldn't take the disappointment if it didn't pan out.

Too bad her heart wasn't listening to the part about how it might not pan out.

"Well it certainly looks different than what it did the other day." Mrs. Manley ran her fingertips gently over the barrel-shaped table that had been a splotchy mess of varnish and stain but was now newly sanded blond oak.

"And in a few days you won't recognize it."

"I'm very excited to see it. The décor will look lovely next to the blue chair Mary-Alice Catherine bought me." She looked around the garage. "My, you have a lot of projects going on."

"And unfortunately, no more room to work on the rest of the pieces. I used to have a storage area but it, uh, the lease was almost up and the rent's no longer in my budget."

What budget?

"There's the other half of the garage." Mrs. Manley pointed to the truck.

"That's where Liam parks."

"It's summer. He can park outside. You should make this your studio."

"I don't want to impose any more than I already am." Liam didn't deserve her imposition in his life, but having met his grandmother, she could see exactly why he'd offered to help her out.

"You're so sweet. So thoughtful." Mrs. Manley patted her cheek. "You know, I can help you and my grandson out. I know of a place you could use as a studio. The landlord needs someone to occupy it so the neighbors won't complain to the city about it being abandoned. You could do him a favor by having your studio there. I'm sure he'll be thrilled."

"Oh, but, Mrs. Manl—"

"Don't you dare turn me down, young lady. You think I don't know you're cutting me a deal on that table? I wasn't born yesterday." She arched both eyebrows. "And don't go asking when I *was* born. I won't tell you. A woman has to have a few secrets, you know."

Like the one about her gentleman friend if Cassidy had read her right. Was he the owner of the place she was talking about?

"But, Mrs. Manley—"

"I said no *but*s. I won't take no for an answer. And neither will my, um, friend."

Friend. One word said so much. How could Cassidy refuse?

"But I don't have the budget for it." That's how she could refuse, and it sucked that she had to. This would be the perfect opportunity to get out of Liam's way so he didn't come to resent helping her.

"He won't hear of it, my dear. You trust me on this. If you really feel the need, you could make him a matching table and call it even."

Cassidy resisted looking heavenward, but someone up there was on her side. "If you're sure he won't mind . . ."

"I know he won't. Matter of fact—" Mrs. Manley rummaged around in her purse. "Ah. Here it is." She held up a shiny key. "He gave me my very own key to the place. I think we should go over and take a look right now. If you have a few smaller pieces, we could even take them with us and you could have your own studio by tonight."

The offer was tempting. And Mrs. Manley looked as if she'd be heartbroken if Cassidy turned her down.

"Okay, you're on. Let's go take a look. I just hope your, um, friend won't mind me moving in."

"Not to worry, my dear. He might be a stubborn coot, but he's not stupid."

Chapter Twenty-one

❧

LIAM got out of the work van in his driveway and enjoyed the sounds of his pond in the front yard for a few minutes. He hadn't had the chance to enjoy it for a while, always working, then hitting the sheets once he got home—more to ward off temptation than exhaustion.

Because with Cassidy in the next room, his exhaustion disappeared.

It took everything he had not to knock on her door. That kiss might have started out as a *thank you* kiss, but it could have so easily gone in another direction, and he was finding himself more and more curious about seeing where it could lead.

Maybe he ought to rethink sleeping at home tonight.

Sighing, Liam rubbed his lower back. He wasn't twenty anymore and a couple of nights on a bed made of drop cloths were his limit.

He tapped the side of the truck and headed toward the door to the garage. Had she left another pile of clothes there?

And what would he do if she had?

What he found, however, was nothing.

Nothing.

Well, nothing of hers.

Liam took a few more steps inside, triggering the automatic light.

His truck was there, but there was no pile of clothing, and even more importantly, her furniture was gone.

Did that mean she was?

Liam opened the mudroom door. No little paw prints on the floor and no pile of sawdust-laden clothing to trip over.

He didn't like this. She'd cleared out? How? With what? His truck was still here—

Her father. He must have come for her. Maybe the guy had had a change of heart after seeing the piece in the *Herald* and was planning to parade Cassidy around like her prized show dog to tell the world the report was wrong. It'd be just like the man to use his daughter to do damage control.

Liam couldn't say if it was the thought of Cassidy being used that way or the fact that she'd left without a goodbye that hit him the hardest.

It was over.

What it are you talking about?

He rubbed the back of his neck. There was no *it*. There was nothing. One kiss didn't change anything. She was still Cassidy Davenport, socialite extraordinaire.

Who, as it turned out, just so happened to have a real person inside the fancy packaging.

Mind off the packaging, Manley. That ship has sailed.

Except . . . it hadn't.

He nudged open her bedroom door and there, in the moonlight spilling in through the curtains, was Cassidy, sound asleep in her bed.

Where she belonged.

Her bed, Manley. Not yours. Remember that and get the hell out of here. This isn't a good idea.

It wasn't. He knew that. But it didn't stop him.

But when the fur-ball raised her sleepy little top-knot-and-bowed head, her little pink tongue sneaking out to lick her nose, that stopped him. He didn't need a repeat of the other night when Titania woke her.

Actually, he wouldn't mind a repeat of the other night. With a mix of that kiss tossed in.

Which was exactly why he needed to get out of there. Did he really want to start something? Sure, she was turning out to be different than what he'd thought, but she was still a Davenport. Had still been raised in that lifestyle. How long would it be until she missed it? Until she wanted it again? And he wouldn't be able to give it to her because there was no way in hell he was worshipping at the altar of Mitchell Davenport.

He backed away.

But then the dog licked her bare arm and Cassidy let out a long, drawn-out breathy, "Hmmmmmm," and Liam's good intention dissolved. He could imagine her moaning like that while he licked other parts of her.

Move, Manley.

He didn't.

Now.

He should but he didn't because her fingers curled into the dog's fur and he felt that touch as if she were doing it to him.

God, he wanted her.

He'd wanted Rachel, too, and that hadn't worked out for him. Was he out of his mind? He needed to back away. Now.

Cassidy snuggled into her pillow and slid her leg to the edge of the bed, her toes peeking out. The blue toes. He couldn't see the color in the moonlight, but he remembered it. He didn't know why he was so entranced with blue toenail polish, but on Cassidy, it seemed to say something. Make a statement. As if she'd had them tattooed on in defiance of the image her father wanted her to present to the world.

He smiled. It was a small act of defiance, but he suspected she hadn't had many chances to do so over the years. Or if she had, she'd never been brave enough to take them.

Maybe he could take a chance with her. Maybe, just maybe, she wouldn't turn out to be another Rachel.

He resisted the urge to tuck her toes beneath the sheet because the minute he touched her, all bets would be off. Cassidy was beautiful, but it wasn't just her looks that had a hold on him. And it was those other things that did that worried him.

She wasn't who he'd thought she was.

She was better.

And he didn't have a defense against that.

"*Woof.*"

Liam held up his hand as if the little dog was smart enough to understand him. Of course she wasn't, so she wiggled out from Cassidy's hold, jumped off the bed, and made a beeline straight for him, the little tail going a mile a minute.

He caught her as she jumped into his arms.

Just like her owner had . . .

What would have happened if he hadn't ended the kiss? The possibilities had been bugging him ever since.

"Titania?"

Those possibilities reared their head with Cassidy's tousled hair and sleep-laden voice. And the peach nightie hanging off one shoulder.

Get out! Get out! Get out!

"Liam? Is everything okay? What are you doing with Titania?"

"She must have heard me get home and came to investigate."

Liar!

"I was just bringing her back."

Going to hell, dude. Going to hell.

He was already there.

"Oh. Well thank you." She patted her mattress. "Come here, you little heathen."

She's not talking to you, Manley.

Yeah, he got that.

Titania squirmed in Liam's arms and he debated whether to take her over to Cassidy or set her down to go back on her own.

"Could you put her on the bed? She doesn't like to jump up this high."

Of course she didn't. Why would she? Why *wouldn't* the universe set this up . . .

Not the universe. You made this happen all by yourself. Makes me think you wanted it to.

Yeah, he did.

There. He was honest with himself. He'd been cursing himself since he'd backed out of that kiss.

"Liam?"

"Sorry. Here." He set Titania on the edge of the bed. He might want to act on his desire, but ultimately, it couldn't be a good idea. There would come a point when the newness of working for herself wore off and she'd take that easy-in back to the high life. He didn't know if he could invest emotion in her only to lose out in the end. Again.

"Thanks." Cassidy brushed the hair back off her forehead. "And Liam?"

"Hmm?" God she was gorgeous with the moonlight spilling over her skin and making her eyes sparkle, her lips puffy.

"That opposite sides thing?"

He wanted to taste those lips. "Mmhm?"

"You're breaking it." She nodded toward her door. "This is my side."

"Oh. Right. But your dog—"

"Heard you come in. I get that. But she also knows where she sleeps. She would've come back on her own." Cassidy sat up and *didn't* catch the sheet that slipped from her chest to her lap. "You didn't have to bring her in. So why did you?"

Holy hell. She was stunning and sexy and he got hard just thinking about—

Get the fuck out NOW, Manley!

Yeah, he got *that.*

He turned around. "Pardon me for doing something nice like returning your dog. Won't happen again. Good night."

He stopped short of slamming her door, but he damn well did pull it shut behind him.

Then he leaned back against it and took half a dozen deep breaths. Jesus. That'd been close. For a second he'd been so tempted to go to her, slide a hand beneath her neck and pull her up to him, kissing her so she'd never ask senseless questions again. They both knew why he'd returned the dog, and what the hell was her point taunting him with it? She had to know he wanted her.

So what was he going to do about it?

He knew what he wanted to do about it. He just had to decide how much he was willing to risk.

Chapter Twenty-two

"CASSIDY, about last night." Liam walked into the kitchen the next morning, scrubbing his hair with a towel.

Thank God he'd put clothes on after his shower instead of just a towel. Not that they did anything to mitigate his effect on her, but at least she didn't have to look at that eight-pack.

But she could imagine it. Like she had for the rest of last night.

"Thank you for bringing Titania back." Cassidy didn't want to talk about last night. He hadn't "returned" Titania; the dog had jumped off the bed because he'd been in her room. The question was *why*?

And why had he turned away? Again.

"You're welcome, but, I broke our rule. It's just that I came home and your furniture was gone and I didn't know if you were, too, so I peeked in. Titania saw me and jumped off the bed, and well, that's what happened."

"Oh." So it hadn't been a burning desire for her that had brought him to her room? Boy, was *she* reading the signs wrong.

At least it made her decision for her. She could get the

idea of having any kind of relationship with Liam off the table. He might want her, but not enough to do anything about it. And if there was one thing she knew about herself, one thing she was sure of, it was that she'd never beg for anyone's affection.

She toed Titania's food bowl, hoping the little dog would stop prancing behind Liam and finish her breakfast so they could get out of here sooner rather than later.

Of course Titania didn't. The dog had taken to Liam in a way she hadn't to any of the men Cassidy had dated. And she flat-out hadn't liked Dad.

Liam gave Titania a quick scratch behind the ears, then went to work making his breakfast. "So where's all the furniture?"

Cassidy finished off her toast. "Gone."

Liam poked his head out from the fridge. "Gone where?"

She picked up her plate and juice glass and headed to the sink. "I, um, found a place and moved it there."

"You moved *all* of it? By yourself? How?"

"The portable tailgate lift in your garage and the dolly. I went online to see how to use it and I paid attention in school when we learned about fulcrums and levers. It wasn't difficult."

"But what about the rent? How are you affording that?"

She grimaced. This was the part she didn't want to get into because she had no idea how he felt about his grandmother dating. It wasn't as if she could just come out and ask him if he didn't have an inkling that Mrs. Manley was. And it wasn't her place to spill the beans. So she gilded the lily a bit. "I'm bartering for the space."

He arched his eyebrow. "Bartering?"

"You gave me the idea. This space needs work, so I figured why not? The owner is fine with it." Mrs. Manley had said it was okay, that the owner wouldn't pass up free decorating services when he wasn't even expecting rent.

"So when do you plan to do all of this, Cassidy? You have a lot on your plate."

"The extra space will allow me to work more efficiently and

on more pieces at once. It's easier to keep sanding if I have all the pieces out and prepped. Then I can paint and finish them like an assembly-line. This way, I'll be more efficient, more productive, and have more product to sell faster than if I have to clean up between each stage on individual pieces. Economy of scale. Which means I can, hopefully, sell a lot and pay you back quickly." She picked up Titania's half-eaten bowl and dumped the contents into the trash, then cleaned the bowl in the sink. "And obviously I'll still clean this place and work on the office. That shouldn't take me very long. And then I can get out of your hair so you can get back to living your life."

He didn't want her out of his hair. He wanted her hands in it and holding on while he thrust into her—

Cassidy wanted to get out of his life. Here he was, finally ready to give her the benefit of the doubt and maybe, possibly, see if it could go anywhere, and she'd been looking for a way to move on.

He hadn't seen that coming.

He ought to be thankful for it. It saved him the heartache of finding out when he was already invested.

Too late.

Shut up.

"You're going to need my truck more, then. Good thing I have Mac's van."

"Oh. I hadn't thought about that. I guess we can add it to my tab?" She gathered her hair into a ponytail and twisted the rubber band around it, tugging some hair free that'd gotten caught on her earring. "Or, I can just pawn these. No one's made any offers online, and at this point, I'd rather have the money."

She really was trying to get away from him.

He should let her. She could take what Vito gave her and start her own life, allowing his to go back to normal.

Normal was good. It wasn't an emotional roller coaster and it wasn't this up-all-night wanting.

"Okay, let's do it. Let's go see Vito."

Unfortunately, Vito had a nasty surprise for them.

Chapter Twenty-three

❧

"THESE ain't real, sugarpuff," Vito said as he removed the eye loupe. "Somebody pulled one over on you. They ain't worth what you're asking. I'll give you two for them and not a penny more."

"Two thousand?" She'd been hoping for at least five.

Vito snorted and rolled the stones in his palm like a pair of dice. "No, sweet thing. Two *hundred*. These are CZ and barcly worth even that to me, but you look like you could use a break."

Cassidy stared at the stones. Two hundred dollars? Cubic zirconia? These were *not* the earrings Dad had bought. Or if they were, he'd wanted to go cheap on the *Flavor du Jour* who was supposed to have gotten them.

It'd be funny if he hadn't given them to *her* instead. How he must have laughed at her for being happy with a pair of worthless pieces of glass.

She didn't know whether to be horrified or sad. Insulted, definitely. Who *was* her father? She'd thought she'd known him. Thought he'd only been a bastard to the outside world and his control over her life had been for her well-being when she'd been younger, then for his image when she'd gotten older. But what good was giving her fake diamond earrings? All she'd had to do was take them to an appraiser and the jig would've been up.

But she hadn't. Why would she? She'd had no reason to think they wouldn't be real.

It was a good thing Vito didn't know who she was or dear ol' Dad's name would be smeared across the front page.

She ought to do it. Play his game and leak the story. But that wasn't who she was, and it'd let him know he'd gotten to her. Plus, it'd take too much time and energy, both of which she'd need to make her future happen on her own merits now.

After she took Liam up on his generosity yet again.

"Well?" Vito clinked the earrings against the glass countertop. "Whatddya think? I'm sure I can sell 'em to a prombound teenager, but other than that, there's not a big call for these. Those who can afford to buy diamonds this size don't buy 'em here, and the kids who do ain't gonna pay big bucks for 'em. I can retail 'em for about two-fifty if I'm lucky. Two's the highest I can go. Sorry it ain't more, sweetheart, but a guy's gotta make a profit. Might want to take it up with your sugar daddy."

She was so upset she didn't bother to correct him about the sugar daddy thing. What would be the point?

"I'll keep them. Two hundred dollars isn't going to get me far and I have a feeling keeping these could get me a lot farther. Thanks, though." She stuck the earrings in her pocket, nodded at Liam, then strode out of the shop, all the while trying to pull her dignity back together from the shroud it'd become. God, she was going to have to take down the online listing before someone *did* bid on them. One more thing to add to her To-Do list.

Liam, thankfully, kept quiet all the way to his truck. Then into it. Then starting it and pulling out of the parking spot until she couldn't take it anymore.

"Go ahead and get it over with."

Liam glanced at her, but she couldn't meet his gaze.

"Get what over with?"

"The gloating. The I-told-you-so's."

He zipped the truck into a parking spot and turned it off. Then he angled himself so his right knee rested on his seat and his hand gripped the corner of hers. "Cassidy."

She blew out a breath and tried desperately not to cry. She hated crying and she especially hated crying in front of anyone. Crying was a sign of weakness. She'd learned that lesson early on at boarding school and had been sure to never let anyone see her cry again. She wasn't about to start with Liam. "What?"

"Look at me."

She so didn't want to.

But she did. "Satisfied?"

"Sweetheart, I'm not going to gloat. I'm sorry your father is such a prick that he lied to you and gave you crap jewelry."

She didn't even bother trying to defend Mitchell. *Prick* pretty much summed him up.

"I'm not going to say not to be upset or take it personally, because, yeah, it was a shitty thing to do. But the fact is, it's done. You're no poorer than you were a half hour ago, but you have your work, a roof over your head, and food on the table. And my offer's open for as long as you need it."

Dammit. *He* was going to make her cry.

"Why are you being so nice to me, Liam?"

She tossed the ball back in his court because she needed time to work on her composure. She'd been *hoping* for the recriminations so she could take all her anger and mortification at her father out on someone and Liam was the one who happened to be handy.

Too damned handy.

Liam scrubbed his chin. "It's no big deal, Cassidy. I've got the room, I need the help, and you've got the skills. It works for both of us and, frankly, I can't stand when people take advantage of others. Your father really pulled the rug out from under you and that just sucks. So, if I can lend a hand, I'm happy to."

And there went a tear.

Cassidy tried to sniff it back, turning her head so he wouldn't see it track down her right cheek. She had to stop it before the same thing happened on her left. "I'll work so much you'll never see me so I can get those pieces ready for sale and get out of your life. You've been more than generous."

He touched her shoulder.

Really? She didn't have the fortitude to take all this niceness when her emotions were bouncing all over the place.

Just don't kiss him again.

Right. She wouldn't.

"It'll be all right, Cassidy. Stay as long as you need. Don't rush your painting; you want to do your best work. Remember what you told me: it's all about your brand. Make your Cass Marie furniture the best it can be."

"C. Marie."

"What?"

"C. Marie. That's the name of my brand. The minute I stick Cassidy on it"—she'd never use Cass—"is when the world knows that I'm Cassidy Davenport. I'm not cashing in on my father's name for all the sales in the world. He'll think I won't because he told me not to, but it's really because I want to do this on my own merits. And I've got them. That first sale—hell, the offer to carry them in the gallery—was proof. He's not going to deter me from my dream."

Liam squeezed gently. "That's the spirit. You can do this."

She pasted that Showpiece smile on and looked at him, tears fully in control. "Not without you, I couldn't. And I'm more grateful for that than you'll ever know."

H E didn't want her gratitude. He didn't want the tears she was holding back, and he especially didn't want her looking at him like she was.

Remove the hand, Manley.

He turned back around and put all body parts firmly on his side of the van. "So, do you want me to drop you off at your new place or take you back to mine?"

"Yours. It's closer and I need to get the truck, otherwise you'll be going out of your way later tonight, and I'm not sure what time I'll be done. I had incentive before, but now I have even more. Plus, I need to get Titania. I'll keep her with me so you don't have to worry about her when you come home tonight."

Two things hit him at once as he started the van. One, she called his house *home*, and two, he would miss the little mutt when she left for good.

When she left. Cassidy *was* getting out of his life at the first decent sale she made and that was a reality he had to face. It was a reason not to get involved with her. He didn't need another broken heart.

Chapter Twenty-four

❦

WHEN Cassidy said she was going to work so much he'd never see her, Liam hadn't thought she'd meant that literally, but it turned out she did. The only way he knew she was actually keeping her part of the cleaning bargain was that he purposely messed things up so she'd have something to clean. But she was up and out of the house before he was, and came home after he'd gone to bed. He figured she stopped back during the day to clean up and set the automatic timer on the oven so his dinner would be warm when he came home.

He'd heard her come in late last night, but hadn't gotten up. No sense tempting fate. He needed to keep his distance.

Easier said than done.

And, annoyingly, he'd missed her. And her little dog, too.

His cell phone rang and he answered it as he yanked the van door closed and started the engine. "Yo, Jared. What's up?"

Jared, longtime friend and professional baseball player, was staying at his grandmother's house—Gran's best friend Mildred—recuperating from a car wreck. "Hey, Lee. I got tickets to the ball game tonight. Suite seats. You interested?"

Perfect. Keep him from staring at the four walls. "Cool. Yeah, count me in."

"What about your brothers?"

"I'll give 'em a call and let you know."

It'd be good to hang out with the guys. Talk sports, eat some dogs, swill some beer. A manly night with zero thoughts of anything remotely feminine.

YEAH, that wasn't happening. There was no getting away from Cassidy Davenport. Her father advertised heavily at the stadium and her gorgeous face was on placards all over the damn place.

Bryan nudged him. "That's her? She looks familiar."

"Other than the fact that her picture's all over the place, I'm sure you've been to the same parties." Liam couldn't help the sarcasm. Rachel had bugged the shit out of him to get tickets to the same events his brother would be at. He wasn't jealous of Bryan, but he had a huge problem with his girlfriend being a hanger-on, so he'd told her tickets weren't available even though Bryan could've gotten him as many as he'd wanted.

Bryan rolled his eyes. "I told you, Lee, I have to go to those things. Good for the image and for PR. And backing, too. Those rich guys are always looking to invest and they like the idea of being part of a movie. Know what I mean, Jare?"

Jared twisted around in his wheelchair. "Yeah, and the catering and top-shelf drinks aren't bad either."

"Hey, aren't you Bryan Manley?" A kid ran up beside them, tugging a giggling teenage girl beside him.

Liam shouldered Bry. "Looks like you're up, baby bro."

"Don't call me that," Bryan muttered as he handed over his food carrier before stopping to talk to the kid. "Yes, I am. Would you like an autograph?"

"Yeah. On my sister's arm. She says she'll never wash it again if you do and I wanna see that fight with Mom."

Liam handed Bry's food carrier to Jared. "Here, make yourself useful. That bogus injury's not getting you out of doing some work." He started pushing the chair.

"Bogus? If I could get out of this damn contraption, I'd show you bogus." Jared repositioned the three food carriers on his lap, trying to keep the beers upright. "And trust me, I'm working these days. Your sister . . ." He shook his head.

Liam smiled. Jared and Mac had been butting heads since forever. "Don't tell me she's put you to work."

Jared swept a hand over the chair. "Sorry, Lee, but she's a pain in the ass even if she is your sister."

"Hey, you don't have to tell me." Maybe he'd feel Jared out about doing some sleuthing to see how Mac had won the game. After all, Mac was cleaning Jared's grandmother's home, which was where Jared was recuperating.

Liam couldn't help but chuckle. He'd pay to witness that. The place was probably a disaster from all the plaster falling off the walls during their verbal sparring. He didn't know what it was, but Jared and Mac had rubbed each other wrong from day one.

Bryan caught up to them. "Thanks for abandoning me, guys."

"Aw, come on. You love it. Isn't that why you got into the business? So you could get all the women?" Liam elbowed him.

Bryan shook his head. "That's just wrong. The kid was fifteen."

"Long time to never wash an arm."

"I signed her T-shirt—the one she'd just bought, not the one she was wearing. What kind of pervert do you take me for?"

Jared shrugged. "Just your average, run-of-the-mill pervert, I guess. What's the difference?"

Bryan slapped the back of Jared's baseball cap so it fell over his face. "Watch it, you. I say your name just a little louder and we'll have a swarm crawling all over you, too."

Jared's head turned so quickly the cap spun to the other side. "Don't you dare, Bry. I don't need that nightmare."

Bryan held his hands up and stepped back. "Backing off here. No need to get psycho on me."

Jared straightened his cap. "You're all about publicity

these days and I get that, but me? I'm all about recovery since the accident. I don't need cameras and mics in my face asking me how it's going or when I'll be back. If I knew, they'd know, you know? I'm so sick of the intrusion into my privacy. Do they think I *like* having to relearn how to walk? That I *want* to show up in a stadium in a wheelchair? Or hear what my ex-girlfriend who did this to me is doing these days? Why the hell is any of it news? Can't they just leave a guy in peace to do his job?"

Bryan looked at Liam. Liam said nothing. He wasn't on the publicity wheel they were, and seeing their lack of privacy, didn't want to be.

Cassidy was just as much a publicity magnet as these two. Yet another reason to stay away from the woman.

Not that he could because she was staring at him as they headed toward their seats from yet *another* poster. Jesus, had her father blown his entire advertising budget at the stadium? Seriously, how many guys coming here for a game were in the market for luxury condos?

Then he was actually in his seat and she was staring at him *again*. This time from a giant billboard next to the scoreboard, dressed to the hilt in a sparkly nude-colored (good God, why?) outfit. Even when he *tried* to get away from her, he couldn't.

"Damn, that's a gorgeous woman." Jared got out of his shitty mood long enough to appreciate her.

Yeah, Cassidy could have that effect on a guy.

And damn if it didn't piss Liam off that Jared had noticed. Jared wasn't exactly the most monogamous guy—not that he had a harem, but he always had a new woman. Perks of the job, Liam guessed, but Cassidy wasn't going to be another notch on Jared's belt.

And not yours either, loverboy.

"Steer clear, Jare," said Bryan, helping Jared maneuver out of the chair and into a seat. "Woman like that . . . I don't know if you've got enough bank to keep her happy. And if you do, she's only after it. Not the marrying kind."

"Who says I'm in the market to get married?" Jared lifted his leg onto another chair. "But she might be the perfect incentive to get back on my feet."

"On your feet isn't where you're planning to be with her." Bryan picked up a cup. "Lee? Here's your beer. You look like you could use it. I bet she's a pain in the ass to work for, right?"

Liam took the beer and let them think that was it. He wasn't going to tell them about her getting evicted and he sure as hell wasn't going to let on that she was living with him. And he definitely wasn't going to mention that little kiss.

And its really big effects.

"I pity the guy who ends up with her." Bry handed Jared his beer. "We learned to steer clear of daddy's-girls. Right, Lee?"

Liam chugged half the beer. Why the hell couldn't Bry let it go? He really didn't want to have this discussion so he let his beer drinking speak for him.

"See what a hardship it is?" Bry asked. "He's gotta chug a few after spending the day cleaning her froufrou shit. I bet it's all pink and lacy, am I right?"

Liam wiped his mouth with his arm. Usually he was right there with the guys, doing guy things and occasionally bordering on being an ass. Tonight, not really. He didn't want to talk about Cassidy and he didn't want to talk about Rachel. "What about the place where you're working, Bry? How's that going?"

"How? Well, let's start off with: Beth's a widow. And a mom. Of five." He said it as if it were a mantra.

"*Five*?" Jared choked on his beer. "Who has five kids anymore? Who'd *want* five kids?"

"You don't like kids?" Bryan asked him.

Jared shrugged. "I like kids well enough, I guess. But five? That's a little much."

"It's a basketball team."

Jared picked up a dog and slathered it with ketchup. "It's not enough for a baseball team, so what's the point?"

"Hang on. You want *nine* kids?"

"No. I'm just saying. If you're going to go for five, what's another four?" He downed half the dog.

"Uh, a lot more mouths to feed," said Bryan. "Diapers to buy. College tuitions to pay. Ballgame concession stands to go broke at. I can't imagine having even one."

Jared grinned and finished off the dog. "Yeah, but once you get beyond two, it's just numbers."

Liam looked at Bryan with new eyes. Bryan said he was never getting married because it was impossible to find someone who could deal with his lifestyle. Apparently that meant he was never having kids, either. Liam hadn't thought their childhood was *that* bad, so he was surprised to hear his brother didn't want to repeat what they'd had. Not the parents-killed-in-a-car-accident thing, but the four of them had been close. And very much loved by Gran. He definitely wanted a family someday. It was a shame Bryan didn't.

"But a widow, huh?" Jared asked, picking up his next dog. Liam had been wondering how long it'd take him to pick up on that fact. "How long's she been single?"

"Seriously?" Bryan's eyebrows almost touched his hairline. "Did you not hear me? I said *five* kids. Need I say more?"

As long as he wasn't saying it about Cassidy, Liam was fine with ending the discussion before he did. "So what's the prognosis, Jared? When're you gonna be back in the game?"

Jared sucked the inside of his cheek and grimaced. "I have to wear this damn brace awhile longer and do a shitload of rehab. Doc says nine months. I'm planning on it being sooner."

Bryan chimed in about listening to the doc, which segued to some injury he'd sustained while doing a stunt in Sri Lanka and the lack of medical care, and pretty soon Cassidy was forgotten.

Well, by everyone but Liam.

Liam kept hearing Bryan and his "five kids" and he wondered if Cassidy wanted kids. She'd have to have them to keep the Davenport dynasty alive and well—he could see her father paying his son-in-law for each male heir. Making that heir wouldn't be a chore for the lucky bastard who got to marry Cassidy.

He wondered what it'd be like to be that guy.

Chapter Twenty-five

❧

CASSIDY was in his bedroom. His closet to be specific. On all fours, if one was getting technical, with her butt covered in stretchy nylon shorts that hiked up over the curve of her cheeks, wiggling as she backed out.

Liam shook his head and raised his eyes heavenward. Seriously? He was a good person. Nice to little old ladies and small children. Helped princesses-in-distress. Walked the occasional purse-candy dog. Why was he subjected to this torture? What in God's name was she doing in his bedroom in his closet? Honestly, he'd put up with the dust if it meant getting her out of here.

"Come on, Titania! You can't stay in here. God only knows what you could get into in here." Cassidy was inching backward on her knees, dragging the little moptop from its hips while the thing held on to . . . one of his boots. So that's where it'd gotten to.

The dog was trying to pull her legs free while stretching her pink claws down toward the carpet, apparently trying to get a toehold so she wouldn't have to give up her prize, little muzzled growls accompanying every shake of her head as the boot jerked after it.

"Titania, no! That's not yours. Give me that." Cassidy sat back on her legs, let go of one of the dog's, but Titania seized the opportunity, hitting the carpet running and managing to undo the past few seconds of forward—backward?—progress.

Cassidy huffed, propped herself back up on all fours, and crawled back into the closet.

He ought to get out now. While he could.

But he needed his truck, so he had to talk to her. "Cassidy."

Her butt stilled. "Liam?"

"Unless you were expecting some other guy?"

She backed out a lot quicker, this time without the dog. "I wasn't expecting anyone."

"I live here."

If her father could see her now. If the fiancé-wannabe could see her—

Liam didn't want to think about the guy her father had chosen for her to marry.

She got to her feet. "I'm sorry I'm in here, but Titania ran back when I let her out of her pen and I was just trying to get her out. I know it's an opposite sides violation."

He arched an eyebrow. "Wearing my T-shirt is, too."

"Um . . ." She flipped her hair off her neck in a sexy move that he had a feeling was designed purposely to get his attention off the question, but which wasn't going to work on him. And the kicker was, he didn't think she even realized she was doing it. So far, he hadn't seen the disingenuous Cassidy he'd expected when he'd first walked into her condo.

Matter of fact, he hadn't seen *any* of the Cassidy he'd expected.

"I'm sorry. It was on the shelf in the laundry room and I only have one decent outfit left. If you can call it that."

"You *can* do laundry, you know. I have a perfectly good washer and dryer."

She winced and looked at Titania, who was sitting there, her little tail wagging and bit of leather hanging from the corner of her mouth, looking up at the two of them as if she had a secret.

Liam had a sudden flash of what that secret was. "You don't know how to do laundry, do you?"

"No."

He shouldn't be surprised. The Davenports of the world would have someone do their laundry. "Come on. Get your stuff. I'll show you."

"You don't have to."

"Why? Because you're going to hand them over to your father's butler?"

"Valet."

"Excuse me?"

"His valet. Hendricks. He takes care of the clothing and linens."

"Of course he does." Liam didn't even bother hiding his sarcasm.

Cassidy sighed. "That sounded pretentious, didn't it?"

Liam headed out of his room—the last place he needed her to be—and prayed she was following him. "Pretentious? No. Unrealistic to the average working man, which I happen to be? Yes. People don't have butlers and valets."

"You might be surprised how many do."

"Sweetheart, nothing's surprising me these days."

He was lying, of course. She was surprising him. Every time he turned around.

Like now, for instance. He turned around and she was right behind him. Close enough that his quick turn hadn't stopped her forward momentum and the next thing he knew, he had Cassidy Davenport plastered up against him.

Her hands were grasping his biceps, her hair was tickling his nose, her scent was taking his legs out, and the rest of her was doing insane things to his insides.

"Liam—"

He practically shoved her into her room. "Stay away from me, Cassidy." Granted that was a little harsh, but he couldn't help his reaction. He wanted her so badly he couldn't bear her touch *and* keep his sanity. It was one or the other and he was kind of attached to his sanity.

"You're the one who stopped moving. I was just going to get my laundry. Which *you* ordered me to do, if you remember."

"I didn't order you."

" 'Come on. Get your stuff. I'll show you.' That's not an order?"

He exhaled. "Okay, so I might have been a bit harsh. The thing is, you do something to me. And I don't want it. I don't like it."

"Bullshit."

"I—what?"

"Bullshit. Isn't that what you said to me when I kissed you? You said I knew why I'd done it; well, I say the same thing. You *do* want it. You *do* like it. But for some reason you don't want to pursue it."

"We aren't doing this."

"I gathered that."

He crossed his arms and leaned against the door frame. "Look, I am not going to be your boy-toy. Your downtown dude to rub in your father's face."

"My—?" She stared at him for a few heartbeats too long and he almost caved. "My *downtown dude*? Did you really just say that?"

"You can't deny it."

"I most certainly can. I am *not* interested in you."

"I was there for that kiss."

"So you're hot." She shrugged as she turned away, and Liam wanted to kiss that disinterested look right off her face. "That's not news. I'm sure you've kissed your share of women."

Right this minute he couldn't think of a damn one. Cassidy's Irish was up, and it was a mighty fine look on her.

She picked up the T-shirt she'd been wearing yesterday and tossed it onto her bed. "I told you, it was a spur-of-the moment thing. And just now? The only reason I touched you, the only reason I was even *close* enough to touch you, is because you stopped walking. I was on my way to get my laundry for this little impromptu home ec. class of yours and you stopped." She grabbed the denim shorts that he remembered all too well off the chair. "Maybe you *did* want it and just needed a convenient excuse so you wouldn't have to shoulder the blame for taking it."

"You're crazy."

"I must be to stay here." She balled up the shorts.

"You don't have to."

"You're right." She raised her arm to toss the shorts onto the bed. "I don't."

He arched an eyebrow.

She chucked the shorts onto the bed underhanded, then raked her hair off her forehead. "Look, Liam. The place is big, but it's not that big. Even with the opposite sides rule, we're going to run into each other. So can we make a pact to not automatically assume that the other one is putting the moves on? That it was an accident and means nothing? Please? Despite what you think, that kiss was one of gratitude. I wasn't coming on to you. It just happened."

His ego didn't like the logical explanation, but for the sake of their living arrangement, he was going to accept it. "That's fine. Ready for your lesson?"

It depended on what lesson he wanted to give her . . .

Cassidy exhaled. So much for the pact. "Sure."

She sighed as she hiked the laundry basket onto her hip and followed him to the laundry room. There *was* something to be said for living in Dad's world, but hey, if she was cleaning toilets, she surely couldn't complain about cleaning clothes.

Actually, after Liam got done explaining about separating the clothing and different water temperatures and pretreatments and bleach and drying temps and speeds, yes, she could complain about it. She should have given her dry cleaner a bigger tip during the holidays.

"So, any questions?" Liam asked, shutting the lid to the washer as the machine kicked on.

"Not about laundry, no. Thanks for showing me how to

do it. But I *am* wondering what you're doing here. I thought you were working at my old place today."

"I am. But I got a call that the toolbox I ordered for my truck bed is in and I want to get it installed. So I thought I'd drop you wherever you need to be today first, since you can't drive Mac's van, and then I'll go take care of the truck."

"I know how to drive a van. Just because I've never worked a washing machine doesn't mean I don't know how to do other things. I'm surprised you trusted me with your truck if you don't think I can drive a v—"

He put a finger on her lips. "I meant that you're not insured to drive Mac's van, so you can't get behind the wheel. I'm sure you're fully competent to drive it." He took the finger away. "So where do you need to go?"

"Actually, nowhere. I'd planned to stay in and clean."

"All right. If you need anything, give me a call. I'll be out all day but can swing by if you need me. And I have dinner plans tonight, so I won't be back until late."

She wanted to ask with whom but it was none of her business. "That's fine. I'll be painting your grandmother's table. I brought it back here to work on during my downtime. You know, like during loads of laundry?" She was going for teasing and after a couple of seconds, Liam got it.

His eyes crinkled at the corners when he smiled, a look guaranteed to knock the socks right off of her. Well, if she'd been wearing any.

This no-contact thing was going to be harder to adjust to than getting tossed out of her home.

Chapter Twenty-six

❧

LIAM was atop a fourteen-foot ladder cleaning the glass transom over the French doors in Cassidy's old bedroom when he heard Mitchell Davenport enter the condo. Crap. He didn't remember anything about not having to be here today.

Liam dug out his phone and brought up the calendar app. Nothing there. He checked his messages. Nothing there either. Hopefully Davenport wasn't planning to show the place because cleaning supplies were all over the dining room table.

Liam quickly finished the transom he'd been working on—the last one would have to wait. He climbed down the ladder and collapsed it so it rested in front of the doors, then headed toward the dining room to gather his stuff.

"Burton, calm down," Davenport said as he pulled the cord to open the curtains on one of the million-dollar views the guy was known for, standing there as if he were king of all he surveyed. "Cassidy can play out her little tantrum for as long as she likes, but she'll be back."

Liam plastered himself against the wall. Either Davenport hadn't seen the cleaning supplies or he didn't care that Liam could hear him. And given that the vacuum cleaner was in the center of the living room where Titania's pen had been, Liam was going for the latter. Davenport was the kind of guy who had butlers and valets and cleaning people and maybe even someone to wipe his nose for him, so he'd probably gotten used to talking in front of "the help." Paid them good money to *not* listen to conversations, too.

But this was one Liam wanted to hear.

"Yes, I know it's been over a week. She must have found some friend of hers willing to take her in and they're holed up somewhere. I would have thought I'd have heard from her after the *Herald* ran the story, and this whole childish adventure would be over with by now. She's really screwing up my plans."

He'd probably been the one to leak the story in the first place. Talk about a shitty thing to do to his daughter; trying to make her look like a spoiled, self-centered, air-headed brat in front of everyone she knew. Nationally, too, because Liam had seen a glimpse of it on one of the celebrity news programs before he'd turned off the TV in his bedroom last night.

"No, she isn't out of the country. I have her passport." Davenport swiped a finger along the sofa back table and looked at it. Liam was surprised there was no white glove in attendance. "She'll make it to the dinner, Burton. She's not going to let me down."

But he could let her down? Jesus. This guy was a piece of work.

"I've already cut off all her cards and her phone. Her jewelry is in my vault, and all my bankers know they're to contact me if she shows up. You know Cassidy; she can't live for a week without her credit cards. She'll come crawling back soon. Might even be today." Davenport skirted the vacuum cleaner as if it were a bomb. "I do know my daughter, Burton. And you'd better learn how her mind works if you're going to marry her. She's not stupid, just emotional. Takes after her mother."

No one but Liam would ever know that the look that crossed Davenport's face at the mention of his ex-wife wasn't anger, but . . . pain.

"You'll have to keep her on an even keel. I've suggested medication, but she refuses to take it. Said it made her head fuzzy." Davenport snorted. "I should've had her nanny crush it into her breakfast every morning. Hell, I should have done that with my wife."

Liam wanted to shake the man until his head got screwed on right. Drugging his wife and kid? The man had more than just obsessive greed and self-aggrandizement going against him. Father of the Year he was not. No wonder Cassidy wanted nothing from him. Liam didn't even want his business, but that wasn't his call to make. And since Mac needed the income from this contract, he'd keep his mouth shut and provide the kind of service Davenport—and Mac—were expecting from him. But, God, he'd love to punch the guy's lights out.

"No, if she shows up, let her sweat it. No need to propose right away. She's going to learn to appreciate what my money can do for her." Davenport picked up a crystal knick-knack off the end table and looked at it. He puffed on it, brushed it against his coat lapel, then set it back down.

Pretentious SOB. Liam had polished every facet of that thing, knowing the guy would be anal about it. There wasn't a smudge to be had; he was sure of it. Seemed that nothing was good enough for Mitchell Davenport.

Poor Cassidy. Liam had known the guy was a hard-ass when it came to business, but what must it have been like growing up with him for a father? And without a mother to mitigate the emotional damage.

Liam glanced back at the bedroom. At the bed frame where he'd found that bracelet and picture. He needed to give them to her. Maybe they did mean something to her after all, and seeing how dismissive Davenport was of her feelings, Liam could see why she'd kept them hidden.

"Yes, yes, Burton. Of course you'll get your bonus regardless of when she shows up. Can't have my future son-in-law driving a mid-class sedan much longer. You have to look the part. Now, did my lawyers contact you about the name change? Can't have Davenport Properties without a

Davenport, can we?" He inspected the mantle, too. Liam ground his teeth.

"We'll make it official the day you marry her." Davenport fiddled with the knot of his tie. "I'm sure Cassidy will be thrilled not to have to change her name. After all, Davenport does open doors."

Liam wanted to puke at the play on the company's slogan. "A Davenport Property Opens Doors." It was all about the lifestyle. All about the appearance to this guy. Everything. Including his own child. Bastard didn't know how lucky he was to still *have* a daughter. What Liam and his brothers and sister wouldn't *do* to have had all these years with their parents, yet this bastard was playing with his family as if they were part of a contract negotiation.

"I'm telling you, Burton, I know my daughter. She'll come back. She's not stupid, just stubborn."

No, Davenport was the stupid one. The guy didn't have a clue what it meant to have his daughter out of his life. He still thought it was about money.

Liam got it. As he hadn't before. She *wasn't* like Rachel. Cassidy wanted her father's love and acceptance and all his money couldn't buy it for her, whereas Rachel would've taken the platinum credit card and run—off to Monte Carlo or L.A. or somewhere equally as expensive.

"She had a tantrum. She does that every so often. A bit high-strung like her mother. But one doesn't just buy one's daughter off the way one can with an ex-wife, so I have to put up with these moods of hers."

Liam bit his tongue. Literally bit it, because figuratively doing so wouldn't stop him from saying what he wanted to say. The guy was completely missing the *Father* gene and *Human* was in question as well.

"She'll come back, Burton. She always does. Her *kind* always does."

If it weren't the exact same thing Liam had said about her himself, he'd take offense at the man's smug condescension.

Now, he just found his own conclusions about Cassidy condescending. And wrong.

"Cassidy's used to the best in this world." Davenport rearranged a picture frame on the top of the baby grand. "It's all she's known. Her friends can't hope to compete with what I can give her. Not many people can."

The guy just didn't shut up. Good God, the hubris. What would take Davenport down a few hundred pegs?

What Liam wouldn't do to get the chance.

But . . . why? Why was he so mad on Cassidy's behalf when he'd thought the same things about her?

Maybe that was it. Maybe he was mad at himself. For being wrong. For judging her. For not taking her at face value. He always gave people a chance, but he'd seen the high-rise, had heard all the press coverage about her, and, hell, had *Rachel* for a template for these sorts of relationships . . . It was no wonder he'd jumped to those conclusions, but that didn't mean he had to like it about himself. He'd always prided himself on giving people that chance. On giving them a break, but he'd judged her. Wrongly.

"Oh, she started with these little fits of temper about a year ago and they've become quite the chore. This time she'll learn who holds the cards, and if she wants to continue wearing the high-end designer clothing and shoes she loves, if she wants to vacation at the most beautiful resorts in the world and eat at the most famous restaurants and have the best seats and meet celebrities, she'll get herself under control and come home. Or she'll have to learn how the other half lives."

As a representative of the so-called *other half*, Liam wanted to walk in there and tell this pompous ass that the other half wasn't doing so bad. Wouldn't the guy shit if he knew that, right this minute, Cassidy *was* living like the so-called other half and doing a damn good job of it?

But it wasn't Liam's place to enlighten him, so he snuck into the dining room and tucked everything back into the Manley Maids tool tote, plunked a baseball cap onto his head, shoved the mop, dust mop, blind cleaner, and extension rod under his arm, picked up the tool box with his other hand, and swung around—

And smacked Davenport across his midsection.

There was more than a small measure of satisfaction in that, but still, there was Mac's contract to worry about.

"I'm sorry. I didn't see you standing there—"

Davenport held up his hand. "Hang on a second, Burton." He hit the MUTE button on his phone. "What are you doing here?"

"Cleaning."

"Weren't you here last week?"

"Yes, but dust comes back. Since you're selling the place, I thought you'd want it to be in tip-top shape."

Davenport arched an eyebrow and studied him, his lips pursed. "How much of my conversation have you overheard?"

"What? Me? Eavesdrop? I'm sorry, sir, but that wouldn't be professional." Firmly entrenching himself in the *peon* category of Davenport's estimation, Liam added that "sir." Gran always said he could get more flies with honey; Liam was sure the same applied to rats. Besides, it was Cassidy's right to tell the guy where to shove his condescension.

"Hmmm." Davenport clicked his tongue, then reached into his interior jacket pocket and pulled out—

His wallet.

Oh this was rich.

"Burton, let me call you back." Davenport slid the phone into his pants pocket, then flipped the wallet open and withdrew a hundred-dollar bill. "I'd appreciate it if you wouldn't say anything to anyone." He flicked his wrist, presenting the cash in one fluid motion, as if he'd done it dozens of times before. "A nice dinner, perhaps, to take your mind off my little problem?"

Liam should have cleaned out Cassidy's closets. Taken everything. This ass, with his pious condescension in wanting to teach his daughter a lesson, deserved to be shorted a few thousand dollars by losing her wardrobe. The hundred was nothing to him.

But Liam took it anyway, though not for the reason

Davenport would think. Cassidy could use this. It wasn't as if he had any intention of telling people what he'd just heard; *he* was trying to forget he'd heard it.

For the first time in his life, he was feeling *sorry* for a spoiled little rich girl—who maybe wasn't so spoiled, and who was definitely nowhere near as rich as he and his siblings were when it came to what was important in life: having someone who loved them enough to take them in.

Not kick them out.

Chapter Twenty-seven

❦

IT was a thought that stayed with Liam throughout the dinner with Gran and his brothers that evening. Sean and Bryan were at each other's throats—figuratively, that was. The three of them were as close as could be, but one couldn't *not* rib the other about anything and everything.

Funny, though, that they knew to draw the line when the subject of Cassidy came up.

"How's Cassidy?" Gran asked, effectively shutting down the conversation about the issue with Sean's project and getting their focus on him. She might as well have said Rachel, because the reaction would be the same. His brothers had been his support system when that relationship had gone to hell and he knew they'd be there for him even if he fell off the wagon and into Cassidy's bed.

But too bad they didn't know the Cassidy he did.

But he wasn't ready to share that Cassidy yet. Wanted to make sure she really was what he was coming to think she was before he sprang her on the guys. They'd be naturally cautious, and he had enough on his plate without them looking over his shoulder. "She's Cassidy." He just hoped Gran didn't bring up anything about her staying at his place. Then again, Cassidy hadn't given her the correct name, so Gran wasn't supposed to know who his houseguest really was.

"Now, Liam, don't judge her by what everyone says about her. I mean, look at Bryan. Do you really think everything they've printed about him is true? He hasn't dated all those women."

It was not his place to disabuse his grandmother about Bryan's supposed lack of prowess. Because Bryan didn't lack any prowess and the tabloids made good use of that.

"Don't worry, Gran. I'm letting Cassidy prove herself."

And what a surprise she was turning out to be.

"Good. I'm glad to hear it." Gran waved her glass around for a little more wine, and Liam recognized that gesture for what it was: a change of subject. Gran never had two glasses of wine.

Her tactic worked and the rest of the dinner was all about Sean and the heiress, Bryan and the widow, and Liam's latest property-flipping project. And racquetball. Specifically, Sean challenging him to a game tomorrow night.

Blowing off some steam on the court and kicking Sean's ass at the same time sounded like just the thing to take the edge off. He'd imagine Davenport's face on the ball. A win-win in his book.

"You know, Liam," said Gran after serving dessert, her homemade apple pie. It brought back all sorts of memories from his childhood—Gran had been one of those who'd put her pies on the windowsill to cool. He and Jared had stolen a pie only once. The whooping she'd given them—verbal, not physical—had been enough to make them never want to do that again. Well, that and the threat that she'd never give him another slice for the rest of his life. Thing was, Gran had meant it, so he'd learned to respect her orders.

Had Cassidy ever had someone bake her a pie? Sneak her a piece when she'd fallen off her bike or gotten tackled in the big game, or whatever the boarding school debutante version of falling down during a clutch game was?

He had a feeling she hadn't. Her father, as evidenced by

that phone call to the man he'd chosen for her to marry, had no concept of how to raise a child. No concept of family.

No wonder she'd lived the life she'd lived. With a man as shallow as Davenport raising her—or leaving others to raise her—what chance had she had?

And the fact that she was trying to change . . . Couple that with the whole attraction thing, and the situation was just getting more complicated.

Gran wasn't helping matters. "I met your houseguest, Liam," she said after Bry and Sean had left.

He'd been two steps away from making a clean break. "She mentioned it."

"She seems nice." Gran was going to drag it out.

"Yes."

"She's painting a piece of furniture for me."

"She told me."

"It'd be nice if you could help her deliver it. I'm sure it's too heavy for her to do by herself."

Message received. Still . . . "Oh she's pretty good at doing things by herself, Gran. Is kind of insisting on it, actually."

Gran patted him on his arm. "Just because someone can, doesn't mean they should, Liam. She's a nice girl and ought to be judged on her own merits. Remember that."

It wasn't something he was likely to forget.

Chapter Twenty-eight

❦

"YOU brought *Cassidy*?" Sean whispered as Liam was taking his racquet out of his bag for their game.

"It's not like I had a lot of time to come up with someone else, and she overheard."

Liam glanced at the girls who were on the other side of the court doing whatever girls did when they first meet. And this had to be the first meeting for the two of them; Sean's Gypsy-Chick would never run in the same circles as Cassidy.

"She's in pink," Sean stage-whispered. "Rhinestones."

"Tell me about it." They'd had to run out and buy her a pair of sneakers courtesy of Davenport's hush money, but she'd refused to take any extra cash to buy an outfit. She hadn't wanted to be in debt to him any more than she already was, and Liam had been ready to *give* her the cash because he didn't think anything could be more inappropriate for a game of racquetball than the rhinestones. But then he got a look at Livvy, Sean's partner, in her beaded skirt and stomach-flashing half shirt, and realized he was wrong. The Gypsy-Chick won.

Yet despite this, Sean had the balls to ask, "She does

know that this is a sport, right? That you get hot and sweaty and the makeup will slide off her face?"

"If she doesn't, she soon will. That could make this whole thing worthwhile." He meant the hot and sweaty part. He wouldn't mind seeing Cassidy like that—

Damn shorts suddenly got tight. He crossed his arms with the racquet hanging down, hoping to hide the evidence. "Any progress with the Gypsy-Chick?" Livvy's grandmother had changed her will, leaving the estate to Livvy instead of allowing Sean to buy it at the below-market price they'd previously agreed on *if* Livvy completed some strange scavenger hunt thing the old woman had devised. Liam, Bry, and Sean were all hoping she failed.

Actually, Sean was doing a little more than hoping. He was kind of helping the failure along.

Sean rolled his eyes. "We're following the clues. Tomorrow we're chasing down baby cradles."

A jolt shot straight through Liam's gut. Babies. It seemed to be a theme lately. His assistant was on maternity leave, his housekeeper was on maternity leave, Cassidy's father was selling her out like a brood mare . . . "You realize that's a dangerous line of thought around any woman, right?"

"Trust me," said Sean. "It's not an issue."

"Famous last words." He wasn't talking to Sean. He smacked his bro in the chest. "Come on. Let's get this going." He needed to concentrate on something other than Cassidy in those short shorts that hugged her ass in a way his palms were itching to.

He gripped his racquet. At least he could get a good workout in so thoughts of her across the hall from him tonight wouldn't screw with his sleep.

FIVE minutes into the game and that was a lost cause. Hell, *two* minutes into the game, with Cassidy's slim, toned body eating up the court, and her hair swishing all over the place, and the determined grunt she made every time she returned the volley . . . Liam was going to have all

sorts of dreams and probably be up all night. In every sense
of that word. God, even with those crazy rhinestone-studded
protective glasses she used for painting on for safety, the
woman drove him crazy.

"Woo hoo! Score one for me!" Gypsy-Chick, er, Livvy
high-fived Sean, getting Liam's head back into the game.
No way was he going to lose this one. The last game he'd
lost had been the poker one, and look where that'd gotten him.

"Don't get too comfortable with a one-point lead. Cass
and I will have you eating our dust." He looked over at
Cassidy while tossing Sean the ball.

She tossed her ponytail over her shoulder. "Cass-i-dy,
Liam. I don't like Cass."

He did, though. It suited her: tough, to the point, ready
to take on the world and come out a winner.

He liked that in a woman.

Head in the game, Manley.

"Serve, Sean."

He kept his head in it for a while actually. Cassidy was
as good a player as he was. And Livvy was no slouch either.
Both women could have used some help in the athletic attire
department, but they had their game faces on. The match
was as even as if it were just him and Sean.

"You need a break yet, Cass?"

She glared at him but didn't answer.

He hid his smile. He liked teasing her.

He was liking a lot of things about her.

Yo, Manley, chill. Just because she seems *to be different
from Rachel doesn't mean she is. It's been, what, two
weeks? Not exactly the longest track record. Slow down,
dude.*

His conscience had a point. Rachel hadn't shown her true
colors at first. Or maybe he hadn't been looking closely
enough.

He was, however, looking very closely at Cassidy.

"Sean, you gonna serve it or stare at it? I don't have all
night, you know." He lunged from side to side, twirling his

racket in his palm, his nerves stretched thin. Time to get this game over with and go back to his house where she had her side and he had his and he could think things through before he did something he'd regret.

"Come on, Sean," said Livvy, smiling at him. "I'm ready."

Whoa. When that woman smiled . . . Sean would have to be dead not to notice her.

And with the way his serve fell short . . . He'd noticed.

Ha. His brother had a weak spot. Good. Now, as long as he didn't figure out that Liam had one as well.

"One more, Sean," he taunted. "You lose the serve and you can kiss this game goodbye."

"You're not that lucky, Lee." Sean smashed the serve, and he and Livvy managed to pull two points ahead, dammit, before the serve changed hands.

"Ladies first." Liam bounced Cassidy the ball. "Let's show these two how it's done, Cass."

And then he could show *her* how it was done—

Damn, he almost missed Sean's return. He had to get his head in the game so they didn't lose the match. Sean would never let him live it down.

Luckily, Livvy gave up their fifth consecutive point, and after that, she and Sean couldn't touch him and Cassidy. The serve volleyed between them, but Cassidy managed to get as many points on the board as Liam did. They were well matched.

Slow, Manley. Slow.

He was trying, but watching her bounce around the court . . . That tight T-shirt and those short shorts hid nothing from his imagination and he had to work really hard, totally focus on every point, or Sean would have the physical proof for the questioning look he kept sending Liam's way. One Liam was not about to answer.

He gritted his teeth and raised his hand over his head, gearing up for the serve. Sean had a weakness on the left and Livvy was too far away to cover it.

Cassidy glanced at him, nodded toward the corner where

he'd been planning to serve, then faced the wall, her racquet passing between her hands as she bounced from one foot to the other, her adrenaline literally keeping her on her toes.

He glanced at Sean, trying to keep him guessing where he was going to serve it. Then he looked at Livvy while keeping Sean's weak spot in sight out of the corner of his eye, and served.

It hit the floor, hit the wall, and veered off exactly how he'd wanted it to, way out of reach for either Sean or Livvy.

"Score!" Liam raised his arms in a V. "You're going down, Sean," he said, allowing himself to crow after high-fiving Cassidy. "Ready to cry like a baby?"

"Bring it on, bro." Sean was all business, lined up and waiting.

Cassidy earned them a point with another wicked serve, then it was Liam's turn again. He smashed it, sending Sean all over the court and Livvy diving to save a shot.

It was the distraction of her *thud* as her shoulder hit the floor that Liam was looking for. He slammed the ball so hard he heard it whistle.

Unfortunately, Sean heard it, too, and managed to make a solid return.

Cassidy went after it with a powerful shot that almost got by Livvy, but again, Gypsy-Chick went all out for the ball, smacking her hands on the floor as she landed. That outfit wasn't the best design for taking a dive.

Liam took the shot, smashing it past Sean so the bounce-back would hit him if he didn't move—

Damn. Sean made a half turn and managed to catch a piece of it, enough to get it back to the wall for Cassidy's return.

Cassidy, braced for a spike, had to adjust quickly to reach the ball before the second bounce, lobbing it beautifully. Not that a lob would earn them the point, but her form for the shot was incredible.

Hell, her form for *anything* was incredible.

Livvy returned the volley, and Liam followed the arc, doing the logistics as he ran toward the right corner. One point from taking the game and with Sean back over his left shoulder, he could take the easy shot to the center front to keep the ball in play, or rebound it off the side wall and try for the win.

He went for it, smashing the ball to the side and, yes! Sean missed!

"Winner!" Liam tossed his racket to the floor and swept Cassidy up in his arms, twirling her around.

"We won!" She shook her ponytail down her back, laughing as she wrapped her arms around his neck and—

The celebration got serious in a heartbeat. Matter of fact, he could *hear* his heartbeat. Or maybe it was hers.

He stopped twirling.

She stopped laughing.

He didn't let go.

She didn't either.

He did, however, set her down on her feet.

In a long, slow slide down the front of his body.

There wasn't one damn thing left to his imagination. Hers either if she was paying attention.

The darkening of her eyes said she was.

The quick lick of her lips said she was.

The tightening of her breasts against his chest said she was.

"So, Lee. You and Cassidy want to—"

Yeah he and Cassidy wanted to and Sean's cut-off sentence said it was a secret from no one.

Liam cleared his throat and stepped back while Cassidy practically stumbled away at the same time.

"You guys want to go grab something to eat?" Sean glared at him, challenging him to say nothing was going on. That what Sean had just witnessed wasn't true; that he and Cassidy hadn't almost locked lips right here in the middle of the racquetball court where anyone walking by could see.

Not that there was anything Liam could say. A dead man would know what'd been in his mind a few seconds ago and Sean wasn't dead. He was also a pretty smart guy and he'd been there for the hell after Rachel.

"Thanks, but I have to get home." He didn't need the

lecture or the looks. "Billing's backing up with my assistant out on maternity leave, and if the bills don't go out, money can't come in." He didn't dare glance at Cassidy. One look and Sean would know he was lying through his teeth. Money wasn't what was on his mind.

Sean stared at him a few seconds too long. "If that's what you want . . ." He tossed him his racquet. "Give me a call when you get a moment. I need to remind you about a few things."

"Yeah, sure. No problem." He didn't want to hear Sean's *things*. He knew what they were, but he wasn't about to discuss this situation with his brother before he figured out what he wanted to do.

He grabbed his gym bag and looked at Cassidy—who looked like a million dollars and not because of her father's money. An honest-to-God sweaty workout made her light up. No makeup, sweat glistening on her skin, messy hair that he wanted to comb his fingers through, and lips so damn puffy and kissable that he had a feeling one night with her would never be enough.

But . . . maybe . . . Maybe it'd get her out of his system.

Chapter Twenty-nine

GREAT game."

Cassidy kept her eyes on the road. "Yes."

"You're really good."

"Thanks."

"Did you have fun?"

"Yes."

"Am I going to get more than a one-word answer out of you?"

"Sure."

Liam glanced at her and Cassidy realized what she'd said.

"Oh. I mean, yes. You will. How's that? Better?" She was rambling. But at least she was coherent. She was surprised that she was because, holy mackerel . . . What just happened back there?

One minute she'd been jumping for joy, thrilled with their hard-won victory, and the next . . . The next, she'd been in his arms, smashed up against his hot, sweaty body, his scent calling to her like a siren's song, and she'd forgotten where they were. That they were in a public gym where anyone could see them, with his brother standing not five feet away.

But the moment she'd looked into his eyes and felt his arms go around her, she'd tuned out everything but what had been happening between them. It'd been different than when she'd kissed him before. Stronger.

Mutual.

She'd known that even before he'd pressed his erection against her. Or maybe she'd pressed against it, but regardless, Liam wasn't going to be able to call bullshit for that.

He'd wanted her and she wanted him.

Question was, what were they going to do about it?

"You want to get something to eat?"

She shook her head. "Not like this. I need a shower."

Oh, God. The images flashed in her brain and she couldn't get rid of them. Her, naked and wet under the spray, and Liam shoving the curtain aside, equally naked but nowhere near as wet . . . until he stepped into the stall with her. Pressed her up against the cool tile and started nibbling on her neck.

She gripped the truck's door handle and squeezed. Hard. She had to squeeze something and she couldn't exactly squeeze her legs together when he was watching her.

Which only made the ache between her thighs stronger. And made her want that fantasy to come true.

"I don't think it'll matter, Cass. We're both pretty sweaty."

"Hey, I take offense to that. I don't sweat. I glisten."

He arched his eyebrow and, man, it was sexy. "Glisten? Nice try, sweetheart, but that's sweat. Good-for-you, hard-earned sweat."

The words themselves weren't sexy, but the images they conjured . . .

So what was she going to do about it? Her gut was telling her to go for it; her brain was saying *back off.* She was staying in his house and had no other place to go. If they got involved and things got weird, what then? They'd already tempted fate once with that kiss; wasn't that what the "opposite sides" thing was all about? It wasn't a good idea to risk temptation any further.

That thought worked until Liam pulled into the garage

and cut the engine. They stared at the back wall until the cab light dimmed.

"Liam."

"Cass."

Someone made the first move. It could have been her. It could have been him. It really didn't matter because the next thing she knew she was in Liam's lap, her hands tangled in his hair, his hands cupping her face, and he was kissing her until she couldn't see straight.

Given that she had her eyes closed and it was dark in the garage, that wasn't exactly a surprise, but the way her head was spinning with the taste and feel and scent of him . . . Colors and lights flashed behind her eyelids like fireworks.

Oh wow. Liam gave her fireworks.

Then he plastered his palm to the side of her face and dragged her hair back as he cradled her head, nipping kisses along her jaw, and the fireworks were joined by butterflies. Millions of them, fluttering in her belly so much that she could swear she heard them hum.

Oh, that was her.

"We said we weren't going to do this." Liam licked an incredibly sensitive spot beneath her ear.

"I know." She gasped as shivers radiated from that spot, and she dug her fingernails into his shoulder, never wanting him to stop.

"Both of us agreed." He showed no signs of stopping.

Good. "I know."

His teeth scraped her earlobe, eliciting a whole new round of shivers. "This isn't a good idea."

She grabbed the back of his head and let her fingers curl into his hair and held him tighter to her. "I know."

"We should stop." He nibbled his way along her jaw toward her mouth.

She tilted his head just enough and looked him in the eye. "I know."

"Cassidy, I—"

She kissed him. Sucked on his lips, swept her tongue inside, and never wanted to come up for air.

She moaned when he did.

"Let's take this inside, Cass."

"Mmmm hmmm," was all she could manage. At least one of them was coherent.

Actually, Liam was more than just coherent; he was surprisingly competent, given what had erupted between them. But he managed to get the door open and carry her cradled in his arms through the mudroom door and into the hallway, only stopping when Titania went ballistic in her pen.

"Tell me the dog doesn't need to go out," he groaned.

Oh hell. The fireworks sputtered. "The dog needs to go out."

"And that's going to happen how?"

Cassidy nipped his jaw. "Let me down. I'll open the door, she'll go out then come right back in. She wants to be around me."

He kissed her neck as he stood her on her feet. "I know the feeling."

Titania barked and hopped around them, almost tripping Cassidy as she let her out to do her business.

She stood in the doorway, trying to catch her breath and think this through. Was this a good idea? Or was it just going to invite disaster?

Liam wrapped his arms around her from behind and rested his chin on her shoulder. "I can hear you thinking."

She leaned her head against his. "That's not possible."

"Not true. You were doing some pretty heavy sighing that I could clearly hear."

"Sighing happens for different reasons, not just thinking."

"I know. You were sighing for other reasons in my truck. Moaning, too." He nuzzled her neck.

Both of which she was going to do again if he kept that up. He did.

"I want you, Cassidy," he whispered against her throat, the vibrations of his voice rippling through her. "It's not a secret and it's not a surprise and I'm tired of fighting it. We can deal with the aftermath later. Tell me you want this as much as I do."

"I do."

Thankfully, Titania came back then. They penned her up and Liam led Cassidy to his room.

He stretched out beside her on his bed. "Last chance to stop if you don't want this to go any further," he said, kissing his way down the middle of her chest, nuzzling her neckline as low as it could go.

"Don't stop." She wiggled beneath him to get her hands on the hem of her T-shirt. She wanted this thing off. Now.

The darn rhinestones kept getting caught on his shirt, then snagged in her hair. "Rip it off." It was either that or her hair, and she could always buy another shirt.

"You don't have a lot of clothes, Cassidy."

"So I'll wear yours. Or none at all. Just get it off me."

"None, huh?" Liam's smile lit a slow burn inside her—that went to raging when he *did* rip the shirt apart.

The rhinestones that didn't go flying off were still caught in her hair, but she didn't mind because he lowered his head to her nipple and rhinestones became the *last* thing on her mind.

"Ahh, God, yes. That feels so good."

"You are beautiful. And you taste so good," he said, never taking his lips from her nipple, his tongue circling it until it was as tight and hard as he was against her.

She slipped her hand between them and stroked the length of him.

"Ah, Cassidy," he groaned against her skin, the vibration sending shivers all over her once more. "Careful, woman. I don't seem to have a lot of control where you're concerned."

She smiled and raked her nails up his length through the silky basketball shorts. "Good. The better to torture you with, my dear."

He looked at her, her nipple still between his lips, and tugged, a wicked gleam in his eyes. "And this is better to taste you, my dear." His tongue did some quick flicker/stroking movement and *ohmygod* . . . Cassidy dug her heels into the mattress and grabbed the comforter to keep from flying off the bed.

There was no place she'd rather be and she wasn't about to get off this bed until the earth moved.

His fingers slid down her stomach, over her hip bones, to exactly where she needed him to be.

The earth moved.

The heavens sang.

Birds wept, lions roared, and somewhere in all of her scattered thoughts, Cassidy knew she was helpless to do anything but go with the wave of pleasure Liam's fingers and lips were giving her.

"Liam." She whimpered it. Or maybe she breathed it. Or maybe she moaned it . . . Possibly all three; Cassidy wasn't sure. All she knew was that Liam was giving her the most intense pleasure of her life and she never wanted it to end.

And then it ratcheted up. He cupped her breast, leaving her aching and wet and throbbing between her thighs, a state she could take huge issue with except for the fact that when he cupped her breast, his thumb slid over her nipple with such torturous pleasure that every nerve ending in her body roared to that one point, all energy, all desire, focused there—then shifted when he tongued the other one again.

She grabbed his head, holding him there, arching into him, muted pleas begging him to never stop, to give her this intense pleasure for the rest of her life . . .

He shifted, moving on top of her, pressing his erection— thankyougod—against her aching center, and she just wanted to pull him into her and keep him inside her long enough to fill this void that had been there for so long she hadn't ever really known what it was like to *not* have it. But Liam could make the void go away. Make it disappear for good.

She'd never thrown herself at someone. Had never felt the overwhelming urge to do so. She'd never had to because men had always come on to her and she'd been the one to say no. Thank God Liam was saying yes because it was as if the very act of living was dependent upon him touching her.

It scared her, this depth of what she was feeling for him. To give someone so much power . . . It was the exact opposite of what she'd said she wanted in her life now.

But it didn't stop her from wanting him. From wanting his hands all over her. His lips, his teeth, his tongue all over her skin. So she was going to go with that and deal with the rest later.

She slid her hands up his back, enjoying the sweat beneath her palms, the way it smelled on him, the way it slicked their bodies so they could slide against each other with just the right amount of friction—

"God, Cassidy. I want you."

Thank the lord and pass the popcorn. Cassidy tugged his face to hers and kissed him with everything in her.

His tongue danced over hers, his teeth nipped at her lips and his tongue . . . Dear God he had a talented tongue. What would it be like if he moved lower . . .

She gripped his shorts, wanting to find out. Wanting to know what it was like to be joined with someone so intimately—and she didn't mean physically. She'd had sex before, but this, what Liam could do to her . . . she'd never had this.

"Take your shorts off," she muttered, trying to shove them down his hips and giving up, sliding her hands beneath the waistband and curving them over his butt instead.

He had a great butt. So firm and tight and muscular . . . Perfect for hanging on to or grasping to her as he thrust inside of her . . .

"I want you, Liam. Inside me. Now."

"Bossy thing, aren't you?" He didn't sound annoyed. "Give me a second, sweetheart."

He crawled over her some more, his lower half now in the vicinity of her chest.

Cassidy nibbled on his hip.

"Holy—!" Liam fell onto the bed. "Cassidy, honey. Give me a chance here. You do that and I'm not going to get one of these on in time."

She looked at "these." Ah. Condoms. Good. "Grab a bunch."

He arched an eyebrow. "Define a bunch."

She smiled back at him. "As many as you think you can handle, big boy. Then add three."

He laughed and shook his head, the almost desperate edge taken off. Oh, she still wanted him, but at least now she could think.

And then he stood on the side of the bed and dropped his shorts.

Thinking went out the window.

"My God, Liam. You're beautiful."

"That's my line." He didn't move, just stared at her.

Cassidy looked at herself. Her nipples were two hardened pebbles, there was some brush-burn on her chest, her shorts were half shoved off her hips, and her socks and sneakers were still on. Oh, and her shirt was still tangled up in her hair. She had no makeup, had been sweating like a pig, and her lips were probably swollen from his kiss. "I guess beauty truly is in the eye of the beholder." She kicked off her sneakers and shimmied out of her shorts.

"Baby, you're gorgeous. From the first moment I saw you, you've only gotten prettier."

If she'd needed anything else to melt her bones, that might have been it, but she didn't. She wanted Liam not because of what he said to her but because of who he was. *How* he was. These past two weeks, she'd come to learn who *he* was. How *he* thought. His generosity, his compassion, his talent, his smarts, and his heart. His love for his family and his unselfishness in helping her. Then there was this chemistry thing and it was as if Liam was too good to be true.

"Please, Liam." She held out her hand, inviting him to join her. To join *with* her. To be with her in this moment.

"I'm right here, Cass."

He slid beside her, cupped her hip, and rolled her to face him, and she didn't mind the nickname. Not from him. Hearing him say it . . . It was different from when Mom had called her that then left. Liam wasn't going anywhere. Not now and maybe, not later.

"You're sure?" Liam brushed his fingertips over her cheek.

She caught his hand and brought it to her lips. She kissed

his fingers. Once. Then she sucked his index finger into her mouth and rolled her tongue around it. "Does that answer your question?"

His eyes darkened and that sexy smile slid over his lips. "Hell yeah, it does."

And then he rolled her onto her back and was on top of her, with only the condom between them.

Liam cupped her face and brushed some hair off her forehead with his fingertips. "You are so incredibly beautiful, Cassidy. And I don't just mean the physical. God gave you the beautiful structure, but there's a light inside you that shines through. It eclipses everyone else around you. And you aren't even aware of it. You don't even know how you affect others."

God, the words were nice, and she really hated to disabuse him of his fantasy, but the reality was . . . He didn't recognize what he was looking at when he saw that supposed light.

"That light is the lure of being a Davenport, Liam. Nothing to do with me and everything to do with my last name."

Liam shook his head. "That's what you think, but it's not true. The same light doesn't shine from your father and he's had the name longer. It's you, Cassidy. It's what's inside you, the goodness of the person you are, that shines through and draws people to you like a moth to a flame. Don't let yourself become so jaded that you don't see the worth of who you are. I know your father has pulled one over on you, but you're still you. In that condo, in my house, in your studio . . . It's all you and that's who I'm here with now. Not a Davenport, not a socialite, not someone who's met people I've only ever heard about on the news, but Cassidy Marie Davenport. Furniture refinisher, artist, and a pretty good housekeeper after two weeks on the job." He nudged her nose with his. "I want *you*, Cassidy. You. No one else."

It almost sounded as if he was trying to convince himself or make some sort of declarative statement about something, but Cassidy was going to take him at his word. Liam was one of the few people she'd met who she *could* take at his word.

She pressed her palm to his cheek. "Then have me, Liam. Make the rest of the world disappear."

Liam didn't need any more urging. He'd barely kept himself contained with the feel of her beneath him, her soft skin cradling his hard taut body that was ready to explode with desire.

One night. That's all he needed. One night with her.

But what about all those pretty things you just said to her? Were they merely to get into her pants?

He shoved that door closed in his mind. He hadn't said them to get in her pants. Hell, he was already in her pants. He'd said them because they were true.

And he wasn't analyzing it any more than that. Not here. Not now.

He shifted his hips and she opened to let him in. "Jesus, Cass, you feel amazing." He gritted his teeth to stop himself from plunging straight into her. He wanted to savor this moment, feel every inch as she took him into her wet, hot heat, her muscles clenching around him, releasing him only to tighten again, urging him onward.

"Oh, God, yes," she gasped and arched her neck as he slipped inside.

Liam couldn't help himself; he sucked on that exposed flesh. God, she tasted so good. Felt so good.

He pulled out, smiling at her gasp, then surged in again, going deeper.

"Yes, Liam, like that."

Her nails raked his back and she locked her ankles over his ass and did some amazing wiggle thing that almost had him going off like a rocket.

He tugged on the skin of her neck with his teeth. "Holy hell, Cass. You're going to get me off before we've had any fun."

She ran her hands down his back, fingertips giving him shivers the entire way, and grabbed her ankles. "There's lots more fun where this comes from."

She arched and Liam hadn't believed it was possible to go deeper. To feel more, but the way she was taking him in . . .

He pumped into her. His body wouldn't let him not. He couldn't fight the urge and he did it again. And again. Once more. Twice, and he could feel it start. Feel the tightness in his balls and he couldn't stop it. She kept moving under him, kept rocking him forward, clenching him, and Liam, who'd always been so proud of his famed self-control, lost it. All of it. He became a feeling, moving, pounding, thrusting, love-starved being, wanting to take everything she had and then more.

"Jesus, Cass . . . I can't . . . I . . ."

"Come for me, Liam," she whispered against his jaw. "Let me feel you come."

"But you . . ." He tried to draw a breath, but it wouldn't happen. Sweat trickled down his forehead, between his shoulder blades, and in the small of his back where her heels were urging him into her.

"Just come. We have all night. You can take care of me after."

It was utterly selfish of him, but Liam didn't honestly think—when he got a few seconds *to* think—that he could stop. There was just something about Cassidy—

His orgasm took that thought and every other one out of his brain in a blinding flash of light. He arched back, might have cried out, and let the pleasure roll through him, almost too intense to take.

But he took it. And took some more. Wrung every last drop from it, even shifting a bit to prolong it.

And then she ran her fingertips up his chest, curled them into a whirl of hair over his breastbone, and tugged.

He collapsed on top of her as he slipped from her, barely remembering at the last second to catch his weight on his elbows.

"Liked that, did you?" she whispered with a smile against his ear.

He chuckled. Well, if a puffed-out breath and a flash of smile could be called a chuckle. Given the fact that he was able to even *think* that movement, the action itself was momentous. "Yeah. You could say that."

And four words. He wouldn't have thought he'd had them in him. Not after that. Not after Cassidy.

"I'm too heavy for you." He tried to will his limbs to move, but lethargy was creeping along them.

"No you're not. You feel amazing right where you are." She stroked his sides and more shivers ran through him—and put another part of him right back in the game.

"Mmmmm." He was back to being incoherent. Ah well. Incoherency had a lot to recommend it.

Especially when she circled her fingertips over his shoulder blades then buried them in his hair.

"Kiss me, Liam."

For that, his muscles moved. For that, the lethargy took a hike and energy came roaring back, and he propped himself up on his elbows and kissed her.

It was more than a kiss. It was a meeting of two souls. A moment where the physicality of their touch was outshone by the meaning and the feelings behind it. When everything in his life seemed to coalesce to that one point of contact, and he couldn't ever have enough of it. Of her.

He angled his head, thrusting his tongue into her mouth as he'd thrust into her moments ago. Had it been only moments? It seemed like a lifetime.

Uh, dude? Are you listening to yourself?

Liam thrust that nagging voice out of his head. Yeah, he was listening to himself. As he should have been listening all along.

Cassidy wasn't Rachel. She wasn't even *like* Rachel. None of this was anything like it'd been with Rachel and he'd been a fool for trying to force Cassidy into the same mold when they could have had this all along if he'd been able to get beyond his past.

He slipped his lips from hers and nipped her jaw, then down to that sweet spot behind her ear again to see if he could send shivers all over her body as she'd done to him.

"Liam—"

"Ssh." He tugged her earlobe into his mouth. "Trust me, Cass. I'm going to make this good for you."

"Mmm, yes," she moaned when he flicked his tongue over the shell of her ear.

There were those shivers.

He kissed his way down her throat and over her breasts, taking sweet, incredible time with them, making her moan and writhe beneath him.

"Liam . . . I want . . ." Her head thrashed on the pillow, her hands clenching his hair, holding him in place.

That wouldn't do.

"Grab the headboard, sweetheart."

"Mmmmm . . . wh . . . what?" Her eyes drifted open and her bottom lip, wet and plump, got sucked between her teeth.

He smiled. "Put your hands over your head and grab the headboard." He licked her nipple. "I promise you'll like it."

Her smile just about did him in, all sexy and knowing and very turned on.

"Like this?" She drug her hands up along her body, arching her back as she lifted them above her head and gripped the cross-board.

Oh yeah, he liked.

"God, Cassidy, you're beautiful." He had to catch his breath. "Inside and out."

The thought ought to scare him; she had the power to strip away the strides he'd made since Rachel, but it was worth the risk. *She* was worth the risk.

"Make love to me, Liam."

Make *love* . . . The words, the implications, threatened to take him out at the knees—so it was a good thing he wasn't using them to support himself.

Yet.

"I intend to."

He kissed her lips hard. Slipped his tongue between them to tease hers, sucked on it for barely a second, then pulled away from her.

"Hey—!" She reached for him, but Liam caught her hand.

"Ah ah ah. This"—he tapped her hand—"is supposed to

stay where it was. And this . . ." He trailed one wet fingertip along her collarbone, then angled it down over one of those perfect breasts he'd been kissing. "Is supposed to be here."

He circled her nipple, getting harder when he felt it tighten and heard her gasp.

She put her hand back on the headboard.

"Like that, did you?" He tossed her words back at her.

"Yeah." She blew out a long breath when he repeated the action on her other breast.

He raked his nails over her skin, knowing firsthand how it felt, how the shivers felt.

He stroked lower, dragging them lightly over her rib cage, liking that he could do this to her. Wanting to be the only one who could.

He shuffled backward on his knees, swirling his fingertips over her belly, smiling when it fluttered and she sucked in a harsh breath.

Then her hips moved under him.

He bit his lip but couldn't help the smile. Her hips would be moving all right.

He moved backward again, this time resting on her thighs. She was ready for him. She wanted him.

He dragged one finger down from her navel, right to the very part of her he wanted to get to know intimately.

"Yes, Liam," she gasped. "Please."

"Please what?" He circled his finger.

"That!" she gasped, her hips jerking.

"You're sure?" He flicked his finger.

"Yes." Her voice was hoarse, her breathing picking up speed.

"Or would you prefer this?" He slid one finger inside her, then a second, and felt her clench them. Oh no, she wasn't going to have it that easy.

He pulled his fingers out, smiled at her whimper, then slipped down to her feet.

Then onto the floor.

She lifted her head, her green eyes half-hooded, her lips puffy and wet.

He tugged on her ankles, bringing her down toward the bottom of the bed. "You ready?"

She groaned and her head dropped back. Her hands were too far from the headboard, but she didn't bring them to her sides, twisting them instead into the comforter above her head.

He couldn't wait to give her the same pleasure she'd given him.

He took his time, savoring every movement of her body, learning what she liked, what made her breath hitch, what made her gasp.

What made her moan.

He stroked and he sucked, and he slipped inside, his tongue and his fingers bringing her to that same writhing pleasure he'd been out of his mind with. He wanted her there. Wanted her to forget everything, everyone, anything but him.

"Yes, Liam, yes!" Her head was thrashing, her hands clutching whatever they could find, and her body was awash in the flush of desire that was so erotic as she jerked and flexed, quivering on the edge until she was begging him, so that finally he had to take her over.

She screamed out his name. Literally screamed it, making him glad he lived far enough from his neighbors that no one would be sending in the cops because he wasn't about to end this for anyone.

She came again, her thighs trying to close against the pleasure, but he wouldn't let them. He kept her legs parted and gave her every ounce of pleasure he could, tasting her until the last tremor subsided.

He kissed her thigh, then just below her navel, crawling up her body as she quivered in the aftermath, each kiss bringing another shiver.

He kissed his way up to her breasts, loving them once more.

She opened her eyes when he sucked the second one into his mouth, his tongue making lazy swirls around her nipple.

"Like that, do you?" she mimicked, a soft smile curving her lips.

"Don't get too relaxed on me, baby. The night is young." He reached for the condoms he'd dropped on the bed at her challenge and rolled onto his side to put a new one on. "Round two is just about to start."

Chapter Thirty

❦

SHE lost count of how many rounds there'd been, but the number didn't really matter. What he'd made her feel, what he'd given her . . . How was it that one of the worst moments of her life had been the start of this? Of meeting Liam and getting to know him enough that she'd not only considered going to bed with him, but had? And wanted to stay there?

It was almost funny that Dad's eviction had given her this. This moment, this place, this man. If not for that one event, she and Liam would have been ships passing in her hallway, a polite "Hello, have a nice day" relationship.

She wanted *this* relationship. She wanted him.

Finding herself was the reason she'd wanted to leave her father's house; finding Liam was a gift she'd never dreamed of.

She curled closer to him, loving the feeling of him next to her. He hadn't let go; his arm was beneath her shoulders and he was rubbing a few strands of her hair between his thumb and index finger. The tug on her scalp felt good. Made her feel wanted. Desired.

"You're quiet," he said.

"I thought I more than made up for it a few minutes ago."

She felt his chuckle. "True."

"Why? Is there something you want to talk about?" Suddenly, she was worried. He'd said they'd deal with the aftermath later. Was this that aftermath? Was he not feeling like she was?

"There is." Liam shifted so that he was on his side, but still kept his arm around her and her hair in his hand.

She liked it there. Liked that he wanted to play with it. Liked that he didn't want to let go.

"What made you the way you are, Cassidy?"

That wasn't a question she'd expected. "What do you mean? I'm just me."

He inhaled and tickled her cheek with her hair. "That's what I mean. You. How did you get to be you growing up with him?"

"Ah." Now she got it. But wasn't so sure she wanted to answer it. Not truthfully anyway.

But she didn't want a relationship without honesty between them. If he didn't like the truth, she'd be better off knowing now.

"I wasn't always like this. I used to be caught up in the society life. I liked going to parties and buying clothes and vacationing at exclusive resorts. I mean, who wouldn't, right?"

"It sounds like a shallow existence."

If she were still in that world, his words would hurt. Or maybe not since she'd been too shallow to care.

The fact that he felt that way, however, was encouraging. The first man to see through the BS and want her for her, *not* for her father's money.

You sure about that?

Cassidy shook off the thought. Liam wasn't like that. He was a stand-up guy. He was honest and hardworking and she'd bet he'd never take a handout from anyone. Liam was the kind of guy to make it on his own.

Unlike the woman she used to be.

"I'm not proud of who I was then, Liam. But that's how I was raised and it's how my world operated. Then I met Franklin."

Liam stiffened against her. And not in a good way. "Franklin?"

She rubbed a hand over his chest. Felt his heart beating beneath her palm and she left her hand there. If he only knew how symbolic that was for her.

"Franklin was a thirteen-year-old boy with a lot of medical issues. Issues that could have made him mean and bitter and nasty to be around. I sat next to him at one of the hospital's charity dinners."

"They wheeled him out to solicit donations?" Liam's jaw tightened.

"No. Nothing like that. It was one of Franklin's life wishes. That's what the foundation who'd sponsored him calls them instead of last wishes or dying wishes. They like to focus on what's left of someone's life rather than the approaching finality." She pulled her hand from Liam's chest and curled it into her own. She had a hard time talking about Franklin without welling up.

"Franklin wanted to wear a tux and go to a fancy event before he died. The dinner fell at the perfect time and he came as a guest. Sat at my table. I knew everyone there except him, and I'd grown jaded. It was just another event to me where I presented my father's donation with a lot of fanfare and smiled and looked pretty for the cameras. I made small talk with Dad's cronies and his wannabe-associates." Same old Tuesday night gala that happened too many times a year. And she'd had a new dress for each one.

"Then along came Franklin for whom everything was new and shiny and sparkly and happy. He was like Cinderella at the ball, seeing glamour in what we'd all grown so blasé about. Seeing him in his wheelchair, with his oxygen tank and his bald head that was such a contrast to his big smile and wide eyes, with his interest in everyone and everything . . . I couldn't *not* want to get to know him. But the others at our table couldn't have been bothered. He was an outsider and, even worse, underprivileged and sick. I was embarrassed for them. But the thing was, if he noticed, he didn't care. He was just happy to be there and in the moment.

And that's what got to me. What made me open my eyes. To me, he wasn't a curiosity because of his medical condition, but because of his optimism and acceptance and sheer happiness at doing something I'd started taking for granted and even resenting."

She sniffed as she remembered how his eyes had widened when the serving staff had brought out dessert. To her it'd been a piece of chocolate cake that would go straight to her hips, so she'd pushed it away. To Franklin, it'd been ambrosia. A bounty so sweet and so precious he'd had to fight himself not to gobble it up in one bite because he didn't want to miss tasting it.

She'd given him her piece and that'd sealed their friendship.

"Franklin had such an amazing outlook on life. And on death. He wasn't afraid of it. He obviously didn't want it, but when it finally came calling, he was ready to embrace it."

She, however, hadn't been and it still choked her up to remember how he'd patted her hand and smiled as best he could with the little strength he'd had left. "He'd packed a lot of living into those months I knew him, and he taught me what was important in life. Not money, not things, not other people's awe and grudging acceptance because of what you have or what your last name is or who your father is. Even when his family abandoned him to live in the group home and let society pay for his treatment, Franklin wasn't bitter. He chose to focus on the positive."

"They left him? Sick? Dying?"

She nodded. "But he didn't judge them and he taught me not to." She exhaled. "It was hard not to."

"Like when your mom left you."

"You know about that?"

"There's not much about you that hasn't made the news over the years."

She was torn between liking the fact that he'd been interested enough to pay attention and remember, and sad that he'd heard her dirty laundry.

He touched her cheek. "Hey, don't let your parents' actions

define who you are. You're your own person. Stepping out on your own, right? You don't have to be who they are."

It was the perfect thing to say. "Thank you."

"My pleasure."

Hers, too. One of the things she'd vowed when Franklin had died was to spread his message of acceptance and love and letting go of a bad past.

"Franklin was rich in friends if not family. And they became his family. Everyone loved him because he loved everyone. He accepted them as they were, even those who ignored him. He never had a mean thing to say about anyone and always had a joke or a compliment. Because, as he'd said, everyone he met was part of his journey, and since his journey wasn't going to be a long one, there was no sense focusing on the bad or dwelling on the mean. This was his one chance to experience happiness. For however many months he had left, he was going to enjoy every minute, everyone, and everything."

Franklin had been all about paying it forward, about living the life he'd been given to the fullest, and he'd been her inspiration. Her catalyst for change. Her new world view of how little her life had meant until meeting him.

She swallowed, her throat clogging with the tears she was trying hard not to shed. *Smiles, not tears.* That's how he'd wanted her to remember him.

"He was thrilled when people started bringing him plants as gifts instead of flowers." She'd never told Franklin it had been her idea because plants lasted longer than flowers. Nor that *she'd* stocked the gift shop with them and had enlisted the staff's help in having random visitors drop them off for Franklin. "We'd research every plant online and he'd decide where he wanted to plant it on the grounds. He wanted to know something would live on after him."

She lost the battle with a couple of tears then, remembering how solemn he'd been when he'd figured out that the plants would go on after he was gone.

"Hang on." Liam tilted her chin up. "Hospitals have landscape departments and boards of directors. He would have had to get approval for this, and that would have taken time. Not just anyone can plant whatever they want on hospital grounds."

She exhaled. "They can if they're backed by a Davenport donation."

"You used your father's position and money to help Franklin? Gotta love the perks that go with being a Davenport."

She tensed. People always thought that. Always thought that money made problems disappear. It didn't. There were just different problems. Case in point: her father. And Burton. People wanting what they could get from her, wanting to use her for their own benefit.

That was the beauty of her relationship with Franklin; it had been predicated on her being there for him in spirit and friendship, not for what her money could bring him.

"It allowed me to make Franklin's dream happen. He was allowed to plant whatever he wanted wherever he wanted. When he died, I had plaques made for each tree, shrub, bush, and flower so everyone would know. So he'd never be forgotten."

LIAM tried to breathe around the lump in his throat. He was right; she could never be like Rachel. He'd bet that, even before Franklin, Cassidy had had a heart and a soul she wouldn't admit to. It'd probably gone into hiding so it wouldn't be crushed by the shallow people who'd inhabited her world. "What'd your father say?"

"He . . . ah . . ." She nibbled her lip and glanced away.

"He doesn't know."

"Oh he knows that I had plaques made. He even thinks the sizable donation I made to the hospital came from the corporate charitable-giving account."

"It didn't?"

She shook her head. "It was from my bank account, not the company coffers. It was important to me that *I* do it, not the corporation, so it could be all about Franklin, not the donation. That's why the plaques don't say Davenport anywhere on them. Dad'll be mad when he finally takes the time to actually *look* at them."

Her money. That's why she didn't have any. Not because she'd spent it on fashion shows or parties or exotic locations.

Was it possible that Cassidy *was* the woman for him? That she had—aside from her father—what he was looking for?

But there were still differences between them. Big ones. Glaring ones. Million-dollar ones.

Right now, things could be easy, since it was just the two of them, but once ol' Mitch got back into the picture—and he would; the press would have a field day if this estrangement continued—the game would change.

He tilted her chin and the sheen of tears tugged at his heart. He didn't want it to change. He wanted her just like this. "So how do we do this, Cassidy? You a Davenport; me . . . not. I'm not from your world. Where do we go from here?"

The change that came over her shocked him. One minute she was all pliant and melting into his side, her arm slung peacefully across his abdomen, her fingers lightly stroking his side, and the next . . . She was scrambling off of him and not meeting his eyes.

"I'm thinking a shower and then some breakfast." She got off the far side of the bed. "I'll see you in twenty."

She practically ran out of his room—in all her naked glory. But all he could see was that she was leaving him.

What'd he say? All he'd asked was what was next for them and she'd shot out of his bed as if she couldn't get away from him fast enough.

Shit. Had the disparities in their lives sunk in just now? Was that what this was? She realized that he would never be able to give her what men like Burton and her father could, so tonight became a one-shot deal?

Had he completely misjudged the situation *again*?

Chapter Thirty-one

C ASSIDY blinked the tears back under the hot shower spray. He'd *had* to bring up the differences between how they lived, hadn't he? Had to see it. Had to ask about her father, mention her last name. Just when she'd thought her life could be different . . .

But she was still her father's daughter, which put the ugly thought in her head: had Liam taken her in out of the goodness of his heart or because of a possible financial reward? Was there a payout in this for him? Was he like Burton but using a different angle? Hoping to get on her father's good side so Dad would help his business? And how would she ever know the truth?

She hated this. Hated questioning him and his generosity, but it didn't take a genius to figure out that whoever married her would have a shot at the brass ring and she wasn't stupid. Arm candy perhaps, but there was a brain in her head, and once guys had started going down the happily-ever-after-to-the-bank-account path, she usually cut them off. She certainly hadn't let one of them get under her skin enough to sleep with him without making a few things clear up front. Well she sure as hell would now. If Liam really wanted this to go somewhere, he was going to have to prove to her that it was for the right reasons.

None of which had to do with her last name.

LIAM confronted her at the breakfast table. She didn't get to turn his world upside down, then bow out with the silent treatment. Not when he needed to know what kind of woman she was.

You know what kind of woman she is. The kind to make a sick little boy's final days everything he wanted. And not take the credit. A woman who'd rather start at the bottom than give in to her father's demands. A woman who has lost so much, but still has so much to give.

He placed a plate of scrambled eggs in front of her and put a small portion down for Titania after he'd let her out of her pen. "So you mind telling me what happened back there?" He tapped his fork on his plate, the eggs holding no great appeal at the moment.

She shoveled a forkful in, then looked up at him. "Um, we had sex?"

"I know we had sex. I'm wondering why you took off the minute I mentioned continuing it."

"Oh. Well, you know. That can get awkward."

"Awkward? Come on, Cassidy. I was in that bed with you. That was *not* awkward and you can't tell me one night is going to be all there is."

She blinked and bent down to pet Titania. He heard her inhale once more, then she looked up at him with that fake-ass smile he never wanted to see across his breakfast table again.

"Okay, Liam, suppose we do get involved. Where, exactly, do you see it going?"

"Why do I have to have a master plan? Why can't we just see where it goes?"

"Because everyone has a master plan when it comes to me. But my father isn't going to reward you for being with me. He'll only accept someone who went Ivy League and has the connections he does, or a pedigree that beats out the Rockefellers.'"

"Are you *kidding* me?" Liam dropped his fork onto his plate with a teeth-grating clatter. Maybe he *had* misjudged her after all. "You think last night was because of who your father is? Of all the fu—er, messed-up—" He sucked on the inside of his cheek. "I don't think I've ever been more insulted in my life."

Or hurt, dammit.

And that crack about Ivy League . . . Hell, he'd worked his *ass* off to put himself through college *and* get his business going. If she knew even half of what he'd done to get where he was today, she'd choke on her Ivy League.

He got up from the table and walked to the sink, looking out the window without seeing anything. Jesus Christ. Here he'd gone and let himself hope, let himself believe in another woman, and she thought *he* was using *her*. Yeah, yeah it was ironic. He'd misjudged her at the outset and now she was doing it to him.

He sucked in a breath and turned around. "I don't, you know."

Her eyes narrowed. "You don't what?"

"I don't have any ulterior motive regarding your father's company or his money or your bank account."

"That's because we both know I don't *have* a bank account."

"You know what I mean."

"No, actually, I don't." She shifted on her chair, then shoved some of her eggs around with her fork.

Titania plunked her butt on the floor and was looking between him and Cassidy as if they were playing racquetball again.

They'd made a good team on the court. And painting his office. And definitely in the bedroom. She couldn't fake all of that.

It was that last thought that made him head back to the table. He took the chair catty-corner to her and removed the ever-moving fork from her grasp. Then he tilted her chin with his finger.

There was a sparkle in her eyes that came from unshed tears. Or—as his thumb moved up her cheek—shed ones.

"I'm not like the others, Cass."

"Don't call me that."

"You didn't mind a while ago."

"A while ago I was out of my mind."

"With pleasure."

"With insanity." She got out of her chair and picked up her plate, intending to pass him on her way to the sink.

He caught her arm. "Don't, Cassidy."

She looked at his arm. "Let go, Liam. You don't own me." She cleared her throat and straightened her shoulders. "No one does. And it's going to stay that way."

He let her go because it was so important to her. He could see that now, her pride in being her own person. She didn't like being her father's little dress-up doll.

Just as he didn't like being lumped in with her father's sycophants.

He stood and headed toward her. "I'm not like those other men, Cassidy. I'm not out to get what I can from you. Or your father."

"Good because right now I'm not worth very much to him."

The pain behind her words got to him. She wasn't pushing him away because she didn't want him; she was pushing him away because she did. Because she was scared of getting hurt. Hell, the one man in the world who wasn't supposed to hurt her, the guy she ought to be able to count on for anything, had let her down. Big time. It wasn't surprising that she was leery of *his* intentions.

He put a hand on the counter on either side of her. "You're worth a lot to me."

Another tear slipped down her cheek and she quickly swiped at it. "Stop saying things like that."

He brushed the residual moisture. "Like what? Like I care about you? Like I enjoy being with you?" He took a deep breath and went for it. "Like I don't want you to leave after you sell your artwork?"

"Why?" Cassidy swept the next tear away, then crossed

her arms and cocked her hip to the side, knocking his arm off the counter. "Good sex isn't an automatic invitation to move in."

"It was great sex and you already had the invitation." He tucked some hair behind her ear.

She brushed his hand away. "I'm serious, Liam."

"You think I'm not? You're not getting it, Cass. Trust me, I don't ask just anyone to move in here."

"That's not true. You asked me and you didn't even know me."

"That was for an entirely different reason. And now I do know you."

"You *think* you know me. That"—she nodded toward his room—"isn't who I am."

Jesus. He almost wished she *was* like Rachel. Rachel would have taken him at his word and moved her stuff in before he'd said another word.

But he didn't want someone like Rachel. That's what Sean had wanted to remind him about last night—

Shit. Sean. He was supposed to have called him.

"I'm more than someone to fool around with, Liam."

He'd deal with Sean later. Right now, the woman in front of him needed him more.

He gripped her upper arms and was glad she didn't shrug him off. "I know, Cass. But that"—he repeated her nod toward his bedroom—"is part of who you are. Part of what makes me want you. I'm not going to deny that. I want you." God, did he. "But not just sexually. I like you. I want to get to know you better. I want to explore this thing between us and see where it can go. It has nothing to do with who your father is and everything do with who *you* are."

THERE. You see? You don't have to go all worst-case-scenario on the guy. Give him a chance. Give this a chance. Don't make your demons his, for crying out loud. You'll never get anywhere with anyone if you do.

Cassidy took a deep breath and let the tingles his touch evoked work their magic. Maybe she'd jumped to conclusions. Wrong ones. Liam had a successful business; he didn't *need* her money or her name.

Not that she had either at this moment.

Right. She didn't. And there was no guarantee her father would ever take her back—and no guarantee she'd go. Dad might expect it, but then, he didn't know her.

Liam did. Or, at the very least, wanted to.

She was being paranoid. Liam hadn't given her any indication that he aspired to be her father's son-in-law. He was a good guy. He worked hard, loved his family and his grandmother. Helped damsels in distress. Walked little dogs without fearing for his masculinity.

Goose bumps shivered over her skin. Liam had nothing to worry about when it came to his masculinity.

"So can we please can get beyond this morning and move forward?"

She took a deep breath and a leap of faith. "I don't want to get beyond this morning."

He released her arms and let his hands drop to his sides. "You don't."

The crushed look on his face spoke volumes—and *not* dollar signs.

It was what she needed to see. "Well, the last twenty minutes or so, sure. But the rest of this morning was pretty spectacular."

His eyebrow arched and he cocked his head. "Are you saying you want to give this a shot?"

She nodded, a little afraid to voice it. So many people had let her down in her life . . . What if she was opening herself up for another fall? What if Liam broke her heart?

Because he had the power to.

He reached for her hips and tugged her closer. "God, Cassidy. I can't believe you thought—"

She put a finger on his lips. "I was wrong, okay? Haven't you ever been wrong about someone before?"

He kissed her fingertip. "Like you wouldn't believe."

"So, then . . ." She traced his lips. "*Can* we get beyond this?"

"Yeah. We can." He nipped her finger. "As long as it means you're not going anywhere."

She put her palm on his cheek. "Not unless you want me to."

She squealed when he scooped her up in his arms.

"The only place I want you to go, lady, is back to my room."

Poor Titania had to finish her breakfast all by herself.

Chapter Thirty-two

CASSIDY and Liam spent the weekend working on his office project—well, during the day. Nights were spent at his house. In his bed. And his shower. She'd finally gotten the chance to make that fantasy a reality, and, honestly, the fantasy was a pale substitute for the reality.

"So what are we going to do today?" She stretched beside him in bed, loving the hair on his legs and chest rubbing against her skin.

He cupped her breast. "What do you say to doing nothing? Just staying here and seeing what comes up."

She slipped onto her side and ran a hand under the covers. "I have a pretty good idea of what's going to come up, Liam." Yup, sure enough, it was.

"God, Cassidy. I don't think I'm ever going to get enough of you."

The words warmed her heart. And a few other places. Places that'd gotten quite the workout over the past thirty-six hours.

She slipped her hand away. "Much as I'd like to take you up on that very impressive offer, we both have a lot to do today."

"About that." He propped a pillow under his head with one hand and grabbed hers with the other, interlacing their fingers. "I've been giving it some thought and, well, you're right."

She arched her eyebrows. "About?"

He tugged and she tumbled down beside him, catching herself on her elbow. He put their joined hands on his chest and she could feel his heartbeat, strong and steady. "The office could use some color."

She couldn't stop her smile. Nor rubbing it in. "I'm right."

He rolled his eyes. "At the risk of creating a monster, yes, you are." He released his pillow and cradled her head with that hand. "So will you paint the walls?"

It was her turn to roll her eyes. "Is this just a ploy to get out of having to paint?"

He leaned up and kissed her quickly. "Sorry, sweetheart, but I only offered because your suggestion was a good one. But, since I'm not ready to let you out of my clutches yet, this gives me the chance to have you nearby and still get the place ready. Plus, you look awfully cute on a ladder."

"Were you checking out my butt?"

"Well, sure. It's a nice butt. Sue me."

She half turned and plopped onto her back next to him. She stared at the ceiling, the feeling of Liam trusting her judgment making her giddy. "You're sure you're not just saying this because we're . . . you know?"

"You think I'd let you turn my place into a monstrosity because of sex? Cass, this is great, but I do still have to pay my bills."

Yes, she'd been teasing, but only on the outside. On the inside . . . Why was it so hard for her to accept that someone actually believed she had something to contribute? "I'm sorry for questioning you, Liam. I'm just not used to—"

"You're not used to people wanting you for you." He rolled onto his side this time and brushed her hair back from her face. "Well, get used to it, Cassidy. You've got a lot of potential and I believe in you. You can do anything you set your mind to."

He leaned down and kissed her, and Cassidy had a hard time catching her breath. The kiss was part of the reason, but the rest of it . . . His words. His meaning. His intent. If she didn't look out, she'd willingly give up her independence to spend the rest of her life with Liam Manley.

CASS, can you toss me that rag, please?" Liam was on top of the ladder, finishing scraping the shelving unit that'd been the bane of his existence for the past couple of days. She'd told him not to worry about the top—no one would see it—but he'd just raised his eyebrow and said, "Branding."

It'd made her smile again. Her work at Davenport Properties had been predicated upon her being Mitchell's daughter. She could have suggested painting the walls black—windows, too, for that matter—and no one would have said anything against her. Word would most assuredly have gone up the ladder to her father, and he would have squelched it, but no one would've been honest to her face.

Liam was more than happy to tell her when he didn't agree with her. Like dinner tonight. He'd wanted burgers on the grill; she wanted his grandmother's stew.

"I can't eat all the food she makes, Cassidy. I always end up throwing most of it away because it goes bad."

"Liam Neil Manley, don't you *ever* throw out what your grandmother makes for you. The kids at Franklin's group home would *love* to have this. If you're not going to eat it, you need to take it there and let those less fortunate than you enjoy it." She put the final brush stroke on the last wall, then tossed the rag at him.

He caught it just before it hit him on the nose, chuckling. "Place looks good."

She brushed some hair that'd escaped from her ponytail off her forehead with her bicep and smiled. "Told you so."

"So you did. Now if you're finished, I've decided I'm going to let you do the sideboard and hutch you were talking about."

"You're *letting* me?"

He winced. "Sorry. Bad word choice. I'd be honored if you'd paint the sideboard and hutch like you suggested. But they're only on loan, of course."

She set her brush in her paint tray. "That's better. And I'd be happy to do it for you. On loan, of course."

"Good. Thanks."

"My pleasure."

"Oh really?" He tossed his rag on top of the sawhorse table and the teasing in the room disappeared as her heart suddenly beat triple-time at the gleam in his eye. "Wanna come here?"

"Come . . . here?"

"Yeah. Here." He took a step down the ladder.

"For, um, what purpose?"

"You know what purpose." He took another step down.

Man, when he said that . . . *Like* that . . .

"Liam, it's broad daylight and there's not a window treatment to be found."

"I don't care about window treatments." He was off his ladder—and off his rocker, too, if he thought she'd do . . . that . . . in front of a window where anyone could see them. Especially anyone with a smart phone and an internet connection.

Still, she wouldn't mind seeing what he had in mind. Didn't mean they had to do anything tabloid-worthy, but she could have a sample . . .

She exhaled and tightened her ponytail before climbing down the ladder. This was fun, this teasing. Being able to be herself whether it was goofy or sexy or covered in paint or whatever. Liam liked her whoever she was.

She was just about to step off the bottom rung when the front door banged open.

"Liam!" A short bundle of energy barreled through the opening. "I've got a problem. I need to talk to you."

"Mac." Liam glanced at Cassidy and the teasing light in his eyes was replaced with regret. "Uh, meet Cassidy. Davenport. Cassidy, my sister, Mac."

Mac came to an immediate halt. "Oh. Uh, hi." Mac plastered a smile on her face in a matter of seconds. An impressive feat, given that it wasn't a Showpiece smile but a *genuine* one from what Cassidy could tell. "So nice to meet you. We've spoken on the phone, I believe."

"Actually, that was Deborah. My father's assistant." Because Deborah always handled issues with "the help." God, the first time Cassidy had heard a friend refer to someone that way after she'd met Franklin, she'd been horrified. People were people no matter what their bank accounts said, and to hear the open derision . . .

She brushed off her hands and held one out. "Hi. Yes, I'm Cassidy. It's nice to meet you."

"Liam told me what happened, but I didn't think he'd make you do manual labor to pay him back."

"Oh I'm not—"

"Mac, that's not what this is." He put a hand behind his sister's back. "Come on. Let's go into the kitchen and you can tell me what you need. Cassidy has to get to work on her own projects, actually." He looked at her as he headed into the other room. "Do you mind, Cass?"

"No. You're right. I do have work to do." And she wasn't going to begrudge him time with his sister.

Until she overheard what Mac said.

"I got a call from Davenport, Lee. That Deborah woman Cassidy mentioned. Davenport's interested in contracting me to handle all of his buildings in the tri-state area."

"Hey, that's great! Congrats!"

Cassidy had a feeling it wasn't as great as Liam thought. She didn't believe in coincidences when it came to her father. He was up to something.

"No, Lee, you don't get it. I can't sign the contract knowing you have Cassidy in your home."

"Why the hell not? What does it matter what your brother does with his life when it comes to Davenport hiring you?"

"You're not that naïve, Lee. He's dangling this carrot because he knows where she is."

"So? Cassidy's a grown woman; she can live where she

wants. It's not like he's going to put something in the contract about his daughter."

Oh he very well might. Dad always got what he wanted in business. He knew how to exploit a weakness, and having the Davenport properties would put Mac's business in a whole other league and Dad knew it. A smart businesswoman wouldn't turn it down.

Mac exhaled. "On second thought, maybe you *are* that naïve. He won't *have to* put anything about her in the contract; if he wants her back, all he'll have to do is threaten to badmouth my company. The guy's got clout. I don't need my business getting bad PR, and I certainly don't need my clients questioning my ethics. I can't risk everything for this one contract."

"And of course you want it."

"Wouldn't you?"

Liam sighed loudly. "You want me to kick her out."

Cassidy's stomach thudded. Liam was choosing between her and his sister, and while she would've liked to have won, she couldn't blame him for choosing his family first. Especially when it was in a face-off against her father.

"Well, no. Obviously I don't want you to have to do that, but how much longer is she going to be staying with you? I don't want to have to keep pretending I don't know. This is a really big opportunity for me, Lee. It could make my company."

But Cassidy was standing in the way.

Her father really was a manipulative, controlling bastard to do this to her. His own flesh and blood. She didn't understand how or why her parents had walked out on her. *Both* of them. She barely remembered Mom leaving, except for the tears and the incredible sense of abandonment and loneliness. Dad had actually been good back then, buying her ponies and taking her to Disney World and on cruises, spending all sorts of time with her so that she didn't miss Mom quite so much. She'd carried that damn picture with her for so long. The one of her and Mom on the beach. And the bracelet they'd made together. She'd thought Mom had left them behind so Cassidy wouldn't forget her, but when she hadn't even called—not once—Cassidy had realized that she'd left them behind because she hadn't cared. And she, idiot that she was, had kept them.

Well, good. Now she was glad she'd left them at the condo. Ending all of it in one fell swoop. Time to move on.

With Liam?

Obviously not. It was one thing for her to stand up to her father and walk out, but she couldn't jeopardize Mac's business.

She needed her get-out-of-servitude money right now. And there was only one way she was going to be able to do that.

She let herself out and closed the door quietly behind her.

The fairytale was over. Prince Charming Liam might be, but it was up to *her* to save him from the evil father.

Chapter Thirty-three

❧

AT the studio again. I'll be back late. Don't wait up. ~C.
This was getting ridiculous. Liam put the note down
that Cassidy had left on the kitchen counter *again*. Five days
in a row now. It was as if they weren't living together, hadn't
started something together.

She'd slept in his bed; that much he knew because her
scent lingered on the pillow, and he might have imagined a
kiss or two, but that was it. She even took Titania with her
when she left.

She'd overheard Mac's problem and was working as much
as possible to remove herself from her father's bargaining
table as leverage.

He liked that she was getting her life in order. Moving
forward. Working for her future. He got that, but the quick
conversations—"Working." "Paint's drying." "Gotta run."—
weren't cutting it for him.

He crumpled the note and laughed at himself. He certainly couldn't say she was using him.

Still, he brought up her number on his phone just to hear

her voice and was about to hit CALL when another call came through. "Liam Manley."

"Manley, Mitchell Davenport. I have two prospective buyers coming by this afternoon and there is a layer of dust all over this condo. Be here in ten minutes."

The call ended before Liam had the chance to respond.

Which was a good thing because what Liam wanted to say to the man would have killed Mac's contract in two not-so-nice words.

CASSIDY heard the phone but couldn't pick it up. She was in the middle of linking the vines from one door to the other and needed a steady hand to complete the stroke, and talking to Liam made her less than steady. It'd been torture to have to fall asleep next to him each night and not wake him up. But two A.M. was a rotten time to rouse someone, especially when she got up three hours later anyway. She didn't know how much longer she could keep up this pace, but at least she'd finished a few of the pieces.

Not enough of them, however.

She'd finally mustered the courage—or rather, desperation—to call Jean-Pierre and, thankfully, he was willing to give her another shot—*if* she could get the pieces to him by Tuesday.

Since he'd had an artist back out of a show—that guy would never work in this town again—she'd figured Jean-Pierre was desperate, too. So even though it was an insane turnaround time, she wasn't going to blow the opportunity. Liam would still be there once the show was over.

She smiled. Yes, he would. She knew that as surely as she knew that she wanted him to be.

So she was working fifteen, eighteen, twenty-hour days to get it all done. Drying time was a pain because it was the one thing she couldn't control. She'd found a fan in someone's garbage—wouldn't her father just love to hear *that*—to help with the drying process, but it was a poor imitation of an industrial one. Still, beggars couldn't be choosers. And a beggar was what she could be if this didn't go well.

It *had* to go well. Not just for her, but for Liam, too. And Mac. Cassidy had to make it on her own so she could get out of their lives to protect their businesses from her father.

Titania growled as the back door opened.

"Titania, hush!" Cassidy wiped up the smudge her brush made when she'd been jarred by the noise, then brushed off her hands, and stood. "Hello?"

"*Bonjour, ma chèrie.*" Jean-Pierre walked into the studio, the look on his face speaking volumes as he glanced around.

It wasn't the nicest place, but at least it wasn't messy. She'd gotten more organized now that she was on her own—now that her father wasn't looking over her shoulder. Sure, it'd been childish to mess up the inside of her cabinets and drawers, but it'd made her feel good. Had given her some semblance of control. Now she really had control and could live her life the way she wanted. "I know these aren't the best digs, Jean-Pierre, but the light is good and so is the space." Not to mention the price.

"This is the piece you told me about?" Jean-Pierre cocked his head and walked around the hutch, tapping the side of his mouth. "I like the composition. The design is eclectic enough to appeal to a broad audience, and the skill is impeccable." He kissed both of her cheeks. "You have talent, *ma belle*. Pity your father can't pull his head out of his ass long enough to realize it."

Say what? Cassidy did a double take. Jean-Pierre felt like that about her father? There weren't many people who'd vocalize their dislike for Mitchell Davenport. If she'd known he felt like that, she would've called him weeks ago.

"So where is the rest? I still have the ones from before, but they aren't nearly enough for a show. You do have more, *oui*?"

She led him behind the Japanese folding screen someone had put out on the curb. So many people discarded quality pieces when all they'd need to do was replace a dovetail joint or hardware or hinges and do some touch-up work. But

Cassidy wasn't about to share that secret with the world; it gave her the inexpensive—free—"canvases."

"*Excellent!* This mirror, *c'est merveilleux.*" Jean-Pierre ran his fingers a millimeter above the "magic mirror" she'd created. "This will sell. I know someone to call already. She has been looking for a special piece for her daughter's room. *C'est parfait.*" He made the quintessential French move of kissing his fingertips. Cassidy thought Jean-Pierre sometimes overplayed his nationality just for the drama.

"And this armoire. I like it. I have a few people in mind for it. As I did for that bombe chest your father insisted on buying back." The word that followed was one of the foulest in the French language.

But then he exhaled, grabbed her by her arms, and air-kissed both cheeks. "The exhibit, she will be *magnifique*, Cassidy. I shall have everything set just so for Tuesday night. We will sell each piece you make, and perhaps . . ." He looked around the studio and found a few pieces she had yet to work on. "*Oui.* You shall bring these as they are. Unfinished. We shall have a silent auction for the highest bidder's personalization. You will be a sensation."

And she'd have her walk-away money.

"Sounds good, Jean-Pierre. I'll prep two pieces for the auction."

"*Magnifique!*" He air-kissed her cheeks again. "Then I shall leave you to your painting. As many as possible by Tuesday morning. That will barely give me time to stage them, but, at the last minute, we shall do the best we can. Thank goodness you were available. It has worked out well."

"Yes, it has." Almost *too* well, but maybe Franklin had put in a good word for her with St. Peter or something.

This was going to be it for her. Her big break. She'd show her father.

Not that he'd show. He never attended these events; they were her responsibility. Tuesday night, that would work to her advantage. Her art would sell on its merits, not her name, and there was nothing her father would be able to do about it without it coming back—very publicly—to bite him in the ass.

It was about time something did.

JEAN-PIERRE brushed some lingering abandoned-building dust off his one-hundred-percent silk sleeve, and suppressed a shudder as he walked back to his Aston Martin. Mitchell Davenport could cry all the way to the tabloids about Tuesday's event, but *no one* bought back a piece Jean-Pierre had sold, it didn't matter for *how* much money. Jean-Pierre had slaved and sacrificed to build his name and his gallery on this side of the Atlantic, and a crass new-money man like Davenport was *not* going to sully it. Let him publicly cause a problem for his daughter and he'd be the one who came out looking like a fool. The girl had talent, as the world was about to find out.

He smiled at the hum of his prized car. A car paid for by the hard work of the artists he'd helped launch. Mitchell Davenport had no idea who he'd messed with, but he was going to find out.

Jean-Pierre picked up his cell and dialed a number he knew by heart. C. Marie was going to have a bigger name in her art world than her father had in his. Jean-Pierre would see to it.

Chapter Thirty-four

❧

SOMEONE was licking his toes.

Liam squirmed in that half-sleep/half-wake moment, the tongue on his skin registering instantaneously.

As did the hard-on under his covers.

Then little teeth gnawed on his toe and he shot up in his bed, yanked his toe away, and was glad as hell that his erection shriveled up when he saw it was *Titania* who'd been licking his toes.

"What are you doing here, mutt?"

"Titania?"

The dog dove under his pillow when Cassidy's hoarse whisper echoed in from the hallway.

"She's in here." Liam arranged the covers over his lap, then wondered why. Cassidy had already seen it. Though much too long ago.

She poked her head around the doorframe, soft brown waves cascading over her shoulder, and he wanted to scoop her up in his arms and reacquaint her with what was beneath the covers.

Except he had to go to work.

For her father.

"I'm sorry. I didn't mean for her to wake you."

He grabbed his cell and checked the time. "It's seven and you're still here? Are you taking the day off?"

"I wish, but no. Jean-Pierre's counting on me."

"He's selling your work again?"

"Better than that." She plopped her butt on his bed beside him and oh what he'd like to do with her if they had the time. "I'm having a show tomorrow night."

"A show! That's fantastic! I'm happy for you."

And for him. Cassidy was doing it; she was putting her money where her mouth was—or, more specifically, her actions where her money was going to be.

Cassidy was making it on her own.

Funny how when he found a woman who would, he didn't want her to have to. He wanted to share the burdens with her. And her triumphs. And a lot more, as well.

"Thanks. That's why I've been working nonstop. I need to get back now, too; I'm almost finished. But little Miss Houdini here"—she felt under the pillows for the mutt who was scooting backward toward his headboard—"managed to escape her collar and ran back to see you."

Thank God for the mutt. "I don't mind if it gives us a few minutes to talk." He ran his fingers along her arm. "I've missed you."

She tossed her hair over her shoulder, and the look she gave him was a few degrees away from setting his sheets on fire. "I miss you, too."

Awareness swirled around them and Liam was just about to lean in and say to hell with the day job when he could have Cassidy instead, when Titania stuck her cold nose out from under the pillow, right into the small of his back.

"Holy hell!" Liam wriggled to the edge of the bed so fast it was as if he'd been shocked with a live wire. "Jesus. That dog's nose is *cold*!"

Cassidy scooped the little terror up. "Well you know what they say about cold noses and warm hearts."

"That's cold *hands* and warm hearts."

Cassidy touched his hand. "Hmmm, I certainly hope that adage isn't true or I'm out of luck where you're concerned."

He stroked her cheek. "No way, baby. You'll never be out of luck where that's concerned."

"Good. Hang on to that thought. Once tomorrow night is over, we'll see how well my luck's holding out."

That was the thing with luck; sometimes you could help it along.

LIAM set the bucket of cleaning supplies down to unlock the door to Cassidy's old condo. The place didn't need any more cleaning thanks to Davenport's little command performance phone call, but since he was doing the other one, he thought he'd make a pit stop and wanted to look legit.

While he took more of Cassidy's clothes.

She needed something to wear tomorrow night and he could tell from her work-focused brain this morning that she hadn't gotten that far. Her jerk of a father had created this mess; he could damn well pony up a dress and a pair of shoes for his daughter's big night.

Just as long as he didn't show up to ruin it.

The door opened and Liam grabbed the bucket. He took that first doozy of a step into the place when, suddenly, his day went straight to hell.

"My daughter is off limits and I want her out of your house by the end of the week." Mitchell Davenport stood by the fireplace, an arm resting on the mantel as if he was Daddy Warbucks. "And don't think for a minute that you'll be getting your hands on any of my money."

"Well happy Monday to you, too." Liam hefted the bucket of supplies and headed to the right, glad he'd planned for this possibility, though he'd been thinking more along the lines of neighbors seeing him go into the place, not Davenport himself. "I'm just going to get started in the bathroom." Since he was already dealing with crap.

"I'm not finished speaking to you."

Liam cocked an eyebrow. "I'm contracted to clean, not listen. And since I'm on the clock, I better get to work."

"Don't walk away from me. What I want, I get. And I want you out of Cassidy's life."

Liam's grip tightened on the bucket handle. "What do you care?"

The asshole dropped his arm from the mantel and walked toward Liam, his eyes narrowed. "My daughter is my business, not yours, and if you don't want to see your sister's company go down in a hail of bad publicity, I suggest you follow my orders. I always get what I want. Remember that."

Yeah, well after tomorrow night, he'd be getting what he deserved: Cassidy making it on her own with no help from this guy.

But he had to protect Mac as well as give Cassidy the time for all of it to come together.

"Okay. Fine. I get it. Cassidy out. Are we finished?"

Davenport smiled and Liam actually wanted to cringe. There was no warmth, no amusement, nothing but cold calculation in that smile.

"If she's not out by Friday, *you'll* be finished. Got it? And your sister, too. I want my daughter back where she belongs."

It was on the tip of Liam's tongue to tell the guy to go to hell—where *he* belonged—but that would only satisfy him for a few seconds. Seeing Cassidy pull off tomorrow night and have fuck-you money to toss in her father's face? That satisfaction would last forever.

Because he planned to be a part of that forever.

Chapter Thirty-five

୧᠁ᢀᢀᢀᡒ

"DO I look okay?" Cassidy fidgeted with the fake diamond earrings for the fifth time since getting into his truck.

"You look beautiful, Cassidy. That dress looks great on you." He'd pulled half a dozen from her closet with shoes to match, bundling them up in a garbage bag, giving himself a laugh. Especially when he'd seen Davenport's car still in its reserved spot when he'd left. Taking the merchandise out right under the guy's nose. Davenport would never miss it, and if he did, he wouldn't create a scene in public. But Cassidy would come off looking like a million bucks—hopefully while *earning* a million bucks.

He wanted to tell her she didn't need the money. That he had enough for them to get started together and she'd make more once her work started selling consistently. He wasn't going to ask her to pay him back for staying at his place—he was going to ask her to stay permanently. But not tonight. Tonight was her night. Her chance to make it on her own, to prove that she could. He'd waited this long; he could wait a little longer.

"Come on, sweetheart. We don't want to be late for your

big night." He opened her door, then tugged the sleeves of his tuxedo jacket down. Been a while since he'd had to get this dressed up. The last black-tie event he'd been to had been with Rachel.

It was much better going with Cassidy.

"Okay, I'm ready." She took a couple of deep breaths and tugged the neckline of the midnight blue gown up a little.

Damn. He liked it lower. Then again, he didn't want anyone else liking it lower.

"But remember," she said as she slid her hand into the crook of his elbow, "this isn't *my* big night. It's C. Marie's and she's not here. Bit of an introvert, apparently. But I hear she does beautiful work."

He closed the truck door and covered her hand with his. "I heard that, too. Maybe we should buy one to get the process started."

He'd been teasing, but when she put her hand on his chest and looked at him, there was no teasing about anything.

If they weren't standing across the street from the gallery and she hadn't just spent an hour doing her hair and makeup—which she hadn't needed to do—he'd kiss her senseless.

"Thank you, Liam, but no. You are not to buy anything. I need other people to so they can have it in their homes and talk about it when friends come to visit. Word of mouth and actually seeing my work, that's what'll get people interested. I just hope I sell *some*."

"Not Gran's piece."

"No. I had Jean-Pierre mark it as sold."

"What about the hutch and sideboard? I know you need the cash, so if they don't sell, I'll rent them from you."

"You're not paying me anything for them. You've done more than enough."

He wanted to do so much more.

He had to chuckle at himself. He'd almost let her slip through his fingers, but when had Cassidy Davenport crept under his skin and touched his soul? When had this woman he'd thought the worst of become one he could see the best in? When had he fallen in love with her?

"Liam? You ready?"

"I am." For so much more than she knew.

CASSIDY took a deep breath, clenched Liam's arm a bit tighter, and walked into the gallery.

It was packed. Cassidy hadn't realized that the other artist who was supposed to have been here tonight had such a big following. If all of these people had come to see *her* work, there'd be no way she'd pull out of the event, artistic temperament or not.

"Cass, some champagne?" Liam waved the glass under her nose. "Might help calm you," he whispered, his breath on her skin doing *nothing* to calm her.

She took the glass and drank about a third of it because champagne flutes were too small and she was *wired*. The frenzy to get everything finished while maintaining quality . . .

There were two pieces she'd refused to include. They hadn't been up to her standards and, as she'd told Liam, branding was all about giving people a certain experience. If her work didn't pass the C. Marie standards she'd set, they hadn't gone into Jean-Pierre's moving van.

"Cassidy? It *is* you. What are you doing here? I didn't think you were, well, that you were representing Davenport Properties anymore."

Carolina Hutchinson was one of her "circle," someone who'd gone to all the same events, shopped at the same stores, had attended the same boarding school. Cassidy wouldn't exactly call them friends, and with the speculation going on in Carolina's eyes vis-à-vis the piece in the *Herald*, Cassidy would go with *frenemies* to describe their relationship.

But she slapped that Showpiece smile on, handed her champagne flute to a passing server, and worked the moment like she used to. "Oh you know the rumor mill, Carolina." She tugged Liam beside her. Nothing could change Carolina's focus quicker than an attractive man. "Carolina, may I present my date, Liam Manley? Liam, this is Carolina Hutchinson. We went to school together."

Liam's bottom lip twitched and she prayed he wouldn't laugh. He'd understood her relationship with Carolina immediately.

As predicted, Carolina latched onto Liam and the topic of Cassidy's life was forgotten in the face of trying to then pull the woman off him in the figurative sense. Carolina had sat through far too many etiquette classes to make that sort of spectacle of herself, but Liam was hot and Carolina wasn't blind. She was, however, opportunistic, and it was all Cassidy could do not to tell her what Liam did for a living. While it didn't matter a hill of beans to her, Carolina would have a stroke being seen talking to a general contractor. In their world, they *hired* general contractors, not *dated* them.

Cassidy looked around. There were a lot of familiar faces. People from her previous life who were caught up in being out and being seen. A typical Tuesday night gathering like the ones she'd come to abhor.

Interesting how being on the other side of it wasn't so abhorrent. No, it was thrilling, actually. Fun. Exciting. Would people enjoy her work? Would they like it enough to purchase it? Would this be her one and only show, or would it make a name for her, er, C. Marie, so that her dream of being on her own and supporting herself this way actually came true?

She smiled, she talked, she commented on C. Marie's work, all the while supremely aware that she wasn't the same person who'd been at the last art exhibit here. Nor was her date.

Liam was beside her the whole time. It might be because he didn't know anyone, but Burton had always been off networking, making contacts to fit in with Dad's view of who he should be. It was nice having a man beside her who was comfortable in his own skin and not trying to be the person someone else wanted him to be.

Jean-Pierre gave his welcoming speech and spoke about the artist, then schmoozed his way around the place as he usually did before slipping beside her and pressing another glass of champagne into her hand, making it look for all the world to see as if she were just another patron.

The whisper in her ear told a different story.

"You are a hit, *ma belle*. The pieces are selling. The auction is higher than I'd thought it'd go, and the night is still young. You are a sensation. There will be demand for C. Marie's furniture for years to come. Congratulations." He kissed her cheek. "And I do get to tell you I told you so."

She blinked the tears away. No need to make a spectacle. Cassidy Davenport shouldn't have tears at this event. "Thank you, Jean-Pierre. I owe it all to you."

"*Non, ma chère.* You owe it to your talent and your hard work. I am just the vessel by which your message is conveyed to your admirers. Here's to many more exhibits together."

He *chinked* his glass to hers and for a moment she allowed herself to feel the joy and the satisfaction. She was going to be okay.

But then her father walked in.

"What's he doing here?" She reached for Liam, but he was a few feet away, trying to extricate himself from Carolina's clutches yet again.

"Who?" Jean-Pierre raised his glass and looked around the gallery. "Your father? He was invited, of course. As always."

"But he never comes to these things." He couldn't have known she'd be here.

She was trying not to hyperventilate. It was one thing to tell Dad that he was wrong, to enjoy the moment when she could throw sales figures in his face and tell him she was on her own, but another to do it in a packed gallery where everyone could overhear them.

She worked hard to plaster that damn smile on, but for the first time in her life, she wasn't sure she could. Why'd he have to come tonight? Why, this one exhibit of all of

Jean-Pierre's exhibits, did he decide to show up? Was it because it was hers? And if so, how had he known?

"Cassidy." Her father strode over to her with poor Burton in tow, and Cassidy could swear the noise level in the place dropped a few thousand decibels.

"Dad. Burton."

"Cassid—"

"How could you, Cassidy?" Her father cut Burton off. Burton had better get used to it if he planned to have a future at Davenport Properties—and that would be the only future he'd get with Davenport attached to it. "I specifically told you not to."

Cassidy linked her arm through her father's to throw off the pack of gossip wolves and tried to nudge him away from the crowd. She was not having this conversation in front of everyone. "Perhaps we could discuss this somewhere else?"

He wasn't budging. "Why? Have something to hide?"

She didn't know what to say. That was the first time she could ever remember him calling not just her, but *anyone*, out publicly. Usually he did it with such panache that the person on the receiving end of his anger never realized it until it was too late.

Was it too late? Was this the end of her new beginning? Was Dad going to cause such a scene that people would rethink their purchases? That they'd be too scared of Mitchell Davenport's reach that they'd pass on her work simply to keep him happy?

Oh, no. Not this time. He didn't get to do this to her now. She'd had no choice when he'd removed her from the design team because it was his company, but now, this, tonight . . . this was *hers*.

"No, I don't have anything to hide. Including the fact that C. Marie and I—"

Her father grabbed her arm, spun her a hundred and eighty degrees, and stormed off with her toward Jean-Pierre's office—with Burton in tow. Again. "Don't say a word."

"But you asked me a question and I was answering it."

Her father practically shoved her into the office. "Burton, close the door."

It was yanked open not two seconds later and Liam strode in. "Leave her alone, Davenport."

"Oh, good God." Her father rolled his eyes. "You've gotten yourself another puppy, yet you throw an infinitely more acceptable man out to the curb. What is wrong with you, Cassidy?"

He was talking about *her* collecting puppies? Of all the ridiculous accusations . . .

"Look, you arrogant son of a bitch." Liam shoved his jacket sleeves back. "You don't get to talk to her like that. Not anymore. Not after the stunt you pulled with the *Herald*. Backfired on you, didn't it?"

"The *Herald*? What's he talking about, Dad?"

Her father didn't answer her, but he pushed his sleeves up as well. "You don't know what you're talking about."

Cassidy had to step between them. Her father would press charges if Liam so much as brushed by him, and Liam wouldn't be able to beat—or afford—Dad's lawyers.

"Don't I?" Liam took a step closer.

"Dad, Liam, stop." She pushed both men's chests to separate them. Liam's was heaving, but Dad was Mr. Cool. It'd always annoyed the hell out of her that she couldn't get a rise out of him even when she'd purposely done something wrong. No, Mr. Analytical had let her have her temper tantrum and would only speak to her when she'd "gotten it out of her system." There was no winning with him if anyone went off emotionally.

"Liam, I appreciate you defending me, but I can handle this. He is, after all, my father." She rolled her shoulders back and stared her father in the eye. "How did you know about tonight? I can't believe that you suddenly decided to patronize the arts tonight of all nights."

"He probably had you tailed." Liam took a step closer to her and, man, it was nice having someone have her back.

Her father adjusted his jacket, the supposed epitome of style.

Style came in many forms and his was sorely lacking.

"You'd like to think that, wouldn't you? But the truth is, Cassidy, that your buddy Manley, here, gave it up when he walked out of the condo with a bag of your gowns." He glared at Liam. "Did you really think I wouldn't notice that you stole them? Or did you *want* me to come after you so I could take her off your hands?" Dad did that little smirk she'd always found so irritating. "Unbelievable. You had the brass ring in your hand and you're giving her away."

"Brass ring?" Liam obviously found it irritating, too. "Brass *ring?* Are you out of your fucking mind? She's not some trophy to be won. Not a prize to auction off to the highest bidder. Or in this case, the most malleable one."

Burton looked as if he was going to say something, but thankfully, thought better of it. Her father had chosen Burton for a reason and having a backbone wasn't it.

"You mean like that cheap publicity stunt going on out there? Auctioning off her services like a, well, I don't have to say it." Her father looked at her as if she was exactly what he was intimating. "At what point, Cassidy, do you plan to reveal who C. Marie is? I'd recommend doing it before the auction closes. The Davenport name will raise bids considerably."

"She's good enough to have this exhibit on her own merits, Davenport."

Cassidy had to grab Liam's arm before he hauled off and decked her father. Not that she wouldn't applaud, but neither of them needed the nightmare that would entail.

"She doesn't need your name to make one for herself."

"Oh really?" Dad crossed his arms, looking so damn smug that *Cassidy* wanted to haul off and deck him. "Then explain the invitation I received today. The one saying you'd be hawking your wares like a common street vendor."

"Invitation?" That took the wind out of her sales. Someone had intentionally told her father what she was doing? *With an invitation?* "What invitation? I didn't send you an invitation."

"Well Deborah handed one to me."

"Where'd she get it?"

"I didn't ask. I presume from the manager here."

"But that's not possible. Jean-Pierre didn't send out invitations with my name on them. This was a last-minute show."

"I knew it wouldn't be long before that opportunistic immigrant tried to capitalize on your name. He probably expects me to buy back every piece you sell tonight at the exorbitant price I bought the last one for."

"Don't you dare." Cassidy got in his face and wouldn't back down. Not about this. She didn't have to kowtow to him anymore. "I want you to leave, Dad. You'll only make a scene and neither of us wants that."

"You think they're not already talking out there? The *Herald* saw to that weeks ago."

"And you're just fueling the gossip. Why, Dad? Is all of this worth the clean-up you're going to have to do *if* I were to do what you want?"

Liam put his hand on her waist and she squeezed it. No way was she doing what her father wanted. And *not* because she had Liam. But he was another reason not to.

"You need to leave, Dad. Without making a scene. Just let it go. I'm not going to marry Burton." She looked at Burton. "I'm sorry, Burton. You're a nice guy, but I'm not in love with you."

She was, however, in love with Liam.

The thought flashed in her brain and at that moment, Cassidy knew it was right. There was no big fanfare, just a warm tingly feeling of acceptance. She was in love with Liam, and her father could never take that from her.

"Think very carefully about what you're doing, Cassidy. If I walk out that door, I won't give you another chance. Burton will be gone."

Oh she was thinking carefully. Of a future with Liam. A future where she could be who she'd become.

"Dad, don't make it like this. Accept that I'm not going to marry Burton and let it go. You have to do some damage control, since everyone out there is talking about you throwing me out. I can't believe you didn't see that coming."

"You weren't supposed to go. And you definitely weren't supposed to stay out. You were supposed to come back. Any sane, rational woman would have come back."

"Mitchell, what is going on here? What are you doing to my daughter?"

Everyone turned to the back door where a woman in an evening gown stood.

A woman who looked a lot like an older version of Cassidy.

"*Mom*?" Cassidy felt around for a chair to sit in before her knees gave out.

There wasn't one, but Liam was the next best thing. He put both hands on her waist and leaned her back against him. "Stay strong, babe," he whispered in her ear. "You can do this."

She wasn't so sure about that. She had mixed feelings about her mother. There'd been no contact for years; why on earth had she shown up tonight of all nights?

To see her now . . . It was too much. This whole night was too much. What had begun as her triumph was fast unraveling into a nightmare of epic proportions.

"I came as soon as I could, Cass." Her mother walked toward her, tears in her eyes. "When I learned you were finally out of his house and on your own, I came as quickly as I was able to. He can't touch you anymore, honey. He can't keep us apart."

Her father took a step closer. "Elizabeth—"

Liam tensed behind her, and Mom held up her hand. "No, Mitchell. We're through. My daughter made her decision. She left. You have no hold on me anymore."

"Hold?" Cassidy really needed to sit down. Things were happening too fast. It was as if all her worlds were converging at once. "What are you talking about?"

"He—"

"Don't do this, Elizabeth." Her father clicked his heels together and stood straighter, that demanding tone Cassidy had heard for years even sharper now. More lethal.

Her mother tilted her chin. "Your threats won't work anymore, Mitchell. You can't do anything to me now."

"Don't be so sure of that."

"Will one of you please tell me what you're talking about? What happened that was big enough to send my mother to another country to get away from me?"

Mom cleared her throat and glared at Dad. "It's done, Mitchell. I'm telling her. I suggest you send your little toady out of the room if you don't want the world to know."

For the first time ever, her father actually backed down. "Burton, if you wouldn't mind."

"No problem, sir."

Cassidy rolled her eyes as he left. *Sir.*

"You, too, Manley. This conversation is private."

Liam squeezed her waist. "Cass?"

She thought about it. She should face them on her own. This was, after all, her life and they had yet to define Liam's place in it. But she didn't want him to leave. She wanted him to be here. It was as simple as that.

"Liam stays." He might as well know the bad with the good.

Mom actually clapped. "Brava, Cass. Stand up to him. Be your own person."

Cassidy looked at her mother. A little older, but still exactly how Cassidy remembered her. Cassidy had searched online for her over the years, but never found any mention of her after the divorce. It'd been as if she'd disappeared. Cassidy hadn't known if she'd died or had another family, or had ever tried to contact her.

Well, obviously she hadn't. With all the publicity her father had gotten over the years and the fact that his company was still in the same building, Cassidy would have been easy to find. Yet her mom never looked.

"My name is Cassidy. You don't have the right to call me anything else. Why did you leave? What happened that made you leave your four-year-old daughter?"

Her mother took a deep breath and blew it out. "I didn't want to. I wanted to take you with me. But Mitchell threatened to destroy me if I did."

Cassidy crossed her arms and looked at her father. "Gee, there's a surprise."

Dad scowled and for once, he wasn't the arrogant, in-charge, alpha guy she'd always known. "Don't do this, Elizabeth." He was almost pleading.

Cassidy's stomach went hollow. Maybe she *didn't* want to know what they were talking about.

God, what she wouldn't give for her previous shallow, hedonistic lifestyle. Maybe that's why that world was that way, so no one would have to deal with emotions.

"I had an affair and as punishment, your father refused to let me see you."

Emotions like betrayal. Who kept a child from her mother?

"Goddam it, Elizabeth! I warned you if you ever came back that I'd—"

"What, Mitchell? Cut me off? You did that anyway. From the only thing that ever meant anything to me. My daughter."

"You were more than willing to walk away with a nice fat checkbook if memory serves."

"I had no choice."

"You had every choice. You had the choice not to sleep with that, that . . . that man."

They were arguing, but Cassidy couldn't get beyond the fact that her father had kept her from her mother as *punishment*. And not just her mother's punishment but hers as well.

"I needed a mother, Mitchell." She couldn't call him Dad. Not now. She wasn't sure she'd ever be able to again. Not after the eviction and not after what he'd put her through back when she'd been four. And five. And six. And all the other times a girl needed her mother. All for his damned pride.

"Look, I get that you two got a divorce, but someone please explain to me why *I* had to pay the price. The divorce wasn't enough?"

Mitchell waved his hand as if she was an annoying gnat—a feeling she'd had all too many times over the years. "You wouldn't understand, Cassidy—"

"Don't tell me I wouldn't understand. I was a child. A *child*. And you took my mother from me. Just like you're trying to take the rest of my life away by forcing me to marry someone I don't love. Who *are* you? What sort of control freak does that to a person? I was innocent. And scared. And alone. And you pawned me off on nannies because your ego had been bruised because she wanted someone else over you."

"And you." She faced her mother. Her mother wasn't getting off any easier. "You let him. With your big divorce settlement, you certainly could have afforded to come visit me. It's not as if he shipped you off destitute to a penal colony. So where have you been all these years?"

She was close to breaking. Anger could only sustain her so far, but oh my God, all the wasted years when she'd asked for her mother and been ignored.

Well, dammit, she was going to be heard. For the first time in his life, Mitchell Davenport was going to hear her.

Liam obviously did because he tugged her back against him and wrapped his arms around her waist, giving her his strength.

Her mother pulled the chair out from behind Jean-Pierre's desk and sat. "Mitchell and I should never have gotten married. I wanted a family; he wanted an empire. Guess who won that battle?"

Mitchell said nothing.

"He got his empire and I got lonely. I'm not proud of it, but, yes, I had an affair."

"With my head of security." Condescension dripped from Mitchell's words.

"He was a good man, Mitchell."

"Don't give me that bullshit, Elizabeth. I was building our future and you threw it away."

"You were building your empire, Mitchell, and I was the pretty little wife who was supposed to host your parties. I was supposed to keep your house and go to garden parties and charity events and sing your praises."

All of which sounded sadly familiar. Cassidy wrapped her arms around herself. He'd made her into her mother—and then taken his anger at her mom out on her.

"I hated you for that, Mitchell. I hated your coldness, your way of making *me* feel inadequate. Of feeling as if you'd reached your potential and I was still the same small-town girl you'd married. You looked down on me and I knew it." She cleared her throat and her voice softened. "Jim . . . He didn't look down on me. He liked me. And then, he loved me."

"That doesn't excuse what you did, Elizabeth. Why you tore this family apart."

"I—"

"Enough." Cassidy left the haven of Liam's arms. She wanted to stand on her own two feet, and by God, she was going to. "You two should have had this conversation twenty-five years ago and given me the family I deserved. So someone please tell me why the hell I had to grow up without a mother?"

"I wanted to see you, Cassidy, but—"

"But if she did, I'd cut you off." Mitchell nodded toward Mom and didn't take his eyes off her. "Elizabeth is well aware of how you've grown up. Of the things and opportunities I could give you that she never could. She wasn't about to deprive you of that."

"That's why you left me with him? For *things*?" If Cassidy hadn't had the epiphany she'd had with Franklin, this statement alone would have done it. What the hell kind of people had created her?

"That's not why I didn't take you, Cass. If you'll let me explain—"

Mitchell unbuttoned his jacket and put his hands on his hips. "To hell with the niceties, Elizabeth. Let's not sugar-coat it. You had an affair and tried to have your cake and eat it, too. Only I wasn't playing along. You took my family from me; I was taking yours from you."

"Did you ever stop to think that you were taking mine from me?" Cassidy wanted to be sick. He was talking about her as if she was an asset like his car or his home. "I not only lost my mother, but I lost my father, too."

Her father actually looked as if he had no idea what she was talking about. Which only highlighted the fact that she was right.

"I gave you a life others only dream about, Cassidy. I gave you anything money can buy."

His dream had been her nightmare. "Exactly. Anything money can buy. But not love. Not family. Not the sense that I was ever good enough. Look at her. Every time you looked at me, you saw her. No wonder you shuttled me off to boarding schools the minute I was old enough. And all those summer camps. I'm surprised you kept me at the company, but then, I had her job, didn't I? The party hostess."

"And you." She looked at her mother and loathed using the term in conjunction with the woman who should have loved her above everything else. "You gave me away for money? You *sold* me?"

"No, sweetheart. It wasn't like that. I couldn't give you what Mitchell could on my own. I had my mother to take care of as well, and he demanded I stay away or he'd stop paying for my mother's nursing home and end my support payments. I couldn't take care of her and look for a job and raise you. I didn't want to subject you to that kind of life. Not when you had the chance to live like this."

As if *this* was some big prize. "I have to get out of here."

"Cass, honey—"

"No." She held up her hand. "You walked out on me; I don't care about the reasons. They may have made sense to you at the time and maybe someday they'll make sense to me, but right now, I need to get away from both of you. I need to think." She reached for Liam's hand. "Can we go?"

"Sure thing, sweetheart. Let's go home."

Chapter Thirty-six

HOME.

Liam had brought her *home*. Not to his *house*, not to *his* home, but *home*.

And it was. This was the closest thing to a home that she'd ever lived in. And it was with someone she'd known for less than a month. How sad was that?

"You want to talk?" Liam finally said something when they were in his kitchen and he'd pulled a pair of wineglasses from the cabinet.

She snorted. "What more is there to say? I have the most selfish, clueless parents on the planet and I'm actually mourning the loss of them."

He set the glasses on the breakfast bar in front of her. "That's understandable, Cass. I lost my parents, so I know how much it hurts."

"But yours didn't choose to leave you. And you had your grandmother."

"I know. Thank God. I can't imagine what it would have been like growing up without her around."

"Lonely. Sad. Cold." She twirled the wineglass stem

between her palms. Too bad there was nothing in it. She could use a good belt or two right about now. "And that's when they *were* around. Well, when my father was. I barely remember my mom."

Liam sat across from her. "At least they were trying to give you a better life."

"Were they?" Cassidy set the glass down, a little worried she might snap the stem with this conversation. "These were two people who thought of themselves first. Mom had the affair because she didn't feel loved. Really? Did she ever hold me? Ever see the joy in her child's eyes? Babies don't see dollar signs; they see love. How do you turn your back on that? And my father . . . It's no surprise that he thought of his ego first. That he sought to punish her by keeping her from the thing she supposedly loved so much. God forbid he think about what I'd want. What I'd need. Selfish, both of them."

"So what are you going to do? They are still your parents."

She sighed. "I don't know. This is going to take some time to think through."

"Well." He pulled something from his back pocket and placed it on the breakfast bar.

An envelope.

"It looks like you'll have that time."

"What's that?"

He slid it toward her. "Jean-Pierre gave me this on our way out."

Cassidy opened the flap, took out a check—and started to cry. "Oh my God."

"Nice, huh?"

She looked at Liam. "You know how much?"

He shook his head and pulled a bottle of champagne from the wine fridge. "Jean-Pierre wouldn't tell me. Said it was none of my business, which technically isn't true, since some of that is mine, but I figured I wouldn't argue with him when he said it'd make you cry." He winked at her. "So I guess I owe you dinner for our bet about the credenza."

Cassidy drew in a shaky breath, not sure what she was supposed to feel at this moment. Today had been a day of all-over-the spectrum emotions and she was still reeling. Now with this check . . .

"I'll pay for dinner, Liam. And I can pay you back. With interest."

"True." Liam popped the cork and filled her glass. "But I don't want your interest." He filled his and tilted it toward her. "Not the monetary kind."

She picked up her glass and *chink*ed it with his, waiting for him to clarify that last part.

He took a sip of champagne.

"What other kind are you talking about?" She didn't have the patience for riddles. Not after all she'd been through tonight.

The glass was at his lips for another sip when he stopped. His blue eyes stared at her over the rim, igniting several thousand fires all over her body.

How did he do that with just one look?

"You don't know, Cass?"

Her mouth dried up and her heart rate went into overdrive. Ah. She got it. But she wanted to hear him say it.

She took a quick sip of champagne, catching the lingering drops on her lips with her tongue. "Why don't you tell me."

Liam took her glass and set his on the counter beside it. Then he walked around the island and sat on the bar chair next to her. He swiveled it to face her, turning hers enough that she faced him.

And then he cupped her cheek and drew her in for the lightest, barest kiss. "This kind," he whispered. "This is the interest I want from you. Forever."

He went in for another kiss, but his words had already stolen her breath.

"Forever?" she whispered as his lips barely touched hers.

He smiled and, God, it was the best smile. "Yeah, Cass. Forever. I figure that since your father cut you off, you can't accuse me of wanting you for your money, so maybe you'll see that your money was never the draw. It's you I want, babe. Only you. Cassidy Marie, Cass, C. Marie . . . I don't care what your name is, but I'd like to add my name to that list."

"I don't think I look like a Liam, Liam." She worked hard to keep the smile off her face. She knew where this was going and she was going to enjoy the ride.

He grimaced and rubbed his temples. "I guess I'm not doing such a good job of this."

She put her hand on his. "I think you're doing just fine."

"You do?"

She smiled then. "Is there something you want to ask me, Liam?"

He smiled back and that smile—the look in his eyes— undid every nightmarish event of the night. He cupped her face with both hands. "Yeah, Cassidy, there is something I'd like to ask you. Would you take my last name as yours? To have and to hold, in sickness and in health. And in moments of extreme emotional upheaval like art gallery exhibits, condo cleaning, and office flipping?"

"Liam, are you—"

"Yes, woman, yes. I'm asking you to marry me."

"I gathered that. But I want to make sure you're sure. You haven't known me very long."

"I know you, Cass. I know *you*. It's all right there." He touched her heart. "It's always been right there. *You* are right there. And I love you. From your generous heart to your strong will, to your compassion and caring, to your talent and your confidence, to the way you smile, and the way you nibble your lip when you sleep. Even to the love you shower on your little stuffed animal arm ornament and the way you keep going when the going gets tough. I love *you*, Cassidy." His fingers slid into her hair and held on.

Good. She never wanted him to let go.

"Say yes, Cass. Say you'll marry me."

"I don't deserve you."

He put his finger on her lips. "Never say that again. Say yes to me, Cassidy, and you'll get a man who loves you and admires you and wants to give you the family you've never had. Say yes and you'll get *exactly* what you deserve."

He was wrong. He was so much more than she deserved. But she wasn't going to let Liam Manley slip through her fingers because with everything her father's money could buy, Liam hadn't been for sale.

"I love you, Liam Manley, so yes. I say yes."

Those were the last words Liam let her say for quite a while . . .

Epilogue

❧

THE community center was a hive of activity the last Saturday of the following month, with the indoor community room holding a buffet that stretched the length of the stage, and a seating area stocked to capacity. Local companies had donated drinks and paper products; everyone else had brought a covered dish or dessert—or Gran's thawed-and-re-heated gourmet meals to share. There was a petting zoo—courtesy of Livvy, Sean's former-client-now-girlfriend—and pony rides on the right side lawn, with a local dairy giving out homemade ice cream. Team sporting events were being held on the left side lawn, a scaled-down summer Olympiad was happening around the pool area out back, and a carnival with rides, concession trucks, and booth games was holding court on the front lawn.

The balloon darts booth was the main attraction for the Manleys and their friends, since last night's poker game had been cancelled. Needing to feed their competitive spirit—as well as Mac's now-vacant "manly" maids positions—Liam, Sean, and Jared had roped in a couple of buddies for a few killer rounds of balloon darts, bets included.

Cooper Wexford put down his five bucks and picked up his six darts. "Last round. Liam's got fourteen, Sean twenty, Jared eleven, Kellan ten, Kirk nine, and I'm at ten. Loser buys rounds tonight at O'Grady's."

Liam held out his hand in front of Coop before the guy could take a shot. "Let's make this a little more interesting, guys."

Sean snorted. "Here we go." He adjusted the new official Manley Maids baseball cap and saluted them. "I'll catch you guys when this is over, since there's no way I'll be last. Livvy needs some help. Rhett is trying to get into Scarlett's pen and the alpaca doesn't like to take *no* for an answer. Not really something you want the kids to witness, you know?"

"Horny bastard," muttered Jared, tugging Mac to his side.

"You're one to talk." Sean knocked Jared's cap off and nudged his sister as he walked by.

Liam winked at Cassidy and mouthed, "Later." She winked back. It'd only gotten better between them. He hadn't thought it was possible to *be* better, but life was good.

Wedding plans were going full steam ahead for the weekend before Christmas, the office he and Cassidy had created had gotten three offers over asking price, and Cassidy was in full work mode at her new studio, which, thanks to Gran, helped him out, too, because it was *his* property she'd had the key to. And demand for Cassidy's work had gone through the roof after the incident at the show.

Cassidy was still trying to come to terms with her parents' actions. He'd given her the photo and bracelet one night when they'd been talking about what she should do. The photo had shown up a few days later in a frame beside their bed, so Liam was hopeful that she and her mother would work things out. They had help from Deborah, Davenport's now-former assistant who, unknown to Mitchell, had taken huge issue with him cutting a mother out of her daughter's life, and had taken it upon herself to keep Elizabeth apprised of her daughter's life all these years. Including an invitation to the art show. When Davenport had found out, well, Cassidy had told him she'd been surprised at how betrayed her father had felt. There'd been some justice in it for her, but it was going to take a while for her to heal.

That was okay; Liam would be with her every step of the way.

He'd found out that Jean-Pierre had sent the invitation to Davenport in order to rub Cassidy's success in his face. Even though the night hadn't gone as planned, Liam had sent him a bottle of champagne anyway. It took a lot of courage to stand up to Mitchell Davenport, and those who did needed to stick together.

"So what's the interesting part, Lee?" Cooper set down his darts and cracked his knuckles.

"Well, it's—"

"It's like this." Mac pulled herself out from under Jared's arm. Business first with Mac. Always. "Loser owes me a month of cleaning services."

"Are you out of your mind?" Cooper asked. "I work full time, munchkin."

Mac glared at him. Cooper had known her her whole life and knew she hated that nickname. Which was probably why he'd called her that. "I didn't say it had to be full time, Coop, but one client for a month."

"I don't see *you* playing," said Kellan. "Why should we bet something for your benefit?"

"I'm playing for her." Jared stood a little taller on his rehabbed leg.

Liam had to nod. Jared wasn't who he'd have chosen for his sister—he knew him too well—but if the guy was going to fly straight and do right by Mac—and Mac was all for it—Liam couldn't say anything. Still . . . interesting. He'd love to hear that story.

"Okay," said Kirk. "So what do we get if we win?"

"A month of cleaning services," answered Liam, Cassidy, Jared, and Mac in unison.

Coop handed his darts over to Kellen. "Sorry, guys, but a month of cleaning service isn't worth the risk of losing."

Kellen snorted. "That's because he only cleans every other month."

"Ass." Coop gave him the finger.

"Chicken." Kellen held out the darts.

Cooper shook his head. "Dick."

"Loser." Kirk, Kellen's twin, got in on the action. The guys always had each others' back.

Cooper looked at all of them. "Okay. Fine." He swiped the darts off Kellen's palm. "I'm a good shot, and *when* I win, I want you guys in a serious maid costume."

Liam clapped him on the back. "Oh, don't worry, Coop, we have them. And they're really cute."

As Cooper was going to find out firsthand, since he was the one who came in dead last.

Acknowledgments

I honestly have no idea how authors wrote before the internet came along. But as wonderful as the internet is for research, sometimes you just need someone who knows what the heck they're talking about. Many thanks for the hours I *didn't* have to spend researching tailgate lifts to Nicole at Northern Tool & Equipment. She was very helpful and went way beyond what I needed to help me find something Liam would have in his garage that Cassidy could operate—and figure out *how* to operate. To Nicole's boss: Please give her a raise. ☺

To my editor, Leis, who waited for this so patiently as surgery kicked my butt. Okay, not my butt, but close enough.

To Marci, who came through for me one Saturday night when my world—and the dogs—skewed left. To Michelle for the b*tch sessions, to Janice for the text hugs, and to Steph for the parenting gripes. To The Survivor Girls for the meals, the friendship, and the wine. What would I do without all of you?

And to my readers. It's really all about you. I couldn't do what I love without you reading and loving it. Thanks so much for your enthusiasm, your love, and your emails/letters. Keep 'em coming!

TURN THE PAGE FOR A SNEAK PEEK AT
THE NEXT MANLEY MAIDS NOVEL

What a Woman

*COMING IN MARCH 2015 FROM
BERKLEY SENSATION!*

Guys' Night . . . Plus One

❧

THREE hunks in aprons were the best advertising in the world for a maid service. Make one of them a Hollywood movie star, and there was no way Mary-Alice Catherine Manley could fail to get the publicity her fledgling business needed.

Make all three of them her brothers, and the picture only got better.

"You really won?" Gran gripped the doily-covered arm rests and leaned forward when Mac returned from the watershed poker game with her brothers. "Oh Mary-Alice Catherine! I wish I'd been there."

"Me, too, Gran." Except it'd been enough of a coup to get a "you can play" from the three of them; there'd been no reason to push for an invitation for Gran, too. That would have raised too many red flags and maybe given their plan away. "You should've seen the looks on their faces when I told them they'd all have to be fitted for Manley Maids uniforms. I wish I'd had a camera."

She'd make sure there were plenty of cameras around when her brothers started work on Monday.

"So who are you going to pair them up with?" asked Gran, who was on board with the plan in hopes of getting her brothers married off. Whatever worked. Mac just wanted the publicity. "We have to plan carefully. You know the kind of crazy that follows Bryan around."

Bryan was the Hollywood movie star, and Mac didn't think he minded crazy. He'd taken to that lifestyle like a duck to water. 'Course, you had to teach a duck to swim, as odd as that sounded, so maybe she and Gran could teach Bry a thing or two about women, since his recent choices were about as feather-brained as ducks.

Mac plopped onto the sofa that'd been in the same spot for the twenty-six years she'd lived with Gran, the worn depression cradling her butt as usual. "I was thinking I'd tell them when they pick up their uniforms. That'll give you some more time to figure out where you want them. Though Sean's already called dibs on the Martinson estate. I didn't see any reason to object."

Gran tapped her bow-shaped lips. "The Martinson estate? But it's empty. He won't meet anyone that way, Mary-Alice Catherine."

Mac let her full name go by. Gran was the only one who used it since she'd dubbed herself Mac, back when she'd done anything to be like her brothers—male name included. Given that tonight's poker game was her attempt to catapult her company into the same kind of success her brothers had earned for themselves, she hadn't gotten over that competitiveness yet, had she?

But tonight was her win, fair and square. Well, maybe not quite so fair. She *had* spent a lot of hours learning to play poker online and to count cards to improve her chances, but her brothers played together every month. She'd had to even the odds.

Tonight she'd beaten them at their own game; she was going to enjoy every minute of her victory and the possibilities it meant.

And Bry had said she had nothing comparable to what he, Sean, and Liam had? Clearly he had no idea. Yep, she was definitely going to enjoy the win.

"Actually Gran, the Martinson house won't be empty. Merriweather's granddaughter is moving in. Besides, Sean specifically requested that place. It would have looked odd if I'd said he couldn't have it. Maybe he'll fall in love with the granddaughter." And maybe pigs would fly, but if it kept Gran's spirits up and created enough word-of-mouth, this was worth every bit of her hard work.

"The granddaughter, huh?" Gran tapped her forefingers together. "It just might work. But what about Bryan? We can't assign him to just anywhere. It'll have to be someone who won't mind having Mr. Movie Star around."

Gran said it with more love than the rest of them did when ragging on Bryan about his stardom. Ever since he'd gotten a part with one of the biggest female leads in the industry, they hadn't been able to resist teasing him, and Bryan hadn't been able to stop smiling. Until tonight.

"I really think he should help that widow you just had a call about. The one with all those children."

"You want me to send Bryan into a house with five kids? Gran, that'll drive him nuts."

"Or teach him tolerance. We don't want him getting too big for his britches, do we?"

Gran had a point. And Mac *would* like to see Bryan try to clean a house overrun with five kids. None of her brothers was the quitting type, but this would test Bryan's mettle. She owed him a lot more than that for the pranks he'd pulled on her over the years.

"Okay, so what about Lee, then, Gran?"

"Oh I know the perfect place for Liam. That nice Cassidy girl. She's going to be lonely when Sharon leaves to have her baby. Liam can keep her company."

"What do you have against Liam?" Cassidy Davenport was as spoiled and high-maintenance as they came. More Bry's type, but if Bryan went there, the only thing he'd end up cleaning would be Cassidy's sheets. And the shower stall. And the table top . . .

"Now, Mary-Alice Catherine Manley."

Mac winced. The first time Gran had said all four of her

names in that tone, she hadn't felt the layer of skin it sliced off for about an hour until she realized she'd been severely chastised. The effect hadn't lessened over the years.

"That Cassidy girl simply needs someone to pay attention to her. And our Liam needs to get his head out of his—well, off himself and into the rest of society. Have you noticed how preoccupied he's been since he broke things off with Rachel? It's not good, and if anyone can take Liam out of himself, it's that Cassidy."

The problem was, Cassidy was just like Rachel, though on a far bigger scale: all designer-this and celebrity-event-that. Rachel had put Liam through the ringer, and Mac wasn't so sure shoving a replica-on-steroids in his face was all that kind. Still, he definitely wouldn't fall in love with Cassidy, so she'd actually be doing Liam a favor by thwarting Gran's matchmaking attempts.

She felt sorry for the guy. He was the only one of her brothers to have come close to the altar and the fallout had been tough to witness.

"Okay, but if he wants to bite my head off, you need to talk him out of it."

"Never fear, honey. Your brother will love it."

Mac wasn't so sure about that, but she wasn't about to argue with Gran. Her grandmother had raised four grand-children on meager savings, love, and not much else. The woman had grit.

"Oh. I forgot to mention something."

"What, Gran?" Mac hid her worry. Gran had been for-getting a lot of things lately. That was one reason she'd agreed to Gran's wacky plan of trying to marry off her brothers while having them work for Manley Maids, even if the chances were as slim as . . . well, as Mac being able to pull off a win tonight. And lightning rarely struck in the same place twice. Still, it'd give Gran something to keep her mind occupied.

"Mildred's grandson moved back home this week." Mil-dred was her grandmother's childhood friend whose recent move into an assisted living facility had spurred Gran to do the same. "You remember Jared? The one who was injured in that car accident?"

"Yes, Gran. I remember Jared." As if she could forget him. Besides being a professional baseball player who'd sustained season-ending injuries in a bad car accident that was *still* all over the news, and being Liam, her oldest brother's best friend since forever, Jared had been her first crush. And her longest. And her most embarrassing. She'd followed him around like a star-struck teenager. And that'd been *before* she'd been a teenager. God, the time she'd fallen out of the tree fort once when she'd been spying on him, only to land *on* him and his date and, well, it hadn't been her best moment.

It also, sadly, hadn't been her worst.

"Well, Mildred and I were chatting and it came up that now that Jared has moved back, he could use help, what with the house being so old and his injuries. It's been tough for her to keep ahead of it, and, well, one thing led to another, and she wants to hire you to clean it. Isn't that wonderful? I got you some business and you can help Jared out, too."

That was her grandmother: kindest heart this side of the Make-A-Wish Foundation. Too bad it was *her* biggest nightmare.

Mac gritted her teeth. Refusing would be too childish and petty—and it'd make Gran ask too many questions. Besides, it wasn't as if *she* had to do the cleaning. She wouldn't even have to see Jared. "Yes, Gran, it sure is. When does she want someone?"

"Not *someone*, dear. You. I told her you'd come. Mildred doesn't want just anyone in her home."

Great. So much for that rationalization.

She couldn't do this. She couldn't. To see Jared . . . All that humiliation hitting her right in the face again . . .

But arguing with Gran was fruitless; she'd win in the end. Mac had learned that early in her teenage years, which had saved them both a lot of angst.

But she was going to end up with angst no matter what, apparently. Best if it was temporary with Jared rather than hurting her grandmother in the process.

She just hoped she was lucky enough that Jared wouldn't remember.

Then again, she might have used up all her luck in the poker game.

She sighed. "When am I supposed to be there, Gran?"

"Tuesday, dear. This Tuesday."

Which gave her three days to gird herself to see him again.

It wasn't going to be enough.

But she was a big girl; she could do this. After all, she wasn't that same girl who thought Jared was the only man alive. And considering his relationships kept par with his homeruns, she wasn't the only one to think so. And if there was one thing Mac Manley could never abide, it was being one of a pack. Jared no longer held any thrill for her.

"Okay, Gran. Tuesday it is. I'll be there with bells on."

Chapter One

❧

THE woman had bells on.

Jared blinked, then rubbed his eyes and looked out the front window again.

She wore bells.

Then she rang his bell.

And, yeah, she was a pretty little thing, so she did kind of ring his bell.

She rang it again—the doorbell, not *his* bell.

Jared shook his head and willed his legs to move. Well, the working one. The other just still hung there and let his crutches do its work. Funny, though, how he still thought about the mechanics even though his muscles now made the involuntary actions on their own, but then, habits you taught yourself when re-learning to walk tended to stick.

He opened the door just as she went to knock on it with the pot in her hands, and Jared had to jump back to avoid hot soup—which sent pain shooting through him and almost took the crutches right out from under him.

Damn. His body might have been repaired by the best surgeons in the country, but idiotic moves like that reminded him real quick of what he'd gone through—both during *and* after the accident.

Other things he'd learned when re-learning to walk also stuck.

The woman's bells jangled. "Hello. I'm—"

"Wearing bells."

"Not exactly." She hefted a pot of delicious-smelling something with a "Here. Hold this" at him, and he had to shove his crutches into his armpits to balance on them and his good leg. "Actually, I'm carrying them. My grandmother thought your grandmother might want them back." She hefted a leather slab of sleigh bells off her shoulder, knocking her baseball cap askew. "Where do you want 'em?"

The woman was about five-two yet entered the house like a tornado. Jangling bells included.

"I don't know. I wasn't planning on bells in my future." Jared waved the pot toward the left. "Just drop them on the chair over there."

She did. Dropped them right on the chair. Then they slid off and hit the hardwood floor with a nerve-destroying reverberation. He hoped to hell they hadn't destroyed the floor.

And then he saw her outfit. Matching green pants and shirt with MANLEY MAIDS embroidered over the left breast pocket.

Oh shit. He knew exactly why this woman had entered the house like a tornado—she *was* a tornado. Mac Manley could stir things up like only acts of God and Nature could.

And now she'd brought her particular brand of terror to his life. He'd seen it first-hand as a kid, with her brothers jumping to do her bidding. And apparently she was still pulling their strings from what his grandmother had told him about a little poker game escapade they'd allowed her to win.

Nothing had changed in all these years. Little Mary-Alice Catherine Manley could still wrap the men in her life around her little finger.

Jared had had enough of women like that. One had landed him in the position he was in: dashed dreams, career on its way down the toilet, and way too much time on his hands. Not to mention busted ribs, a couple titanium rods, a bum knee, and the prospect of arthritis at an early age. He'd learned his lesson. Triplefold.

He was staying far away from women like Camille. And Mac Manley, too. When he started dating again, it'd be someone like his grandmother. Someone warm and loving and giving, who didn't care how many zeroes he had in his bank account as long as the two of them were happy and healthy.

No, the Mac Manleys and Camille Johnsons of this world could be someone else's problem.

Jared took two crutch-swinging/hop steps with the pot, and—yeah. That wasn't going to work. Some sloshed out from under the lid and damn if it wasn't hot. "Hey, a hand here?"

She looked at him as if he had two heads.

He picked his crutches up by clenching his arms against his torso and lifting them with his armpits. "Injury?"

"Oh. Crud." She grabbed the pot and carried it into the kitchen, steam rising from the pot when it bounced as she set it on the counter. "Sorry. I wasn't thinking. You okay?"

Okay? Hell no he wasn't okay. Any moron could see that.

Unfortunately, the only moron around here was him. He had Mac Manley in his house when he was at a physical disadvantage.

And a sexual one, too, because that soup wasn't the only thing that was hot in this kitchen.

Jared hobbled away from her as fast as he could. As if he'd been burned. By the soup or by her, he didn't know. Didn't care. Because he'd seen Mac in action and it was comparable only to the car accident that had almost killed him.

And she just might finish the job.

JARED Nolan had certainly filled out nicely.

It was Mac's first thought at her first up-close and personal glimpse of the baseball hero who'd filled her dreams long before that last time she'd seen him when Mildred had invited Gran, her, and her brothers to the going-away party his parents had thrown to kick off his major league baseball career—a career that looked to be in jeopardy if those crutches and that leg brace were anything to go by.

But he could work those crutches something fierce, and his flexing chest and biceps were a nice result. Abs and thighs, too. Physical therapy had done good things besides getting him upright again because he certainly didn't look as if he'd come close to death. Matter of fact, he looked to be the picture of health, the perfect cover model for the men's health magazine he'd been on before the accident.

She was very sorry to admit to herself that she had looked at that cover. A few times.

But she wasn't here to ogle the client. She never ogled clients. She never ogled *anyone*. Especially Jared. She'd worked too hard to make Manley Maids successful, so by the time she *could* look at anything other than work, her eyes were crossed with exhaustion.

He, however, definitely straightened them out.

Get over him, Mac. Remember your embarrassment? Remember his derision?

Right. She did. Still, he didn't have to know that. And the best way for him *not* to know it was to pretend everything was just fine between them. "Are you sure you're okay? The soup didn't burn you?"

"I'm fine."

That he was.

Mac rolled her eyes just as he turned around and shoved his fists onto his hips—a really good look on him that she didn't need to notice, because if she did, Gran's hopes would skyrocket.

Hey, wait a minute . . . Did Gran actually think she could hook Mac and Jared up like she was trying to do to Liam, Sean, and Bryan?

Jared leaned against the counter and crossed his arms, his crutches falling against the butcher block. "Are you really here to clean?"

That was the idea. But was it Gran's?

"I'm certainly not here to cook." Mac nodded at the pot. "That's from my grandmother."

A ridiculous idea because chicken soup was a cold remedy, not a cure-all for broken bones. And even if it was, Jared had been out of the hospital for a while; he was certainly capable of getting around if he'd moved in here to get the place ready to sell for his grandmother.

"That was kind of her. Please thank her for me."

"Or you can give her a call while I get started. I know she'd love to hear from you." Ever since Mildred's request for her to personally handle this assignment, Gran had done nothing but regale Mac with Jared's wonderfulness, seen fully through the eyes of his grandmother. Gran and Mildred loved talking about their grandkids.

Now Mac was wondering how much of that regaling was because Gran was thrilled Jared was doing okay or because she wanted Mac to be thrilled about Jared. Too bad Gran wasn't aware of their history, or the lack thereof, though not for Mac's fervent wishes—and that one time she'd made a complete idiot of herself—when she'd been a kid. The embarrassingly obvious wishes that she'd wished to hell more than once that she could take back and pretend had never been. Especially since the object of those wishes had been aware of them all along.

Mac picked up a misshapen blue ceramic mug. Mr. Davison's fourth grade project. She had the same one, though hers was a little more even than Jared's. "How about if I start upstairs and work my way down? Will that interfere with your schedule?"

Jared looked at her as if he didn't understand a word she was saying.

She set the mug down next to a picture of thirteen-year-old Jared with Mildred at one of Jared's Little League games. Mac knew exactly how old Jared was in that picture— actually knew it to the *day*; that's how infatuated she'd been with him. Her poor deluded, prepubescent self . . .

"Mac, what are you doing here?" He laid the dishtowel on the side of the sink, folded up all nice and neat.

Who did that? She cleaned for a living and didn't do that in her own house.

"I'm here to clean your grandmother's house."

"No. I mean, why are you *really* here?"

"*Really* here? I don't understand the question."

Jared stared at her as if he were trying to figure her out, but finally shook his head and turned away.

And winced.

He stumbled a little and Mac was at his side, under his arm with hers wrapped around his waist before he could protest.

Not that that stopped him. "I've got this, Mac. I got the crutches. You don't have to try to carry me."

"I'm not trying; I'm doing. I don't need you breaking something on my watch." She grunted with the effort it took to keep him upright. He might not be aware of it, but he was no light-weight. All that muscle put some major poundage on him.

Not that she was paying attention or anything.

"So you're saying it's okay if I break something later?"

Wow. His tone put Gran's skin-slicing ability to shame because Mac figured out right away that he wasn't her biggest fan. Still harboring resentment that she'd practically been his shadow all those years ago? She'd love to tell him to get over himself—that she had—but Gran and Mildred wouldn't be happy if she blew this contract, so it was time to cut her losses.

Hands up, Mac backed away. Let him fall; see if she cared. "Okay. Fine. I'll just get started and you go do what you do and I'll stay out of your way." Far, far out of his way.

He gripped the countertop and worked the one crutch under his arm. "Fine. You do that."

"Fine. I will." She should probably hand him the other one that was by the sink, but screw it. If he was so "I got this" then let him get his own damn crutch.

She spun around and strode toward the back steps. She'd find the farthest corner of the house from here, and take out her emotions on the dirt—

Except she needed her cleaning supplies that, between

the soup and the bells, she hadn't had enough hands to carry in. Which meant she had to go back downstairs. Past Jared.

Great. Fabulous.

Executing a ninety-degree turn that would stop an army drill sergeant in his tracks, Mac strode toward the front door.

"Leaving so soon?" He didn't have to sound so happy about it.

She turned around. "Look, Jared, I'm here as a favor to your grandmother and mine. If you have issues with that, take it up with them."

She so would have loved to slam the door behind her, but it was Mildred's front door, not Jared's, and she wasn't about to let him see her sweat.

Because, damn it all, he actually *could* still make her sweat.